STILL MORE STUBBORN ★ STARS

A NOVEL BY PAUL N. GALLANT

ACORNPRESS

Cover design by Kenny Vail
Cover illustration by Stephen B. MacInnis
Interior design by Cassandra Aragonez
Editing by Penelope Jackson
Copyediting by Jennifer Graham

Printed in Canada by Rapido

Library and Archives Canada Cataloguing in Publication

Gallant, Paul N., 1969–
Still More Stubborn Stars / Paul N. Gallant
Identifiers: Canadiana (print) 20210313919 |
Canadiana (ebook) 20210314486 | ISBN 9781773660875
(softcover) | ISBN 9781773660882 (HTML)

Classification: LCC PS8613.A459545 S75 2021 | DDC C813/.6—dc23

The author gratefully acknowledges the generous support of
The Ontario Arts Council.

ONTARIO ARTS COUNCIL
CONSEIL DES ARTS DE L'ONTARIO
an Ontario government agency
un organisme du gouvernement de l'Ontario

The publisher acknowledges the support of the Government of Canada,
the Canada Council for the Arts and the Province of Prince Edward Island
for our publishing program.

P.O. Box 22024
Charlottetown, Prince Edward Island
C1A 9J2
Acornpress.ca

For my dear friends, the best in the world:
Andrew, Jared, Stuart and Sujata

In honour of my grandparents Loretta and Melvin,
Lillian and Howard, all of whom I wish I had spent
more time with

"There are men who can see one star break
Momentarily through a rake of clouds;
Guess which it is and thereupon stake
Course, life and many more thumping loud
Human pulses on a line more tenuous
Through an incoherent stagger of shocks,
Than one by which a new spider launches
His wee red splot of life over world-tops."
—By Still More Stubborn Stars, Milton Acorn

"Nothing is ever lost."
—I Trawl the Megahertz, Paddy McAloon

CHAPTER 1

NO WONDER THERE WAS dirt everywhere, blowing across yards, against the vinyl siding of homes, onto the front steps where it'd sit waiting for somebody careless enough to track it through the porch and across the living-room carpet. Farmers in a more enlightened age, before everybody was running into town every time they took a notion, would never have been foolish enough to have plowed their fields so late in the fall. Everywhere you looked, bare red dirt checker-boarded the brown and the brown-green. The late September wind peeled off precious topsoil, as if it were in infinite supply, throwing the Island's earth and pesticides at everyone's good clothes.

The funeral cortege was behind schedule leaving Corcoran's in O'Leary, which was about a half-drive from the church on Palmer Road, and if it started pushing up against an imaginary limit of about ten minutes late, something that would set people to checking their watches, the mourners waiting at St. Bernard's Church would likely engage in what Father Michael Chaisson called "further unhealthy speculations," an abyss from which it would be hard to retrieve them. Father Michael Chaisson was pleased to have the last word at this particular funeral, but things were off to a shaky start. Already the muttered conversations echoed off the ceilings at decibel levels considerably above his comfort level.

"She can't not come," said Angela Gaudet (Ellsworth), who had never been able to shake the habit she had picked up in the fish plant of repeatedly wiping her hands on the front of her skirt as if they had been dampened by fish oil and guts though she hadn't worked in the plant for more than a decade. She twisted around in her seat to check the door. "Have you talked to Sherrie?"

"No, I have not talked to Sherrie. For God's sake, we haven't talked since tenth grade. Anyways, it might surprise you, Mom, that not everybody worries about what everybody thinks." Janet Gaudet had three months ago decided that university wasn't for her but hadn't decided what was, other than the Friday trivia at The Glenn, Saturday karaoke at the Legion, and the odd visit to the Walmart in Summerside where they sold cranberry cocktail by the three-litre jug. Roger Niese's death and its fallout were the most excitement she'd had since she moved back home.

"It's a grey area." Janet repeated a phrase she heard on the news.

"Some things are black and white," said Angela. "Pregnancy... AIDS...."

"I knew a girl once who was only half pregnant," said Janet.

"You believe everything you hear," snapped her mother.

Oh, the stories. Roger had been sleeping with Kate Pineau for years and was father to her daughters, Sherrie and Krystal. After a break then there was little Bethany. Or Roger had been sleeping with Kate for years, but Sherrie was somebody else's. Or Krystal was. Or Bethany. What was known for sure was that Kate had had sex at least three times in her life.

Roger had, perhaps, started sleeping with Kate only when her marriage with Arnold Crozier fell apart, though his friendship with her had made her marriage unstable from the start. Perhaps Roger and Kate never had sex, but they might as well have been, they carried on so much, pretending it was all about music and some such nonsense.

Perhaps Kate had seduced Roger into giving her money and boosting her career, whether he'd gotten any sex out of her or not.

Roger Niese was a sexless gorm who likely never had sex in his life. No—there was sharp-tongued Tracey Shaw (Tillard) from New Brunswick. Maybe Roger had cheated on her with Kate. Or cheated on Kate with Tracey. There were those years that Roger and Kate were barely speaking—there had been something up then.

Janet liked all the options. It certainly made the Pineaus seem a little more exciting. Sherrie had been dull; dull, volunteer-in-the-canteen, join-the-debate-club dull all through high school and, even now, never went to either of the two clubs in Summerside. She had probably never bloodied a nose with her own hands. Sherrie mostly seemed to like clog dancing, which made sense if you thought about the world Roger had created around Kate, her daughters, and the whole community. Clog dancing was a trend Up West these days. There was even money in it.

"Kate Pineau's a schemer," Janet told her mother. "If I were her, I'd park on the road so I didn't get trapped in the church parking lot.

You know we're going to be here forever, don't you, Mom, because you had to park so close? We didn't have to get here so early. I wasn't one of Roger's pets. The solos I got, you could count them on one hand. Oh, I was no Kate Pineau!"

"The hearse is coming all the way from O'Leary," said Angela, rolling her eyes. "They could take a while."

O'Leary, a predominantly Protestant farm town, was not so well tied to the community of St. Louis-St. Edwards, the home of St. Bernard's Church and the Acadian Cultural Centre and Fun Park that had brought Roger Niese to public attention.

"Who arranged that, with the St. Bernard's Funeral Co-op right here? Makes no sense to me."

"That's enough," said Angela. She had been on the board of the Centre for years, and though she never attended board meetings, she did go to events and parties at the Centre, which was right across the road from the church. They had the best surf and turf menu this side of Charlottetown. Angela didn't want to jeopardize anything.

Since it was built in 1864, St. Bernard's, also called Palmer Road Church, also called St. Louis Church, had twice been on fire, once by accident and once on purpose at the hands of a priest who, months later, was running a bakery in Souris with a divorcée. The altar, a white and gold replica of a baroque church façade, was the only thing not rendered in honey-coloured maple.

"It's filled up," said Betty Ann Pineau (Getson) to her husband Noel. They were sitting a few rows in front of Angela and Janet. Noel and Roger had been buddies when they were younger. "Roger will be well remembered. God bless his soul. Hard to forget him. The guy who built the fixed link—that man from Italy or Toronto or wherever he's from. He's here, thank you very much."

"So's the crazy lady who tried to stop the fucking bridge," said Noel. "Maybe she came in a kayak."

"And Léonce and Réné LeBlanc," said Betty Ann, who knew better than her husband who was worth mentioning and who wasn't. Léonce had been one of the most long-standing members of the Legislative

Assembly, as well as the founder of one of the Island's biggest construction companies. His son Réné had taken over the company, and then Léonce's seat in the legislature, when LeBlanc senior retired from each position. Réné's son, Joey, was also with them, looking anxious and awkward, not quite ready to take his place in the family legacy.

So many names showing up at a funeral was an excellent measure of the quality of a Prince Edward Island life. And there were lots more names there inside the church. Some were, as of late, notorious. Betty Ann knew better than to mention Kate, Noel's sister. They had made a pact not to discuss whatever her role in all this might be. She hadn't taken Betty Ann's calls.

When the cortege arrived, Roger Niese's blood relatives barely filled one of the remaining empty pews; they were all from away, anyway. The front row seats were reserved for the senior staff from the Acadian Cultural Centre and Fun Park, who were also driving in the cortege.

It was 11:13am. Betty Ann took a deep breath through her teeth, a Maritimer's sigh, which sometimes turned into a resigned "Yep."

The elder of the Niese brothers, David, all business, hardly seemed the type to cause a delay with tears or theatrics. His wife ran the roost, though, you could tell. The younger Niese brother, Allan, was harder to read as he paced, smoked, disappeared, and was looked for. Susan Kennedy, who was sitting a few pews in front of Betty Ann, had watched the surviving Niese brothers accept the terms of the women's auxiliary luncheon, four hundred plates at a buck a plate; they didn't bat an eyelash at the cost. The two of them had arrived at Thursday's family viewing in jeans and a polo shirt the same dark blue, as if they had agreed on a uniform, though the older one was husky, the younger one slight.

Roger Niese had been tall and lanky, always leaning down to hear what people had to say, those few times he listened. You'd wonder how they got the body into the casket. His face always had a question on it, and a bit of panic, but at the wake, everybody was saying he looked serene. Satisfied for once.

The Vancouver brother, David, had come straight from the airport, his wife, Emily, scowling at him; she had been denied the opportunity to fix her hair and change her top before marching into Corcoran's, blankly taking in faces Emily Niese had glimpsed once or twice decades ago, when she was more flexible about where she would go on holidays. Back then, she shamefully crammed her mouth full of butter-drenched lobster, the dribbles down her chin forgotten in a daze of pleasure. In recent years, it had been Miami—not even Orlando, which Islanders might have appreciated—the south of France, the Caribbean. Perhaps her mind was in these places now. Emily had looked right through everybody at the Friday wake. At least she had gotten them one of the nicest suites in Up West: the bridal suite at The Glenn, with a view of the golf course and, beyond the pristine greens, Mill River, slowly filling with algae gone viral from fertilizer runoff.

The Ottawa brother, Allan, the pouty child in him still showing at age forty-two, had driven down with a buddy who had not balked at a fifteen-hour drive through the dullest parts of Quebec and New Brunswick.

Father Michael Chaisson was very strict about cellphones in the church. So at 11:17am, nobody at St. Bernard's knew the hearse had already pulled out of the freshly asphalted parking lot of Corcoran's Funeral Home in O'Leary. Ronnie Corcoran was behind the wheel, having gotten his licence back in August, just two weeks before his father Gerald lost his. While the penalty that came with driving drunk was finite, the bad eyesight and inattentiveness that often comes with old age was not; Gerald Corcoran was never again going to be in the hearse's driver's seat.

Ronnie Corcoran turned left and headed up O'Leary's Main Street, the mourners in their dirty cars behind him. They drove past the Scotiabank. Past the old hospital which had been converted into a manor. Past the old manor which had been converted into a summertime flea market where they sold the kind of junk not worth stuffing in a leaky basement. Past the Co-op, buckets of fertilizer, canisters of Roundup pesticide stacked in its display windows. Past the old train station, which Arnold Crozier, Kate's ex-husband, had turned into the office for his "Captain Haddock's Putt-Er-Inn" mini-golf after the provincial tourism information centre was relocated to the main road. With candy bar wrappers and plastic bags blowing across the miniature ramps and bridges, the mini-golf looked abandoned. The mini-golf at the Acadian Cultural Centre and Fun Park, with its castles and spaceships and pirate ships, put Arnold's to shame.

Drivers in O'Leary pulled over when they saw the hearse coming, its glistening shine (Gerald Corcoran the elder had to do something to keep himself busy) recognizable from a great distance. Men coming out of the pharmacy, walking down the sidewalk, getting in their cars all took off their hats, held them at waist height till the convoy passed. Women lowered their heads, some of them making the sign of the cross. People stopped and, for a moment, forgot the cable bills they were paying, the sales at the drugstore, the hamburger-with-the-works special at the café. The 21st century had robbed Prince County of its manners, just like everywhere else. Until that hearse drove by. A passing had to be acknowledged with the greatest vigour modesty allowed. Especially somebody so young. When somebody died at forty-seven, you couldn't pretend it wasn't a deep cut in the local fabric, even if he had been born on the wrong side of the Northumberland Strait.

And then there was the fact that the deceased was Roger Niese, a man who, not inconsequentially, had already been mentioned in six local history books, though he had authored a couple of them himself. Nobody could call Roger a drama queen—he was low-key to the point of oblivious—but he brought out the formal and the grand in people, like a schoolmarm whose eyes transformed every forgotten "please" and "thank you" into an opportunity missed for living life the right way. Roger had done so much, too much for some people's taste. When the drama over the newspaper death notice—oh, that death notice!—was over and forgotten, all the other bruised feelings and grudges would dry up too.

A graphomaniac from beyond the grave, Roger made sure that even his own funeral proceedings were something of a show, laid out in pages and pages of instructions, poems, and diagrams tucked into a crusty plastic folder he had left in the top drawer of his office filing cabinet, a file he had been secretly filling since he was in his early twenties, an age when most young men were doing all they could to avoid thoughts of death.

Roger had chosen the Corcoran Funeral Home, more than thirty kilometres from St. Bernard's, because Gerald Corcoran had given him a loan to get his first book published: *The Life and Times of Father Sylvain-Ephrem Poirier*. Roger had also been troubled by the thought of giving Father Michael too much control over his funeral. He couldn't not be buried in St. Bernard's. That would be unthinkable. But he wanted to make sure his body was properly disposed of, considering how much say Father Michael had at St. Bernard's Funeral Co-op. For a long time, Roger believed that Father Michael had tried to sabotage his vision. Those close to Roger had, in recent years, come to understand that this was likely true. Forcing the priest to coordinate things with the Corcorans introduced a level of civilian oversight. Because the Corcorans were of an Irish background, rather than Acadian, Roger perceived them as being neutral about internecine matters.

A teenage fiddler whom Roger had befriended during some meeting down in Rustico played all three sets of visiting hours at the wake at Corcorans. She was good. Though, of course, not as good as Kate Pineau. Live music at the wake might have been considered a sweet touch, though Roger had selected startlingly lively tunes. A step dancer arrived with her fold-out wooden clatter-racket to jump upon. From Rustico, too, likely, because nobody recognized her, and nobody wanted to ask. Roger's funeral guidelines had tried to keep the duties light for the people who had been closest to him, and that included most of the young people Up West who had attended the Acadian Cultural Centre and Fun Park's music and dance classes, worked at its restaurants, shops, rides, and stages.

Through all the visiting hours at Corcoran's, the crowds swelling, the two performers never stopped. The wake made a dent in the bar sales at the Legions in O'Leary, Bloomfield, and Tignish. The locals—those who lived in, say, a ten-kilometre radius of St. Bernard's—chattered easily among themselves as if they were attending one of Roger Niese's shows. The unfamiliar faces, who arrived in ones and twos, kept to themselves. Vince Amato, the man whose company built the bridge between the Island and the mainland, came through with his firm handshake, writing a cheque for five thousand dollars to the Acadian Cultural Centre and Fun Park on his way out.

The Member of Parliament, Ed Montgomery, sent regrets from a conference in Italy. Premier Duke Milligan also sent regrets via an email that Ronnie Corcoran printed up, sealed in a textured, cream-coloured envelope, and handed to the family. Emily Niese went to stick the premier's regrets in her purse when Ronnie grabbed it back from her, as if he had never given it to her in the first place. He tacked it to the photo montage by the coffin.

The parlour's bulletin board was overflowing with images. Roger Niese donating giant cheques. Roger receiving giant cheques. Roger and a parade of politicians breaking ground at the Acadian Cultural Centre and Fun Park. Roger giving instructions to two pole climbers at an Acadian festival in the early nineties. The photo montage was composed almost entirely of published clippings, and his face and bulbous head were often lost in the shadows of splotchy, fading newsprint.

The funeral cortege turned left again onto Route 2. Drivers along the highway, some of them trying to make good time doing a run down to Summerside, were less inclined to pull over. It was a good test of the paved shoulders.

"Will they give Kate part of the estate, do you think?" Janet asked her mother. It was 11:45am. "The Vancouver brother and his wife look like they'd sue the pants off yah if you looked 'em in the eye."

"How do you know she's not in the will herself?" Angela sucked air through her teeth.

The bells were still ringing as the hearse backed up to the church door. Two sharp taps alerted the choir in the balcony to get ready. Three songs off the top, ten altogether for the mass. Father Michael had vetoed "Spirit in the Sky" and "Wind Beneath my Wings," though he permitted the just-as-secular "Au chant de l'alouette" as a treat for the die-hard French speakers. The volume of unhealthy speculations finally dropped as the organ breathed its first chords.

Angela twisted in her seat and glanced toward the back of the church just at the exact right moment. There she was. With a roll of her broad shoulders, white leatherette purse held out in front of her, a fleeting female figure squeezed past the pallbearers lining up between the hearse and the open church doors. Those who hadn't been looking might have sensed the small diminishment of light in the doorway, the sound of rushed, tentative footsteps.

Kate Pineau wore heavy, black-plastic eyeglass frames, which gave her face the look of a 1950s-era stenographer. Her sculptured hair, with its layering and feathering, highlighted peaks, and diagonals you could ski down, was a new thing. She had shed a lot of weight after she'd split with Arnold Crozier, but she was still considered a "big girl." Her own girls—Sherrie, Krystal, and little Bethany—were not with her.

The rear pew was full on both sides. Kate Pineau cut across the back where the eighth station of the cross guarded the confessionals. She found a place hidden on the far side of a pillar, made the sign of the cross, and kept her purse on her lap. The organ's chord revealed itself to be the beginning of "How Great Thou Art." Kate Pineau breathed what one imagined was a sigh of relief. Only a handful of people had noticed her.

Roger had suggested a dozen readings for the mass. Father Michael, not wanting to ask for papal permission to rewrite the liturgy, edited it down to the traditional two. The Old Testament reading, Job 19:1, 23-27, was a no-brainer: "I know that my Vindicator lives, and that he will at last stand forth upon the dust; whom I myself shall see: my own eyes, not another's, shall behold him, and from my flesh I shall see God."

Beatrice Perry, the general manager at the Acadian Cultural Centre and Fun Park, was to read that one. She was in a state, feeling bereft, not just about losing Roger, but about her role in his death and the subsequent mess. But she could always be counted on to perform her duties with grace.

The coffin proceeded down the aisle of St. Bernard's. Kate Pineau was sobbing. Hyperventilating even.

"Please be seated," said Father Michael. Feeling a further disruptive presence in the church, his eyes sought its source. He found it gasping for air from behind a pillar. The congregation caught his eyes and followed them. There were a few tongue clicks but mostly a chorus of silent inhalations.

They were lost to him now. Nobody was paying one iota of attention to the mass.

Father Michael, prone to taking things personally, now wondered if Roger had intended his death notice to cause this drama. If Roger had made a grand effort to blur any difference between here and the hereafter, between the living and the dead.

Was there a way to get their attention back? Father Michael could be the priest who called out from the lectern to Kate Pineau, "What have you done?" Cruelty had its uses. But Father Michael didn't have the nerve. He had lost it years ago. And he had his own reason to be embarrassed and anxious about the events surrounding Roger's death. It was best not to cause discussion of them.

"Peace be with you." Father Michael stretched out his arms. Roger Niese had won. Again.

★

St. Bernard's Parish Hall, which had burned down and been rebuilt once since it was built in 1975, was considered one of the nicest in West Prince. It had been expanded many times, particularly when the rivalry between Father Michael and Roger had been at its peak. The spacious dining room was used for the church picnic lobster suppers in the summer. The main hall, the size of a professional basketball court and flanked by a stage and two kitchens, had a year-round café and was in demand for wedding receptions, bingo fundraisers, and, of course, concerts. There were weeks St. Bernard's Parish Hall hosted as many events as the Acadian Cultural Centre and Fun Park, which was diagonally opposite at the intersection of Palmer and Thompson roads. Though the Parish Hall wasn't as big and modern as the Centre, the ceiling was high, the windows were tall and airy, and the floor bounced as if it was made of firm rubber, all conditions which lured even the most reserved dancers onto their feet after just a couple of drinks. Out the side door, there was a little porch where you could stand and smoke, and a table where you could leave your drinks if the party hosts, owing to a lack of foresight, had failed to obtain a liquor permit.

From the side porch, you could see across the intersection where the hulking hodgepodge of structures that comprised the Acadian Cultural Centre and Fun Park sat behind a white picket fence that ran all the way up Thompson and back to Church View Road. That week, everybody from Tignish to Tyne Valley had found an excuse to drive by the place, as if expecting to see a For Sale sign out front. But the Centre was as lifeless as its founder. Everyone had been given two weeks off to mourn.

It had been suggested by those without firsthand knowledge of the funeral-planning process that Roger would have wanted his funeral re-ception to be held at the Centre, the empire he had dedicated so much of his life to building and maintaining, which was listed in the Lonely Planet, Frommer's, Fodor's, and other less-renowned travel guides. But the obvious was sometimes obviously inappropriate. The Centre's three senior staff members—Beatrice Perry, Mitchell Gallant, and Tracey Shaw (Tillard)—mourned Roger with a depth that was particularly debilitating, rendering unreasonable any call on them to get things set up, then cleaned up. Asking the staff to host the luncheon would have been like asking a widow to dance a jig. Beatrice, Tracey, and Mitchell wept all through the mass and huddled together at the gravesite like children orphaned by a car accident caused by a drunken uncle. People had never seen the likes of it. Three full-grown adults acting like that. Of course, Mitchell, who played the part of all-purpose yes-man at the Centre, was a little simple, brain-damaged from all the falling down he'd done in his life. But Beatrice, the Centre's general manager, was famously unflappable. And people suspected that Tracey, the Centre's retail manager (whatever that was), didn't have a heart at all. When the burial ended, the three of them ran to compose themselves in Tracey's car. The rest of the mourners ambled across the road from the grave-yard to the reception at the Parish Hall.

"Here they come," said Elis Getson, who had, some of the other mem-bers of the Women's Auxiliary noticed, drunk almost half a pot of tea, and eaten half a plate of sugar cookies as the ladies waited for the burial to end. Elis had been leaning out of the window—watching a car turn in her driveway, which was the next up from the rectory—when she saw the herd coming over.

"I certainly hope they're not hungry," Susan Kennedy shrugged, her comment thrown carelessly into the room as if it had no target. Susan was the youngest member of the Women's Auxiliary but, having missed decades of squabbles and grudges, considered herself its babysitter. An import from Charlottetown, she had married Earl Kennedy, who owned a big house near Profit's Corner and managed the Scotiabank in O'Leary. The strain of all Susan's efforts to fit into Up West life, join-ing every group that would have her, had prematurely given her the demeanour of a senior. There were times she wondered if, instead of following her husband Up West, she would have been better off starting up an affair with a younger man and running off to Montreal, a city where her undergrad degree in English would count for something.

"I wonder if I should start cutting the sliced meat in half?" said Susan.

"Too late," said Elis, pulling her head back inside and letting it wobble like an excited little girl. The front doors flew open. The adults leading the way plodded as people who have just left a funeral should, but five or six children bolted in, their scramble to the food table immediately filling the room with the energy of low blood sugar rising.

"One each!" barked Susan. She positioned herself at the sweets like a goalie in a Stanley Cup net. Her eyes greeted the adult mourners one by one. She bowed her head and bit her lip.

Many of the Centre's students, summer staff, and young alumni had skipped the funeral and come directly to the reception. Alone or with their bored parents, they had been waiting in the parking lot or at the Palmer Road strip mall, which occupied another corner of the intersection and provided home to a bakery, a dollar store, a souvenir store, and a restaurant, called KFD, which, as legally as possible, resembled Kentucky Fried Chicken.

Because so many students had passed through the Centre's music and dancing classes, and had had summer jobs there, Roger's was a death that affected the young as much as the old. You could see it as a teachable moment, though instructive of what—who could say? Don't mess with a parish priest? Don't get too big for your britches? Don't meddle in other people's business? Don't get so worked up about things that people thought your head was going to explode? Get yourself a wife and hunker down for a quiet life?

Perhaps such searching questions were for effete city people.

"Nice homily, father," said Janet, who didn't know what to say when the priest took a seat in the chair next to her. She hadn't paid attention to a word of it.

"You think so?" said Father Michael. His eyes darted around the room. He did not like to enter a conversation where criticism was possible. He felt safe at this moment. He thought Janet, despite her post-secondary studies, was a little simple.

The fiddler and the dancer from the wake were setting up. The Niese brothers, the Vancouver wife, and the Ottawa buddy ambled uncertainly into the Parish Hall, surveying a scene with the discomfort of outsiders. Father Michael excused himself from the Gaudets and went over to comfort the blood relatives yet again. He could take refuge in the family's ignorance of his struggles with Roger's life, death, and funeral proceedings.

"Please enjoy the hospitality of the parish's local ladies," said Father Michael. "I hope you found the mass to be healing."

"Of course," said Emily Niese, looking the priest in the eyes.

"Is this all the food?" asked David Niese.

"I guess this isn't licensed?" said Allan Niese.

"I wish we could say we're glad to be here," said David.

"David did like growing up on the Island," said Emily.

"When I was a kid and didn't pay much attention to things," said David. In his rare adult visits years ago, he had seen his brother living in squalor, how his eccentricities could be off-putting to people. David was unable to figure out how Roger had managed to end up so celebrated. The Acadian Culture Centre and Fun Park, and the centrality of it, didn't seem real to him, though Roger was certainly not capable of arranging such an elaborate deceit or any deceit at all. Perhaps it was all a government project, and Roger had somehow been chosen as its spokesperson.

"And why should any kid have to pay attention?" said Emily, her eyes still locked on the priest's. There was something about him. And it wasn't so much the light of the Holy Spirit as something sexy.

Without so much as a head-nod of warning, the dancer from Rustico sprang to her tiptoes, extending her arms. The fiddler played. Something by the Rankin Family, which most of the room received with pleasure.

If anybody had been looking for signs of what happened next, they may have surveyed the arrangement of people around the St. Bernard's Parish Hall. Each distance had a meaning. People had gravitational forces. Some people could turn into black holes. Some people got too close. A few metres here, a few metres there would have saved some embarrassment.

At first glance, Caroline MacPhail, the *Spectator-Herald's* star reporter, looked too downcast to cause much trouble. Although she was not carrying her notebook or camera, people moved away from her as she made her way toward the snack table, perhaps afraid she would start asking sharp questions, the answers for which no one was in any mood to see appear in *The Spectator-Herald* the next morning. Roger Niese—oh, now that was a man who loved to answer questions! Or try to, as best he could, considering the conditions under which his mind worked. Caroline felt as if she had spent the better part of her journalism career trying to get a straight answer out of him. Some wondered whether Caroline was relieved to be free at last from constant nagging. Roger hadn't put the Acadian Cultural Centre and Fun Park on the international map—it had been mentioned at least three times by *The New York Times*—by ignoring the local press. But then, Caroline had tormented Roger all through his life. Wasn't it fair that he got her back?

Caroline, who was daintier than you would have guessed from her take-no-prisoners writing style, was tempted to skip the reception except for her curiosity.

Kate Pineau, too, would have preferred to have been elsewhere. She had hoped to tiptoe in unseen, a funereal broad-brimmed hat pulled down over her face as if she could disguise herself. Here she was, a safe distance from Caroline—hadn't they squabbled, back when Kate was the Centre's number one star? Had Caroline grown tired of taking pictures of Kate in those days?

The senior staff of the Acadian Cultural Centre and Fun Park, Beatrice Perry, Tracey Shaw, and Mitchell Gallant, were wandering dumbfounded around the Parish Hall. Mitchell was a big man, taller and more athletic than Roger. He always wore a hockey helmet in case he had an epileptic seizure and fell. Here he was sobbing into Beatrice's butterfly brooch. Tracey was giddy with grief, her limbs and head flinging about recklessly as she hyperventilated. Beatrice, who would normally be issuing orders and greetings, looked like a hologram: every hair was in place, her perfectly appropriate black shawl draped symmetrically over her shoulders, but she was also not there at all.

As the morbid trio came near her, Kate made a purposeful beeline toward the Niese brothers' circle, extending her hand to offer condolences. Kate said something, though, that caused Emily to turn away sharply. David nervously shifted his weight back and forth.

The Centre staff noticed this tense encounter. Beatrice whispered something into Mitchell's hairy left ear. The Centre's general manager was in her eighties, the janitor was in his early forties, and the connection between them was as strong as mother and son. Mitchell nodded solemnly. With Tracey, they approached the Niese family circle. Chosen family made contact with blood ties.

At first, the words exchanged had the fake lightheartedness required by a funeral luncheon. But then the tone sharpened; the voices got higher, easily heard over the fiddling and the step-dance clomping.

Suddenly, Mitchell's hand snapped shut on the Vancouver brother's throat and, if you could have pulled your eyes away from the fingers clawing into the stubbled flesh, you might have seen an expression of satisfaction stretching across Beatrice's face.

The Vancouver brother fell backward. Kate extended her arms to catch him, then thinking better of it, stepped back, and let David fall on the floor. At least, he had managed to release himself from Mitchell's grip.

Over the next few moments, ears were yanked, faces were slapped. Mitchell, somehow ending up on his hands and knees, chased David, also on his hands and knees, under the snack table. Scuttling along, Mitchell's helmet caught on the thin plastic tablecloth, sending a flurry of dishes, mostly hand-me-downs from parish ladies who had upgraded their own tea services, onto the polished wooden floor.

"Lordie," said Elis Getson, scurrying to catch an airborne teapot she had, presciently it seemed now, emptied into her gut over the course of the day.

Kate found herself holding the right sleeve of Allan Niese's suit jacket in her hand. Tracey tried to slap Caroline, not for any reason in the moment, but taking the opportunity to pay back some bad blood. The *Spectator-Herald* reporter caught Tracey's wrist before contact was made. Caroline held onto that wrist like an athlete holds onto a trophy.

"She's fast, that Caroline," said Angela, who struggled to remain seated.

"Don't know what all this slappin's about when you can bite," said.

Beatrice Perry, who had maintained a medicated decorum throughout the scuffle, made a non-violent intervention. She found Allan, the Ottawa brother, took him by the arm, and led him out of the Parish Hall. She knew Allan. It was the polite thing to do. The Vancouver Nieses could find their own way out.

Outside, the air was cool and clear. The smokers, those who had already fled the Parish Hall and those who, hearing the screaming, had delayed entering, all stared at Allan Niese, who pulled a flask out of his pocket and solemnly offered a swig to anyone who wanted one. Each onlooker took a silent step back from him. Allan sucked the contents of the flask into his own guts.

Most of the other scrappers made their way outside and, already regretting their behaviour, pretended not to notice each other, standing an appropriate distance apart.

"Roger'd know how to fix this," said Kate.

"Roger'd think he'd know how to fix this," said Tracey.

"Roger, God bless his soul," said Beatrice.

"Roger, oh my poor dead brother!" said Allan. "I hardly knew yah."

Allan eyed the car his brother David had rented, parked in the handicap spot. Allan decided it might be a refuge from grief and the insanity that had broken out around him, especially once he saw that the keys had been left in it. Allan heaved the empty flask into the ditch before installing himself in the driver's seat and driving off.

"Littering!" bellowed Beatrice.

Back inside, Allan's Ottawa buddy realized he was the only non-Islander left. All those remaining in the Parish Hall were on their feet now, deciding whether or not to leave. The Ottawa friend bowed to the room and calmly left the building, heading on foot up Palmer Road toward Route 2. He was never seen again. Nobody got his name. Nobody could even really describe him. Years later, when she had had too much to drink at a party, Tracey claimed he had been Dan Ackroyd. The rumour stuck for a while, until it reached a generation of young people who had no idea who Dan Ackroyd was.

"Everyone, we should say a little prayer to bring our hearts and minds back to what we're here for," declared Susan to the people remaining. She had been a substitute teacher and 4-H instructor for years, callings primarily dedicated to preventing injury.

"Indeed," declared Father Michael, who, during the clash, had been in the kitchen checking that the ovens and stovetops were off. "Join hands!"

Nobody moved.

"Gather round," said Susan. The fiddler, who had not ceased playing throughout the ruckus, dropped her fiddle to her hip. The dancer stopped clicking her heels. A lopsided circle formed.

"The Lord's Prayer," called out Father Michael. Even among those who had no regard for prayer, it was as if he had given codeine to an injured person. The room went slack, breathed a sigh. They had a purpose.

"Our Father," began the priest. "Who art in heaven" came the thundering response.

For a few moments, Susan prayed along with everybody else. Then, growing restless, she removed herself from the circle and went quietly into action. She wiped up spilled juice and set the coffee urn right side up. She moved some sandwiches to the kitchen. She up righted chairs.

Near the decimated snacks table, where most of the mess had been made, she saw a large black vinyl purse open on the floor with a folded copy of *The Spectator-Herald* hanging out like a tongue out of a dog's mouth. She removed the paper and looked at the column of newsprint someone had circled in red. She did not have to read the whole thing. Susan, like pretty much everybody Up West, had read it so many times she could recite it by heart.

The death occurred at the O'Leary Hospital, O'Leary, on Wednesday, October 17, 2007, of Roger Niese, of St. Louis, aged 47 years. Born in Ottawa, Ontario, September 15, 1960, he was the son of the late Raymond and Sarah (Potts) Niese. Survived by his brothers David Niese, North Vancouver, British Columbia; Allan Niese, Ottawa, Ontario; sister-in-law Emily Niese (nee Parker), niece Bridget and nephew Gary; and by special friend Kate Pineau, Skinner's Pond. Resting at the Corcoran Funeral Home, O'Leary. Visiting hours will take place at the Corcoran Funeral Home on Friday, October 19, 2007, from 7:00pm to 9:00pm and Saturday, October 20, 2007, from 2:00pm to 4:00pm and 7:00pm to 9:00pm. Funeral service will be held at St. Bernard's Church, Palmer Road, on Monday, October 22, 2007, at 11am. In lieu of flowers, memorial donations to the Acadian Cultural Centre Foundation would be appreciated (that includes free performances).

Susan sighed. She had always thought Roger was a presumptuous attention-seeker. Sometimes she thought all his accomplishments meant as much in the grand scheme of things as a paper hat meant to New Year's Eve. She'd been around. She grew up in Charlottetown. As a young woman, she had spent some time in Cavendish, waiting on tables and hawking T-shirts. She'd seen supposed "world class" tourism attractions—amusement parks and museums and miniature golf courses—reclaimed by woods and swamps after a hard winter and a few bounced cheques. Who knew what would last?

After this eruption of ill-will, though, Susan realized Roger had gotten deeper under people's skin than they realized. That had to account for something, even if you didn't care about the Acadian Cultural Centre and Fun Park's endeavours, government-funded boondoggle or not, Acadian or not. You could hardly blame Roger for the mess. He was from away. He didn't know what the rules were here Up West, no matter how long he had lived here.

Anyway, Roger wasn't here to defend himself anymore, was he?

Kate's marriage to Arnold Crozier had ended, that was true. But when you counted back the days, like you'd count the days back to a premarital conception, you had to wonder how long the end had been brewing, and whether the removal of Roger from the equation would have saved the marriage. You probably couldn't have gotten an answer out of Roger, even if he was alive. He'd talk about literature and music and give examples of songs or poetry quotes and you wouldn't be able to figure out if a kiss passed between his and Kate's lips. You found out more in that obituary than Roger Niese would ever tell you.

"You know who wasn't here," said Elis, interrupting Susan's thoughts. "Debbie Arsenault!"

"Don't say that name aloud," hissed Susan.

"Oh, Susan, Roger's dead," said Elis. "He's not going to hear."

"No, but she might. That's all I need, walking through that door now. Debbie Arsenault."

"I thought Kate Pineau was the problem."

"She was supposed to be the solution."

CHAPTER 2

BEING AWAKE CAN FEEL like being asleep when the spring pollen
has swelled your head up so much you can barely keep your eyes open.
One flicker of the eyelids at your school desk and you're crawling along
the jungle floor or standing with a baton in front of a symphony full of
grimacing faces. Roger Niese plodded along Bank Street with his hands
extended in case he took a nosedive, which he surely would, with all
his sneezing on his walk from school to home. Roger thrilled about his
ability to teleport so easily into the world of dreams—other people's
silence about their having such an ability suggested to him this was a
special power—but worried he might get addicted. He had heard about
addiction on TV. He himself had fallen prey to the vice of excessive milk
consumption and now limited it to his breakfast cereal. No, he did not
want to be the rat at the button. He might get trapped in other soft-
edged dimensions, which would be fine, really, if Roger could count on
people to navigate politely around his prostrate body and, from time to
time, stick a chocolate chip cookie in his mouth so his flesh would not
dissolve into nothingness as his subconscious flitted from elaborate set
piece to set piece.

Having realized as a precocious preschooler that people didn't carry
cookies around with them to give to strange kids lying semi-conscious
in the street, he didn't trust his fellow citizens on this latter point.

Nine-year-old Roger knew where his orchestra conductor dream
came from. At a yard sale on First Avenue, he had bought, along with
three watercolour paintings and a salt-and-pepper shaker set shaped
like mushrooms, a ten-album collection of Beethoven's greatest hits,
all for a dollar-fifty. The merchandise, laid out on pink and orange bed
sheets spread over the damp grass, had been a virtual buffet of arcane
pleasures embedded with virtues only Roger could see in it. The seller

was a man who looked like a Tintin character, goateed, big-nosed, and ready to fly off at a moment's notice, perhaps having brought the loot to Ottawa from seedier harbours.

The Beethoven albums were an especially exciting find, primarily because each of the album covers was emblazoned with its own colourful drawing of a dancing couple in some fantasy location with palm trees or mountains or quaint houses visible in the distance through an arch; even if he didn't like the music, he could tack the covers to his bedroom wall. Another perk: he could override his mother's intolerance of loud music. She wouldn't dare protest against classical music, would she?

"It all sounds the same to me," his mother would moan, standing arms crossed in front of the record player. She was more of a Tammy Wynette fan, though she always changed the radio station when "D-I-V-O-R-C-E" came on. "Stop being so giddy! You're all wound up."

"I'm conducting. Very seriously!" Like Bugs Bunny before him, Roger put his whole body into the motions, occasionally losing grip on his paper-towel-cardboard-roll baton which several times came close to hitting his mother's collection of Red Rose tea figurines on top of the television.

"Roger, just stop it!"

The porcelain animals were so small and compact, they'd break no easier than rocks, but Sarah Niese used any excuse to avoid references to high-brow culture. It reminded her that she could have finished high school, gone to college and married a man who had a library full of leather-spined books. She had watched enough soap operas to have an idea of what it might have been like.

"Do you understand any of it?" Sarah looked at her son with defiance and skepticism. Roger had made it to grade three without her being able to figure out if he was particularly smart or lamebrained.

"You don't understand it, you feel it," Roger giggled. He had heard somebody on TV say that.

Sarah looked at her sister, who was drinking Red Rose tea. "It's all noise to you, isn't it?"

"I like clarinets," said Aunt Margaret Bird, who had studied the instrument in high school. "I think I can pick them out of the mess. They're pretty good."

After Sarah's limits had been exceeded, the albums were placed in an upper kitchen cupboard, to be brought down at prescribed times, namely those rare occasions when Roger finished his homework before 7pm. He soon enough forgot about the records. But he remained a conductor in his dreams, tapping his baton, his fingers fluttering to any music that wafted from the radio or through his imagination.

Roger hopped off the Bank Street sidewalk, into a bulk-food store. It was one of the few neighbourhood retail outlets from which he had not been barred, but that did not mean his shopping expedition was a done deal. Roger flinched as the glare of the clerk fell on him. But he did not retreat. Roger had faced so many naysayers in his short life. He ducked down the beauty-products aisle while some stiff-haired lady occupied the clerk with questions about herbal tea.

He approached the bins of nuts and dried fruit with great solemnity. The results were always the same, of course. Every time he left the store, it was with fifty cents worth of peanuts and raisins. Every time, though, the process was a little different. During his first visit he had been caught using his bare hands. Now he scooped small quantities each of peanuts and raisins, weighed them on the scale, and then sifted meekly through them with the scoop, too nervous to do a proper count while on the premises. A perfectly equal number of nuts and currants was the ultimate goal. Roger came within eight once, but it was a dubious achievement; the raisins, which he didn't like, were the surplus. He had eaten all eight of them with the cool dignity of a martyr.

Wrinkled black nuggets rubbing against smooth, beige ovals. He held open the paper bag for the cashier to see inside.

"You still don't sell by the piece?" he asked the clerk, trying to pre-empt criticism.

"Does your mother know you're here being crazy?"

"Nope," said Roger, doing his best imitation of a Little Rascal. Now those were the kind of boys that adults liked, even if they were dirty all the time.

"Look," said the clerk, a coatrack of a man, who might have reminded Roger of a vampire except Roger hadn't yet learned about vampires, "I'm going to sell these to you this time, but it's more effort than it's worth. It'll be a one-dollar minimum next time."

"Ahhhh," said Roger, who was trying to remember when the other clerk, the nice lady in the flowered dresses, had her shifts. He should carry a notepad to write down such vital details. He couldn't very well ask now. It would give the game away.

"Thanks, Mister," he said, sounding appropriately cheerful and waving frantically as he headed back to the street. He ended most conversations that way when he could. A moment you were prepared for, a moment from which you had eradicated anticipation because you had already lived it in your imagination—that was a moment that couldn't crush you. That was a moment when you wouldn't blurt out the wrong thing, a snide, "We'll see," that would upset the apple cart.

"I'm home," Roger called out, running as fast as he could to his bedroom. Out of the bottom drawer of his dresser, he pulled one of the metal mint tins he had obtained from his grandmother, who, in her forties, had discovered she had horrifically bad breath and amassed a vast collection of mint containers. Roger poured his treasure into the tin with his treasure. All but six peanuts and fourteen raisins fit inside. He took the excess nuts and raisins in his hand and, as was his ritual, tossed them as far back in his mouth as he could. Just in time.

"What took you?" barked David. Roger's older brother was in grade seven and the intermediate school went later than the elementary. David may have ceased to exist for a half hour, Roger figured, not having anybody to pick on.

"I was...."

"Don't say 'with friends.' Don't even."

"I was... I wasn't. Oh, leave me alone, will ya? Where's Mom?"

"Where else, doofus? Down the street. With Allan." David rolled his eyes. "The stinky little troll."

"That's not a nice thing to say. He's only five." Each of the three brothers had a massive chin, jutting out like a crescent moon. Roger's forehead scampered back, ceding every inch his chin gained. David's forehead jutted out bulbously, his eyebrows seemingly supporting a heavy weight. Allan's face was still cherubic, the essential bone structure hidden by pink flesh, and would remain so until middle age.

Roger's defence of Allan was purely on principle. Working intensely on various grade three projects, mostly about bats, he had been ignoring his little brother for some time. When a screaming Allan caught his attention the previous weekend, Roger was genuinely startled to see a strange boy, slightly older than the one he remembered, sitting on the sofa, playing with a ping-pong ball.

"If it makes you feel better, you're a troll too."

"Where's Dad?"

"Where else?" David said. "At school. At the farm. It's still light out, as you might have noticed."

"What are you watching on TV?"

"Nothing."

"I wanna watch *Hogan's Heroes*."

"Maybe I am watching something. Maybe I am!"

David ran off to the living room to guard the channel knob on the TV set.

Roger wasn't sure if he really wanted to watch *Hogan's Heroes* or just get rid of his bossy brother whose torments had grown more elaborate with the onset of puberty. The week before, David lured Roger to the attic with the promise of three cans of Play-Doh. David played something like a game-show host, wearing a clip-on bowtie he had found somewhere, while Roger played something like a model, dressing up in different combinations of their mother's long-abandoned wardrobe choices: vests as shorts, skirts as capes, blouses as pants and anything else as a wrap. To wear a dress as a dress was mere cross-dressing and not eligible for prizes. Allan, who showed up mid-competition, played something like an audience, clapping when a particular headdress (because no outfit was complete without a headdress) pleased him. Though less painful than the game of human croquet wickets David had invented, Roger felt more anxiety about their getting interrupted by adults.

Their mother spent most of her time visiting her older sister, their aunt Margaret, whose family lived on the same side of First Street, just five doors down; an all-weather underground tunnel would have made everybody's lives easier. When she first married Raymond, Sarah thought it was sweet that her husband wanted to set up housekeeping so close to her kin; her parents lived six blocks away, on Thornton, and her first cousin lived on Second, just on the other side of Bank Street. But fifteen years into their marriage, Sarah had come to suspect that the location was more a freedom for him than a courtesy to her. Her sister's was somewhere Raymond could park his wife when he was running around the city doing anything but being a husband and father.

Whatever Raymond's motivation, Sarah had grown tired of being embedded in her nuclear family. She had realized years ago that she didn't like her sister much. But she could not think of a way of extracting herself. Margaret's teenage daughter was mentally challenged—not offputtingly so but enough that she could not be left alone for more than a few moments without her trying to rip up shrubbery. It never seemed right for Sarah to complain that visits and favours always seemed to flow in one direction, nor did it seem wrong to treat her children like anything more than clocks that needed only an occasional winding up. Sarah failed to realize how proficient her sons had become at winding themselves up.

They were in the midst of doing so. *Hogan's Heroes* was not on. There was hell to pay, and it was Roger who would cough up. David came stomping into the kitchen. Roger started running in a panic.

Usually, it was Allan who got to take it all in, as David chased Roger around the house for one reason or another. But on this afternoon, it was their father who quietly entered the front hallway and stood silently until he had gathered enough aural information to be sure it was his own blood, not sinister home invaders, squawking and hurling items around the living room.

"Boys," said Raymond who had, for months, not been in the house before 9pm. Lit by sunlight, he might as well have been a hologram. David released Roger from an ear-chafing headlock, letting his little brother roll into a brass ashtray stand that held a black glass ashtray, which Roger quickly learned was heavier and sharper than he could have imagined. The 1970s backlash had not yet begun, but Roger learned right then about the dangers of smoking. Roger's rolling head wiped blood onto the side of the beige sofa.

"Roger, the upholstery!"

"My neck isn't working."

"Well, get up then."

Head still drooping like a flower on a broken stem, Roger scrambled to his feet.

"Go get yourself cleaned up," his father told him. "David, where's your mother?"

"She's at...."

"Ah right. Yes. Yes. David, could you go get her?"

The eldest Niese boy, still out of breath, scanned the room for signs of fire or for the ax in his father's back. He looked at Roger to see if his brother was damaged seriously enough to require the presence of both parents. David had always wondered if it was possible to go too far. This little bit of body leakage hardly seemed like an outer limit.

"He's fine!" decreed David, absentmindedly rubbing the bruise that was erupting on his own calf. "He's perfectly, perfectly fine."

"Who?" Raymond was already in the dining room, looking through the stationery drawer for lined paper.

"Roger cries if you look at him."

"I'm bleeding," said Roger, too fascinated by his father's arrival to feel much pain.

"David, get your mother. Roger—Do something about, ah, that." Raymond's hands went up and down, as if illustrating the height of a waterfall.

Within ten minutes, the family was gathered in the dining room. Sarah had to be persuaded to stop washing Allan's ice-cream-smeared face. Both David and Roger, whose forehead was still sticky with a smear of dried blood, eyed their little brother jealously. Nobody had mentioned there was ice cream at Aunt Margaret's.

"All right," said Raymond. "Sit down, Sarah. Please."

If Raymond was home and awake, chances are he was sitting at the far end of the dining table, his back to the picture window which looked over the backyard. The dining table was his desk and newspaper reading podium. He leaned onto his elbows, using his hands to support his large head—there was no doubt he was the boys' father—by his ears. Raymond pushed the magazines in front of him off to the side. The boys weren't permitted to look at the National Geographic without his supervision. He hid it under the Saturday Evening Post.

"I could put something on. There's stew ingredients here." Sarah dashed to the kitchen, haphazardly opening and closing cupboard doors.

"Come in here and sit. We'll go out to eat," said Raymond. "I could use a club sandwich."

"I have bread I can toast. And tomatoes...." David and Roger's hearts fell at their mother's words. Restaurant eating meant milkshakes, fries, unlimited ketchup and not having to do dishes.

"No, it's a special occasion, mother." Raymond got up, walked over to his wife, pulled her out of the kitchen and into the dining room. He put his arm around her, an action their sons had witnessed before only when their father had had too much wine at a wedding. He looked sober now. Jumpy even. "We need to celebrate."

"Celebrate?" Sarah giggled nervously. Wasn't that how she had announced her unexpected third pregnancy? She wondered what surprise celebration a man might so unexpectedly and cheerfully declare. They had no place for a pony.

"Your pop, well, he's got a new job." Raymond pulled himself up and pushed his chest out like someone who had been instructed on the proper way to receive a medal.

David, who understood where money came from and what it could buy him, lit up. Roger, who knew the shakiness in his father's voice was that of a confessor, not of a victor, sat hands clasped, patiently waiting for the other shoe to drop.

"Darling!" said Sarah, not quite pulling herself from her husband's grasp.

"It's a great new job. For me. But see... No, no buts.... You like animals, don't you, Roger?"

Roger looked sharply to the right and then to the left. His parents looked for what had caught his attention before realizing it was a theatrical gesture.

"I like owls. I suppose," Roger finally said.

"And David, you like to run around!"

"Ah, sure," said the eldest skeptically. "You're not coming to teach at my school, are you?"

"No, no, no. Teaching, you know. I've never loved teaching very much, have I, Sarah?"

"But you're good at it. They respect you."

"Respect? Lordie." Raymond's eyes rolled. There was a moment of silence during which one could guess Raymond was recalling key examples of the sort of respect he was shown in his wretched high-school classroom. This was a happy announcement, he reassured himself. No matter what had happened last week, the broken ruler, the student's bruise, he was pleased he was able to move toward something. The moving away from something was a bonus. He sighed. "But you know my true love?"

"Farming," the family said in unison, even Allan, who threw his arms in the air at the word. They offered no encouragement to continue; they knew what a bore the topic could be. Roger rolled his placemat up into the tightest tube he could. David, unable to catch his attention, started kicking randomly under the table, hoping to make contact with his brother's leg.

Sensing he was losing the tougher members of the audience, Raymond let go of his wife, leaned down, swept Allan into his arms, and heaved his son around like he was a newborn.

"We're moving to PEI."

Blank stares.

"Prince Edward Island. Canada's smallest province. The garden of the gulf. The million-acre farm." It might have been his introduction to grade nine geography.

"For how long?" asked Sarah.

Raymond realized he was going to have to start all over again from scratch. "No, no, mother. Dad's going to be happy now. No more teaching. PEI—that's it."

The farming thing hadn't come from nowhere. Raymond started volunteering at Ottawa's experimental farm the year David was born. At first, he had been a member of a small gang who conducted the diplomatic tours, pointing out to ambassadors and their wives the various hybrids and the more subtle innovations in soil conservation and water management. After the tours were over, all the hands shaken, Raymond lingered in the fields. The researchers and groundskeepers had gradually learned to be patient with his questions and, as the paid staff moved onwards and upwards to bigger and better projects, Raymond became guardian of what they had told him. Maintaining an extensive database of farm-related information in his brain, he became the resident expert in pesticides and fertilizers, easily identifying types of insects and diseases by their ability to help or, more likely, hinder a given crop. He dropped by the farm before school and after, winter and summer. He formed a Friends of the Experimental Farm group, which the employees tolerated as flattery. They developed an informal policy not to read any of Roger's unrelenting correspondence except for his annual report, which he mailed out each December, like a family Christmas card, to their homes and the homes of each visitor who had foolishly left his or her address in the guest book.

Raymond had tried to bring his obsession with him into the classroom. You might not cover so much territory teaching a subject that held you in raptured awe, but what you did manage to cover was more likely to hold their attention, more likely to forestall disciplinary problems, more likely to sink in. He had proposed an agriculture class to his high-school principal. Smiling and politely saying he'd see what he could do, the man had not even bothered to bring it to the school board. Ottawa may not be a metropole, but it was not a hick town either. The parents of Glebe Collegiate students were raising future civil servants, not hay-chewing farmers. And the children had no tolerance for Mr. Niese's yardstick-slamming when their attention understandably wandered.

"The university there has taken over an experimental farm in Charlottetown, the capital city. Capital to capital for us. And they've.... Well, I'm going to work there."

"You are?" asked Sarah.

"I am. We are. This is the opportunity I've been waiting for."

The thoughts in Sarah's head failed to take shape. They were coffee grounds swirling around a sink and down the drain. She thought of Margaret and what she would say. She remembered when they were growing up, talking about taking a trip to PEI but never getting around to it because their mother had a sister in Boston who monopolized their family's vacation time. Sarah knew Boston better than anywhere outside Ottawa. PEI was poor, wasn't it? They lived in falling-down farmhouses, no neighbours for miles. They milked their own cows.

"For what?" She wasn't looking for a reason she could argue against; Sarah did not like to argue. But maybe her husband, if she got him going, would talk himself out of it.

"You know that, Sarah."

"Me? I don't know what's happening right now." The problem was that she knew exactly what was happening. But if she pretended she didn't, maybe it would stop.

"Is this a fight?" asked Roger. "I don't like fighting."

"I wouldn't know what it's about, dear," said Sarah.

"What do you think, boys?" Raymond figured the young absorbed new information more quickly than the old.

"You work at a farm, don't you, Dad?"

"This is different, David. I would be able to put my passion into it and be paid. I'd be one of the bosses. Not a volunteer."

"And where would we be?" asked Roger.

"It'll be so much fun. PEI is a great place for boys. The beach will be so close. The farms. The fresh air."

Raymond's two eldest sons got that they were moving—and their faces flushed with panic. Their mother, meanwhile, stood up quickly, a rush of blood surging to her head. Her vision blurred. She stumbled on her feet.

"Don't be so dramatic," snapped Raymond. "You don't have to rain on my parade, do you?"

"No, no, it's not that." Sarah grabbed the back of a dining room chair and lowered herself to a sitting position.

"What is it then? Why aren't you happy for me?"

"You always have something to say, don't you?"

Allan, who didn't understand anything that was going on but noticed the room's emotional temperature had risen, started to cry.

"Daddy," said Roger. "If we're going somewhere, can I take everything with me, even my turtle?"

"Yes, yes, of course." Raymond's mind was on his panicking wife.

"Might it be possible for me to have my own room?"

"I think so, yes. There's more room to spread out in Charlottetown."

"I suppose I should call Mum," said Sarah.

"Let's figure out how to put it to her first."

"Like you figured out how to put it to me?"

"Can we get a horse?" asked David.

"It's possible, boys. Anything is possible."

Yes, thought Sarah. Anything is possible. I could run down the street in my nightgown and run up the canal to that experimental farm and I could set the whole thing on fire and I could fling myself into it.

"That's the spirit," said Raymond, loosening his grip a bit too much on Allan, who was, much to the relief of his parents, when they picked him off the floor, not the bleeder his brother was.

CHAPTER 3

IN OTTAWA, THE NIESES had been too caught up in quotidian concerns to bother with recreational activities. Like joining the circus or panning for gold, neither camping nor picnicking occurred to them. Sarah could count the times in the run of a year when she left the Glebe, never mind Ottawa city limits. The few times she agreed to a road trip, perhaps to Montreal or Kingston to visit Raymond's equally insufferable kindred spirits and colleagues, were rushed and poorly thought-out, their ill-timed arrival coinciding with dinner or, preferably, their hosts' departure.

But the family's increasingly utopian-minded patriarch believed that Prince Edward Island would transform them into outdoorsy people who would fill their time with nature walks, cross-country skiing, and bird watching. The fresh country air would envelop them, delivering a pleasant and wholesome head-rush that would, self-perpetuatingly, send them out to commune with intoxicating flora and fauna. So, as they headed east on the TransCanada, their '67 Valiant hauled a pebble-shaped Play-mor camper, a purchase Sarah would neither acknowledge nor discuss. At least the thing had kept Raymond out of the house while she packed and repacked, removing all dead space from each box and bag so there wasn't a square inch of air left among their possessions.

The services of a proper moving company had been commissioned. But the at-first-glance spaciousness of the camper, with its narrow-assed toilet, cleverly stacked bunk beds, and nooks and crannies that would have excited a squirrel, proved too much of a temptation for Raymond. The small appliances, workshop tools, knickknacks, and a substantial selection of the adult wardrobe were packed inside the Play-mor for the twenty-four-hour drive. Sarah would not camp in the thing. Roger accepted the plausibility of his mother's argument: humans and their tightly packed stuff cannot occupy the same space at the same time. Moving around inside the camper was something only Allan enjoyed, oblivious as he was to the risks of suffocation. An exasperated Raymond finally splurged for a room at a cheap hotel in Drummondville, Quebec. Its coin-operated vibrating bed was an object of fascination for the eldest son, who spent the evening pleading for quarters.

Aside from the expected disputes over colouring books, a drying up of ideas with eye-spy, and the loss of a dozen playing cards, the journey was mostly uneventful. The spring weather hummed clear and warm. The three times Allan threw up, they were close to a comfort station or safe pull-over point. The traffic was so light on the TransCanada, the highway seemed a holdover from a busier past or optimistic planning for the future. Its present desolation served Raymond's nervous driving habits. A panicked brake-slam coming out of Rivière-du-loup did no more damage than sending Allan into another round of retching.

Roger, who tolerated the long trip and his brothers' odorous excretions by remaining well inside his own head, arrived at the Cape Tormentine ferry terminal with expectations that were about right for an arrival at Pompeii, the Taj Mahal, or a moon space station. Through most of New Brunswick, he had stared at the PEI visitors' map, imagining the infrastructure that would be needed for marine vessels to carry cars and passengers across an eight-mile span of the Northumberland Strait. He expected that, as they drew nearer, the dense pine woods would thin, giving way to a glistening array of cranes, freighters, and tall ships. To markets where exotic spices, fruit, and reptiles were bought and sold. To a place where farmers—and his father had promised many, many farmers—sold their wares off trucks or out of medieval-looking tents. Pirates and minstrels would not have surprised him.

Roger grabbed onto his mother's headrest to pull himself up to adult height as they approached the toll booth. He scanned the horizon. The terminal, no bigger and no more glamorous than a strip mall of non-chain stores, sat between a woods and field, not unlike the ones they had been driving past for hours on end. He looked at the toll collector, a buxom woman in a dirty blue man's shirt. She was no guardian of a magical world.

"It's just a parking lot," Roger moaned.

"They've got vending machines, if somebody'd care to give me a quarter." David glared at his brother.

"You've had enough junk," replied his mother absentmindedly. Her mind was still in the Glebe. Her sister hated her. Sarah Niese could tell. Margaret would never manage on her own. Their mother was having migraines. Perhaps the house sale would fall apart and Sarah would have to return to Ottawa to relist it. There was always hope.

"You can see it from here, Ma," said Raymond, pointing to a sliver of ruddy brown that separated the pale blue sky from the murky blue water. "Huh, Ma?"

The boys did not have much time to explore the terminal's meager offerings. Ten minutes after Raymond Niese parked them in the fourth lane of waiting cars, the ferry arrived. The vessel, of a breathtaking size that made Roger think of an iceberg, looked seaworthy enough to get them to the Baltic. Its grandiose greasiness overwhelmed the makeshift scale of the treed landscape. As their car and trailer bounced on board, Roger thought the car deck might have been an ancient cave retrofitted with metal plating, the stalactites encased in metal tubing, clumps of wiring providing a home to bat colonies. A maze of portals led starboard and stern, topside and further down below sea level. Every surface had a highly articulated yet unimaginable purpose. Roger, lightheaded from lack of sleep and excess sugar, was spellbound, imagining living there forever, food and comic books appearing courtesy of passing fishermen. He would get used to the fumes, the poor lighting, the driblets of water trickling along the grooves on the floor.

A ferry worker in a fluorescent vest shattered Roger's daydream.

"That way to the passenger decks! The fries won't do you as much damage as a tractor-trailer rolling on your toes!" he bellowed. "Parking brakes, people, parking brakes!"

Like refugees making their way through a border town, the five Nieses followed a grey-bearded man who seemed like he knew where he was going. They zig-zagged around the cars to a hatched door that opened onto a staircase as narrow and steep as a ladder. Their final climb, though, was on a compact oak staircase that might have been ripped from a Victorian-era five-star hotel built for children. In a gasping blink, the grimy lower realm revealed itself to be a mere backstage to the sensuous and well-lit theatre set that was the passenger deck. Roger wanted to squeal with delight as they ascended into a quintes-

sentially nautical lounge, wood panelling here, brass there, lushly upholstered seating pulling it all seamlessly together. Tempting corridors
led off in all directions.

"Can we...?" asked Roger, his eyes taking it all in.

"Stay with your brother. I don't want you falling overboard," snapped
his mother, who had just realized how dirty Allan's face was. She
needed a sink. And, it must be said, a clean toilet for herself. The drive
through New Brunswick—a province of burnt-out car bodies, old fridg-
es sitting on unpainted front porches, broken swings, and dirty-faced
children playing in swampy ditches—did not give her much hope for
what she'd find on board.

"The two of you meet back here at these stairs in half an hour."
Raymond scowled at David, who was harrumphing at the babysitting
duties.

"Let's go." Roger wanted to squeeze as much adventure as possible
out of the next thirty minutes.

"I have an idea," said David when their parents were out of earshot.

"Yes?" said Roger skeptically.

"Let's look for spies. I know there has to be a few on board, stealing
state secrets, sabotaging our national achievements."

The deck was filling with passengers. Although the boys hadn't yet
developed the insight to see it—and it might be suggested that Roger
never developed this insight—the passengers could easily be divided
into two categories: locals walking around in circles to see who they
knew was on the ferry that they could chat with; and tourists serenely
ecstatic that the passage over water signalled the official commence-
ment of their holidays. Roger's initial doubts about his brother's
motives gave way to enthusiasm. There had to be secrets available to a
sharp eye.

"Okey dokey!"

"Look for anything suspicious. Maybe somebody who's trying to get
information back to the Russians."

"Who are the Russians?"

"Anybody who shouldn't be knowing things about our way of life."

"Great!" Roger was pleased by such an open-ended definition. David
rarely made things this easy. "What do we do with them when we find
them?"

"You have to gob on them." David pantomimed the acts of aggressively spitting, the act of drooling on a shoe, and the act of a fake sneeze. "Tag him so the cops can identify him."

"Ewww."

"Seriously. It's easier than trapping and torturing them. It'll be fun, Rog. You have to do it, man. You have to do it. I'm going to do it. You have to do it."

"Shouldn't we interrogate them? Try to get them to confess?" Roger had started carrying a notepad around in his back pocket, in which he wrote down all the ideas that came to him.

"Do it right and I'll give you two of my dinkie cars, my red one and my black convertible, one for every dozen you hork on. We'll meet by that lifeboat in twenty minutes. Okay?"

Roger would have agreed to anything in order to have twenty minutes of his own on the ship. Spying was a perfect task, one in which his stealth and careful observation would also help him avoid his parents, who would not be pleased to spot him on a solo mission.

On the open deck, the wind nearly ripped the baseball cap off Roger's head. The heavy door clanged behind him, making him feel he might be trapped there forever. A couple, maybe in their twenties, was leaning on the railing, their arms around each other. The woman wore a flowered wrap around her shoulders. Roger thought it might be covering up a wound from a knife fight or a scar from acid spilled during an assassination attempt. Her suitor turned around, noticed Roger, and glared at him as if the boy had invited himself along on their honeymoon. Further on, a young family took turns posing for pictures.

After one circumnavigation of the ship's deck, Roger's bladder was distracting him from his mission.

He ducked back inside—yes, the heavy door could be opened from the exterior—and scurried down a tight corridor, passing the temptations of the pinball room (which made no sense on the high seas) before finding a men's washroom tucked away behind the cafeteria exit. Like the car decks, the utilitarian design of the loo had no pretense and might have been inspired by military vessels. A long, narrow, and low-ceilinged compartment held two rows of equally narrow toilet stalls. Once seated—a necessary position because of all the bobbing, shuddering, and heaving of the vessel—one would have to keep his knees clamped together, elbows tight to the hips. Roger used his hands to stabilize himself as he walked the distance to the end stall; he was extremely pee shy and did not want to be distracted by passersby. Roger was glad for the quiet moment.

His peace was short-lived.

Midstream, Roger became aware of a rush of motion into the next stall. With all that choice, only an animal would choose a stall so close to another pair of shoes. For distraction, Roger silently sang "Harper Valley PTA." A few more glugs of pee landed in the stainless-steel bowl. Next door, more rustling, then a sharp, echoey clank. The ferry waned, triggering several smaller clanks. An open bottle of rum rolled into Roger's stall, nudging against his sneakers. Like a boozy slug, the bottle left a trail behind it. Roger's urinary tract seized up.

"Fuck," said the gravelly voice on the other side of the partition. "Give that here!"

"Swearing!" said Roger. It's what his mother would have said. He pulled up his pants quickly and tried to manoeuvre himself into a less vulnerable position.

"You, there! My fucking rum's spilling all over the fucking poop deck, for God's sake. Fucking pick it up or we'll be swimming in it."

It was true; half of the rum had spilled over Roger's shoes, mixing with the misdirected urine already coating the metal floor. Hating waste more than he hated being ordered around, Roger righted the bottle, setting it by the metal toilet tank. His then mind turned to something more pressing: escape.

"Give it here, you little shit. I'll beat your ass." The voice, with its squawky high notes and low rumbling bass notes, was half-drunk already. A fist pounded on the metal partition.

"What are you doing over there?"

"Spare me the lip, kiddo. Hand it the fuck over." These waters had once been traversed by rumrunners bringing booze from Saint-Pierre and Miquelon to dry U.S. markets. It was entirely possible, thought Roger, that the stall next door was a portal to that time.

A hand shot through the gap between the partition and the floor. Shrieking, Roger grabbed the bottle and jumped up onto the toilet seat. He watched the arm dart around like a poisonous snake. Mid-tricep was as far as it could go. Roger leaned forward to check the lock on his stall.

"Gimme, fucking bastard, fucking asshole, cunt."

"Language!"

This prompted a stream of profanities that made the first round seem mild. What it did not trigger was a siege on Roger's stall. The man did not want to come out. For all his verbal shamelessness, perhaps he did not want to be seen.

"Tell me when you're ready to talk nice."

"Fuck you!" said the pirate. A moment of silence when the ferry shuddered. "What do you fucking want, you little twerp?"

"Say it nice," said Roger. He wondered how much time he had left before he had to meet David and return to the car.

"What, then? What!"

"Who are you working for?"

"I work for meself!"

"I see," said Roger. "On the high seas?"

"I'm from fucking Palmer Road, for God's sake. Do you know where that is? Didn't think so, you fucking little tourist."

"Are you going to, um, do any damage to this ship?"

"The only damage I'm going to do is to your eff-ing head if you don't give me that bottle. Where are your bloody folks, anyway? Taking pretty pictures, I'd guess. So romantic!"

Roger thought for a minute. He regretfully decided it was time to break character.

"It won't fit under without spilling more. Give me the cap."

"The cap's.... Fuck the cap. Don't you be giving me any orders. Give my bottle here."

"Let's meet at, ahhh, the sinks."

When Roger stepped out of his stall, the bottle, in a flash, was ripped from his hand.

In person, the pirate looked like he might have started out as a dough-faced farm boy who experienced too much dough and too little farming. Marked by veins and sun, his face, neck, and bare arms might have been smeared with berries. His eyes had a dangerous glare.

"You're a cocksucking little thief," said the pirate, holding the bottle at his hip like a pistol.

"I have to go. My parents are waiting for me."

"I'll tell you when you can fucking go, you little cocksucker," shouted the man. Pirates, it seems, changed the rules whenever they wanted.

There was a beat—no, there were several. Eyes remained locked. Then the man's shoulders dropped a little. Holding a nine-year-old captive in the washroom of a car ferry was not something he had set out to do when he went to take a piss.

The pirate walked unsteadily backward toward the exit as Roger followed.

"Don't try anything or I'll say you touched my penis." Ready access to words like these were the sole advantage of having an older brother.

"You are a total little know-it-all twat, aren't you?"

Roger had been picked on at his school, it was true. He had always blamed his classmates for being cruel, crazy barbarians. He had always figured his victimhood was random, like those poor kids born on February 28 or on Christmas Day, a small accidental fact delivering crushingly real repercussions. This move to PEI, if he could conceive of it as a good thing, would put that behind him. Some other sucker would take his place, chasing after the chocolate bar snatched from his lunch bag, guarding his underwear against wedgies, searching for boots that were snatched away and hidden. Now this man was telling Roger it was not the victims who were interchangeable; it was the bullies. His tormentors would manifest themselves in some new Island boys unless Roger did something to prevent it.

He had to leave part of himself behind on the mainland. Roger offered a meek smile.

"Okay, give me a drink of that."

"Go fuck yourself."

"I'll tell."

A muffled chime over the P.A. system was followed by an announcement for passengers to return to their vehicles.

The pirate sighed an elongated "fuck" and handed the bottle over. Roger wiped the bottle's mouth on his shirt sleeve and, taking a breath, took a big swig. Most of it he spat out, splattering the pirate.

"Fuck!" said the pirate, but the new Roger didn't care. He dropped the bottle in disgust, spilling the remaining gulps over the sticky floor. The man bellowed again. Roger pushed past and out the door.

"Drinking is bad for you," Roger said, dashing out into the hallway.

Raymond was waiting for Roger at the top of the grand staircase. He grabbed his son's arm to show his displeasure.

Sarah was fuming in the car below deck.

"Roger! I have been…. Where have you…?"

"I got lost…."

The oldest brother punched the middle brother in the leg. Roger was tempted to scream and ask why he should be placed in the custody of someone who willfully did him physical harm. Instead, he quietly started to cry so his parents would leave him alone. And they did. He wondered if anyone could tell that he wasn't really upset.

The car and trailer wobbled on the ramp. The Niese family had arrived in their new homeland, though becoming Islanders, it would turn out, was not an option.

CHAPTER 4

AN OTTAWA TEACHER'S SALARY was extraordinarily comfortable compared to that of an agriculture researcher at a newly established experimental farm. Nor did the affiliation with a newly established university provide prestige, funding, or expense accounts.

Island farmers were in the early stages of consolidating what had been small parcels of land, divided amongst sons at each generational turn. Bigger was increasingly better. Also with the government's encouragement, the farming enterprise itself was being sliced into mechanized components of an efficient capitalist enterprise—why would a dairy farmer have pigs?

In this environment, Raymond's views were seen as quaint. A generation of Islander farm families seemed eager to wash the soil from their hands, while those in it for the long haul dreamed of larger and more powerful machines. There was little time to pay attention to the birds.

The Niese transition to their Island home took months. The boys suspected that what was called the "Island way of life" was a sort of befuddling limbo. Perhaps their neighbours also kept their socks in suitcases and ate off paper plates while the CorningWare lay in storage. For two weeks, crates and boxes and a beloved heavy oak dining set sat lopsided on the lumpy front lawn, waiting to be crammed into the tiny bungalow.

"What do you want for that hutch?" local bargain hunters would ask, assuming it was a yard sale. Sarah would exasperatedly fetch her husband so he could talk at them until they finally gave up and walked away empty-handed. This was how, for a time, she was reputed to be mute.

For the boys, the green vinyl siding on the three-bedroom prefab home was excitingly modern. The house's yard was more spacious than their Ottawa yard. They were delighted there was enough room to play off to the side of a house, where there were no windows from which their mother could watch them. Unlike in Ottawa, property lines were not so defined; only the length of the grass told you where their lot ended and the neighbours' began.

Inside, the bedrooms were bigger, even if the kitchen, living room, and dining room were more cramped. The walls were thinner. With slippery hallways perfect for running slides, the brittle wooden bedroom doors quickly developed ankle-high indentations and holes.

The massive picture window in the living room looked across a road—someone might call it a street—to a butterfly-inhabited meadow and, beyond that, to the red brick buildings of the newly formed University of Prince Edward Island. Ottawa was no metropolis, but, to Roger, Charlottetown seemed to have more pastureland than architecture.

Raymond would not need to drive to work. But for the first few months anyway, he gave in to societal expectations that he commute by car. On PEI, to not drive was to arouse suspicions of a criminal record or worse. It was Raymond's responsibility to adapt. His family saw him try. He arrived on his first day at work in denim overalls; his three coworkers, all in their twenties, wore polyester shirts and ties. They worried that this old fart (Raymond was thirty-seven at the time) would get in the way of what should be a very slack job; supervision was almost impossible in the fields and unlikely in the lab, so long as the paperwork was done right. Raymond tried to avoid gushing about his horticultural passions for fear they might intimidate the younger fellows. Yet they soon placed him in the most readily available category they had for him: Ontario nature-lover who had used his political connections to get a retirement-ready job. Though why he would exploit connections for a banishment from a province where money and strippers grew on trees was a mystery.

Setting up housekeeping, Sarah found herself doing as much re-packing as unpacking. Her face fell when she realized their home was a bungalow; it offered few places to escape to. With the large front windows, it was like being on constant display. Even closed curtains gave others too much information about what was going on inside.

"We'll find another house soon. A century home, something with those stairs they used to have for maids and a kitchen you could feed an army in," Raymond promised her. The grandfather clock, oriental rugs, and a half-dozen occasional tables could wait in the extraordinarily dry basement till the upgrade.

The backyard gave way to a corn field beyond which, as they would discover when the corn was cut in late August, was another road and then a potato field, then another road, a golf course and then a body of water, and then more farmland. Although Roger had not yet fully manifested his compulsion for knowing where everything was, he was sure there were no 7-11s, no candy stores with collectible cards. Charlottetown itself had only a sad Slurpee-less imitation of a 7-11 where they had bought milk before his mother settled on a proper grocery store.

David found many places near the house where his younger brothers' screams would not be heard. Sometimes his torments took the form of something gross, like his shoes after he mistakenly stepped in a cow paddy. Sometimes they were about endurance, like assigning Allan to cling to a tree as long as he could if he wanted a partner for a game of catch.

But all these sibling harassments could not dampen the new feeling of freedom. These were halcyon days for the Niese boys. Three weeks before starting at their new school, the three of them were running around the countryside like a pack of feral dogs effortlessly discovering fresh chicken carcass after fresh chicken carcass. They took their bikes on the road, visited a convenience store without permission, collected dirty bottle caps from ditches. Roger gathered lupins, pink and purple and mauve, ripped them apart, and added rainwater to produce a magic potion. As long as the boys showed up for lunch and dinner—and these were delightfully lazy meals of mac and cheese, grilled cheese, hot dogs, soupy hamburger mix, and fries—as long as they spent the long, sunny evenings parked in front of the television, whatever else they did was their private matter.

It was a shame their parents lacked interest. If the boys had been given the opportunity to recount their adventures, they would have contributed to a much-needed family mythology, vignettes that would have fortified the spirit of graduations, weddings, and funerals. But in those weeks, the brothers lived concisely in the present. Other children might as well have been unfamiliar tribes camped on the opposite side of the canyon; forming alliances was not worth risking unexpected hostilities. They were all old enough to know that school would be a major reset.

School supplies appeared on the kitchen table the Wednesday before school started. They sharpened coloured pencils, tested erasers, and installed scribblers in binders. On the Friday before, the boys were taken for haircuts. On the Saturday, the boys were ordered to clean up their rooms. And on the Sunday, with the sun's brightness ringing in the cooling September air, Raymond announced an expedition. They would go to the beach. Islanders went to the beach as much as they could each summer, but for the Nieses, a trip to the shore would mark the end of their orientation as newcomers.

"I don't want anybody tracking sand into my carpet," said Sarah.

Finally caving in, she put a change of shoes and some towels into two brown paper bags; chopped vegetables, cookies, and a thermos of cherry Kool-Aid in another two. The boys had not contemplated the possibility of living close to a beach. They were beside themselves with giddiness. Roger flapped his hands. Allan skipped. Even David brightened. They were too excited to consider their father's motives, which grew out of late-night arguments, one of which ended in this cheerful plea: "We're on an Island, ma! Won't it be fantastic to go to the beach anytime you want, the sea wind in your hair?"

"What would I want a beach for?" All Sarah could picture in her hair were bird droppings. "Give me a good grocery store, a decent fabric shop. The light, will you?" She could never figure out how her husband got it into his head that beaches, those large swaths of filth and debris, would warm her to Island life. Still, she would go and get it over with before Raymond got other ideas, like winter walks, hunting or, she shuddered, installing a swimming pool in the backyard.

★

By the time they got to Stanhope, the late afternoon air was pulling heat from land. Raymond Niese parked the car on the road that ran along the backside of the dunes. The family marched up the park's wooden walkway. From the deck at the top, the cool-white beach swept out in front of them.

Roger was mildly resentful of his exhausted state; it had taken so long to get here.

The beach was busiest near the walkway from the parking lot.

Couples and families and groups of young people drinking beer were scattered like tribes between the dunes' peaks and the edge of the slate-blue water. The Nieses pitched their modest camp not far from a large family gathering whose territory was marked by an assortment of tents, blankets, depleted food stations, drink coolers, sandcastles, and beach toys. The family made a show of how close it was. Granny passed a beach ball to a three-year-old, who threw it to the German Shepherd puppy who dropped it at the feet of a middle-aged man who stuffed the ball under a blanket on which a baby sat kicking its legs.

Sarah lay on her back on the bedspread she had brought, a woman on an examining table waiting for a doctor's cold hands. Allan immediately fell asleep beside her. Raymond sat primly on the corner of a brown bath towel, looking in the direction of the family gathering. His ears were cocked for stray phrases that would provide him with an opening conversational gambit.

"Not too far, boys," he called out at David and Roger. His sons were already out of earshot, walking quickly and calmly so as not to trigger more warnings. Their decorum soon gave way to a footrace, then a shoving match. The dunes got larger as they headed west. There was no one on this part of the beach. They kept to the waterline looking amongst the rocks and faded lobster shells for more exciting treasures.

"Be a seal! Walk on your hands!" David ordered Roger. "Do it and I'll feed you fish!"

David's bossiness was much less threatening under all that blue sky. The same blue sky that was over Africa, Malta, Antarctica, and China, places Roger had seen on TV, places he was sure he'd visit someday.

Roger made a run for it.

He sprinted up the beach and would have clapped his hands with delight if he could have seen the sand shooting out from under his feet, like jet-bursts from a rocket. Roger zipped past an old lobster trap, orange Styrofoam buoys, and some plastic oil containers. David's yells crumbled in the sunlight. The brothers, for once, had not been instructed to stay together. Roger splashed in and out of the freezing shallow water as he ran, the smooth, flat rocks pressing painlessly into his bare feet. David did not have to be obeyed.

When Roger ran out of breath, he turned around. David was a mere matchstick in the sand, head barely discernible from his shoulders.

That also must be how Roger looked to David. Unrecognizable. He ran further. The dunes swept on.

He ran past a massive piece of driftwood, grey and twisted.

And then, there it was. Partly hidden from view by the log. It took a moment to figure out what it was and what its being there meant.

It was the same colour as the log, waterlogged grey. Dry and wet. Sand and clay clung to its fur. What must have been sad, stuffed-animal eyes—fodder for anti-fur campaigns—were closed. Roger was thankful. Otherwise, he would not have been able to do what he did.

It was still fat. It was still breathing, very slowly. The seal was a long way from the high-water mark.

Roger got as close to the seal as he dared. He had never seen one up close before. Here was a playmate of whales and dolphins and walruses. A real clown. Roger picked up a thin twig. He poked. The seal did not twitch. A sputtering sound from inside. Roger's heart raced. Perhaps something gross was happening. Perhaps he'd be blamed. He found new energy, more breaths. He ran.

Roger scrambled across the beach and heaved himself up the slope of the dunes. They were steep here, sand cliffs. His feet cutting deeper and deeper into softer and softer sand. Nearing the top, he grabbed at the sharp marram grass, which came loose in his hand. Roger stumbled onto a narrow plateau at the crest of the dune and collapsed on his knees, a castaway arriving at long last on solid ground. The small circle of bare sand was surrounded by grass, stretching down toward a swampy lagoon and a scraggly woods. He did not know the little circle had been caused by the repeated visits of nudists, whose blankets, towels, and beach umbrellas had killed the marram grass.

"Oh God," he thought to himself. He inhaled deeply. Molecules of dying seal breath were in his nose. He was breathing them in.

"Hey! Hey!"

The sound popped into his ear. Was it a word? It couldn't be another human.

"Hey! Get out of here!"

Something rose up out of the rolling green marram grass. The eyes might have been a fox's. It was not until Roger saw the mouth that he realized it was a girl. Her dress of tiny brown flowers made her look like she was wrapped in rusty aluminum. It slowly dawned on him he had caught her peeing and that the right thing to do was turn away. By the time he did so, twitching with shy panic, she had already composed herself. That composure took the form of a taunt, delivered in a sharp voice that, Roger worried, echoed for miles.

"Peeping Tom trying to catch a peep! Peep! Peep! Peep!"

Roger turned his back to her. He was too agitated to take in the sprawling blue of the Gulf of St. Lawrence; his visual cortex held the girl in plain view. She wasn't budging.

"Peeping peeper! Peep! Rapist, that's what!" Her voice was full and confident, like a star solo vocalist at a music festival hitting all her consonants. "Rapist. Rape! You're raping me!"

Roger did not know what this meant but he was sure he didn't want to be caught at it. He suspected the police would come, something he feared more than any punishment his parents might mete out. Shame welled up inside of him. Aside from a few haggard seagulls and the half-dead seal, they were totally alone. He said exactly the wrong thing.

"Don't tell!"

The girl took a step toward him. Roger was frozen. He could see her raise and lower her eyebrows, perfectly formed arches that defined her face even more than her eyes. Her forehead was enormous. She was about his age, but had poise and confidence Roger had never seen before in another kid.

"I love to tell! You should hear me tell. Your face is red already. Guilty! Peeper! Rapist!"

"Don't!" Tears streamed down Roger's face. He could hear his voice, stretched full of hysteria. Hyperventilation seemed the most natural next step. She might take pity on someone unconscious.

"Don't what?" There was already a sense of disappointment in her voice as Roger's tears rolled off his face onto the sand; there was almost no place for her performance to go. Almost.

"Have you seen a girl pee before? Have you?"

"I didn't see anything! I didn't see!" Roger was filled with the dread he felt when David threatened to show him the magazines he had shoplifted from the convenience store back in Ottawa. Roger believed that if he had absorbed the magazines' garish glossiness, he would be irreversibly changed. The loss of innocence he imagined was not sexual—Roger lacked even a street knowledge of sex—so much as catastrophic. Something torn inside you. Roger had, so far, failed to absorb from other men any sense of lust, admiration, or sexist belittling that marked women as different. Femaleness darted just outside Roger's field of vision.

"I saw nothing."

She came closer. "I'll have to read your mind to find out."

"What?"

"You have to promise not to touch me when I do it. Or I'll tell. I'll say you raped me and then touched me. I'm clear-voyant. My IQ dwarves yours. My teacher told me. All my teachers."

Roger cringed hearing the word "tell" again. Slowly and ceremonially, like a veterinarian trying not to startle a farm animal, the girl stepped forward and raised her hands to his temples. Roger did not move. Her fingertips hovered there, grazing the tiny hairs at his temples. Roger inhaled sharply through his runny nostrils.

"Shhhh."

"What are you... Oh!" Roger pulled his head away. "No!"

"If you didn't see anything, this is the only way to prove it."

"You can't. Can you?" The possibility excited and frightened Roger. He wanted clairvoyance to be true, but he didn't want her to have it. Why had he been passed over for this gift?

"Believe me." She squinted. Roger clenched his jaw and held as still as he was able.

"You're not from PEI. Not at all."

"Maybe."

"Bad liar."

"Maybe."

"Your family will be worried if you don't show up soon."

"Sure."

"But not too worried. They like the others better."

"No!"

"A lot better, I can see."

"No."

"I can see you don't know much about girls. Nothing, really."

"I don't know."

"But you are curious. You want to know. You are a little pervert." Her fingertips made contact with his temples. "You... Oh, your future is bad. Very bad."

"You can't!"

"Do you want to know your future? Do you dare?"

"I don't do dares." Because of David, dares were strictly forbidden.

Her fingers released his skull but hovered over his skin like magnets.

"Hrph," she growled, her best impression of a wise old man. "I can see inside your mind. I know you're afraid to take a dare. Little boy is afraid."

"Not."

"Fear's seeping out of you." She smirked. Her button-pushing would have been transparent to most people, but not to Roger. He had reached his limit.

Without grazing her fingertips, Roger whipped his head from between her hands and, as if he had been pushed, hurtled himself down the dune, barely keeping himself upright until he reached the beach's flat sand.

The journey here, beyond the limits of civilization, had taken ages. His sprint back to his family felt instantaneous, filled only with the blur of sand and sky and the whisper of wind in his ears. He didn't look back.

Roger had not been reported missing and, in fact, had not been missed. He had been gone for twenty minutes, tops. David was writing profanities in the sand. Allan was still sleeping by his mother. The only change in the familial mise-en-scène was Raymond, who was now talking to the alpha male of the nearby family gathering. Roger joined his father; being alone could invite more disaster.

Raymond was about four hundred miles into recounting their trip from Ontario. "... And the gas station in Rivière-du-loup, now they had the most expensive gas that you'd ever encounter this side of the Atlantic because, if you read the news, you know that the Europeans pay a lot for their gas...."

The man nodded patiently. Several minutes passed before Raymond registered that Roger was standing sheepishly at his side. Raymond's cue was the man's eyes, which lowered to Roger's and stayed there, fixed on the young man, until Raymond followed his gaze.

"Your son?" His tone was that of a teacher correcting a mistake in an oral presentation, the error being, it seemed, Raymond's failure to make an introduction.

"Oh, yes. Yes. This is Roger. The, ah, middle one."

"I'm Reverend MacPhail," the man told Roger, extending his hand. He had a square head, grey moustache, and eyes full of unsolicited opinions. "You can call me Reverend or pastor, if you like."

"Hello, Reverend, I'm enchanted to meet you, totally enchanted," said Roger, as if reciting the first few lines of a favourite poem.

Raymond looked at his son, mystified. The pastor looked amused by the formality.

"Our ice cream melted," said Reverend MacPhail, "or else I would invite you to come and partake."

"That's okay," said Roger.

"Not to say that your father's not taking care of you or that you wouldn't want to wash your hands first," said the Reverend. Roger felt the man's eyes crawl over his stained shirt and the seaweed clinging to his legs.

"So, your parents made the right move. Got you out of the Ontario rat race. The getting and spending. Makes you forget the important things. Family. Our Lord. The fresh air."

"Yes, sir." Roger, for his part, could not imagine a more corrupting influence than this very beach.

"I grew up in Kensington. You know the place? But my congregation is Up West. Near O'Leary. Do you know where that is, Roger? How well do you know the Island? Do you have any family here, besides your mom and dad and brothers?"

"O'Leary?" asked Raymond. "Big potato town?"

"I'd say," laughed Reverend MacPhail.

"Reverend!" said Roger. "Do you know anything about tides?"

"A bit."

"When's the next really high tide here?"

"Not for a while, I think."

"Thanks, Reverend."

Father and son returned to their spot on the beach. Waking his wife, Raymond began recounting everything that had popped into his head while she slept. Roger looked back at the MacPhail clan. He wondered what it would be like to be one of them. He noticed that Reverend MacPhail had attracted a cluster of kids. Magic trick? Candy?

There was a girl among the other children. Roger gulped. The Peeper girl. She had come back right on his heels. Followed him? She hadn't registered him. She was surrounded by her family, smiling and laughing with the same ease as her father. One moment she was talking to the whole group, then to people singly and directly. She did nothing to catch anyone's attention; each person held it in waiting for her to address them. Reverend MacPhail beamed at her.

"I have to pee," said Roger. "Be right back!"

"We're leaving soon!" his mother called to him, but he was already running as fast as he could into what he now realized was wilderness.

He arrived at the driftwood log sooner than he expected. His brain had been too busy to notice the scenery.

The seal was still there. Now you had to get close to hear the breathing. It was fading.

"Poor thing. So much pain." The distance between the seal and the water's edge was substantial. Roger tried to push it toward the water, to no avail, but the futility was immediately obvious. He stepped back. He stood there quietly. He thought of his science book's chapter on sea mammals. He thought of his comic books. None of it was much use to him now.

Finally, Roger found a club-sized stick by the log. He lifted it and brought it down hard on the seal's head, repeating the motion frantically like he was chopping wood. Tears flew from his eyes. He had never hit anything so hard before. He didn't notice the horseflies around his head. He was moving too fast for them.

There was no blood that he could see.

When Roger stopped clubbing the seal, he knew it was dead. His own breath was ragged.

"Won't tell," he muttered to himself. He felt heroic and ashamed at the same time. He sat beside the log for a few minutes to catch his breath and compose himself before returning to his family.

The rest of the Nieses were packing up when he arrived. They did not ask Roger what had taken him so long. The sun was low in the sky and, though it would not be dark for hours, the day felt over. The adult women among the MacPhails were also cleaning up their camp. The children, Roger could hear, were begging for a bonfire.

As the Niese car pulled out onto the road, Roger stared out the back window and saw the first few sparks and puffs of smoke rising up over the dunes, like a dragon exhaling. The fire must be beautiful, lighting up the faces of the MacPhails, even Caroline, as horrible as she was.

When he got home, his mother made him lay out his clothes for his first day of grade four, but his heart wasn't in it.

CHAPTER 5

ROGER NIESE'S EARLY SCHOOL years were relatively uneventful, especially when it came to making friends. His studies weren't much more fulfilling. He could recall little of the classroom learning he endured in intermediate school: determining varieties of potatoes, sewing a pillow shaped like a van, and knowing what to do about wet dreams (ignore them). But he remembered every inch of the geography of St. Louis-St. Edward Intermediate until the day he died. Even after a 2003 renovation transformed it into a French-language elementary school, Roger could tell you how many steps it was from the science room to the library, the quickest route from the detention room to the bus parking lot, and the only way from the cafeteria to the front entrance that did not take you past the tough kids. Managing to avoid the tough kids was an impressive feat—they might have constituted sixty percent of the school's population, drawn from the fishing villages scattered around the remotest part of the Island. Living in the low scrubby land beyond where the British dared chase the Acadians, their families established their rough habits long before lobster was a luxury food, in the days where a trip to the nearest Zellers department store, an hour away in Summerside, was an extravagance. St. Louis and St. Edward—both located in St. Bernard's parish—was not where someone from, say, East of Bloomfield, casually found themselves. Not for fun, unless you loved getting in a fight, nor job opportunities, which were scarce.

Roger was both a come-from-away and a townie, by way of Ottawa and Charlottetown. West Prince kids did not hide their suspicion of outsiders nearly so well as the kids in the provincial capital, who themselves were resented by country kids. In Charlottetown, the children of civil servants and shop owners wore clothes from off-Island retailers.

They boasted about multiple TV channels, travels to Disney World, and going to the mall. At St. Louis-St. Edward Intermediate, the kids would throw rocks at you if you showed up in sneakers that looked too exotic. When Roger showed up as a mid-term registrant just after the Christmas break of grade seven, he quickly read the mood and learned to avoid wearing clothes bought on visits to Ottawa. If you did your shopping anywhere east of Summerside, you thought you were too good for the room.

Halfway through grade seven, he and his father had moved to the trailer on the John Joe Road, a dirt road off Union Road, a pot-holed stretch of St. Louis-St. Edward that nobody in Charlottetown had ever heard of. Roger was given the trailer's tiny bedroom while his father slept on a bed created by the rearrangement of the dining-bench cushions. For the first few months, home life meant watching a single channel on a tiny rabbit-ear TV and eating from his father's bottom-less pot of boiled dinner: soggy potatoes and soggier meat. Unlike Charlottetown, there was nothing within walking distance except more trees.

The move had two causes, one professional, one familial. Rogers' parents' break had been acrimonious. No name-calling or raised voices, which made it all the more mysterious to the boys. His father's job had changed. He was no longer at the experimental farm in Charlottetown. Nothing was said about Raymond Niese's performance, but his position was eliminated. He was reassigned to a woodlot management pilot project sponsored by the university and the provincial government. This job paid less, which certainly affected Roger's life and his future. But more profoundly, the woodlot management pilot project was located in Montrose, almost a two-hour drive from Charlottetown. His first day at work was the first day Raymond had ever ventured that far west. The day Raymond and Roger eventually moved to the John Joe Road, so that Raymond could be closer to his new job, was the first day Roger had ever ventured that far west. This flat new territory would be surprisingly hard for both men to leave.

The sons were split so they wouldn't have to be shared. Roger ended up with his father Up West. David and Allen stayed in Charlottetown with their mother while she figured out her next steps. It never oc-curred to Roger to ask how the division had been decided; he was fatalistic for his age.

At school, hapless at connecting with peers, Roger focused on the architecture. His intimate knowledge of the school's narrow, ill-lit hall-ways stemmed purely from his desire to stay out of them. Their social function was lost on someone who had nothing resembling a social life. For someone without a clique, they were galleries where you submitted yourself to unwanted judgments. You had to pay so much attention to what the other kids were doing around you, you could barely think.

The classrooms provided little refuge during lunch and other breaks. Smart teachers kept the rooms locked when they were away, otherwise, they'd return to find that students had broken into desk drawers to steal a hidden pint of vodka or reclaim a confiscated pack of girlie play-ing cards. It was the unclaimed spaces, the quirks produced in the gap between the architect's vision and the school's use, that Roger exploit-ed. His first discovery was a small room, about the size of a tight galley kitchen, off the east staircase, with an easily picked lock and an array of rarely used cleaning supplies. Good location, but too cramped to be much more than a safe place to hide from oncoming bullies. The alcove behind the mimeograph machine in the principal's office offered a place to duck if Roger was interrupted making unauthorized copies of school-dance flyers and posters.

But the ideal headquarters was hidden up behind the auditorium stage. Not the shadowy wings where the curtains were, which had been claimed by students who used the space to lurk, grope, push, chase, giggle, and get dizzy during their free periods. No, at the very back of the backstage, a stairway led to a little-known mezzanine-level room. The stairs were hidden by both a protruding backdrop wall and an up-right piano. The room itself: maybe six or eight people could fit around the table that was its main piece of furniture. Two dozen electrical out-lets freckled the walls. Perhaps the provincial education minister who had supervised the school's construction in the 1950s had a grandiose idea for it. Say, a lighting or sound room for staging large-scale musical productions rather than the annual St. Louis-St. Edward no-fuss-no-muss beauty pageant and the odd performance by the school's rickety band. The necessary mechanicals were never installed, nor was any security other than a pickable doorknob lock.

Roger discovered the room near the end of grade seven. As an alter-native to carbon-dating the last human presence in the room, he stud-ied its graffiti. The phrase that repeated the most was "R. P. G. hearts

K. S. D." A search of the yearbook archives indicated that an R.P.G. had not attended St. Louis-St. Edward Intermediate for at least three years; in his twinkly-eyed photo from ninth, Ricky Peter Gallant looked like someone with a great capacity for love, sex, and trouble; he was all easy smile.

Roger began making his own contributions to the décor. He brought posters of the Osmonds, David Cassidy, and KISS; an orange table lamp; a plastic-domed portable record player; a wooden carpenter's toolbox full of poster paint and other decorating supplies. His scratchy yellow curtains covered the distasteful graffiti of R.P.G.'s less soulful cohorts. Over the summer holidays, Roger left behind a few items as something of a test. In September of grade eight, he found the room untouched. The smell of the tomato and cheese sandwich he had forgotten back in June had failed to attract the attention of the janitor, dear Mr. O'Brien. The backstage room, part refuge, part prison, was officially his.

Roger cared little about grades, which came easily, or popularity, which didn't come at all. Roger felt no parental pressure to succeed in school. But any living person must fill his or her time one way or another, and Roger focused on what might be loosely defined as school spirit.

In the first week of grade eight, Roger's campaign for school-council president failed to take root; his own lunchtime poll gave him three percent of the popular vote. Michael Chaisson, the alpha male of the advanced D-stream class and a volleyball star, commanded eighty-two percent. The rule book did not prevent Roger from abandoning his nomination a few days before the election, allowing him to put his name forward as treasurer. That race was uncontested. Most students left the treasurer section of the ballot unmarked, but a few made a check by his name. Power without popularity was still power. The yearbook photo of student council showed a grinning Michael Chaisson in the centre, thick-lipped and unarguably handsome, surrounded by what, in other cultures, might be considered a harem of smitten pubescent girls. Roger stood rigidly at the upper-left edge of the photo, his face with the serious expression of a peace-treaty broker. His body was already much bigger than other boys of his age, but he was given no credit for it, as he had little capacity for moving it around with any panache. His build was too wispy. No matter how tall he got, tall like his father and his father's father, he still might blow away. His forehead made him seem too cerebral as did his heavy eyebrows. Even at the age of thirteen or fourteen, it was easy to imagine him bald. Girls thought his big, deep-set eyes made him spooky looking.

Officially, the treasurer position came with a key to the student council room, nominally supervised access to the mimeograph machine, and a guaranteed spot on the dance committee. Unofficially, Roger stretched his privileges much further. As treasurer, he controlled the council's biggest generator of revenue, the monthly dance. The committee's advertising budget meant access to paints and paper, so Roger controlled the poster-making. This duty, in turn, allowed him to duck out of classes taught by the less strict teachers—namely Mrs. McLellan's social studies and Mrs. Gallant's history—and move around the halls without a pass. No other student in St. Louis-St. Edward Intermediate's history had been able to claim more time, space, and public funds.

Michael had run for president more to please his father, a member of the provincial legislative assembly, than any desire to serve the student body. He never questioned anything Roger did. If poster paint cost fifty dollars a month—who cared? Michael was more concerned which girl council member said what about him to whom. Michael's worldview could not include a come-from-away as any sort of a challenger or even peer. If you didn't know who someone's grandparents or great-grandparents were, what value could that person possibly have? Roger's motives were a mystery to Michael and, until new evidence was presented, were probably just fine. To bring out the competitive side of Michael someone would have to be playing the same game.

The day the girl—the girl Roger would become obsessed with—came bursting into his secret room, Roger was using a ruler and magic markers to draw grids and flow charts onto white Bristol board for a presentation on the student council's chocolate-bar fundraising campaign. The sharp chemical smell of the marker filled every corner of the room; the girl's stomping up the stairs and out-of-breath arrival would have panicked Roger if he had not been experiencing a fuzzifying high. He merely fell off his chair.

"Hide me!" cried the girl, throwing the door open. She stumbled in, almost crashing into the metal legs of the table. Until now it had never occurred to Roger that his refuge could be a hiding place for someone else.

"You can close the door," he declared meekly, "and please sit down." She might be a spy for the principal. If so, his respect for authority would make it impossible for him to put up a fight. But he would not confess to anything. It would be a matter of quietly collecting his things and leaving. If she really was a fugitive, then she had thrown herself at the mercy of the right person.

The wild-eyed pixie before him was not the first visitor he had entertained in the room or even the first girl. Roger had revealed its location to fellow dance-committee members Marissa Gallant, Michael's girlfriend, and Betty Ann Getson under terms of the strictest secrecy. Marissa and Betty Ann were quiet, obedient girls, both from clean-scrubbed farming families. They both believed, through suggestion more than lies, that the keys to the room and bluntly prohibitive terms of use had been given to Roger by the principal. Marissa was going steady with Michael and so had considerably more status than Betty Ann. Neither of them would have blabbed and, if they did, it certainly would not have been to this girl, from whom they might avert their eyes if they passed her in the hallways.

Her long dark hair contained a good dozen unmatched barrettes, ties, and clips, none of which managed to correct her hair's contempt of gravity. Her denim skirt was too short for an intermediate-school girl, a fact that no teacher dared point out to her. Her stained white blouse was something a granny might pick for herself until said granny realized how much would be revealed when the top button fell off, as it had. Her maroon footwear, salt-stained from a previous winter or even two, was more slipper than shoe.

These external details were eclipsed, though, by her energy, which was both aggressive and listless. The general measurements of her mass and contours matched those of her pubescent peers, but her spirit seemed to have spent time touring with a circus.

"Who are you?" she snapped, smashing her back against the closed door, then slowly sliding down into a sitting position.

"I'm going to… I'm going to… take a little break here."

"Sit where you want. It's a free world."

"No, it's not."

Roger slowly realized that he did vaguely recognize his visitor, who was in the B stream, officially several IQ points away from him, but not quite as mentally incapacitated as the A stream. She should have been in grade nine, he remembered. Perhaps she had been held back a year.

"Who's after you?"

"Boys!"

"Yikes!"

"Now," she narrowed her eyes, making a point of sizing him up. Her back still on the door, she slid her way back to a standing position. "Isn't this a darling spot? Where did all this stuff come from?"

"I've talked to the principal who...."

"Oh Jesus, please." Her eyes drank everything in with such thirst Roger was thrilled and scared. "You got any Tammy Wynette for that thing?" She nodded at the record player.

"I have Elton John." Roger gave his body a faintly discernible wiggle. The school's regular DJ for dances, a nineteen-year-old from Summerside and future pot dealer, gave Roger his extra copy of the "Crocodile Rock" single as a reward for being such a good customer.

"Spaz!"

Then Debbie shrugged, which would be the closest thing to yes she would ever say to Roger. He fumbled with the lock combination on his record box, carefully extracted the record from its sleeve, and placed it with a proud flourish onto the turntable.

Roger bought the player with his share of the money he and his father earned from collecting beer bottles from ditches. The previous spring, when there were still chunks of unmelted snow everywhere, Raymond had handed him a pair of heavy farmer's gloves and told him to go put on his worst clothes. At first, the enterprise was a welcome distraction. All winter, Roger had gone nowhere other than his new school. Visits to his mother in Charlottetown were infrequent. David had found kids at school to bully. Roger was desperate for novelty. He went picking bottles, dedicating his earnings to his collection of forty-fives.

This western end of the Island was serviced by three commercial hubs, Alberton, O'Leary, and Tignish, the latter being the town where those who lived in St. Louis-St. Edward or the vicinity typically conducted business, including drinking at the Tignish Legion. There were also several small fishing ports, usually a few modest houses clustered around government-run docks. The rest of the Up West population was scattered on roads major and minor, paved, and unpaved, on properties that were buffered by small woodlots and farm fields.

Route 2, a two-lane asphalt spine running down the middle of the Island, was the only connection to the rest of the province; you couldn't get far in Up West without driving along a stretch of, or at least crossing,

Route 2. For their first round of bottle-collecting, Raymond Niese chose Elmsdale corner, one of the busiest Route 2 intersections.

"We'll start here and work our way out to the coastal road." The execution of this plan would have to be measured in weeks and months, not hours.

Roger could feel the nip of cold at his cheeks and uncovered wrists. Some of the bottles were frozen to the ground. He imagined his school-mates looking at him from their backseats as they drove by with their parents. He didn't care, really. But adolescent hang-ups had not completely passed him by. He wished he could tell his peers the backstory. He considered posting a sign wherever they were located. "Making the Island beautiful" or "Father and son bonding," though the two hardly spoke or acknowledged one another.

Raymond took it upon himself to wave at each passing car, as if the area's drivers had chipped in to pay him for this necessary work.

"I'm freezing!" Roger shouted at his father across the road. "Can we go home?"

"Put on another sweater," said Raymond, who was wearing five layers. "It's only just after one."

The Saturday shift ended roughly at six. On Sundays, they picked bottles until five, then went to the M&K in O'Leary for fries with the works and milkshakes. For Roger, this was little compensation for living with his father. Roger prayed and prayed to return to the house in Charlottetown. It was unclear whether that would even be an option for much longer. His mother planned on returning to Ottawa as soon as certain things were sorted out. Until then, she worked at a drugstore near the university and remained mother to David and Allan. Roger wasn't quite sure what she was to him now. On the phone, she was reserved and sensitive to the long-distance charges.

"We're figuring things out, sweetie," she told him. "In the meantime, it's better if your father has some company that's not mine."

Roger supposed that his home life had started unravelling when he was in grade six, around the time of his father's "reassignment" to the woodlot management pilot project Up West. It was a big change for Raymond, who would be the project's only employee. But it wasn't a bad change for such a self-directed man. Working alone in a building the size of a garden shed, where some days his clients dropped by and some days they didn't, Raymond had unlimited time to think about things. Species diversification, erosion prevention, organic fertilizers. Raymond could experiment on the fifteen acres in his care or persuade West Prince property owners to try things out. He could also think about politics and astronomy, ancient Sumeria and British labour strife, new models of automobiles, and Egyptian pyramids. Back in Charlottetown, Raymond's office was turned into a photocopier room.

While still living in Charlottetown, the commute to Montrose gave Raymond even more time with his thoughts. His 1970 Chevy Impala was a temperamental gas guzzler, particularly fond of giving up the ghost on a busy stretch of Route 2, through the Miscouche swamp, where the ditch started at the edge of the asphalt. Raymond was getting up at 6am, arriving home at 8pm. By this time of the evening, he had accumulated so many thoughts, Sarah felt like a dump for her husband's verbiage. And she did not have her sister's to escape to anymore. She began hiding somewhere in the house, sitting perfectly quiet to avoid detection.

You could argue whether the divorce freed Raymond from an unsympathetic marriage or untethered him from reality. At the very least, it allowed him to live closer to his work. For $650, he bought a small lot on John James Road, just off Union Road, in St. Louis-St. Edward. Surrounded by a grey woods, it was a short drive to St. Bernard's church on Palmer Road, to Gallant and Sons grocery store, to the port of Miminegash, and to St. Louis-St. Edward Intermediate School. So convenient for Roger. What more did you need?

For the first few weeks, Raymond and Roger slept in the Play-mor camper that had transported them to PEI, father and son wedged inside like mints in a tin. Then Raymond bought a slightly larger mobile home from a carpenter in Summerside. Red-faced and smelling of chewing tobacco, the man had lived in it himself when his own marriage "went up shit creek."

"I might as well have stuck my thumb up my arse as try to please her," the carpenter told Raymond as if Roger wasn't present. Raymond had no reply to that. He attached the trailer to the car without asking for help. Roger and the carpenter stood watching Raymond fumble with the hitch, pinching the skin on his greasy hands, reluctant to wipe them on his slacks. Roger wondered if all men who lost their wives made such a big jump in the direction of a purely animal existence. The trailer had no running water till spring when a well could be dug.

Raymond's supper menu had four variations, all of which required chewing meat off a bone.

"I don't know if I like that song very much at all," Debbie said when "Crocodile Rock" was over. "Got another one?"

Through the duration of the Elton John hit, Roger had been plotting his next musical choice. He had considered "Bad Bad Leroy Brown," by Jim Croce. If this girl hadn't so intimidated him, he would have been leaning over the turntable with the forty-five in his hands to reduce the waiting time between tracks. But she might have requests. He held back.

"Let me think," said Roger.

A thump on the door. A full-forearm thump. Roger had seen his visitor click the doorknob lock. He didn't want to appear to doubt her by checking it.

"Debbie! Debbie! Arsenault!"

The voice was angry and female, as was the approving chorus of muttering that followed it like an echo. "Debbie! Bitch!" the chorus said. The alleged Debbie Arsenault spread herself flat like a paper doll against the wall behind the door. The doorknob jiggled. Girls, Roger thought. Bobby pins. A few seconds later, there was metallic clicking inside the knob.

Though she had been all movement and noise a moment earlier, Debbie was, it seemed, also good at being still and quiet. She shot him a forbidding look as he stepped toward the door. She would see in a moment the best defence was a good offence, though Roger's offensive style wasn't anything she had experienced before. He held the door with his foot as he cracked it open.

"Can I help you?" asked Roger. Only an open hand, not a fist nor a foot, would fit through the opening he allowed. "The principal...."

"Where is that fucking bitch?" snapped the girl in front. She had straight blonde hair down to her waist.

"Sorry?"

"Did you see her? That little bitch? Is she here?"

"Shhh," said Roger. "Mr. Wedge is conducting interviews. Did you want to make an appointment?" Mr. Wedge was the blotchy-faced guidance counsellor who, according to rumours, used his alone time with students to touch their private parts.

"Oh!" said the girl whose body pressed against the door like an impatient finger presses on an elevator button. Roger could make out the shadowy hairdos of several more girls on the darkened stairs behind her. "No!"

"Then... Mr. Wedge would like...."

"But can you do something?" The girl was now whispering, as if a low volume at this point in the confrontation would keep her out of Mr. Wedge's pervy field of awareness. "Just a little something. That cow is around here somewhere. If you see her, first give her a puck in the mouth for me. A right puck. Then you tell her that Ricky wants his bike helmet back. Right away! Pronto presto. That's a friggin' Kawasaki, man."

"Okay." Roger made as if to look over his shoulder to gauge Mr. Wedge's reaction to foul language.

"Ricky fucking wants it back. Immediatement! Right!"

"Right. Careful on your way down," said Roger. "The school's not insured up here."

He heard some muttering on the stairs, some banging around, some airy movement of the curtains on the darkened stage. Then they were gone.

"Boys?" said Roger, narrowing his eyes at Debbie. "You said boys were after you."

Debbie was now strutting around the room like a scrappy coach exercising dominion over a locker room "They don't do their own dirty work! That's boys for yah. Angela Ellsworth is a skank. A slut! Ricky Gallant! What a friggin' catch! Oh boy! She deserves him. Not a hair on his head! No wonder the helmet fits me." As she spat out her words, Roger could see Debbie's teeth, overcrowded chunks of yellow and silver.

"Did you take it?"

"It wasn't locked up. It wasn't anything. It was just there—how do you call it? Public domain. How exactly do you think I was supposed to know? Helmets all look the same."

"Where is it now?"

"I never touched your songs." She was standing very close to the re-cord box.

"The helmet. Where's the helmet?"

"What's your problem? It's none of your business, is it? Is it? Gotta go."

Debbie yanked open the door and went scampering down the stairs.

Roger checked the record box. "Crocodile Rock" was gone.

Ambling down the school corridor to math, Roger pondered what this breach meant for his future. Although the invaders did not seem particularly amazed by his sanctuary, nothing prevented their return. The thought of eking out long-term lunchtime space for himself in the cafeteria was unbearable. Sitting with his dance-committee colleagues Marissa and Betty Ann was an option in theory only; even Roger couldn't be seen to sit with girls. There was, he supposed, that janitor's closet.

Was there a way to remedy things? Roger did have a passing familiarity with Ricky Peter Gallant, who had some quality that had driven these harpies to do his bidding. Swagger, probably. Ricky Gallant was older—inappropriately older—though he spent an impressive amount of time at the school's smoking corner. He had failed several grades, then quit, and now couldn't stay away. He lived in a tiny house on the dunes by Miminegash Harbour with his younger brother Mitchell, who wasn't quite right in the head. Mitchell was prone to seizures and wore a hockey helmet to prevent his brain from getting more scrambled than it already was. His limbs froze up, so he always crashed like a log. Their grandmother would come and spend time at the house with Mitchell when Ricky was out, and Ricky was pretty much always out. His prowling around was the stuff of legends—his breakneck driving, the stunts he'd pull at parties, like rearranging the furniture in the host's living room when they were out on the deck, his smooth charm with the ladies, though he wasn't particularly good looking. Ricky had made several court appearances for traffic violations that were difficult to define. He was not the kind of guy you provoked, no matter how tempting a motorcycle helmet might be. Debbie Arsenault, as far as Roger knew, did not have any pack of toughs to back her up. Did she even have a motorcycle?

Roger had leveraged his dance-committee duties to escape two of the last four of Mr. Bradley's math classes. Mr. Bradley, a human stick of birch with glasses falling off his nose, had it out for him. Usually, the teacher's method was to ignore Roger's frequently upstretched arm and lob the easy questions at Caroline MacPhail, the captain of the girls' volleyball team. Caroline could already pass for sixteen, maybe even seventeen if she were to wear makeup, though makeup was something she was not permitted nor inclined to wear. But today's equations were not Roger's strength. Mr. Bradley's aggression meant repeatedly calling Roger to the board.

"C'mon, Mr. Niese. I thought the great Ontario school system had kids doing simple equations like this in grade three. Isn't that right?" Come-from-aways could easily be mistaken for one another, with their money and know-it-all pride. Mr. Bradley, who was originally from Montreal, needed to prove there was a pecking order.

Roger stared hard at "$m + 33/4$ when $m = 21/2$."

"I'll get it," said Roger.

"You will, will you? Good for you. Good for you!" Mr. Bradley did not have to tell the class that their laughter was required.

Taking her turn at the board, Caroline was coached through the problem as a virgin bride might be coached by a gentle lover. She took several swaggering breaks from the blackboard to smirk in Roger's direction. The smirk was a warning. As if one was needed.

All through the previous school year, Roger's locker mate, Robert Doucette, had delivered Roger's combination into Caroline's hands. She and her friends came up with ever-new hiding places for Roger's gym sneakers, lunch, and textbooks. Roger's running after them, arms flopping, was a splendid reward.

Roger had failed to recognize Caroline as the girl who had tormented him on Stanhope Beach the summer his family moved to PEI. Unable to make this connection, a line of continuity between his childhood and adolescence, Roger's subconscious invented a way to understand the two encounters: female tormentors were a universal and omnipresent species in all stages of life.

Caroline also failed to connect eighth-grade Roger to that day on Stanhope Beach. When she stumbled upon him at St. Louis-St. Edward Intermediate—her family had eventually moved Up West to shorten her father's commutes to O'Leary—she recognized only his eagerness to be in the right and his ineptitude at doing so, a trait her subconscious attributed to a species of men and boys—perhaps all men and boys. Other young women, looking ahead to love and marriage, might despair at this conclusion; Caroline recognized the opportunities. It gave her permission to have her friends pitch a shoeless young man into snowbanks. Or report random suspects for committing vandalism in the playground. Or identify a possible patient zero for a lice breakout. Drama can be very entertaining. Caroline was a popular, busy girl. She was the senior volunteer in the school canteen. She got around to Roger and his ilk when she had time.

The bell rang. Roger headed to geography and then social studies where the rest of the afternoon blurred by. The bell rang again. His locker had not been infiltrated. Small mercies.

Roger's bus ride home rarely offered much peace. The capricious routing turned what should have been a ten-minute drive into a thirty-minute tracing of every red-dirt road in the school's catchment area before dropping off Roger at the end of the John Joe Road, the only road deemed too treacherous for a bus.

The bus driver, Alvin Bernard, who milked his cows before his morning route and milked them again after the afternoon journey, played an eight-track of last year's hits so loud the students had to shout to speak. The bus's back seats were colonized by the rougher high school kids, who were picked up first on the way home. The front seats were dominated by the elementary kids, who were picked up last. The bus's midpoint served Roger through most of grade seven. This year, however, Michael, realizing the density of girls was higher there, adopted the middle of the bus as his territory, forcing Roger to dance around him.

"Hey Mike," said Roger, casually installing himself in the seat across from the school council president. "The theme is almost finalized."

"Huh?"

"The dance! Three weeks!"

"Right."

The product of what was considered, in more generous analyses, a May-October marriage, Michael had a particularly old-fashioned upbringing. His father had been a successful potato farmer and well-known bachelor before marrying at age fifty-four. Archibald Chaisson entered politics a year later, running for the Liberals in the 2nd Prince Catholic seat. Although the perennially Liberal seat could have been won by a Liberal raccoon, Archibald Chaisson, all bones and combover, was liked well enough. People took his lack of humour as ethics. Eileen Chaisson, a Pineau from Saint Felix, was the warmer half of the couple. Michael's mother had spent her courting years taking care of an ailing maiden aunt in Moncton. Forty-two on her wedding day, she was all accommodation and compliments. Eileen ran the local Catholic Women's League.

While no-nonsense prefab bungalows sprung up across the province like dandelions, Michael grew up in a century farmhouse on Palmer Road, walking distance from St. Bernard's church. It was a home that was only complete and functioning when the wood pile was well-stocked and the outhouse door was not frozen shut. The Chaissons did not own a TV, though they subscribed to both provincial dailies, *The Guardian* out of Charlottetown and *The Spectator-Herald* out of Summerside; the provincial weekly *The Islander; Reader's Digest,* which Michael scoured for jokes; and an uncountable number of political and religious newsletters and bulletins. Eileen Chaisson picked Michael up at dances after the first forty-five minutes, so he could make his curfew and not be tired and cranky during the morning milking.

Nature and nurture may quarrel over who plays the bigger role in making a person, but certain outcomes, like when a dowdy couple produces a child of extraordinary beauty, are probably a fluke. Away from the farm and his parent's propriety, Michael's full red lips, heavy eyelids, and olive complexion suggested a sensual individual of un-derdetermined cosmopolitan origins. It would not have occurred to anyone in 1970s Prince Edward Island to make a living off looks alone. But everyone could agree that Michael was too pretty to spend much of his life shovelling manure. No matter what came out of the young man's mouth, people listened.

"I can't decide on the second-last song," Roger said. "The one before 'Stairway to Heaven.'"

"Up to you."

Roger crawled to the edge of his seat, leaning into the bus's aisle. Michael did not move away from his window spot. The noisy arrival of Robert Doucette, Michael's best friend, and Marissa Gallant, Michael's kinda girlfriend, ended the conversation. Roger sank back into his seat and looked out across the idling buses. Beyond the parking lot, cows wandered through a yellowing fallow field, squirting swampy water where they brought down their hooves.

The bus pulled out of the lot and headed toward the coastal road. Light flickered off the choppy waves like knives being sharpened. Alvin Bernard dropped the Galt twins off on the dead-end Galt Road. Along the route, the collapsing barns, the tiny houses dropped randomly in the middle of fields, the sheds overflowing with brightly painted buoys all seemed such tentative attempts at human settlement. The bus stopped to let off Angela Ellsworth, the girl who had been hunting down Debbie Arsenault. Angela was known primarily for being able to wind her legs in her rivals', knock them to the ground, and then kick them till they stopped crying. Roger could not look her in the eye, but she didn't seem to remember him from their encounter earlier that day.

The bus came around to St. Bernard's Church. It was widely admired for its pencil-elegant steeple and exploding rose stained glass window. In any other part of the world, it would have been the anchor building for a busy intersection; here, two of the other corners were meadow; the fourth was the church's matching white-shingled hall.

The bus turned again. Roger's mind drifted, as usual, to the future. His next step in life was clear. He had to become student council president in effect, if not in name. The treasury and the dance committee were not enough. He worried Michael, sitting there, laughing with Robert and Marissa, might stymy some of his ventures.

At last, the bus stopped at the end of the John Joe Road. The Niese trailer was about a quarter-mile in, down a long gravel driveway that dissolved into a small scruffy yard, surrounded by unhealthy jackpines, their lower branches crispy grey kindling. The Impala was not there. No surprise. Raymond Niese often stayed late at his work shed to be available for people who might drop by on their way home for supper. A farmer would show up wanting to know about, say, the milk marketing board. Raymond would look up from his book—a history of Mexico or St. Thomas Aquinas or an illustrated guide to the birds of North America—before launching into a mini-lecture on whether marketing boards made sense.

The trailer's entrance was via a lopsided front deck the size of a desk. It was cluttered with a torn badminton net, several pairs of rubber boots, a milk can, a cracked planter held together by rope, and an old avocado-green fridge, sold to Raymond by the same coworker who sold him the Impala. Curled up beside the fridge was something Roger first thought was a leprechaun.

"Took yah long enough!" said Debbie Arsenault. She sounded genuinely pissed.

Roger's knees gave out for a second.

"How'd you...?"

"Ran here. As the crow flies, as they say, as you know. What's for supper?"

Roger gulped. His pounding heart jerked around in its cavity. "I'm...."
She must have been torn up about stealing his record and had come to
return it. He had to admire her for that. ".... My dad will be here soon."

"Got nothing against older men, myself!"

Roger squeezed past her to the screen door and lifted his hand toward the screen door's topmost mounting bracket. When he realized
this motion was giving away the key's hiding place, he detoured his
hand to his hair, which was parted on the left and needed an occasional
finger-combing. He was too late.

"Smooth! I couldn't find it. Too much junk to root through, man!"
Debbie sprang up. One minute she was towering over him, the next,
she was inside the trailer. Roger wasn't sure he should follow her in;
maybe she'd just set the record down and leave.

"Do yah have tea? Red Rose please. Or Tetley. I'm easy," said Debbie,
squirming her way to the middle of the U-shaped bench that was both
the dinette seating and Raymond's bed. Grimy sheets stuck up from
behind the cushions.

"It stunts your growth," said Roger, repeating what he had heard his
mother say. He wanted to put his school bag in its proper place in his
room but didn't want her to know where he slept.

"For babies, sure! Put on a pot o' tea, will yah? Unless yah got a beer to
offer me."

Raymond kept a single unopened bottle of sherry in the cupboard
above the range in the improbable event a thirsty priest should drop by.
Raymond hadn't gone to church since he got married but had not ruled
out the possibility the church might come to him. There was a huge box
of Red Rose tea.

Roger filled the kettle to the very top. He became aware of dirty dishes lining the tiny counter, the bag of mouldy bread slices in the sink,
the underwear hung to dry on several of the trailer's surfaces. There
wasn't a single woman's touch. Debbie was unfazed.

"You're Debbie, right?" Roger decided to take charge. "Who's your
father?" In his time on PEI, he had learned the question that takes
precedence above all others. It resemb2led the way dogs automatically
sniff each other's butts.

Debbie burst out laughing. "If I told yah Errol Arsenault, do yah think
yah'd be much further ahead? Yah don't know him or yah wouldn't
being asking."

"I don't?" There were at least eight Arsenaults in Roger's grade. It was true. He didn't know who was related to who, if they all were or none were.

"You're from Tronna?"

"Ottawa. We moved when I was little. Close to Toronto. Kinda."

"I was in Tronna once, you know. We went by train. Reclining seats and everything."

"Toronto's only the provincial capital."

"We ate hot dogs from a cart and saw somebody sleeping on the street. Can yah imagine!" Through the little window, the sun was coming down behind her; Debbie's face was indiscernible. "And they have tall buildings and parks and a pool. The lifeguard was such a dingbat."

"We had a pool near my school. And a stadium."

"Ooh, stadium! I don't even know what the hell that is, loser!"

Roger looked at the silent kettle.

"How did you find out where I lived?"

"I ride your bus—how do they say?—temp-a-temp. Didn'tcha notice?"

"Huh?"

"It's French. I suppose you're still stuck in Je suis un garçon. Figures. Grade Seven French, whoop-de-doo."

"Grade eight!"

"Come over here and sit by me. That kettle ain't boiling any time soon."

Roger sighed and slid himself onto the bench, still holding his school bag. He could feel the heat generated from his corduroy pants dragging across the floral upholstery.

"Why did you leave Ontari-ario?"

"Dad got a job. What does your dad do?"

"What doesn't he do! That's what my grandma says. He's a free spirit. Free as a bird. Chirp chirp." She took a breath. "Fishing mostly."

"Lobster?"

"Sure."

"I don't like lobster."

Debbie leaned forward, lips puckered for a kiss. Roger was a couple of feet away and remained so.

"Don't worry, man, I failed a grade," she told him. "I'm legal. They said so, that time in court."

"You were in court?" Roger leaned over, pulling his school bag tightly into his lap. Debbie slid herself away into the opposite corner, pulled her legs up on the bench, and sat with the bottom of her feet pointed at him.

"Have yah kissed a girl before?"

Roger had not. Girls were all a blur. He could smell this one. Like freshly cut spring grass. Outside smelled like dried leaves.

"Yeah," Roger did not pause between words. "Once we stayed at a Keddy's in Moncton and there was a steam room and there was a girl there in her bathing suit. It was a bikini. And we kissed. Her father was in the pool. My brothers were in the pool and we were alone in the steam room."

"Your kettle's boiling." The water glugged out of the spout, sizzling on the stovetop.

"Crikes!"

"Zut alor!" she laughed.

Distractedly mopping up the spilled water with a dishcloth, Roger failed to turn off the gas stove. The dishcloth caught fire. It took a few seconds for them to notice the flames. Very quickly they were large flames, for a small space. Roger feared for his eyebrows. Debbie laughed like a donkey. Then she sprang into action. She jumped to turn off the stove, grabbed the dishtowel from Roger's hands, which had been moving frighteningly close to the polyester curtains, and tossed it into the sink. With an elegant confidence, she poured the boiling water in a long stream over the embers. Peace was restored.

Still flustered, Roger failed to realize how close she was standing to him until he felt her breath on his cheek.

"Calm down, will yah? Your house ain't gonna burn down. Thanks to me." She hung her finger in the breast pocket of his blue-checked shirt. She was just a little taller than him, all elbows and knees. "Will you get a grip?"

"I will." A thread snapped on his pocket. He didn't care. He couldn't look her in the face, she shone so brightly.

The sound of tires on gravel snapped him out of it.

"My dad!" He pulled away, bending at the knees to detach her finger. Debbie stood there sweetly, the eye in his hurricane.

"At least it's not my dad." She dropped back onto the dining room bench, crossed her legs yogi-style, and posed her hands daintily at their junction.

At first, Raymond didn't notice the girl; she slurped all her wild energy into herself and sat still as a Tic Tac. Nor, for that matter, did he notice his son's extraordinary twitchiness. Raymond's brain was full of root systems, chemical compounds, and a slowly forming opinion on the oil crisis. Things in mere physical proximity to him were just buzz threatening to drown out his passions. His shirt was dirty, the left arm of his glasses broken. The few remaining wisps of hair at the front of his head had become long enough to reach his nose if he did not keep them pushed back. He put three bottles of motor oil and a bag of two percent milk on the dinette table.

"Oh," said Raymond. "Oh," he said again, noticing Debbie.

"Roger invited me for supper. Thanks so much! Can't wait!"

Raymond cocked his head. He was a broad-shouldered man and he twisted himself toward the girl as if he was squeezing himself through a narrow passageway. Aside from Allan and David, whom Sarah dropped off at the end of the driveway at random intervals, Roger and Raymond had no visitors in the trailer. A supper invitation was as unlikely as her presence in the trailer. But then, the latter was apparently true so why not the former? Raymond never thought about Roger's life at school, whether he was popular or despised, a great student or a poor one. Now he was glad he hadn't written his son off as a fruit or a loser. Here was Roger with a young firecracker. A real firecracker.

"I see," said Raymond. "What's for dinner, Roger? Filet mignon?"

"Filly who?" laughed Debbie.

"I thought.... Dad. Could you? I think there's some spaghetti."

"Fancy!" Debbie took off her jacket. "I've had it before. Just so yah know. Fine with it."

"Okay," sighed Raymond, noticing the blackened dishcloth in the sink. "You need to clean up this place after your friend's gone home. Roger."

Raymond prepared overcooked spaghetti and canned sauce with fried hamburger chunks, which they ate out of the red plastic bowls that had been left behind by the trailer's previous owner.

"I never seen Roger at catechism." Debbie was knifing butter the depth of cream cheese onto a piece of bread. "You're Catholic, aren't you?"

"Yes," said Raymond, looking at his son. "I've been thinking about that. What time's it at?"

"Saturdays at five. I'd be a year ahead of him in catechism, though. Catechism don't fail yah."

As they finished eating, Debbie took in father and son. It entered her head that she was entitled to tell them that they were pathetic. But they might take it the wrong way. "Do you want help cleaning up this place... Roger, is it?"

"Why don't you do the dishes together?" said Raymond.

Roger washed, Debbie dried. It was astonishing to see she could be gently methodical. He heard a faint buzzing in his ears he had never noticed before. "Excuse me," he said, opening the door of the tiny bathroom and locking himself inside.

Roger was so successful in retreating to his imagination, his musings on what this new friendship meant, where it would go and how it would change his life, that it took him several minutes to realize that he didn't hear anyone in the kitchen anymore. He washed his hands and walked out to the trailer's main room. She wasn't there. He ran to the front door and peered out. His father's humming and hoeing echoed in the clearing.

"She's gone," Roger gulped, disappointed but also relieved. Almost fourteen, he was unsure of his capacity to compromise. Maybe she'd want a bungalow when he'd want a two-storey home. He would carry on.

Roger, newly conscious about the messiness of their home, tidied up the main room, moving papers and books from seating areas to a pile by the TV. He then grabbed his school bag to go do his homework. He'd do it in bed so as not to get waylaid by his father.

There she was in his room, curled up on the little twin, her head twisted so far around she looked possessed. But peaceful. Roger wouldn't dream of waking her.

In a compartment under the bed, Roger had tucked away shoe boxes and other miscellaneous containers full of what his mother mockingly called "Roger's treasures." A mood ring. A pack of cards with dolphins on the backs. Tiny clothespins. Crumpled audio tape. Journals he had written on a multitude of differently sized pads. The roundest stones he had ever found on the beach. Discoloured religious medals of the Virgin Mary. He did a quick check and found the cache undisturbed. He got a blanket and a pillow from the hall closet and tucked himself in on the narrow floor beside the bed.

He heard his father come into the trailer, taking forever to noisily brush his teeth. But Roger slept so soundly he did not hear Debbie leave before he woke at 7am.

He tried not to feel betrayed as he poured milk on his Shreddies, chugged his Tang, and rinsed his dishes.

Debbie had never been part of his school routine, so it was no surprise that he did not see her the next day on his walk from class to class, to his secret HQ for lunch alone, back to class again, and then to the school bus. Ricky Gallant's assorted girlfriends did not ask him her whereabouts, though he had decided he would lie if they did. The day seemed drab in comparison to the day before. On the bus ride, Michael and his posse had already fully occupied Roger's favourite row. The sixth grader he ended up sitting with wouldn't look at him.

Dragging his feet on the gravel and clam shells in the driveway, Roger spotted Debbie sitting on the front porch just where she had been the day before. She had changed her clothes and was now wearing a blue-checked apron dress that might have, to more discerning eyes, been a camp send-up of a 1950s housewife. There were ruffles at the neck.

"I brought some potatoes," she said, holding up a bag. "And some bacon. I can do a fry-up."

"My dad...."

"Loves bacon! I know. Men do." She rose, reached up, and retrieved the key from its hiding place, watching Roger's face for signs of disapproval; there were none.

And with that Debbie became a regular house guest at the Niese trailer, a shaky arrangement that lasted almost three months, until the last day of school before Christmas holidays.

Raymond never asked why she was there or where she was when she wasn't, though there were evenings she showed up late; he'd scowl at her if it was after 10pm. He never asked where she got the odd assortment of groceries she'd show up with—onions one day, a box of breakfast cereal the next. She was a careless cook, too much water in the stew, too little cooking time for the chicken, too much salt in the potatoes. But at least she cooked. It was a bachelor's dream, sort of; within a week, her keenness for cleaning had evaporated.

When they encountered each other at school, Debbie ignored Roger. She'd look past him like someone would look past a concrete post. He did not complain but suffered inside. Roger's school life should have been the same as before, or better, since he knew he'd have a friend to come home to. But it became much worse. Having Debbie at home made him miss her at school. He imagined each lunch together. Imagined passing time together during breaks. Imagined her introducing him to her friends, whom he imagined were plentiful, since Debbie always seemed to be on her way to or from something urgent. That this had not happened tied him up in knots, but he could not think of an action he could take that had an acceptable amount of risk. He did not want to drive her away. If he spent enough time figuring it out, he might be able to turn what they had into something more. He tried everything. He'd be casual. He'd be serious. He'd withdraw. He'd laugh at her jokes. He'd remain stone-faced. Nothing worked.

Even the at-home friendship felt fragile; her moodiness and caprice made it impossible to talk to her about anything, whether it be top-forty music, her future plans, school gossip, or how his father was driving him crazy, and wasn't he driving her crazy too? She'd roll her eyes, make fun of his feet, wonder what was on TV. Everything was shot down in the name of having a bit of fun. "A right busybody today, ain't cha? Lord, feel the heat in this room, heating up from all the busybodying." She could go on like this for hours, the same shtick with tiny variations. Sometimes the teasing wore him down. Roger became withdrawn at school. He did not really have her in his life, but she took up enough space that there was no room for anyone else.

But it was never boring. Every day there was something. She stepped on a nail and had to be taken to the hospital in Alberton. She was almost in tears over the pregnancy of an unnamed friend, who might have been a teenager or who might have been an adult, she was so vague. She was so angry at a TV show, she swore she was launching a letter-writing campaign. She was going to hunt down and kill a girl she suspected had stolen her hoodie (Roger found it months later in a ball in the back of his closet). She was in a rage over the way Ricky had looked at her across the school parking lot. She threw out one night's supper because the canned meat, she declared, had botulism.

Roger got used to the quantity of events in Debbie Arsenault's life, but he never figured out what she would talk about in front of his father and what she wouldn't.

"I saw Ricky...," he'd say over fishcakes and she'd silently mouth "Shhh."

"I hear there's a dance...," he'd say while she was watching him doing dishes. She'd draw her index finger across her throat and throw a glance at Raymond cutting up an apple. Then she'd put on a pot of tea, sigh, and declare, "Mr. Bradley was looking down my top all day today!"

The more outrageous her declaration, the more likely Raymond would fail to hear it and the more graphic Debbie would become. "Finally, I gave 'em a shake. Good for him, I might as well go for it, right?"

On weekends Debbie usually disappeared completely. Roger suspected her official place of residence was her grandmother's. It was harder to determine whether her mother lived there, too, or whether her mother lived at all. If her mother was merely despised, Debbie would have made bitter jokes about her, like those she made about her father, Errol Arsenault.

"Something my dad would do," she would say when there was a report of a coup, murder, traffic accident, or embezzlement on the radio news.

Sarah, David, and Allan never found out about her. Once a pair of her underwear showed up in the wash when David was visiting, but teenage boys don't pay much attention to other people's laundry.

Occasionally, Roger would wake up on Saturday morning to find her still in bed, the sheet and quilts braided tightly around her, a string of saliva connecting her to her pillow. Hearing her bang around in the cubicle-sized bathroom, Raymond would be pleased and invent an excursion. Debbie rarely refused an excursion, whether it was for aspirin, tire rims, or date squares. Debbie sat in front, Roger in back.

When their errands took them to O'Leary or Alberton, Debbie was tense, always looking over her shoulder and muttering fearful epitaphs. On O'Leary's ramshackle commercial strip, she uneasily joked about Protestants with poles up their backsides, preachers who might chase her into h-e-double toothpicks. In Alberton, which had a lagoon, a Catholic-run hospital, some grand old homes, and a fishing wharf to recommend it, Debbie fretted about girls armed with knives, hanging out behind the curling club. Roger would go to Roy Laird's for penny candy while she sat guarding the car from potential vandals and assailants.

In Tignish, though, Debbie was a gleeful tour guide, even if the people that populated her Tignish seemed terrifying. Here she knew every soul by name and relished the citizenry's supposed outrageousness: more crime and violence and betrayal and drunkenness than seemed possible.

The Tignish Co-op, a warehouse of corrugated steel and blown-in insulation, sold fishing gear, car parts, agricultural chemicals, and dry goods, along with a handful of apples and maybe a cauliflower or two. Debbie would stand at the entrance and nod at people going in and out. Some nodded back. One Saturday, an older woman in a heavy coat smiled and waved in her direction. Debbie called Roger over—he was not allowed to stand close to her when they were out in public.

"That one's husband's banging someone else. Everybody knows but her."

She then pointed out to the middle of the parking lot. "You wouldn't believe Noel Pineau doing doughnuts, right there Saturday night after the Legion closed!"

"Wow?"

"Now, look over there. See that piece of plywood on the Esso? Last weekend, Ricky Gallant was so drunk, he kicked the window out."

"How old is he, anyway?"

"Not old enough to be your father. Too old to be my boyfriend." It was hard to tell whether the information she relayed was first-person or hearsay. "See that car? Ricky Gallant's! Clocked her at eighty clicks down Route 2. RCMP caught up to him in the Miscouche swamp. Down a backroad and he was gone!"

Raymond would drop them off at the St. Bernard Church Hall for Saturday evening catechism. Debbie trailed behind Roger, giving him a hip-high wave as he went inside. Roger never saw her go into a classroom. She never brought home catechism handouts but, then again, she never brought home schoolwork either.

Roger found catechism fascinating. Not so much the curriculum: Vatican II banalities about how much Jesus loves us, how the family is so important, how you shouldn't steal or knock over your friend's books, and how a person should let his or her little light shine. No, what fascinated him was seeing who was there and who wasn't. At school, his uneducated eye couldn't tell the Protestants from the Catholics. Sometimes you could see who was especially poor and who was especially rich, but even that was hard in a province where white-collared types were uncommon and golfing widely popular; farmers and fishermen were as likely to play a round as the lawyers and doctors. But catechism was like a primer in who believed what.

Michael and his girlfriend, Marissa, were among the ten or so regular attendees in Roger's grade eight catechism class. The class included none of the student council girls and only two people from Roger's homeroom, two female cousins rumoured to have lice. There were two brothers, fraternal twins, who had different faces but identical haircuts and matching plaid vests with shiny brown satin lining. They went to another school, as did a tiny little girl with curly hair who hardly ever spoke. You could get away with not speaking at catechism.

After catechism, Roger would find his father sitting in the car in the St. Bernard's parking lot. Sometimes Debbie Arsenault would already be in the car with him. Sometimes she'd be killing time standing by the Parish Hall, talking to an older woman who Roger and Raymond presumed to be her grandmother. Debbie made no introductions. Roger was happy to let Debbie keep her worlds separate. She obviously had a few of them.

In early December, Father Euseb Arsenault caught Roger on his way out of catechism and asked him if he would be an altar boy for St. Bernard's. Roger suspected a conspiracy, but Debbie assured him she was not related to the priest, who, as far as she knew, came from Rustico.

"Where's Rustico?"

"Down East. Another nest of Gallants and Arsenaults and Doucettes."

"How many can there be?"

"Too damn many!"

St. Bernard's rectory, painted white with black trim to match the church, was a grand overbuilt structure. Father Euseb Arsenault's living room was full of knickknacks, including a large salt-and-pepper shaker collection. The priest had converted one of the upstairs rooms into a primitive gym, with wooden benches painted the same shiny black as the house trim, and homemade weights made with piping, pulleys, plastic Javex bottles, and sand. Many years later, as an adult, Roger would visit this room under very different circumstances and would be reminded of the Javex bottles, also painted black.

"Is there a hierarchy of altar boys?" asked Roger, who knew very well that Michael, who had been serving for several months already, had a monopoly on the crucifix and the bells. "Or are there some democratic aspects of service?"

"Hm," said Father Arsenault. He was a compact man, his oval head sitting tidily on his square body. "There are some younger boys and some older ones, but they're pretty much interchangeable in my mind. You'd get shifts. That's why I'm asking."

"Do I get to take a class?"

"The mass itself is like a class that teaches us how to love God," said Father Arsenault. "Niese? I can't place the name."

"It's from Ottawa. You're from Rustico?"

"I grew up right on the Union Road. People who say otherwise—they can go to Tignish for mass if they want," said Father Arsenault. "Is Niese French? From Nicoise? It's not Acadian. You do know about the Acadians, don't you? Do they teach you that in school?"

"We're doing England right now."

"PEI used to be Isle St. Jean, Roger. That's French for Saint John's Island."

"I know that."

"Then the British came and they chased all the French people away."

"But the Natives were lucky, they got a reserve, right?"

"Oh, the Indians!" said Father Arsenault, shaking his head. "That's another story. I can't quite speak to that. But the Acadians! They were a threat to the British. They were sent away."

"You're Acadian?"

"All the Arsenaults are."

"You're still here."

"Some people hid. Some people came back when they could. Some people never came back at all. It's a very sad history."

"Do I need to know all this to be an altar boy?"

"It'll help you be a good Islander."

"They say I'm not an Islander."

"That's true! But we all have to make compromises sometimes," said Father Arsenault, who was slowly figuring out how big a compromise he was making to balance out Robert Doucette's unreliability.

A car honked in the driveway. Roger dashed out to find his father waiting for him, the engine running. The moment he was inside, Debbie twisted around in her seat to get the news.

"You're a bell tinkler now?"

"I'm not sure. I think I need to be an Acadian." The car bounced and shifted as Raymond steered around and through the potholes of

Thompson, then Union roads.

"Acadian? Don't think so." Debbie whistled. "Yah know Evangeline and Gabriel?"

"From school?"

"Ah, for God's sake," said Debbie. "The story. On her wedding day, they took her away on the tall ship. She was supposed to be married to a hot man, but she didn't get him till he was old and dying. Yuck."

"Why'd he let her go in the first place?"

"No choice. Brits snatched her."

"What about the queen? Why would she allow that?"

"Get him. You got quite a son there, Mr. Niese."

"Do I?"

"My cousins almost got me going to Evangeline School. All Frenchies, that lot. Sing in French like yah just don't know it. Do their little dances. The bus ride woulda killed me though. Who names a school after such a big loser, anyway?"

"I don't think I want to be an altar boy."

"Only losers serve," said Debbie. "Unless yah wanna be a priest."

"I don't think I do," said Roger. "Does one thing lead to the other?"

"Just know that communion is a reenactment of cannibalism," interjected Raymond, "Meant to denigrate the flesh to elevate the soul."

This shut up both adolescents.

The Saturday before Christmas, Roger woke to find Debbie AWOL again. Though disappointed, Roger also saw an opportunity, which he presented to his father. The two of them drove to Summerside. On the way down Route 2, Roger took notice of St. Anthony's Church in Bloomfield, Immaculate Conception in Wellington, St. John the Baptist in Miscouche, all hulking white buildings, their shiny black trim reflecting the low winter sun. The Protestant churches seemed far more tentative, especially the Baptist chapel in Portage, which had no steeple. They passed shacks along the road where dirty-faced little girls lay on their stomachs on broken swings, little boys played guns in rusted-out cars. Mainstream modern civilization did not make itself known again until St. Eleanors, whose border was signalled by a sudden proliferation of gas stations.

Raymond took them to the new mall that had just opened in Summerside. The Towers department store had, Raymond was told by one of his woodlot owners, a good fashion section for young women.

Father and son stood among the racks of dresses and ponchos until a salesgirl, who couldn't have been more than sixteen herself, steered them toward the accessories.

"Size is important for girls," she told them. "Men will squeeze into anything."

Three belts, four hair clips, two pairs of sandals. The Nieses worked together to assemble a respectable Christmas present for their houseguest. They only absentmindedly remembered that Allan and David would need gifts too. David got a pair of jeans; Raymond guessed at the size. Allan got a tube of Tinkertoys. Raymond's wallet had not opened this wide since the separation.

Back at the trailer on the John Joe Road, Roger fretted about getting the gifts out of the truck without Debbie seeing them. He searched the trailer and found no sign of her. He wandered around with the bags for several minutes. There was no place to hide anything. Raymond agreed to keep Debbie's gifts at his work shed until Christmas.

But Debbie did not return Monday after school or after the Tuesday half day. Debbie never returned at all.

At the last lunch hour before the Christmas holidays, Roger spotted Ricky Gallant out behind the school, flirting with three of the girls Ricky had unleashed upon Debbie the day she took refuge in Roger's secret HQ. Two of the girls were laughing at a story Angela Ellsworth was telling; Ricky was leaning against the wall looking bored.

Roger walked toward them, stopped, and then turned and walked away. If that gang knew what had become of Debbie Arsenault, he didn't want to know.

CHAPTER 6

WESTISLE COMPOSITE HIGH SCHOOL was plunked down on the Elmsdale stretch of Route 2, as had been a grain elevator, a post office, and a convenience store where the chips were always past their best-before date. The population of Elmsdale was about forty-five, depending on whether the McLellans, all nine of them, were at home or at their Mill River cottage for the summer. But local demand played no part in the decision of where to locate the high school, which, even three years after its grand opening, still smelled of paint fumes. One day, there was a potato field. A few botched tenders later, there was a massive single-storey red-brick school buffered from Route 2 by a fragile row of young birch trees.

The most important thing was that Elmsdale was not Tignish, O'Leary, or Alberton. It was, people couldn't help but notice, considerably closer to Alberton than the other two towns. You couldn't blame the Liberal Party itself, which had dominated all Up West since the 1960s, for giving Alberton an educational advantage. No more than you could blame the Liberals for depriving Tignish of its rightful hospital or liquor store; O'Leary and Alberton both had one of each.

But you could blame religion. O'Leary and Alberton were mostly Protestant, and the Protestants dominated the Prince Edward Island cabinet. The Catholic settlers, French and Irish alike, had scattered themselves along the coast, a loosely knit rural apron of Catholicism wrapped around a denser core of Pope deniers living in the towns. West Prince Catholics ran the farms, not the marketplace nor the institutions.

Roger had no idea what subterranean political and religious forces shaped his high school experience. He certainly hadn't read anything about it in *The Spectator-Herald,* the Summerside paper that cared much more about Up West than its snootier rival, the Charlottetown *Guardian*. What Roger knew was that all the social mores that had governed his education up until Westisle had evaporated. Country kids and town kids from various elementary and intermediate schools were thrown together. If you lived west of Summerside, you attended Westisle Composite High School or you did not attend school at all. The latter option, as well as the teenage pregnancy that often triggered it, was not so unusual.

With its sprawling open-concept design and hoggish use of cheap farmland, the school was short on secret rooms, unexplored crannies, and easily picked locks. But Roger, a twelfth grade almost-honours student, found he no longer needed these refuges. Where he had once exploited the shadows to further his ambitions, he had now found a place on or close to centrestage. Roger thought nothing of taking over the teacher's lounge as a base to glue-gun nylon netting to plastic champagne glasses for the grad-class banquet. Or using the principal's office to make long-distance phone calls to possible canteen suppliers when various kids noticed some subtle changes in the taste of Hostess's ketchup chips.

On this particular Saturday night in May, Roger was wearing Mr. O'Brien's ring of janitorial keys on his belt and rummaging through Principal Poirier's desk drawers for rubber bands with which he could bind balloons.

"They're fine," said Caroline MacPhail, standing just outside the principal's office door. She looked at her watch. The dance started in ten minutes. "Leave them."

"One more cluster," said Roger. Both his body and his head had elongated over the past couple of years, leaving Roger looking more imposing and serious than before puberty. Though his words had become more direct, his gaze had grown shier, more uncertain. He was taller than most people—and his shoulders were wider, too—but he carried himself like a much smaller man.

"I already know the shot I want. All your fussing and mussing is not going to make a sweet bit of difference," said Caroline.

The two of them walked to the auditorium where the school yearbook's Nikon camera stood on a tripod facing the riser on which the DJ would sit and where the awards would be given. Every square foot of the auditorium's walls was covered with eagle-inspired decoration—a theme that was a compromise between The Eagles' "Hotel California" and The Steve Miller Band's "Fly like an Eagle." Chicken feathers were pasted on long rolls of paper wrapped around all four sides of the room. Feathers were attached to streamers dangling from cages hung from the light fixtures. Feathers were taped to balloons, chairs, and other surfaces. There were hand-painted murals of California sunsets with eagles flying across them. Each of the long cafeteria tables contained an arrangement of wildflowers and feathers mounted in a slab of birch log.

Tradition dictated that the Grade 11s decorated for the graduation prom, which was in a month's time. Roger had interviewed the prom committee co-chairs a few months earlier. He had not been impressed. His May dance, his last hurrah, would have to do the job the prom was meant to do. The yearbook had been held back from the printing press so its editor, Caroline, could photograph Roger's triumph. The yearbook would feature two shots: one would be pure and undisturbed documentation of the décor, the second would be teeming with teenagers and their accompanying hormones.

Roger attached his final balloon cluster to the podium. The DJ, Michael DesRoches from Tignish, was wary of photos for reasons he didn't mention and went out back of the school for a smoke.

"I know what I'm doing," said Caroline. "I'm down to three shots. I don't have another roll. Go stand over there."

"Should I turn off the fluorescent lights? Or is it too dark?"

"My darling rubbish pile," said Caroline, "I am the editor. I decide. Don't get my back up. You don't want to be on my bad side."

The university-prep stream had brought the two of them closer together in high school, in the same way prison inmates become close. Roger held no grudges over the torments Caroline had directed at him in grades seven through ten. For her part, Caroline found that amount of forgiveness hard to believe and kept her guard up; for her, friendship could feel like an elaborate revenge ploy.

Roger did what she wanted when he could. What she could offer in friendship was this: her mocking and impatience were directed at Roger himself, rather than about Roger to others. If many people would have considered that sort of kindness a form of hostility, Roger did not register it as such.

Roger turned off the cafeteria lights, turned them on again, and then turned them off again. Blue and white Christmas-tree lights were strung along every surface that could endure their weight.

"Freak," she said. "You need to go."

"I'll check on the line-up."

Over the years Caroline's face had grown rounder, her elbows softer, her bossiness tempered by an all-purpose smirk that could be mistaken for good will. Her father, who had a few years earlier formed a breakaway evangelical congregation, took the smirk as a sign of Jesus's love setting up camp in his daughter's heart. Teachers did, too, and cut her a lot of slack, not wanting to provoke any Jesus talk in their classrooms. On moral matters, she was vehemently anti-abortion, like the Catholics, but also anti-drinking, anti-swearing, and anti-mysticism. Transubstantiation, which Roger thought was lovely, was something she could rail about for entire free periods.

Father Euseb Arsenault had, sensing a possible vocation, promoted Roger from altar boy to youth parish council representative, so he did not worry about Roger's openness to Protestant influences. The only person under fifty on the council, Roger Niese always voted for "more": an extension to the church hall, a larger decoration budget, a graveyard renewal project, a more expensive roofer, pricey whole-wheat communion wafers. Father Arsenault admired Roger's enthusiasm but couldn't bear the young man's fascination with the Evangeline and Gabriel story. The priest wished he had never told Roger about it.

"Like Evangeline waiting for Gabriel before they were put on the ships," Roger would say of the children whose parents didn't pick them up immediately after catechism.

"Like Gabriel appearing in the almshouse to say a last goodbye to his great love," Roger said one Easter, looking over the John 21 reading where the resurrected Jesus showed himself to the disciples by the Sea of Tiberias.

"Now wait a minute there," Father Arsenault snapped. "That Longfellow hadn't a single religious credential. And did he visit the Midas Basin? Unlikely."

The lyric poem was not taught in any of PEI's English classes. As far as the Island school curriculum was concerned, Henry Wadsworth Longfellow might as well have been writing about Hindus on the Ganges. But it hit Roger hard. Shortly after Debbie's Arsenault's disappearance, he dug up the original poem at the Alberton library and, discovering that its core protagonist was someone searching the world for her one true love, did his best to commit the tale to memory.

"Still stands the forest primeval; but far away from its shadow,/ Side by side, in their nameless graves, the lovers are sleeping./ Under the humble walls of the little Catholic churchyard," Roger would recite as he scouted the St. Bernard's graveyard after mass, looking for the names Evangeline and Gabriel on the tombstones.

Roger was not alone in his fascination with Evangeline and Gabriel. The tragic love story had also found fertile ground on the other side of Egmont Bay, where there were fewer Irish, Scottish, or English people to dilute the Acadian heritage. The people there had lobbied for and gotten their own French-language school in the 1960s. With the reluctant support of local Protestant MLA, Irwin Murphy, who did not feel anything on the Island should be named after come-from-aways, the school was named Evangeline Primary and Secondary. The Mont-Carmel priest, Father Eloi Poirier, encouraged dressing up as early Acadians during parish festivals and theatrical performances. The seasonal altar banners were embroidered and appliquéd with the red, white, and blue of the Acadian flag, little yellow stars on the lectern pennant.

During the annual stage production at the Egmont Bay harvest festival, a weeping Evangeline would cry for a while before she was picked up and carried off stage by a group of young men with less than honorable intentions. Gabriel was, in those years, played by a pillow-lipped ham, Léonce LeBlanc, who would go on to become a politician and one of the Island's most influential Acadians. Léonce couldn't contain himself when he put on his Gabriel costume. His death coughs rattled across the fairground. When Roger was fifteen, Raymond had taken him to see one of these performances down in Egmont Bay. Roger's immediate emotional response was muted; he had imagined different faces and voices for Evangeline and Gabriel. He had also imagined a much different emotional temperature to their budding romance, something more easy-going and carefree, less coloured by the tragedy to come. He didn't like Léonce LeBlanc's moustache or pantaloons, which were hardly practical for living off the land in the Midas Basin, if the Midas Basin was anything like Up West.

What did shake Roger to the core was the number of people and resources corralled by the community's harvest-festival production.

His heart swelled for what the people on the east side of Egmont Bay had achieved. In the vicinity of Union, Palmer, and Thompson roads, endeavours beyond the bailiwicks of school, church, and women's institute groups rarely gathered momentum. In Egmont Bay, they seemed to have conjured a fourth mode of public life, with shows and public meetings and debates over history.

For his part, Father Arsenault thought there was enough pagan idolatry of the saints without having to paint a holy glow around two self-indulgent romantics cooked up by a Yankee mystic. At least when Saint Paul found himself shipwrecked, he put his feelings aside to serve God. What did Evangeline ever do except bellyache?

"Oh, poor burnt Grand Pré!" said Father Arsenault. "What was there to burn, up here in West Prince? Nothing! We're all here because the land was too swampy for the British landlords to bother about. Tell that to your Kensington potato farmers, all proper-like Irish Protestant royalty, their lace tablecloths and pianos. I dare one of them to give up his New London estate for some rocky piece of earth in St. Timothy's and keep writing his big cheques to the Protestant robbers and liars that sit in the legislature in Charlottetown."

The Evangeline story was fanciful, Roger conceded. Still, it tugged at your heart.

Speedwalking from the auditorium to Westisle's front entrance, Roger stuck his head into the teacher's lounge and gave a thumbs up to the three already-yawning chaperones. Continuing on, he saluted Marissa Gallant and Betty Ann Getson, who had already taken their spots at the ticket desk. The two girls giggled at their dance-committee president as he sped by.

Roger stepped outside onto the concrete slab that jutted into the school's huge lawn like a wharf into a bay. There might have been twenty cars in the lot, shadowy heads behind windshields, some steamy. At dances, it was sometimes necessary to shoo away non-students, too drunk or too young to make it into the Tignish or Bloomfield legions. Last time, Principal Poirier had yelled maniacally at them while Roger stood in the entrance hoping the shadows hid his face. The last thing he needed was for some chippy Doucette or McLellan taking a disliking to him. It could hurt ticket sales.

Tonight, Route 2 was busier than usual, as students drove back and forth in front of the school to see whose cars were there already, all the while chugging the booze they had come into possession of, thanks, mostly, to older siblings. Roger shivered. The blue and yellow tartan waistcoat he wore over his white dress shirt did little to keep him warm. He did not take responsibility for anything that happened beyond the school's doors. He could not tame all the world's chaos.

There was one bit of chaos Roger had accepted into his life. And that was his unlikely friendship with Ricky Gallant. Ricky must have been close to thirty when they met, though they had heard of each other for years. "You're that weird come-from-away" were the first words Ricky had spoken to him. Ricky entered Roger's heart by the most direct route possible, so that any bad behaviour, either rumoured or demonstrated, was immediately set aside.

A few months after Debbie Arsenault's disappearance, Roger had come home from school to find Ricky sitting in his 1974 Trans Am in the Niese driveway, honking his horn at the empty trailer. Roger timidly leaned in the passenger's side window.

"You know, Debbie, right?" Ricky chewed gum so aggressively Roger felt drops of mint on his face.

"I do. I did. Um, why are you?" said Roger.

"Looking for her?"

"Are you?"

"Get in!"

Roger thought back to Debbie's low opinion of Ricky. But then her conflict had been with his various girlfriends and not the man himself, hadn't it? Roger had gotten busy since she had disappeared and felt bad about his lack of effort in finding her. Now here was someone planning to do something about it. It was hard to resist. Roger got in the car.

"You're not going to hurt her, are you? About the motorcycle helmet?"

"That," said Ricky. "Oh kid, you've got to keep up with the news. We're friends now, she and I. I love that girl."

Ricky Gallant was well known from Tyne Valley to Tignish. Some in Summerside had heard of him. His parents, Linus and Rosemary, had died in a car crash when Ricky was in his teens, leaving him to take care of his little brother, Mitchell, mostly by himself. Grandmother Sylvia, who was supposed to look in on them, didn't much like driving. Ricky, though, was in his Trans-Am more than he was out of it. He had bought it with part of his inheritance. A big man, though lean as a boxer, he wore a tight-fitting black toque over his bald head, even in the summer.

On their first outing together, Roger had expected Ricky would take him directly to Debbie Arsenault. But Ricky, it turned out, was looking for direction from Roger. That first night they drove around for hours, visiting parking-lot hangouts across West Prince and staring into front windows of homes where Ricky thought Debbie knew people.

Although they had no success in their mission, they found a sort of comfort in each other.

"I love that you don't know nothing about nothing," said Ricky.

"I'm an honours student."

"Never heard of it." Ricky burst into the laughter of someone who had just won the lottery using the birthday date of a despised ex. "G'way with yah."

A week later, Roger was walking home from a 4-H woodworking meeting at the Kennedys, where he was making a napkin holder. Passing by Gallant and Sons convenience store, near the corner of Union and Palmer roads, Roger spotted Ricky drinking beer in his car. The store was run by cousins of Ricky's. The cousins weren't on speaking terms, though, so Ricky parked in the lot only when the place was closed. Roger crouched down to the driver's seat window.

"Seen her?"

"No.... Wanna go for a ride?" Ricky's pores breathed out alcohol. "She might be out in Miminegash tonight. Could be."

It was as good a place to look as any. Miminegash was composed of a few modest homes surrounding a run-down government wharf. There was a gas station, a convenience store, and elementary school too; some locals boasted they could go a whole year without so much as going to Tignish, never mind Summerside.

Miminegash was considered a tough place for strangers to avoid fights after dark. Roger pictured Debbie on the small beach just north of the harbour, cursing the breaking waves as she scampered to keep her feet dry. There were stars in the sky but not much of a moon.

"Let's check it out then."

"You think so?" Roger walked around the car and gingerly climbed into the passenger's seat. He declined the bottle offered to him, which would eventually become a ritual between them. He held on for dear life as the Trans-Am skied its way down Union Road to Miminegash. Along the wharf, they found a few young people drinking in their cars.

No Debbie.

"Oh fuck, there's Angela Ellsworth," said Ricky, noticing her in the backseat of one of the cars. "Don't fucking want to mess with her."

"Really?" Roger knew Angela Ellsworth was a piece of work. But it seemed impossible that Ricky was scared of anybody.

"I like my fun. My fun is laughs. Her fun is fighting."

"I see," said Roger, his voice trailing off as the car narrowly missed a pile of fluorescent orange buoys on the wharf. Ricky bounced up and down with glee at Roger's panic. Ricky then opened the driver's door to let a couple of beer bottles tumble into a fishing boat named Charlene's Pride IV.

Ricky Gallant quickly came to appreciate Roger Niese. The teenager had just the right amount of anxiety to be successfully teased—you could easily wind him up—but Roger didn't complain, nag, or hold grudges. Roger held it all in. Or maybe it never occurred to him to be bothered. One time when they were out tearing around, Ricky put the car in the ditch on the Mill River Road in the middle of a snowstorm. He sat there in the driver's seat, giggling. Roger got out and dutifully hiked to the Cascumpec Esso for help, walking forty minutes without gloves. When Ricky invited him on another ride the following weekend, Roger accepted as if the last one had been pure pleasure.

At the end of an evening's adventures, Ricky would drop off Roger at the end of the John Joe Road—it was for the best that Raymond Niese didn't see too much of Ricky. Every time, Roger would politely shake Ricky's hand. The joke for Ricky was that it didn't seem like a joke to Roger.

They might not see each other for a month or two, then Ricky'd show up with fried eggs they'd eat on Miminegash shore. Or with a broken vacuum cleaner they could throw at the side of Westisle Composite High School until it was in splinters that Roger would gather into a plastic garbage bag.

Sometimes they'd wonder aloud about Debbie's whereabouts, but neither of them ever had gossip or sightings to share. They were poor detectives that way. Ricky sometimes talked about moving into a van or trailer he could take to Ontario in the winters. His brother, Mitchell, would like it there. It was easier for people like Mitchell to get into programs in Ontario. Maybe people would be less likely to notice Mitchell's hockey helmet. Maybe in Ontario they'd have some medical treatment to fix Mitchell's scrambled brain.

Roger had been warned by Betty Ann, whose older brother was Ricky's age, that Ricky had a dark side. Roger couldn't imagine what it looked like. Over the last year, Ricky had shown up in the Westisle parking lot during school dances. When Ricky caught a glimpse of Roger surveying the parking lot, Ricky waved from afar, got back in the car, and drove away.

The friendship had done wonders for Roger's reputation, especially among the school's rougher crowd, who nodded at him and emitted appreciative snorts as he made his way down the smokers' corner steps to get to his school bus. Since junior high, Roger had subconsciously mastered the art of never being in the same place with the same people for very long. Many students tended to imagine, if he wasn't in their vicinity, that he was spending his time with Ricky, even if he was just sitting at home doing his homework.

The rumours about the drinking and drugs, the video-gambling machines, the STDs, that the hat covered up scars from a knife fight— none of it mattered to Roger. Ricky was just Ricky. He laughed at Roger's jokes. Since Ricky laughed at everything, it didn't seem like he was laughing at Roger's plans.

So, when a burgundy van with tear-drop rear side windows pulled into the Westisle Composite High School parking lot that May evening, Roger suspected it might be Ricky in a vehicle that he had happened upon. A few weeks earlier, Ricky had picked up Roger in a Mustang of unmentioned origins for a two-hour drive to the new Tim Hortons in Charlottetown and back.

The burgundy van pulled into a spot near Westisle's unfinished tennis courts. Roger clasped his hands behind his back and rocked on the balls of his feet like an experienced maître d' awaiting an eccentric regular. It was seven minutes till the dance started. He might have a few moments to chat with Ricky, who would, conveniently, remember a better party elsewhere.

But the figure that emerged from the van was feminine and moved with a tentativeness uncharacteristic of Ricky Gallant, each foot planted carefully in front of the other like it was finding firm spots on a rotten log.

Roger leaned into the darkness and squinted.

"Debbie?"

Roger's heart gained so much speed, he could feel the blood in his hair follicles. He could barely keep standing for all the activity inside him. He knew he was right the moment the name passed his lips. Debbie hadn't heard him.

"Debbie!"

"Rog?" she said, a nickname she had never used before. No one had.

Roger's feeling that Debbie Arsenault would eventually return to him, a feeling he and Ricky had kept fresh in one another, made recognizing her easy. His brain was primed.

After more than four years, he was still able to see the Debbie he remembered in this womanlier body. Her short hair was cut at sharp, almost avant-garde, angles. Her eye makeup was dramatic, but her face was covered in a light powder that flattened every other facial feature. Her face was rounder, though her nose was still sharp. She wore jeans and a too-light-for-the-season short-sleeve V-neck blouse. What Roger recognized best was the grin spreading across her face.

"Rog? My God," she said, clutching a little handbag under her arm. "I can't believe it's you." She hugged him like a delicate sorority sister would, for the crowds, hug a hated rival.

"Where have you been? Did you come for the dance? Let me get it." Roger reached into his pocket to show her he had two-fifty for her ticket.

Debbie shook her head emphatically.

"Rog, is there, like, a place we can chat, like, somewhere quiet?"

Roger had never heard more beautiful words. He could call Ricky later. Debbie was here. At last! She had come home. He hadn't had to go to Philadelphia to find her, as Evangeline had found the dying Gabriel. Their story was their own.

Roger tried to think of a place where they could spend a long time together, perhaps the rest of their lives, without being disturbed. The only idea that came quickly was the chemistry lab. Mr. Pineau usually failed to lock it. Since the prom was still ahead of them and Roger did not want to crush the hopes of Betty Ann, who had hinted that she would like to be asked, Roger avoided the main entrance. He led Debbie around to the other side of the school, where he had propped open a door for the delivery of the DJ equipment. They had to walk through shrubbery and a mucky flowerbed.

Four minutes to dance time. This would be the first time Roger was not there to turn on the Open sign, which he had constructed of multicoloured Christmas tree lights.

"Aren't you smart!" said Debbie. Roger pulled her inside the building, kicking away the basketball that held the door open. "You always were. You always were! Weren't yah?"

"'Fly like an Eagle' is our theme. You'll love it. There are songs on my request list that will bowl you over...." Roger pointed in the direction of the muffled music which had just come on.

"Oh, no dancing for me. Not looking for anything but a little peace."

Debbie wouldn't let Roger turn on the classroom's fluorescent lights. The streetlights over the parking lot gave her face a soft glow. They sat down awkwardly on stools by Mr. Pineau's lab counter. Roger's heart was pounding fast. Though Debbie was now frowning, he had seen pleasure in her face when she saw him. He was sure he had. Still, it was taking an increasing amount of effort to banish the dance from his thoughts. Whether the DJ started, as instructed, with Chic's "Dance Dance Dance" was far from his mind.

"Dad would love to see you...."

"Oh Rog, how's your father? Sweet man, very sweet man. Putting up with me. Imagine!"

"He was pissed at me for losing track of you. I could tell. He's not at woodlot management anymore. Did you know that? I guess not. Have you graduated somewhere?"

"Graduating? Wouldn't this have been fun."

"I'll be out of here soon. What a relief!"

"I can just imagine."

"You can, can't you just?"

Debbie laughed just long enough.

"Rog, I need to ask you something."

"Anything! You should see the little trailer now," said Roger. "You'd get lost in it. Trailer de-luxe. You have to see it."

When the university had closed down its woodlot project two years earlier, putting Raymond out of a job, the Charlottetown bosses gave Raymond the little building, wood stove and all, which Raymond hauled to their lot on the John Joe Road. Raymond had built a connecting portal from the building to the trailer, more than doubling the size of their home. The little building became something of a common room where the boots and coats were kept, as well as the TV and two high-backed wooden chairs. The uncomfortable chairs prevented Raymond from falling asleep in front of the TV. He was often exhausted from working as a farm hand for the Gliddens, up on the Dock Road.

The job tested his muscles more than his brain, which was left to think of poetry and how much he liked or disliked the host of the local CBC morning show.

"That would be so nice, Rog. So nice. But right now, Roger, right now, I wanted to see if you could fetch me Michael."

"Michael DesRoches?" asked Roger. At that moment he could faintly hear "You're the One that I Want" coming from the auditorium. Roger thought it was an apt choice by Michael DesRoches, but perhaps Debbie wanted to take issue with the DJ.

"No, silly. No, sweetie. Our Michael. Michael Chaisson."

Roger did not know where she got the "our" from. "Michael, eh? Not sure if he's here yet. Not sure if he's coming, actually."

"Get him, Roger, will yah? For me, darling. For me, sweetie?"

"Sure," said Roger. "Um, what... why... what...?"

The obvious questions about where she'd been all this time were swallowed up broader, existential wonderings about their future. Roger pictured him making her omelets, while Debbie did pirouettes in a spacious eat-in kitchen.

"Please, pretty please?" This time her face went hard. Roger lifted himself off his stool and silently left the room to do what he was told.

Out in the main corridor, students were stopping to pose and take photos under the elaborately decorated archway, all balloons and plastic flowers. Under ordinary circumstances, Roger would not have been able to hold himself back from offering greetings, complimenting women on their dresses, or sniffing for contraband alcohol the inattentive chaperones might have missed. But he needed to be focused so he could get back to Debbie ASAP. Michael might as well have been a safety pin or a can of insect repellent, a small detail needed in order to comfortably continue their reunion.

Marissa had taken a break from the ticket desk and Roger spotted her, and Wendy Gallant, no relation to Ricky Gallant or Marissa herself, checking their makeup in the smudged glass of the school's trophy case. The girls' escorts, of which Michael was one, stood back, laughing amongst themselves as they waited for Marissa and Wendy to finish their primping. Michael wore pleated polyester dress pants, a white-collared shirt, and an already loosened blue-striped tie. Roger waved, and then called out "Hey" before Robert Doucette noticed Roger. Robert elbowed Michael to attention.

Michael, who in a few weeks would play his role of prom king and then, a few weeks after that, the role of valedictorian, did not question why he was needed. What a disappointment for Roger, who had decided to refuse an explanation. Perhaps Michael thought he'd be giving a speech or be presented with some surprise award. He immediately and silently followed Roger to Mr. Pineau's classroom.

"Michael!" said Debbie. In a single word, she demoted Roger to the role of a spear carrier. Yet leaving the room did not occur to him. Roger could not depend on these two to report the outcome with as much accuracy and detail as he desired.

"Where's your father?" asked Michael. "I didn't think...."

"Don't you want to know? Don't you want to, at all?"

"I'm with Marissa."

"Her again! Lord. Does Marissa know? That'd knock her nose right out of the air, wouldn't it?"

"Dad settled all this...."

"The money stopped, Michael. Your father didn't tell you? My old man's back at the trough. So many times. It hasn't been good. Not good at all, I can tell you that right now."

"It's between them, isn't it?" Michael turned toward the classroom door. Roger stared at Michael's ear, thinking it would be nice to whisper something in it now to make him go away.

"I have the van. My old man's van. He's at his friend's place. Woman friend, if you know what I mean. From Cardigan. I can't follow the comings and goings. I can't."

"Why, on God's sweet Earth, would I care what Errol Arsenault is fucking up to?"

Roger had never heard Michael swear before and wondered if this could be used to oust him as student council president.

"It's just that you said it wasn't your fault and I'm just saying—this is me saying it—that I don't think it was either. It was them. Those two old buggers. They took me away and I, well, I haven't been in school for a while. Worked a bit. I did! It's you I'm coming to, but it's not you I'm asking. Not really. It was those two old buggers that got us here and I'm just thinking only one of them can help me out. Michael, your old man's got more common sense than mine."

"More money, I'd suppose."

"It's a girl, Michael. Sweet, sweet thing. Almost four. Almost as smart as you. She could be. Amber. That's her name."

"My father took all this in good faith. I never would have."

Debbie Arsenault burst into tears, thick streaming tears like the run-off that shrank the Island each spring, carrying red soil away into the Northumberland Strait and the Gulf of St. Lawrence.

Roger wanted to dry her face, thinking: everybody should cry when they're wrapping up a chapter, saying goodbye, calling it quits. Debbie was dumping Michael in a very backhanded way, thought Roger. That was kind, but he wondered if Michael was getting it.

The three heard hurried steps clomping down the hallway. Perhaps an overindulging dance attendee was looking for a quiet place to throw up. Then a ball of scraggly grey hair and tattered plaid swept into the classroom, chunks of mud flying from boots, plopping like goose shit on the tile floor.

"Little bitch!" squawked the man, the voice of a parrot well-schooled in disrespect. "You fucking, goddam, scampering wench of a bitch."

The two young men stepped back. Debbie sat down again on a lab stool and slouched like a barbell had been placed on her shoulders. The new arrival, several layers of shirts and vests and jackets hanging off him, put his hands on his hips and whistled.

Roger still did not know what was going on, but at least he knew all the players. The man was instantly recognizable as the drunk Roger had encountered in the men's washroom of the HMS Abegweit during his arrival on the Island so many years ago. The man's face had burnt itself into Roger's dreams and nightmares. That face. That voice. Sometimes Roger was asked why he wasn't much of a drinker (an understatement considering Roger wasn't a drinker at all). Every time he tried to answer, Roger thought of the bottle clanking around on the filthy metal floor of the bathroom while a desperate man swore at a little boy.

He now knew that the son of Henry and Bernice Arsenault of Saint Louis had given up fishing because he couldn't hack working in the early mornings. He gave up work maintaining the grounds at the Mill River golf course when he couldn't hack working in the afternoons, either. Marriage and singlehood, friendship and animosity, fatherhood and bachelorhood had also dropped him between the cracks.

As the swearing went on, Roger's gaze fell to the man's calloused hands. The empty hands were a sign, at least, that Betty Ann and the chaperones had been vigilant in keeping booze out of the school.

"Get out, Papa! Nobody wants you here! Leave me alone."

"Ah fuck," muttered Michael.

"You think you're pretty smart, do yah, missy?" said Debbie's father, spit collecting at the corners of his mouth. "Like I don't know if my own goddamn keys are missing. Like I don't have friends who can give me a fucking lift." In fact, at that very moment, a barroom buddy sat idling in the parking lot, counting the high school girls he thought were fuckable and waiting for delivery of the twelve-pack and pint he had been promised. Debbie had been accidentally betrayed by a friend who foolishly called wondering if she needed company on the drive Up West.

Errol Arsenault scanned the dark classroom. He didn't seem to notice Roger. His eyes stopped and held on Michael.

"The two of you? Behind my back all this time? Still together?" Papa Arsenault turned back to Debbie. "Little arrangement, is it? Taking the money from Old Man Chaisson and still together."

"Go with him, go!" said Michael. "You two go figure it out."

"You're fucking telling me fucking where to go?"

"I'm telling her."

"I'm telling you," said Papa Arsenault. "I'm fucking telling you this. You got off easy, you little pansy cocksucker. Your father and me, we had a deal. He's an established man, surely, but aren't we all seeing he's not to be trusted? Wheeler-dealer, that's what he is. Me, I'm the babysitter. And you, you're the cocksucker who can't keep his fucking cock in his pants when some pussy comes along. That's what you are. What if I told you your father said you'd be paying now? All that big-school tuition you've been scrimping and saving and bumming off your daddy, all of it going to me for peanut butter sandwiches. What if I told you that? What if I told you it was the end of the line for you, cocksucker?"

Roger could not imagine this man making sandwiches.

"Talk to my father. Talk to him."

"When I got here to the school, you know who told me where to find you? She knew exactly where you fucking were, watching you so fucking close. What's her name? Little Marissa. Red hair. Who'd fuck something with red hair like that? Those'd be some ugly babies. Not like your little Amber."

"Marissa?" said Michael, a new panic spreading in him.

This hadn't ended up where Roger thought it was going when Debbie arrived asking for him. The pieces of what he was hearing were terribly slow to fall in place. He was, at first, stuck on the fact that the pirate was Debbie's father, and was, unbelievably, babysitting a child named Amber. That seemed like the most immediate concern, something child protection services might be notified about.

Debbie seemed to be as attached to this child, Amber, as Michael was contemptuous of it. It was their equally strong feelings in this regard that led Roger, amidst all this yelling and swearing, to slowly understand whose child it was. Those nights Debbie had shown up at the trailer so late, it had been Michael's fault. Roger had no recollection of seeing Debbie and Michael together when she was in school. But then, no one would have any recollection of seeing her and Roger together, either. Roger felt a sharp jolt of hate toward his classmate for taking Debbie away from him for four years. He wanted the pirate to knock Michael to the floor, to club Michael's easy charm out of existence.

This burst of anger was short-lived. His urge to solve the broader problem pushed Roger's feelings aside. The future might ultimately be salvageable, especially if the pirate was capable of making peanut butter sandwiches until Amber could make them for herself. Maybe Michael could be the one sent into exile in the eastern part of the province for a while.

It did not occur to Roger that Amber could be part of his future with Debbie; his vision of their life together was too pure for that.

"What did you say to Marissa?" demanded Michael.

"Marissa, oh?" said Roger to himself. The name, a reminder that the dance was happening without him and probably needed his tending, knocked him out of his preoccupations.

"What did you say to her?" asked Michael.

"What didn't I fucking say? Now what's your daddy going to do about that?"

"I didn't see much of the money, I'll tell you that," said Debbie. "Why can't we go away together? Do things proper. We've been living in Montague. It's not a bad town, Michael, except for this one standing here."

Whatever Michael's heart and brain were telling him at that moment, his body had its own ideas of how to react to all this. Michael turned white like the chalk marks on the board behind him. He had the good fortune of his body going limp before he fainted to the floor. Errol Arsenault had once seen a man go down stiff as a board, splitting his head open on a boulder. Michael's was merely grazed by the granite countertop.

"Oh lordie," said Roger, who had convinced student council to create a new award for "best incident-free event" that he had planned to win at year's end.

"Michael! Michael! Are you okay?" cried Debbie, without approaching her baby daddy. She looked at him like a window she had broken. Michael slowly sat up. He didn't seem to require urgent medical help; people's attention wandered.

"Let's get this show on the fucking road. I wanna be back in Montague before midnight," snapped Errol Arsenault, looking for something in his pockets. "You're lucky my Sarah's a sweetheart, looking after our Amber while I track you down."

"As if Amber's safe with your fucking tramp!"

"Oh, you fucking slut!" Errol Arsenault made as if to strike his daughter. But he, in this moment, caught sight of Roger, and saw the panicked expression on the young man's face. The pirate did not recognize him from their ferry ride together but knew a possible witness when he saw one. Errol's hand froze in mid-air.

Errol Arsenault's voice got all proper now that he knew they were being watched by an outsider. "I said, c'mon, dear. Let's go."

Roger, head down, teeth clenched, made a run at Errol Arsenault. He tripped on a knocked-over stool and, in an accidental tackle, Roger's flailing arms ended up wrapped around Errol's hips. The older man stiffened. He could handle himself in a bar fight. A hunting knife sat waiting in the inside pocket of his leather jacket. But what to do about this? He looked down at Roger, whose skinny arms could barely hold up his own weight.

"Jesus, you gotta be kidding me."

"No!" said Roger, hanging like a slack clothesline. "Leave her alone."

Errol hula-hooped his hips until Roger was horizontal.

Roger closed his eyes, as if blindness was as good as a break. He could hear Michael's moaning. Then, right in his ear, he heard Debbie's breathing. She had knelt down to pry Roger from her father's dirty boots.

"Oh, Roger."

"Oh, Debbie. I tried."

"You tried something. You did. You tried to get yourself killed."

Roger was at a loss for what to do next. Perhaps his job was done. He'd have to wait and see. The dance was still at the back of his mind.

Errol Arsenault certainly thought the scene had reached its conclusion. He was wondering if he had it in him to permit his daughter to drive the two and a half hours back. He wouldn't mind a bit of rum on the way. The back of the van had custom seating, with soft lime green cushions claimed from an old couch. He liked to feel the velvet on his face when he was snoozing.

"Maybe we'll stop at the Richmond Dairy Bar," Errol told his daughter, "if you can behave yourself."

Debbie Arsenault had become meek. She nodded at her father and then, as breezily as she could, said "Bye" to Michael.

"Yeah," said Michael, rubbing his head. "I'll talk to Dad."

"Oh, Roger," said Debbie, her strategic cheerfulness building momentum as she spoke. "Sorry for all this. It was great seeing you."

"You're not staying for a dance or two?" Getting himself on his feet, Roger directed the most hostile glare he could at Errol Arsenault.

"I got to sort all this out. I'll call you. I will. We'll have a little dance then."

Debbie moved in close, her face in his.

"Don't be jealous of Michael, Roger. Don't hate him. You have something special. I mean, he has something special, too. But your special is... special."

She took his right hand in both of hers and held it tightly, as if they had been sitting quietly all night on the beach and their slow tentative inching toward and brushing against each other had led to this. Over the years, Roger had had some mildly lustful thoughts about Debbie. These were nothing, nothing at all, compared to holding her hand. He would have let himself be neutered to be assured he'd feel that squeeze again. The brush of her index finger on his wrist could not, in any circumstances, be accidental.

"Debbie!" hollered Errol Arsenault. "Let them get back to their fucking dance. Boys! I don't want to be reading about any of this in *The Spectator-Herald* tomorrow."

Roger straightened his back—the dance. "I'll let you out," he said. He jumped into action, leading father and daughter to the emergency exit. He watched them cross the parking lot to the van, watched Errol Arsenault say something to the man in the Chrysler parked beside the van and watched both vehicles pull out. Then he went back to check on Michael.

"You didn't hear any of that!" said Michael, his lips quivering. He wasn't crying but he was shaken.

"I didn't. I don't think."

"You didn't!"

"I didn't."

"Now leave me alone. Don't you have somebody to nag?"

"You have to close the door behind you. I don't want anybody fooling around in here."

As Roger headed down the hall, his thoughts focused on the future, when Debbie would return, what he'd be doing when she returned, what he'd do for her when she returned. There were so many things to figure out. She'd probably want her own room. He'd need a job. Then there'd be the baby—Amber, wasn't it? Roger'd have to make a list.

But first—walking into the auditorium, Roger saw it was full of problems to be solved. The walls were two layers thick with guys, their sharp collars skewed out over their fathers' corduroy jackets. Girls danced in circles close to the DJ station, each afraid that if she wasn't whispering in her neighbour's ear, some other girl would be whispering about her. "Blinded by the Light" was playing and some of the girls held their arms up to protect their eyes from the bursts of brightness the DJ used to emphasize the chorus.

Members of the grade 11 prom committee sat at one of the long tables, glaring ruefully at the décor they'd have to one up for the June prom. Following their gaze, Roger saw that the feathers on the wrap-around mural were gone. The feathers on the table centrepieces had also vanished. In fact, the lunchroom was bereft of feathers. The room had been plucked clean.

"Who did this?" Roger snapped at the prom committee table. "Where are the feathers?"

"What feathers? Are they going to fall from a net?" said Jeanette DesRoches, her long neck bending back at a severe angle so she could see the ceiling.

"Who ruined my décor?"

"I was the first person here and it was like this when I got here," said Sally Chaisson, Michael's younger sister, who saw herself as student council president the next year, Crown attorney eight years after that.

Roger ran to the entryway where he found Betty Ann reading Peanuts comic books. The rush was over. A rule requiring that the doors be closed at 10pm had been implemented after the incident when remnants of a drunken wedding party showed up just before midnight.

"What happened to my feathers?" Roger wailed.

"Now, didn't Caroline say something about feathers?" Betty Ann asked herself. "I can't keep track of that one!" She didn't notice Roger's tears. "A going concern, that one!"

"And you let that drunk man in!"

"I'm no security guard," said Betty Ann.

Roger's face was tear-streaked by the time he tracked down Caroline MacPhail in the student council office. She was sitting atop one of several black garbage bags of feathers, as was Greg MacArthur, co-artistic director of the drama club. The duo was drinking tea out of fancy-looking China cups Roger and Caroline had bought at a yard sale. Down the hall, the DJ was playing Kenny Rogers' "Lucille." An awful song to dance to, thought Roger, sliding to a halt in front of Caroline.

"Oh my God. My God. What, what happened?"

"Where have you been?" asked Caroline. "We thought we'd lost you. You'll be happy to know everything is under control. They're all as happy as drugged puppies."

"Control? What happened to my feathers?"

"The dance committee's feathers?" Caroline looked searchingly at Greg. "Oh yes. So much has happened since you left us all alone to fend for ourselves."

"What the f-ing h-e-double-you-know-what's happened! The gym.... My work...."

"You should have thought of that before using that tape," said Caroline. "I was making adjustments for the photo. It was all coming apart. Yes,"—she was answering the expression on Roger's face—"they were falling off and the room had become asymmetrical. Hadn't it, Greg?" Her voice was as rich and chocolatey as she could make it.

"I hate asymmetry," said Greg. "In hair, in a blouse, in a painting. Picasso! It just doesn't seem right to me."

"We cleaned it up for you. While you were having your little... I shouldn't mention it. What I will say is—ahem—sound travels very well down the halls of this school. People could learn to shut doors. Speaking of—where's Michael Chaisson?"

"Ooh, Michael. Caroline's got a crush!" squealed Greg.

"Please! He's Roman Catholic!"

"Jesus," said Roger. He was, he realized, hyperventilating. Before Caroline and Greg could mock him, he withdrew from the room. Around the corner, Roger crouched out of sight by a row of lockers. He couldn't go back to the dance. His father wouldn't be picking him up until 12:15am. The only thing he could do was go back to see if Michael was all right.

The physics lab was empty; the only evidence of what had happened was a small splotch of blood on the floor and the smell of sweat and Old Spice.

"Well, now. Yes. Of course. She must be in the phone book," said Roger to himself. He pulled the blue lab stool up to the window so he could look out onto the parking lot. It was drizzling outside. He knew, though, that Debbie Arsenault was not in the phone book. When he was fifteen, he got through calling two hundred Arsenaults before his father saw the long-distance phone bill.

Roger's hyperventilation got worse. He lay down on the floor where Michael had fallen.

They were the same, really, Roger and Michael. Roger was just a little behind. He would work hard and catch up. Valedictorian. Such an easy job. But you got your picture in the paper. Roger thought back a lifetime ago when he was in grade eight. Debbie came into his life too early. He didn't know how to read the signs.

Montague, they had said.

Roger had never been east of Charlottetown. His 4-H woodworking entries were taken to the Down East festivals by Susan Kennedy, who ran the club along with her husband, Earl, though they had no children of their own. Napkin holder in first year. Knife holder in second. Bookshelf in third. Susan Kennedy brought him back ribbons from Montague, Souris, Georgetown, and Saint Peter's Bay. They might have been London, Paris, Berlin, and Rome for all Roger knew about them.

Roger's breathing grew steadier. He was still lightheaded, but he had already exceeded the limits of his patience with himself. He was a man of action. He had to do something. Stumbling to his feet, he knocked over stools as he made his way to Mr. Pineau's desk. He found some pencils and a pile of foolscap in one of the drawers. Roger extracted a sheet.

"Dear Prom Committee," he wrote. "I realize you don't have much time left to fulfill your obligations as Grade Elevens. But just as you would not want the Grade Tens to let you down next year, just as you would want them to do the best job they can, it is left to me to worry that the improvements that can be made to your plans are more numerous than the plans you've drawn up. I've never been one to force my nose into anybody's business, but I would be willing to help anybody who asked me. By this token, I think there are five principles you must follow to put on a successful prom...."

When he was done, Roger folded the eight foolscap pages twice, stapled it twice, and stuffed it through the vent in Sally Chaisson's locker. Raymond Niese, sitting in the car reading a book about entropy, noticed nothing unusual in his son locking up the school behind him at 2:30am.

CHAPTER 7

THOUGH THE DYNAMICS OF their father-son relationship changed little over the next few years, there certainly was physical evidence of the passage of time at the home of Raymond and Roger Niese on the John Joe Road. Not a single flat surface of the house/trailer was exposed to air or light. Magazines, piles of *The Spectator-Herald* and *La Voix Acadienne* (neither Raymond nor Roger could read French very well, but there were photos and names to keep track of), church newsletters, books, collectible glasses from Shell, promotional keychains, graduation photos of David, Allan and Roger, photos of David's new baby Bridget, a surprising number of small appliances including a deep-fat fryer, two toasters, a Christmas manger diorama, an autoharp, a music stand, an always-on police radio scanner, and a chrome floor-model ashtray that held Raymond's pipe and accessories. Winter tires sat in the corner of the kitchen, along with two empty rabbit cages.

To further expand on their living space, Raymond had hauled onto the property a tiny house that he bought off Linda Shaw, who worked at the pharmacy in O'Leary. Originally a Thibidault from Tignish, she was recently divorced from Lester Shaw, who ran the PetroPump where Roger worked. Lester was a local wheeler-dealer who owned a range of businesses and properties one wouldn't have expected him to own, some of which, at the time of the divorce, were in Linda's name. Linda was known to hog the pharmacy's bulletin board with the many items she had for sale, including the Atlantic Canadian franchise rights for the Burger Chef chain.

"If I can live without Lester, I can live without an eight-piece dining room set," Linda Shaw would boast as she heaved bottles of discounted cough syrup into plastic bags.

Lester Shaw—and so Linda Shaw—had inherited the little house from a parsimonious spinster aunt who left behind a structure devoid of smudge or smear, wear, or tear. Raymond Niese connected the house to the existing trailer/shed via a door cut through the bedroom closet. The original trailer became something of a storage area, and a place where father could retreat from son, son from father.

Because using the doorways properly meant circumnavigating his father's bed, Roger used a window as his primary thoroughfare in and out of his bedroom. He nailed ladder steps to the exterior wall to make his comings and goings feel less criminal.

Father and son lived like this for several months when Linda Shaw called up Raymond to see if he wanted another old shed at a good price. With the help of Lowell Glidden, the farmer up on the Dock Road who Raymond was working for these days, the shed was hauled to the John Joe Road and attached to the kitchen for use as a pantry. Each of the home's components was clad in whatever siding it had come with or whatever Raymond found on sale: shake shingles, brown aluminum, off-white vinyl, corrugated metal. The wood frame that connected the two bedrooms had been stuffed with pink Fiberglas insulation and covered with black garbage bags to dampen the draft. No trim was added.

Roger had grown as blind to the house's digressions and ellipses as his father. But today, gathering old newspapers into black garbage bags, Roger started to see the place with the eyes of the visitor who would soon be arriving. He wondered if a match and a can of gasoline might be exactly what was called for.

"Put your best foot forward, they tell you," Roger muttered to himself. "This place is quite the foot."

Roger certainly had all the time in the world to play housekeeper. The five years of his life since graduating had been fitful and unfocused. His current job pumping gas at the Esso out at Union Corner was part-time and not particularly challenging.

His first job after high school, a ready solution for quickly earning money, was as fisherman's helper with Noel Pineau, out of Miminegash. But Roger spent most of that time cleaning his vomit from the deck.

Roger had applied for a few jobs in Summerside: bowling alley supervisor, Chinese buffet cashier, and salesperson at Holman's Department Store. But Roger hadn't saved enough money for his own car and his schedule rarely synced with his father's comings and goings. These were often very sudden. A call about a rare bird or a problem Lowell

Glidden was having with a calf had Raymond Niese bolting for the door.

Some might have said that Roger was using his lack of dependable transportation as an excuse to avoid getting a job he might not love as much as he wanted to love a job. But Roger could provide ample evidence he was trying. For the Chinese buffet job, for example, essentially a busboy, he sent an analysis of the number of available parking spaces in the lot and on nearby streets, suggesting Island beef and pork and chicken farmers who might be able to meet this demand. For the bowling alley position, Roger told the owner about his idea for smuggling canned pop over from New Brunswick and reselling it at the snack bar as a high-margin novelty item, since canned drinks were banned on PEI. His cover letters did not so much outline his work experience, but every idea he had ever had about bowling and, more broadly, the hospitality industry.

Roger expected rejection letters authored with a tone of sharp rebuttal, quoting hard statistics against his blue-sky-thinking. Instead, he got demure phone calls asking him what time would be good for him—and if he had a car. In job interviews, Roger might spend most of the time sharing his father's ideas about whether the Island would ever get a fixed link to the mainland. Tunnel or bridge? Roger presented his father's opinions as his own, said he was sure a fixed link would never happen. The rationale was simple. It was too big a project and big projects never came to PEI.

In the days following each interview, Roger would let the phone ring and ring. Sometimes he'd unplug it. Raymond, who thought phones were solely for women and hospitals, never noticed.

So it was that, in what should be a person's wild-oats-sowing-days, Roger rarely ventured far from St. Louis-St. Edward. He'd go up the Union Road to his PetroPump gig. In good weather, he'd started going regularly down the Union Road to Miminegash, usually with his father's car, sometimes walking.

Miminegash was a rough little place, but it had a nice red-sand beach. The strip of sand ran north from the harbour, where a couple of dozen fishermen kept their boats through various fishing seasons. Roger would sit on the beach facing the water, like a romantic in Miami or San Tropez, even when wind from the northwest blasted sand onto his face.

On summer afternoons, adolescent boys with guts shaped by peanut butter, white bread, and beans and molasses swarmed the wharf, jumping into the icy water before they were pushed. Former and current Westisle students sat in their cars in the dusty wharf parking lot, drinking rum from pint bottles, pawing their way closer and closer to matrimonial dead ends.

The locals would chuckle to themselves when Roger walked by, blue bath towel around his neck like a scrawny boxer, goose-stepping barefoot over the rocks to the same spot near the waterline. It occurred to him, from time to time, to invite Betty Ann or one of the other girls he knew from his school days to join him. Betty Ann was at home in Roseville from the University of Prince Edward Island for the summer. But he didn't want to get into what she had been asking about last Christmas, which had something to do with what he thought of her, which wasn't a lot. It wasn't a bad opinion. It was no opinion at all. So a call seemed wrong. He figured that if he saw her one day at Gallant and Sons Convenience or at the pharmacy in O'Leary and started talking about what she should be studying, then they could go to the beach directly from there. That would work.

After his swim or reading some *Reader's Digests* until the sun went down, Roger packed up his beach gear, pulling his rugby pants over his damp swimsuit for the drive home. That would be the time party animals were arriving, gathering driftwood and dried-out brush for a bonfire that would set local mothers and grandmothers atwitter about the hellions who took over Miminegash at night.

Roger was the right demographic for partying, but never seemed to get the call or otherwise find out the details of what, when, and who. Which was all fine by him. If Roger recognized one of the party people as a good head—say, Ricky Gallant's younger brother Mitchell, who was only sixteen, or Noel Pineau, who still liked to party—he might lurk around the beach party for a while, as long as people didn't start smashing bottles and throwing punches. Standing a safe distance from the fire, he'd occasionally call out conversational topics he considered appropriate: Would the government help a fish canning operation get off the ground in Miminegash, like they'd been saying in the papers? Would the school board need a summertime janitor now that Mr. O'Brien had the cancer? Would the federal government have the gall to force Islanders to accept a bridge to the mainland?

"You'd have a better idea what the government is up to now, wouldn't cha?" asked Noel Pineau, who, he said, had a girlfriend in Summerside.

Noel had a little sister, Kate, who was considerably younger. Noel, who had worked in Ontario for a while, was presumed to have a lot of money put away, though that didn't stop him from taking beer from other people's coolers.

"The paper said...," continued Roger.

"The paper, as if they know anything, Roger!" said Noel Pineau. "By the time it ends up in *The Spectator-Herald* or, for fuck's sake, *The Guardian*, all the truth has been squeezed right out of it. City boy thinking! Oh, the papers!"

Roger did not think of himself as a city boy. But he had made certain mistakes. Visiting his mother in Ottawa two years earlier, he had spent most of the time walking Ottawa's streets. He couldn't quite put his finger on it but sensed he was an irritant to his mother, so he tried to stay out of her way. Sarah Niese's new husband, Eddie Carruthers, was in middle management at Customs and Immigration. Roger's brother David lived with his wife and baby not five minutes away by car; they came over to Sarah and Eddie's twice during Roger's visit. Roger saw little more of his brother Allan, who, as far as Roger could tell, never ventured more than eight feet from the television in Sarah and Eddie's den.

One day on Bank Street, Roger bought a button-up shirt with an asymmetrical print across the front. The left side of the collar was green, the right side, blue. In the Up West context, it was not recognizably from the Tignish Co-op, Saunders Variety in Alberton, or Zellers or Towers in Summerside. It seemed like a declaration that had access to fancier places to shop than anybody else.

"The newspapers aren't all bad, Noel. They got some good things in *The Spectator-Herald*. Caroline MacPhail writes some good stuff. About the potato diseases, all the talk of the fixed link."

"Potatoes and the fixed link! Man, oh, man. You going into politics?" asked Noel.

"You think I should?" asked Roger.

"All assholes up there in Charlottetown, in Ottawa. Every one of them. Isn't that right, big guy?" Noel nodded conspiratorially at Roger.

"Couldn't say." Roger shrugged.

"But you like it here better," said Noel. "You and your dad. You like it here, don't yah, yah do." It was hard to tell whether he was being sweet or sarcastic.

It was more than an hour's walk home from Miminegash, but sometimes people would offer Roger a lift. If Gallant and Sons was still open, he'd pick up a *Reader's Digest* and a bag of chips. Raymond would be snoring away as Roger crawled through his bedroom window.

This August weekend, Raymond was expecting a visit from a former coworker. The word "friend" hadn't been used, but so much time had passed since Raymond worked in Ottawa that Roger assumed there must be some friendliness between them. The man, Phillip Sinclair, was on vacation on PEI and had looked up Raymond in the phone book. Roger had taken the call and, with father and son shouting back and forth through the door connecting their rooms, it was hard for Raymond to deny an invitation. Whether the guest would eat with them, stay with them, bring a spouse or travelling companion, be there for an afternoon, a day or a week or a month—these were questions that would only frustrate Raymond. Roger didn't bother asking. The visit would be what the visit was.

Roger filled five black garbage bags with junk. He put away dishes that had never before seen the inside of a cupboard. If Raymond had time after working on Lowell Glidden's farm, he said he'd drive to Summerside to pick up some Tetley tea, fresh cauliflower, and tea biscuits. This was as close to slaughtering the prize lamb as they got.

"Raymond? Raymond Niese?" called out Phillip Sinclair from the other side of the aluminum screen door. Raymond had bought the door off Lowell Glidden, who had left it lying in the cow barn for a few years. It smelled like manure.

"Yes, no, it's his son Roger. Come in. Dad's out. He wasn't sure what time you'd be getting here."

"You've been standing guard like a bloody Beefeater. I thought it'd be evening, all those places on the map to see, but I counted all of six houses in Lower New Annan, maybe four in Central Wellington, and, well, here I am, like a backpacker doing all Europe in a fortnight."

The man wore a crumpled white linen jacket and matching pants, paired with a yellow golf shirt. Roger had never seen white pants on a man before, except on television. But the size of him—Mr. Sinclair must have been six-six, measured to the top wisp of his feathery blond hair—would intimidate the toughest guy down at Miminegash Wharf. His pale face was long too, and his skin was tight, except his cheeks which sagged like oversized dimples. The man's English accent was confident but soft, reined in just the right amount, so it did him more good than harm amongst Canadians.

"It's a boring drive up this way, through Portage especially," said Roger.

"*Por-tahj?*" said the man, in a French accent. He dropped a vinyl Adidas kit bag by the kitchen table as he surveyed the house/trailer. "Train station? Anglican church? Dairy bar?"

"*PORT-idj.* Swamp," said Roger. "Mostly just swamp."

"You'd have to wade out of this part of the province if the main road was in any further state of decay," said Mr. Sinclair, sitting down without invitation. "Roger, my dear young man, do you mind fetching me a glass of water?"

"Right, right!"

"You don't remember me at all, do you? I might have come to the house in Ottawa"—the man paused in thorough consideration—"twice. Yes, twice. You might have been yea high." Mr. Sinclair made no gesture to indicate Roger's youthful height. "Your father and I were work friends primarily. I was with the National Capital Commission."

"The NCC?" Roger knew Ottawans spoke in acronyms.

"The NCC, indeed. Landscaping at first. Then much, much more abstract things with fewer tangible results. This water! It's practically effervescent! Delicious, really. You're a strapping lad now. Twenty?"

"Twenty-three. Twenty-four in the fall."

"Time flies, time flies." This banality seemed truer than it should have. Time flew. Roger looked down at his dirty jeans and hands. The man vaguely reminded him of one of his university professors, a professor of English Literature who wore tweed and was always pushing his glasses up his nose. He could not remember the professor's name; it was not an Island name. Roger's post-secondary education had lasted all of four months, barely worth the savings it had eaten through. As a liberal arts freshman, he could barely keep up with his fellow students and their matrix of complicated relationships, the constant flux of new affections and grievances. The Islanders maintained the tight peer groups from their grade-school days; many of the ones who had more social acumen or, the opposite, the ones who had been unable to make childhood friends, had risked education off-island.

Throwing himself into his studies might have worked if his grades had not plummeted, mostly due to uncertainty of his interests, his superficial qualms with the curriculum; his fifteen-hundred-dollar Léonce LeBlanc Citizenship Scholarship had been indicative of nothing, socially or academically. At the reception for scholarship students, he had talked only to Betty Ann.

University girls did not like how Roger looked at them, his eyes rummaging around their faces as if they were purses containing something he needed. They rightfully wanted their experiments in wardrobe, persona, and sexuality to be glimpsed with indifference and intrigue, not analyzed under a microscope. During orientation week, Roger signed up for debating club, the student union, and, though he had only played the game a half-dozen times, chess club. A week later, he hadn't heard from any of them. He felt downhearted about it. How would he fill the time?

It did not help matters that he shared a smelly two-bedroom apartment with Ken Chin, an international student from China who spoke little English, and a guy named Jason Davison, who was from Kensington and who spent most of his time at his girlfriend's place a few blocks away.

When Roger quit university at Christmas, he gave his textbooks to a classmate. Sarah lost her motherly cool.

"Eddie bought those books for you. He bought David's. He bought yours. They were not cheap. Where are they now?" she snapped into the phone, the per-minute cost temporarily forgotten.

"David graduated. I'm not throwing good money after bad," Roger said.

"What are you throwing, then?"

"Something will come up."

"No, you need to study, get a good job, make a living. Get married."

"It's different here." Roger stared at the clock over the sink. It was a piece of wood jig-sawed into the shape of PEI.

"You don't have to tell me that. Your father has you rolling in the shit down there. But your father can't smell a damn thing, so he doesn't care. But you! You need to get yourself out. I'm sorry I left you there. I'm really sorry." This sounded more like an accusation than an apology.

After that, Sarah's phone calls, which usually came like clockwork at 9:30 sharp Saturday mornings, became random, abbreviated.

The spring after dropping out, Roger ran into Caroline MacPhail at the Alberton Save-Easy. She was studying journalism at King's College in Halifax, where they wore robes and drank wine with their professors during formal dinners. He let her believe he was still at university.

At first, Roger felt like his move back to his dad's place on the John Joe Road was a time to consolidate before he stepped onto the stage of real life. But that stage was not a place he could visualize at this moment in his life.

The man in the white linen suit leaned forward in his chair as if he wanted to be asked something. Mr. Sinclair pinged the empty glass with the smooth curved nail of his left index finger,

"Now, Roger, when do you expect your father?"

Roger looked at his watch. Depending on where his father's head was at, Raymond could be home in three, four, five, or six hours. "This evening some time?"

Mr. Sinclair looked at his watch.

"Hm. Quarter past three now. What's say, you and I? It's such a splendid summer day."

"Yes?" said Roger.

"Surely, there must be some tourist sites in this region. Some attractions upon which two sophisticated gentlemen might cast their attention."

"Well," said Roger, already feeling like he was falling short, "we could go to Cavendish. There's some fun parks and the beach."

"Dreadful kitsch. Mini-golf! That whole Green Gables thing," Mr. Sinclair punctuated with air quotes. "The people of this region, yourself included, must feel like it's a ploy by people in Queens County to hog all the tourism revenue."

"Kinda," said Roger. He had read the first book of the *Anne* series in grade nine and was disappointed. Each jolly moment ended almost as soon as it started. Even Anne's relationship to Gilbert was never more than the promise of better things to come. Except for Matthew dying, nobody really suffered. *Evangeline* had more heart. The relationship was ruined by historical circumstances, not caprice. "Sorry. You've seen Cavendish? I thought you came straight here from the ferry."

The subtlest of blushes crossed Mr. Sinclair's face. "At large, that's what I am. Not tied down to a place, to a schedule. That's what your father and I have in common now. When he heard about my separation, it was so nice of him to reach out." Mr. Sinclair's eyes went up to the left, as if he were recalling a memory packed with a torrent of emotion. "I've taken some hours on my own to explore. It's all quite charming, this island. Really. Perhaps you take it for granted, the contrast of the red soil, the green fields, and the deep blue of the water. But I relish it. I do. And I relish the drive here, to one of the island's farthest corners. And here I am, in the hands of an extraordinarily hospitable host. Where do you suggest for a destination? Of course. Right. My hotel. The Glenn. We can take our afternoon tea there. By which I mean a cocktail. Young Canadian men like yourself don't spend their afternoons with crumpets and doilies. There's a bar there, I'm sure of it."

Roger had spent most of the last few years avoiding alcohol in general and, in particular, its consumption in the afternoon. His early experimentation with booze had been done solo. At fifteen, he made audiotapes of himself talking after two, four, and six beers. After soberly listening to the slurred and nonsensical results—speculation about life on other planets, how sex was nothing more than pleasure caused by friction, and the fantastic house he'd build when Debbie Arsenault finally came back to him—Roger decided to abstain from alcohol. Mostly. He'd hold a beer at a party. But cocktails at The Glenn! What he considered a bad habit felt, as proposed by Mr. Sinclair, cosmopolitan and civilized. After changing into a striped shirt-sleeve button-down, Roger found himself in a Volkswagen Golf, then the Swiss-chalet-style lobby of The Glenn.

The result of more public money than private, The Glenn had been built three years earlier as an appendage to the provincial golf course. The course—situated across from St. Anthony's Church on Route 2 and running along Mill River—had reportedly been admired by Arnold Palmer during a visit in the late 1970s. It seemed like a shame, to the government of the time, to let that endorsement go unexploited. The developer—based in Ontario but using Arnold Crozier as the local point man—went forward with a sprawling, ugly, three-storey building with brown shingles the colour of mainland dirt. At least West Prince could no longer be considered inhospitable to visitors who didn't have family to bunk with.

The owners of the area's two long-standing motels had waged a campaign against the complex. Léonce LeBlanc, the founder and boss of LeBlanc Construction, based in the French-speaking Evangeline Region, owned a little motel in St. Peter's. Lester Shaw, Roger's boss at the PetroPump and ex-husband of Linda from the O'Leary pharmacy, owned the motel in Woodstock. They wrote letters to the papers and to the premier. Both were eventually persuaded to stand down; government tourism infrastructure subsidies can work wonders. With the money, Lester Shaw bought a dozen paddleboats for the sinkhole on his front yard and called it Lester's Leisure World. Léonce LeBlanc directed his infrastructure money toward adding a conference centre to the Evangeline Co-op grocery store in Wellington. This particular piece of tourism infrastructure, which started out with just two small meeting rooms, each with a view of the grocery store's produce department, would eventually play a major role in Roger's life, providing a benchmark he could measure his accomplishments against.

Upon completion, The Glenn quickly became one of the main Up West attractions to take visitors to, rivalling the field of experimental windmills the government had set up at North Cape.

A bar was just one of the functions of the large open-concept space off the lobby. It was also a restaurant, a conference room, party room, and, each summer, staging area for the hotel's entry in the O'Leary, Alberton, and Tignish festival parades. The bar was, of course, called The 19th Hole.

Roger knew where the bar was—straight through the lobby. But Mr. Sinclair didn't pay Roger any attention, preferring to spend several minutes getting directions from the young woman at the reception desk.

"Her shift's not over until eight," said Mr. Sinclair, his accent more British than ever, as they took a seat at a table by the floor-to-ceiling windows overlooking the seventh hole. "Dazzling eyes, don't you think?"

"That's Angela Ellsworth. She's the cousin of the bartender over there, Noel Pineau. Sometimes she dates Robert Doucette. The last I remember of her was her pulling her hair out when she couldn't get Ricky Gallant to pay her some attention."

"She looks fine now." Mr. Sinclair discreetly held his left hand over his pointing finger. "That redhead over there. She's got a splendid figure."

It was Marissa Gallant, Michael's high school girlfriend, Roger's former dance committee vice president. She and Roger had hung out occasionally for the first few years after high school, sat at the same table at classmates' weddings. But Marissa had finished her studies at UPEI, earning herself a business degree and new university friends. Right now, she was manager of The Glenn's gift shop and had a boyfriend in Charlottetown, whom she saw twice a week. He had never come further west than Summerside, so it seemed, if their love deepened, that Marissa would be leaving Up West soon.

"Hi Roger," said Marissa, coming up to their table. Phillip Sinclair ordered a gin and tonic, Roger a Schooner beer.

"There are girls everywhere here and you show no interest. You're not queer, are you? It's not that I hate queers, you see. I just want to avoid the nuisance of it. I hate breaking hearts."

"Me too," stammered Roger, impressed at this man's ability to frame homosexuality as an inconvenience rather than a moral problem. It occurred to him he needed to speak more definitively. "No, no. I love women."

"All men should. It's whether we want to fuck them or not that makes us different."

"Maybe I'm in love with a girl," said Roger. "She broke my heart, but I believe it will work out."

"Romantic, eh?" Mr. Sinclair was amused. He poured at least half of his gin and tonic into his mouth. "That's splendid. She got a name?"

This man didn't know anybody Up West. Roger figured he could trust him. He leaned forward, his elbows making a shallow dent in the cushioned plastic tablecloth spread out between them. "Debbie. Debbie Arsenault. I haven't seen her in forever."

"A Frenchie! Well, there it is. I guess you do live in Acadie, judging by the names on the mailboxes. You and your father must be the only people around here not called Arsenault or Gallant. Parlez-vous français?"

"I try."

"Another drink!"

"Um, si."

"Bloody good sport." Mr. Sinclair got up. "If that red-headed creature comes by, try to hold her attention until my return. An introduction would be appreciated. I can see no greater service to be provided by a young wolf like yourself."

Young wolf, thought Roger. He looked down at his body. Despite some paunch, he could run fast. "Every Breath You Take" came thumping out of some hotel room down the other end of The Glenn, then disappeared when the room door shut.

At the bar, Mr. Sinclair started chatting with Noel Pineau and the guys there, who had been growing louder by the minute. Roger noticed *The Spectator-Herald* on the next table. The below-the-fold headline caught his attention; he discreetly slid it onto his lap and looked around for a possible owner before unfolding it on his own table. The byline said Caroline MacPhail. She'd been at the paper for two years, producing at least six stories a week. One week last fall she had written fourteen, including all four front page stories in the Wednesday edition. Roger always read her stories as if she was writing them for him; every fact, quote, or adjective he disapproved of seemed intended to provoke him. She was beloved in the newsroom for her canny use of off-Island experts to rebut assertions made by locals who needed to be taken down a peg or two. She had once gotten quotes from some guy in a village in southern India, who decried a weapons manufacturer currently in negotiations with the PEI government to set up a factory outside Charlottetown.

By the time Mr. Sinclair returned with two tall gin and tonics, Roger was visibly agitated.

"Did some girl break your heart while I was gone?"

"Oh... No... It's just. This." Roger swatted the paper like it was a mosquito swollen with his blood. "The government gets my goat sometimes."

"You're talking to a senior civil servant. It gets my goat, too."

"It's not fair. The politicians play favourites. In Egmont Bay, they get everything they ask for. The so-called Evangeline Region. They're getting new exhibition buildings for their fair. And more money to expand the Evangeline Co-op and Community Centre. Four more conference rooms!"

"I had a drink at the Wellington legion. It was all 'qui qui, shoo-shoo, monta-balmant.' Couldn't understand a blessed word."

"And a grant to expand the legion."

"Seems to me they're doing well then. Not much to look at, I'll tell you. Didn't see much action, if you know what I mean. Not like, say, Summerside. Rather rambunctious little nightclub in Summerside."

"They've even got a French school. Evangeline School! Have you ever read the poem? It's a beautiful love story. I've read it a dozen times!" Roger's eyes lit up. "Evangeline wasn't even from there. She was from Nova Scotia. What right do they have?"

"Henry Wadsworth Longfellow's verse was painfully hokey," said Mr. Sinclair sharply. "What's amazing to me is that the French are still here, after all these years. The Brits did what they could to drive them away or drive them bonkers. The Irish snuck up the middle and took much of the best farmland—you can see it all there in Queen's County. Beautiful country! But up here, through the swamps and bogs and the clouds of mosquitoes, they're still here, those French. Like weeds! You can't imagine Longfellow caring that much, but he was a bloody git."

"They're pulling some political strings."

"The underdog act only gets you so far," said Mr. Sinclair. He had taken a few sips of his drip, then tossed the rest back in a mammoth gulp. "I expect that they've just applied themselves. Come up with a good convincing proposal, get enough names on it and no smart government can say no. Do you think you'd have liked attending that French school?"

"I don't know. I've never seen it."

"Never seen it?"

"I've never been down there. Never took the turn off Route 2."

"Never been?" Mr. Sinclair snapped his fingers at the bartender. "Outrageous."

"Never had a reason to."

"It's, what, twenty minutes down the road? They must have some pretty girls—at least one or two, since you seem to be over the local lasses. It seems to me," said Mr. Sinclair, his face lighting up as Noel placed the next round on the table, "that there's nothing they're doing there you can't do here. Why, I remember once when I was at Buckingham Palace...."

"In London? Have you ever met the Queen?"

"Oh, Lizzy? That one. Not likely. But what I wouldn't give to be in a room with Princess Diana. Charles doesn't know what a good thing he's got."

Drinking one gin and tonic for every two or three consumed by Mr. Sinclair, Roger became fuzzily enthralled with his father's friend's stories, many of which employed the names of celebrities who did not, in person, appear in the narrative. Here was a new, sharper way to look at the world. One where it didn't seem to matter who your father was, only your ability to get your foot in the door. If you knew the right things to say, at the right time, you'd be successful, or, at the very least, the drama that followed would have a funny ending. Which was as good as a happy ending, according to Phillip Sinclair.

That accident where he wrote off his motorcycle, only to be rescued by two young nursing students! The time in Sicily he had gambled all his money away and had to sleep in an olive grove where a young beauty found him in the morning! That jealous boyfriend of a young Mexican woman who had, in the final moments before blood was drawn, challenged him to a bullfight! No matter how meager or grand the initial goal, life would turn around and hand you a pleasure-soaked adventure if you allowed it.

"And the thing about Brazilian girls...." Mr. Sinclair was saying.

Roger could have spent weeks listening if he were not also struck by a desire to run out and ride motorcycles, learn how to play saxophone, ask girls for their numbers, book airplane tickets. His last few years had not seemed so different from his peers, who threw themselves half-heartedly at adulthood. Now this relief: his fallow years had been leading up to this very moment. PEI, it turned out, was part of a much larger, much more exciting world. The canvas here could be as grandiose as anywhere.

"Brazilian girls, wow!"

"Brazilian girls in bikinis, yes." Mr. Sinclair nodded gravely, as if he were diagnosing a sexually transmitted disease for an itchy friend.

Roger wanted to say something particularly impressive. His earlier confession of obsessive love had not moved Mr. Sinclair much. Perhaps heartbreak didn't merit attention. He had erred in revealing it. He needed subject matter that was more universal, something you'd read about in a magazine.

"PEI's history has been very dramatic," said Roger. "Pirates and Indians! Rumrunners."

"The pirates were British and never set foot on the land. And the Indians. I suspect they've had a sadder time of it than the Acadians."

"But you have to admit, PEI is unique. The old-fashioned way of life. Some of the houses don't even have bathrooms. People stopping their cars in the middle of the road to chat. The farming and the fishing."

"How do you think people on other islands make a living? How do you think PEI's landscape compares to Ireland's? The Caymans and their turtle meat? I'm sure there are lots of people in India who would see the plumbing here as quite desirably conventional." Mr. Sinclair chuckled but was too much of a gentleman not to concede something. "Of course, the salt waters of the Gulf of St. Lawrence are particularly therapeutic. I had a scrape on my knee. Two dips and it was all but gone."

His face flush with excitement, Niese did not notice Marissa till she was looming over him. She put a hand on his shoulder.

"I hate to cut yahs short, but the girls have to get set up for a dinner party. Angela Ellsworth is giving me looks."

Roger looked anxiously at his guest, worried he'd be disappointed. Mr. Sinclair was not going to cause a fuss. The visitor made the bill calculations so swiftly and painlessly, a fifty-fifty split Roger couldn't argue with.

The moment the civil servant went to the washroom, one of the guys sitting at the bar called out for Roger to come over. It was Robert Doucette, who was, these days, considered the second-most handsome man Up West after Michael Chaisson.

"How are you all doing tonight?" Roger asked.

"How are *we* doing? How are *you* doing?" said James. "We're not at Sally Chaisson's wedding, you'll notice."

"I see that."

"Oh, you see that! You and your come-from-away fruit have been watching us?"

Noel shot Robert a "settle down" look.

"Hey, we were just saying something about you," said Robert. "Those days you used to hang out with Ricky Gallant. Running around to the bootlegger's, Arnold Crozier's, that kind of crazy stuff!"

"Ricky would smoke every single one of your cigarettes and you'd be thrilled to watch him do it," said Noel.

"You're telling me," laughed one of the other guys at the bar, who was maybe an Ellsworth from Tignish.

Ricky Gallant had died in a car accident between Red Deer and Innisfail, Alberta, three years earlier. He was on his way to an ill-defined but apparently excellent-paying job on the oil fields, something he had told Roger in a telephone call from Quebec. Between the time he made the decision to go and the time he left, it had been about forty-five minutes.

"That's why I don't smoke," smirked Roger, buzzed and trying to be bright about things.

None of the men at the bar got the joke, but they laughed in honour of Ricky.

Mr. Sinclair returned from the bathroom and the young men fell silent, little boys in the presence of an authority figure.

"That silence is the sound of gossip and intrigue that I've missed," said Mr. Sinclair. "What are you gentlemen up to this evening?"

"They're leaving pretty damn soon!" Marissa Gallant said, impatiently waving her arms in the air.

"May I?" asked Mr. Sinclair, pointing to Marissa's hand. With an eye roll, she lifted it to the come-from-away's lips. He tenderly kissed her knuckles. Marissa blushed. Noel Pineau, Robert Doucette, and the rest of the guys started whooping and banging on the bar.

"Is that it?" said Marissa Gallant condescendingly. She retrieved her hand, turned on her heels, and whisked herself out through The Glenn's lobby.

"I guess that *is* it!" Mr. Sinclair laughed as if he had planned for her to rebuke him. He knocked imaginary chalk dust from his hands.

"Well, I guess we're on our way," said Roger as jocularly as he could manage.

Marissa was long gone before Roger and Mr. Sinclair got to the parking lot. Roger was still buzzed. Before he knew it, Mr. Sinclair was motoring them down Route 2, traces of summer sunlight still lingering in the late evening sky.

"It's so early! No reason we can't go back later tonight! Is there a change of shift, do you think?" asked Mr. Sinclair. They both bounced on their seats as Route 2 took a dip to cross Bloomfield Creek.

By the time they were stumbling from the car to the house/trailer on the John Joe Road, Mr. Sinclair had become mostly incomprehensible. When no one was looking, he had grabbed a bottle of vodka from behind The Glenn's bar. "Glasses, my dear boy!"

Roger was still too blinded by admiration to be embarrassed by Mr. Sinclair's theft. Their time together had triggered something, though not what anyone would guess. Roger was thinking about how his small life could be connected to the larger world. The expulsion of the Acadians separated Evangeline and Gabriel, kept them apart, made it nearly impossible to find each other. In another world, one where the British weren't such assholes, the couple might have married at eighteen and never left Grand-Pré, Nova Scotia, each of their days much like the last, except with more wrinkles, more preserves in the cellar, more children, and grandchildren. Their beloved Acadia might have blossomed into a French New York or Buenos Aires. History was always meddling with what you wanted to do. But you also had to wonder what Gabriel was doing when Evangeline was searching the world for him. Had he been looking for her, too? You couldn't blame history if you didn't roll up your own sleeves.

The two drinkers found Raymond quietly doing dishes. Mr. Sinclair shook his host's damp hand. The two older men sat down at the kitchen table, while Roger discreetly looked for somewhere to hide the vodka.

After twenty minutes of "catching up," Mr. Sinclair declared a desire for a swim. The water was likely too cold for the uninitiated, said Raymond, who thought his old friend seemed a little manic.

"Tosh!"

"Are you sure?" asked Roger. "I mean...."

"I won't hear otherwise," said Mr. Sinclair. "Just point me in the right direction."

This assertion-discouragement banter went on for several minutes. Finally, Roger, who was already sobering up, scrawled directions on the back of a utility bill envelope. The Miminegash beach was the closest.

"He's a character!" Roger told his father, after Mr. Sinclair drove off in search of some buoyancy. That was the kind of bland compliment that was fishing for more information.

"He and your mother had a fling. He's so full of it," said Raymond. "Of course, that was a long time ago."

"Why are you telling me this?"

"You were very young. You wouldn't have even noticed. Did he talk about Brazil? The pickpockets in—where was it?—San Pedro?"

"Could you imagine!"

"You'd hardly have to. He's done all the imagining for you."

"Why did you invite him here?"

"I didn't think I did. He wrote a somewhat interesting article in *The Globe and Mail* on Central American bean production. You'd have seen it if you read anything other than the local rags. I wrote him a letter saying so. I don't bear him any grudge. Next thing you know, here he is." It had never occurred to Roger that his father had any jealousy in him.

"I thought he knew more about women than I do. Apparently, he doesn't. Look at him now. What's this? His fourth divorce?"

Raymond lit his pipe and, puffing on it, looked remarkably like an Irish potato farmer who might have lived on PEI back in the mid-1800s.

Roger waited up till after midnight for Mr. Sinclair to return, but the visitor must have gone from swimming directly back to The Glenn or to the Legion.

The next morning, Mr. Sinclair was sitting at the kitchen table, dark glasses and a hoarse mumble where the bright eyes and devilish giggle had been.

"Do you have any marmalade?" This last syllable rhymed with "odd."

"Just jam," said Roger, who was waiting for a funny story about what happened at the beach or the Legion. Or maybe Roger was waiting for an invitation. Maybe he and Mr. Sinclair could go to Charlottetown, see a play? Roger knew a couple of girls, from his university days, who worked at a restaurant on Richmond Street. They'd love Mr. Sinclair.

"Hm," said the visitor. "I'd better be on the road."

"You and dad hardly got to spend any time."

"Another time," interjected Raymond, pulling a T-shirt on as he wandered into the kitchen.

"I hope to make it up to Ottawa some time," said Roger.

"Your mother will know where to find me."

"Will she?" asked Raymond.

"I'm easily found."

Roger had decided that he had all he needed from the man, and that it was splendid.

CHAPTER 8

TWO STACKING TABLES HAD been stuck together with masking tape and covered with a plastic green-and-red holly tablecloth that was masking-taped to the tables' undersides. All helpless against Mitchell Gallant's bouncing legs. He had sent so much tea flying off the table today, the hardwood floor was permanently stained.

"Still nervous?" asked Roger. Finished with the mopping, he poured three fresh cups.

"Waiting for the music to start. I can hear it already," said Mitchell.

"You're not going to have a spell, are you?"

"Don't think so. No. No. Maybe. No."

"Brain buzz?"

"No, no. Waiting for the music to start."

The table's third occupant, Beatrice Perry, grew stiff in her seat, as if she was about to say something that would create a conundrum.

"I heard our 11am arrive in the porch at 10:50. It's already 11:11. Where does the time go?" Roger knew that was an order. He walked over to the porch door of the Old Union Road Schoolhouse to admit the next applicant.

The one-room Old Union Road Schoolhouse had been converted to the St. Louis-St. Edward Community Centre back in 1976, but local people called it the Old Schoolhouse. Five years after his meeting with Phillip Sinclair, Roger had adopted it as the HQ for his next big idea.

"Thank you, dear," said Beatrice, and then to the young woman who was tiptoeing in, "Good morning, dear."

The young woman might have easily been fourteen as late twenties. Her broadness started at her shoulders and ended at her hips. Her face swirled uneasily around her oversized mouth.

"We have a stand right here, dear, if you need it. Some do, some don't," said Beatrice. She watched the young woman pull a fold-up music stand from the array of bags she had peeled off herself into piles on the floor. Roger had been tempted to help the woman, but worried he'd do something that would undermine the neutrality of the audition.

"No thanks!" the woman chirped. "Gotta use my own stand. I gotta pretend I'm in my basement if I don't want to get all jittery."

"Of course you do, dear. Whatever you need. All we care about is the music," said Beatrice. Roger and Mitchell nodded their agreement.

Once the young woman had set up her stand, pushed her bags up against the boxes of audio equipment on the floor, and placed her fiddle on her shoulder, Beatrice took a deep breath on her behalf. The performer took a breath herself. Beatrice breathed out. So did the performer.

"Now let's introduce ourselves, dear. This is Roger Niese, who you might already know."

"Roger, Roger Niese. From the museum," said the young woman.

"Yes, from the museum." A banana-width grin stretched itself across Roger's face. "Yes, I founded the museum."

"I never went, but I drove by."

"Too bad," said Roger, smile drooping.

I'm Kate. Kate Pineau. You know my brother, Noel. He talks about you sometimes."

"I do know Noel," said Roger.

"And this is Mitchell Gallant," said Beatrice. "Say hi, Mitchell."

"Hi," said Mitchell, theatrically rolling his eyes at Beatrice's patronizing tone.

"Of course, I'm Beatrice Perry, the artistic coordinator for this production."

"So pleased to meet you, Ms Perry," said the young woman, who obviously knew how Beatrice liked to be addressed.

"And of course, you're Albin's daughter," said Beatrice.

"Yes. From Skinner's Pond."

"You're the youngest, aren't you?

"The afterthought. Big gap. Two brothers. Noel. And Chris, he's in Alberta."

"Your mother Regina makes a lovely meat pie," said Beatrice. Her tone implied she could go into great detail about the meat pie and what held it back from being more than merely "lovely," but wouldn't.

Nothing in Beatrice's tone suggested she knew Kate was also a single mother.

"I used to party with Noel, you know," Roger said.

"G'way with yah," said Kate.

"He did," said Mitchell.

"I can right imagine," said Kate.

"Gentlemen," said Beatrice, turning right and left to look at her two fellow panel members. Then she looked directly at Kate. "You may begin whenever you like, Kate."

And so the fourth "Ste. Anne's Reel" of the weekend lurched into motion, the notes crashing into the low ceiling, from which hung three bare light bulbs, and bouncing around the room.

Beatrice had forbidden any coded gestures or note-passing amongst the panel members. It was rude to talk privately in front of someone else. The three panellists sat quietly, saving their opinions for later. Mitchell did all he could to keep his knees from colliding with the underside of the table. Roger, who had been letting his hair grow so he would have something to fidget with when he was trying to look thoughtful in social situations, made rapid-fire notes. He scrawled longhand through the form's many sections, starting with "Attitude." He flipped the sheet over to the back for the overflow and then flipped back for the next section, "Visual Presentation." Beatrice held her pen horizontally. She would not write so much as an exclamation mark until the applicant had left the room.

To start, Kate's playing was pleasant and more energetic than the panel had heard from others. Her tempo crept up, at first hesitantly. Kate took a deep breath and played even faster. The tap of her foot ceased. Instead, her hips swung in a circular movement that took several beats to complete, so she appeared to be moving in slow motion. At this higher speed, the song became less gangly, more baroquely rhythmic. To dance to it would require a high degree of physical fitness. The divide between folk, classical, and the most manic sort of electronic dance music collapsed in the tune's trance-like oscillations. It was overwhelming.

The silence that followed the song's last note was the silence four people needed to reassess their positions in time and space.

"Loved the ending!" said Mitchell, raising his hands to clap above the hockey helmet on his head.

"Interesting," said Beatrice.

"Great!" said Roger.

"Thanks for listening!" said Kate, a closing line she had adopted at age twelve when she took her first recorder lesson. One by one, she gathered her bags to her body again. When they were all strapped in place, it was all she could do to wave goodbye.

There was a moment when each of the three panel members considered putting into words the quasi-spiritual experience they had just felt. It was futile.

"Holy shit!" said Mitchell.

"Indeed," said Beatrice.

"She's our closing act, that's for sure." Roger was still scribbling away on his third sheet of blank paper.

"I'd already penciled in the Buchanan Family Singers. And we have three... no, four more fiddlers to see," said Beatrice.

Roger's artistic director was accustomed to wringing the best out of not much at all. On one hand, he had been lucky to find her. On the other hand, Up West was small enough that it would be strange if they didn't meet eventually.

Beatrice Perry was the product of a mixed marriage. Her father, Albert Perry, had run a tiny grocery store in Tignish. Single into his thirties, he fell in love with a ballet dancer he met during a train stop-over in Montreal en route to Toronto for a meeting with the Massey-Harris farm equipment company. Jeanette Boileau was a tiny thing, who claimed her parents had come directly from France, though there was no evidence in what she owned or how she talked about herself to suggest this was true. Albert and Jeanette met and danced in a night-club off Sainte-Catherine Street and Jeanette met with Albert again during the Montreal stop on the train trip back. Albert picked her up at her tiny east side apartment to take her for a proper steak dinner.

Jeannette already knew that her dance career was not going to happen. She was behind in her rent when she met Albert, who was the gentlest man she'd ever met. Three months later Jeanette found herself picking the dirty laundry off the bedroom floor in Albert Perry's house on Ascension Road. It was a layer cake of a place, an ill-judged attempt at Queen Anne style, hard as hell to heat, that an earlier generation of Perrys had built with fox-farming money. Beatrice was born there on the kitchen table.

After three years in Tignish, unable to make friends with the locals or keep the house clean enough for her own tastes, Jeanette insisted the family move to a more cosmopolitan setting in Charlottetown, where there were at least a couple of hotels and bars. Albert Perry closed the store, rented out the house, and opened a farm equipment business in Charlottetown. The business kept him running the roads. This arrangement kept the family intact until Beatrice was twelve. Up to that point, her life had been dance classes, clothes, and cosmetics imported from Quebec, along with silent pain in her bedroom as her parents spent their evenings in knock-'em-down-drag-'em-out arguments in Franglais. After many threats, Jeanette Boileau moved back to Montreal, sending her daughter nice things once or twice a year. Albert and Beatrice moved back to the big house in Tignish.

Little Beatrice never expressed anything resembling distress when she had been forced to finish her schooling in Tignish, where both the boys and girls mocked her prim demeanour and her broken home; an absent mother was likely to be a licentious woman. In her twenties, Beatrice lived in Montreal for a few years, telling people she liked being close to her maternal family, which, in fact, meant meeting her mother in restaurants every few months. When Albert was killed in a highway accident, Beatrice returned to the Island to claim the ancestral home. Her first few weeks back, she was treated with the respect someone in mourning deserved, a respect that continued well beyond the limits of mourning, even as it became evident she was staying on.

Beatrice was in her thirties by then, and what had originally felt like haughtiness now came across as elegance to Up West people. Besides, she was past her prime in ever finding a husband. Someone who didn't know who was who Up West might have sized her up as a come-from-away, but Beatrice never claimed she was from anywhere other than Ascension Road.

Beatrice's role crystallized in 1972 when she was asked to coach the girls in the Alberton High School Miss Winter Carnival Pageant. The competition had been going steadily downhill for years; even Matheson's Bridal Shop, always desperate for sales beyond prom season, had abandoned its sponsorship. There was little Beatrice could do about the girls' drawls, their disappointed faces, or their contempt for clothes. But she could prod them into improving their posture, being more generous with make-up, walking with purpose, and peppering their speech with niceties. They crammed "please," "thank you," and "if it's okay with you" into almost every sentence uttered in her presence to get her to lay off the constant prompting. The resulting speech sounded pleasing in the ear, but was often nonsensical; as far as Beatrice was concerned, that aspect wasn't much different from where they started. The girls of '72 looked good enough for a two-page spread in the yearbook, one of only four colour spreads that year. The *Spectator-Herald* found a way to run the group shot on three separate occasions before the end of the year, including with a story on the runner up, Angela Ellsworth, when she was charged with shoplifting jeans at the Towers in Summerside that Christmas. Nobody held Angela's crime against Beatrice. In fact, people said that if Beatrice hadn't coached Angela, the girl would have stolen even more.

Beatrice offered her services as far east as Kensington, a town whose awkward farm girls needed more puffing up than reining in. Though she advocated for flowing manes of hair, Beatrice kept her own short, sometimes so short you'd have guessed she cut it herself with two mirrors, correcting mistake after mistake until it was even. She wore heels at all times of the day, a little clutch purse under her arm. When Beatrice went out in the evenings, she wore pearls.

Gradually, Beatrice's expertise expanded to theatrical productions. Visitors to her home noticed her fireplace mantle filled with photos of the likes of Gregory Peck and Christopher Plummer, so lovingly framed you'd never guess they were cut out of magazines. Though she had never studied singing herself, she had a good voice. Music was, by default, included in her coaching repertoire. Because of her devoted church attendance, including doing readings and serving on the parish council when called upon, her esthete ways did not make her as suspect as she might have otherwise been. She was a little fancy, but it was directed to the appropriate channels.

Beatrice and Roger had discovered each other just a few years earlier. For Roger, it had been a revelation; for Beatrice, quite some time was needed for her to set aside her ambivalence. At first, she eyed Roger as an interloper; his baggy purple sweater and cords were something a hippy would wear. He'd talk at you for twenty minutes without knowing who you were, where you were from, or even if you could hear. Beatrice might have avoided Roger like she avoided the Quebeckers who occasionally showed up in West Prince. But after a few meetings at various concerts, book readings, and other cultural events, she figured Roger was no worse than any other man—socially retarded and in great need of clearly articulated limits.

At a murder mystery play put on by the Elmsdale 4-H Club, Roger spotted Beatrice in the front row, where she sat mouthing the words along with the actors. He wanted to praise the precision with which she crossed her legs, like a princess or a model. She was also the play's director, but sometimes praise swells up first and finds it subject as it goes along. He approached her. Mentioning a woman's legs seemed bold. Instead, Roger complimented her scarf, which was so shimmery, the gold paisleys wriggling across the purple.

"Why, thank you, young man."

"Where did you get it?" Roger had come to the play on his own. Not knowing what to do with himself at intermission, he had made a rule that he'd introduce himself to at least one new person every time he was tempted to go hide in the bathroom.

"Oh, I don't know, really."

"Something that beautiful? I've never seen anything like it, even in Ottawa or Charlottetown." His reference to Ottawa granted her special permission to drop names herself.

"Paris," she said, taking little joy in it. "Not that I've been there, oh no. A dear friend sent it. Beverly Wigmore? From Hunter River? Husband is Jimmy Wigmore?"

"Paris! Fantastic!"

"Wigmores?"

"Don't know 'em."

"Indeed! Now, where you grew up...."

"Here...."

Beatrice frowned.

"....and in Ottawa...."

"Yes, there's a beautiful little restaurant on Sussex Drive, near the market. Divine! It doesn't look like anything special." Beatrice skated around snobbery like an Olympian navigates pylons. "Nothing expensive. No more than what you'd pay around here. But, Oh!"

It took a few more sightings before the two of them exchanged any more than polite greetings. Two single people with such a large age gap between them shouldn't be monopolizing each other at the Tignish Co-op or the St. Bernard's church picnic. Those who trafficked in gossip took the friendship as confirmation of Roger's fruitiness, but most people just saw two people of artistic temperament clinging together for safety.

Roger's museum of Acadian paraphernalia had already failed by the time he took up with Beatrice. It was a good thing he had gotten it out of his system. She would have discouraged him every step of the way. The whole enterprise was so ridiculous. Roger funded it entirely from his own savings; Earl Kennedy at Scotiabank wouldn't even meet with him.

The museum, operating out of an old dairy bar where the Deblois Road met Route 2, was an assembly of a handful of Acadian artifacts in what had been the building's ice-cream serving area. A rusty hand-crank drill. A chalice that might have been used at St. Bernard's in the 1960s. A farmyard diorama built of plastic toys from the Summerside Zellers. A large laminate—very professionally printed, nobody said the look of it wasn't striking—depicting intersecting family trees, which Roger created using family names gathered from mailboxes; the family branches often connected to the wrong trunk or, even more often, didn't connect at all. An equally beautifully laminated recipe for meat pie he had copied from *The Spectator-Herald*.

Under strict supervision, Mitchell had painted several verses from Longfellow's *Evangeline* on the walls and across the front window, so the words could be read, in reverse, from the parking lot. "Whither my heart has gone, there follows my hand, and not elsewhere" was written along the front window. Along the back: "Then he beheld, in a dream, once more the home of his childhood; Green Acadian meadows, with sylvan rivers around them, Village, and mountain and woodlands."

The museum's store was the room at the back where the deep fryers and the freezers had been. Roger had issued a call for "crafts, preserves, snacks, anything you make" to be sold on consignment with only a five percent commission. Within days he had more eight-year-old bottles of jam, unwanted bridal-shower doilies, and macramé potholders than he knew what to do with. Not much of it had sold by the time the museum closed eight months later, but a few friends of the quilters visited to admire the colourful polyester canvases. Beatrice went once but paid no attention to the gangly man fretting over the cash register.

The museum's name had been the first stumbling block. The first sign that went up said, "Acadian Museum." But there was already an

Acadian Museum in Wellington, dating back to the 1960s. Its board chair, Léonce LeBlanc, showed up at Roger's museum one day to point this out. Roger had never visited the Wellington museum, not so much out of spite, but out of fear that seeing it would limit the scope of his vision. He had no intention of copying anybody. He'd call his The West Prince Acadian Museum. The Western Evangeline Region Acadian Museum. The Museum of Acadian Life.

"I was at the yard sale when you bought that chalice. The widow in Piusville? She's my aunt Isabelle—see the family resemblance?" It was hard to tell if Léonce was joking or not. "I bought my uncle's golf clubs. Twenty dollars! What a deal! Well, she got that chalice from her uncle— that would be my great uncle. He was a priest in Drummondville. It was never sanctified, if that's what you want to call it. I'm no priest. I let the priest decide what to call it. But, no, well, sir, man, that chalice was never used at St. Bernard's or on PEI at all."

Then there was Roger's claim that the museum was on the site of an original Acadian settlement. Roger declared this based on a few things said by Lester Shaw, who rented him the dairy bar for $350 a month, which he simply deducted off Roger's PetroPump paycheque. Of course, Lester hadn't been paying much attention to what he was saying. He was focusing on bigger things. He had just established a farm supplies depot in Elmsdale and a lumber mill in Tyne Valley and was building a strip mall in Bloomfield.

"The original Acadians were down Charlottetown way. Port LaJoie? That'll take you back to the 1700s, it will. And Malpeque?" Léonce LeBlanc, a quick-tempered man who had gone bald in his twenties, would soon win the Third Prince Catholic seat for the provincial Liberals. His construction firm, the province's biggest, made much of its money off provincial contracts, which made getting into politics seem self-defeating. But Léonce had a plan for everything. His son Réné would take over the business.

"Now these Acadians, as you very well might have read in a book somewhere, because, I can see, you read books. These Acadians didn't make their way up to Bloomfield until...," Léonce waited a millisecond for Roger to try to jump in, then quickly cut off Roger's cutting in, "... until the British absentee landlords—now they were right assholes to the Acadians. Poor damn things! Ended up here, after they were thrown out of everywhere else. Anyway, the point is, your museum, she is a crock. Not a bad idea, son, but still a real crock of shit. Now take down that there sign. Oh, it's a pain in the arse, calling around, running up here all the time."

Before he left, Léonce bought a candied apple and a leather bookmark, both made by his widowed aunt.

Two hours later, Roger's boss and landlord, Lester Shaw, pulled up. Well into his late forties, the man was skin and bones, held together by scabs and randomly distributed body hair. He had money, it was well-known, since his ex-wife Linda had managed to run off with very little of it. But he lived in a sagging two-bedroom bungalow on the Howlan Road near O'Leary.

"I don't know what you've been saying, but I never said what you've been saying I've been saying."

"What's that?" asked Roger, who was polishing the chalice. Its description card now read: "Origin: Unknown. Fits Description of Chalice used at Palmer Road Church (St. Bernard's) circa 1960s."

"I'm not your marketing strategy," said Lester. He subscribed to *Business Week* and had been informed by his postal carrier that he was the only one in Up West who did. "You know what marketing is?"

"Not really."

"Your rent gets you the building, the parking lot. It doesn't get you any fancy stories. Lay off if you still want to be pumping gas for me. I got a pig farm to build. I can't afford to pay through the nose for all that concrete, no matter what you heard."

Not long after, one hot July afternoon, one of the bottles of dill pickles, priced at nine dollars, exploded. It was the only sound Roger had heard all day, except for the cars speeding up and down the Deblois Road. He gave his notice on the museum that evening. Lester Shaw did not return Roger's deposit.

The museum episode taught Roger that physical things could be taken away. Believing in people, that was easier, in a way. People wanted to be believed in and to believe in themselves, even if they were more complicated than putting an object on a shelf.

In the weeks following the museum's closing, Roger, now twenty-eight, would come home from his early shifts at the PetroPump, sit at the dining room table and fill Hilroy scribblers with notes and sketches. The weather was beautiful—the cool clearness of late summer, the kids jamming in their last few weeks of unbridled fun. On the weekends, he couldn't resist driving around, drinking in the crispy Island August with his eyes. After one excursion to the North Shore, along the Cavendish tourist strip, Roger was astonished at all the amusement parks. Cavendish was full of them. Rainbow Valley was the provincial benchmark for a booze-free good time. Parents took their kids there to show what good parents they were. Take Noel Pineau, who had married Betty Ann Getson on their daughter's second birthday. He took the kids to Rainbow Valley once a summer, then paraded them around the O'Leary Co-op so everyone could see the luxury of chocolate smeared on their faces, plastic baubles from the gift shop pinned to their overalls.

Rainbow Valley was a theme park with no theme at all: a space-craft gift shop, a replica of Green Gables house from the Lucy Maud Montgomery books, a scary cave made of hardened foam, pirate-themed mini-golf, each component added according to the whims of the owners, Campbells from Kensington, at the time of building. To Roger, it was all so random. You couldn't build a story out of all the pieces.

A more consistent, singular experience would offer more intense pleasures. Roger could do Rainbow Valley one better, he was sure of it. The world was full of fake castles. Instead, Roger would offer something more deeply rooted. Roger wanted to do something that would soften the hearts of the bitterest adults and make the rowdiest children shudder with feeling.

What was the local story that could move people, tie together high adventure and matters of the heart? Every Gabriel had an Evangeline out there looking for him, didn't he? And every Evangeline had her Gabriel, in the next port or lying on the next hospital bed, didn't she? Life's biggest joys sprang from the ashes of loss. Think of all the people Evangeline must have met, the ornery sailors, the prim ladies, the callous bureaucrats. If "each succeeding year stole something away from her beauty," then the Indian brides of noble French Canadians, for example, might have at least shown her a new dance or raced her in their canoes.

Acadian-themed rides, though, presented the first problem. A rollercoaster representing the expulsion seemed in bad taste, as did an Evangeline maze depicting her wandering around the world looking for her lost love Gabriel. A petting zoo was possible. There could be chickens somebody could theatrically slaughter. Now that would be a thrill!

Then what was possible came into focus. Staff would dress in expulsion-era Acadian clothing. Black vests over loose white shirts for the men, all the better to hide growing potbellies. Dainty white headscarves and aprons for the women. From this emerged the idea that his staff should be in character—the guy slaughtering the chickens should be a "farmer," the guy renting out the paddle boats would be a "ferryman," who would have to be reminded to avoid rough language. A couple of scribblers-full later, Roger saw his staff as characters—Eloi the farmer, Pierre the ferryman. They'd do Acadian things and have Acadian relationships. The chicken beheading could take place every day at noon, with a fresh chicken fricot served at the snack bar at suppertime. There'd be a wedding every Saturday and maybe a rabid dog day twice a summer, to get people's hearts pounding. Late July might be a good time for a simulation of the Mi-Carême celebration, with a masked and silent old woman prowling around giving out complimentary candy. Or selling it? The season could end with a funeral, visitors to the fictional settlement following behind in the funeral cortege, all hysterical tears.

Roger left the trailer and ran to the end of the John Joe Road and back, he was so excited. After he caught his breath, he picked up the phone and called the only person he could trust with his artistic vision. That woman who went to all the plays.

Beatrice agreed to come down to the John Joe Road. She had never seen Roger in any setting other than a public one and wasn't sure she wanted him in her house. Her Royal Dalton figurines were not protected behind glass.

At that first meeting, Beatrice paid close attention to Roger, her eyes drinking in his notes and diagrams, as well as his body language. He was a nervous type, but also gentle. Not quite handsome enough to be pageant contestant consort. Was he a little simple? Well, that was none of her business.

The preliminary amusement park layout seemed dependent on having a large hill in the north, a lake in the south, and farmable land to the west, a topography matching no Up West property Beatrice could think of. And she thought hard. Still, there was something there, she thought. Looking past all Roger's sputter and naiveté, it might be possible to find tiny kernels that just might work. Beatrice had no pension plan and the last man she had seriously dated had died fifteen years earlier.

Beatrice didn't exactly veto Acadia Land. But she put up so many roadblocks, there was little chance of getting around them in the short term.

"Who's going to play your fisherman?" For their fourth meeting, she had permitted Roger to come to her house on Ascension Road.

"A fisherman?" said Roger, sitting uneasily in Beatrice's living room. She was the only person around who received guests anywhere other than the kitchen. Until the arrival of cable TV in the early 1990s, Up West living rooms were usually treated with the reverence of a velvet-roped museum exhibit. Beatrice's was spotless, each bone-white lamp sitting perfectly centred on crocheted amber and ivory doilies. Matching bowls in red, green, and yellow held Gagnon hard candy, which the years had bound together like psychedelic inuksuk miniatures.

"What fisherman is going to let the season pass him by while he's playacting in some woodlot on Palmer Road?"

"Well, somebody else, then."

"Who?"

"Somebody on around here in St. Louis, St. Edward would do it. It'd pay minimum wage, at least. I'll get a grant."

"Give me a name of someone around here who can act at all."

"I can put up posters, see who turns up for auditions."

"This isn't a city. There's a finite number of people. You should know them all by now. One can keep track of most of them—who their father is, how old they are, married or single, working or not working, brain in their head or not. You need somebody for something, you go down that list in your head. There are no surprises. No beauties hidden under rocks down at the shore. You've got to look at who you have and build to fit."

"But then the story wouldn't hold together." Roger scrunched up his face, refusing to consider what spot he held on the master list in Beatrice's head.

"Well, and I don't know about this story. Mad dogs? British soldiers spearing people? Roger, I have to tell you, it's vulgar."

★

Their first show, The St. Louis-St. Edward Follies, held the fall of 1988, was recognized as a smashing success, even before *The Spectator-Herald* published its exclamation-mark-filled front-page story four days later. In the weeks preceding the show, the area's attics and basements were pillaged for decades-old fashions that served as outlandish costumes. Seams were split and resewn. Guitars and pianos were tuned. Lines were memorized.

There was some debate, even years later, about whether the musical portion was more or less successful than the dramatic portion, which took the form of two one-act plays, both comedies about farmers-a-courtin'. An unexpected crowd-pleaser had been when Earl Kennedy, in a turquoise chiffon dress that had been his great aunt's, had waltzed with his wife Susan, wearing a tux of unknown origin, to "The Blue Danube." The number confirmed to everyone that Susan wore the pants in the family and Earl, as everyone had always said, didn't care as much as he should have about the reputation of his bank.

Caroline MacPhail wrote in her review in *The Spectator-Herald* that "residents of the St. Louis-St. Edward area have demonstrated that their talents can stand equally alongside those of other energetic Island communities." Roger was pleased Caroline had not mentioned his MCing, which was mangled by nerves and the two beers he had chugged to calm them. In fact, Caroline had not mentioned him at all, though she praised Beatrice Perry's "extraordinary taste" in performers.

Expectations were high for the 1989 follow-up. People were coming from all over Prince County to audition, some from as far away as Summerside. Yet in this moment, Roger knew that Kate Pineau, the woman who had just scurried out of the Old Union Road Schoolhouse, the sound of her playing still hanging in the air, had to be the closing act. She had to be.

"Please, Ms Perry?" Roger said, anxiously flipping through his notebook in case he needed to present evidence to his colleague. "The Buchanan Family Singers, they're great but they've been around forever. Kate Pineau's a real find."

"She's got a great beat," said Mitchell.

"A find? We'll see. I'll pencil her in," sighed Beatrice. "But no pen yet, please, gentlemen."

"Susan Kennedy is up next," said Roger.

"She's confirmed. She's not coming in today," said Beatrice. "'Music Box Dancer.' Such a pretty song."

"I guess so," said Roger. "Can she play loud enough? This next one is going to be big. Much bigger than Follies '88."

"Dear, we've got a lot of programming time to fill."

"A ballerina could dance next to her or something, just to dress it up," said Mitchell. "Maybe Earl Kennedy?"

Super Summer Follies '89 was scheduled to take place on the Canada Day long weekend at the Union Road ball diamond, right next to the Old Schoolhouse where they were holding the auditions. Stage and sound equipment had been rented, *The Spectator-Herald* had been notified and posters had already been made and posted in Tignish, Alberton, O'Leary, and at Gallant and Sons Convenience store on Union Road, not that there needed to be posters on Union Road to cause a local buzz. This time around, they were looking at five or six hours of programming, three chip trucks, a dunking booth, pony rides, and a pole-climbing performance. Roger had put out a call to all the church halls and community centres in West Prince looking for chairs. Four thousand seven hundred and fifty-six had been secured.

Mitchell was disappointed that so many chairs had been so easily obtained. He had hoped for a standing audience or a cabaret-picnic set-up. For reasons the doctors couldn't guess at, his worst epileptic attacks were triggered when he encountered row seating. His body would freeze, and he'd fall like a log. When Mitchell was a little boy, he smashed his head a dozen times before his parents figured it out. By then, the damage had been done. Ricky Gallant used to joke that it was church pews that made his brother retarded.

"He wasn't born that way, Roger. He knocked all the sense out of himself whenever he was in Jesus's house," Ricky said. "That tells you all you need to know about what the church will do to you."

Mitchell was not going to miss a moment of the Super Summer Follies '89 or any of the planning for it. He figured if he stayed backstage or with the crowds, who'd likely be standing beyond the seating, he'd be okay. His doctor insisted he wear a hockey helmet at all times, especially in public. Too vain to wear it on his head, Mitchell would sometimes carry it around like a woman's purse, straps in the crook of his elbow.

"What if you put the chairs here, there, and everywhere?" Mitchell suggested. "Little clusters."

"Why not? Cabaret style," said Roger. Mixing people all together, so they talked to strangers, if there were any strangers to be found Up West.

"Oh, no," said Beatrice. "I'm not having people crawling all over each other to get pop and chips, and that's how this thing is going to pay for itself. Clear aisles!"

The two men directed their hangdog looks in her direction.

"Or we could abandon chairs altogether and have people bring blankets to sit on."

"Would that work, Mitchell?"

"Maybe. Depends."

"We can ask people to be sloppy when they arrange their blankets," suggested Roger.

"Well, with that lovely suggestion buzzing in our bonnets, it looks like that's the end of our day together," said Beatrice. She had already tucked her agenda into her beaded white purse. "Gentlemen."

Mitchell walked Beatrice out, knowing she'd offer him a ride home. Roger gathered his things and pushed the tables back against the wall. He returned the unused stack of Styrofoam cups to the storage room.

When Roger stepped out of the storage room, someone was standing there in the middle of the Old Schoolhouse's main room.

"Knock, knock," said Father Michael Chaisson. Roger's former classmate was now St. Bernard's parish priest. "Sorry to disturb. Wrapping up?"

"Sure am, sure am," said Roger.

"Lots of talent, I'm sure!" Father Michael let his long black coat fall open as he occupied the room.

"Certainly, yes, you can just imagine." Kate Pineau. Noel's little sister. Who knew? A protégé. A genius. A sorceress. A stirrer of souls. Siren of Skinner's Pond. Roger couldn't even remember what she looked like, whether she'd require a makeup artist or wardrobe consultation. Her playing had scattered his wits. In time, they might return. Right now he was dizzy.

Father Michael made toward the stack of chairs, grabbed two, and arranged them in the middle of the floor facing each other, like some priests did for the new-style confession they heard in their rectories. Some placed the chairs back-to-back, so the confessor didn't have to look at the forgiver. But Father Michael thought if you had made it so far out of the confession booth and into the light of day, it was childish not to take the next step. The young priest was so early in his career he hadn't noticed the drop in the numbers of folks wanting to clear their conscience. Some were going down Route 2 to Mont-Carmel to confess to Father Eloi Poirier, or even as far as Summerside; others had decided to let their sins pile up until there was a change of policy or personnel.

"Beatrice Perry, now there's a going concern! Elegant lady."

"Sure is, sure is." Roger pretended to look for a misplaced item so he could delay taking his assigned seat. Every second he could stall was a second for him to gather his energies in order to deal with Father Michael. He rarely came out on top when Michael Chaisson was involved.

"I imagine she keeps you in line. I don't know how Father Arsenault keeps up with her." Father Euseb Arsenault, formerly of St. Bernard's parish, had been transferred to Tignish parish to make way for Father Michael; the province's youngest and best-looking priest regularly leaned on the bishop for special favours.

Father Arsenault took his homemade exercise equipment with him, leaving Father Michael to figure out what to do with the gym in the St. Bernard's parish house. Already saddled with a reputation for vanity, Father Michael didn't dare do anything to draw attention to his physique. He covered the gym benches with oversized cushions bought at a fire sale warehouse, turning it into a lounge of sorts. Of all the parishioners Father Michael invited up, only the youth group appreciated the privilege of sprawling on the pillows' charred, smoky comfort, crying over their sins, and dreaming of flawless tomorrows.

Father Michael, it was hoped by the bishop, made being a priest seem cool. Look at all the baked goods he was brought by the women's auxiliary members. He was the best hockey, volleyball, and soccer player in the West Prince rec leagues. If handsome Michael Chaisson had turned his back on sexual congress, sexual congress couldn't be all it was said to be. The shock that came from hearing that Michael chose the priesthood over law, medicine, or politics evaporated when people saw him in action. He went about his calling like a spiritual Casanova, wooing the souls of men and women with his sensuous smile, his easy-going challenges to play one-on-one basketball in the rectory driveway. He also played guitar at mass. This Vatican II aesthetic caused tongue-wagging as far away as Moncton.

In fact, he cut such an impressive figure, people failed to notice that Michael had something beaten-down about him since his days as high-school golden boy. Those who hadn't witnessed exactly how this self-doubt had taken root—that is, those who hadn't seen him struggle at Acadia University—might have taken it for priestly humility. Roger, whose long-standing inferiority complex around Michael had hardened into something habitual, didn't see it at all.

To his surprise, Michael's classmates at Acadia University didn't pay him much attention. Nobody in Wolfville knew who he was, and he had no strategy to make an impressive introduction. His desire to be an alpha dog of his dorm, his science classes, or any sports team was soon crushed. He failed to find a girlfriend within his original two-month deadline. He spent his first semester changing seats in his classes, flitting around from cafeteria table to cafeteria table, looking for people who were good-looking, smart and ambitious, and knew how to have a good time. He eventually found such a crew, a clique of friends from Burlington, Ontario, who had known each other since attending the same Montessori kindergarten together. His alliance with them lasted for two months before he realized he did not understand any of their personal alliances or quarrels and couldn't follow their talk about this retail chain versus that one. He distanced himself from the little gang, but it felt more like them rejecting him.

Michael went through a short period of trying to pick fights, both academic and, at the campus pub, physical. The professors started ignoring him and the bouncers barred him. He should have dropped out or changed schools, but his grades were still good enough. Michael spent more and more time alone, more and more time thinking. His assessment of the world grew more and more severe as he struggled to deine his interests and desires. He had a hint of what he was capable of but was increasingly unsure what he wanted.

Service to the church, unexpectedly to Michael and to those around him, occurred to him as an option. His parents were devout; they worshipped every priest they had ever encountered. The priesthood seemed a shortcut to this kind of devotion. Attention was worth more than worldly possessions, wasn't it? Sure, Michael's charm might have made him successful in the world of business (as sure as it would have been an obstacle in the civil service), but religious life would not require so much risk.

"What can I do you for?" Roger asked the priest. Roger still attended church regularly but had not let his name stand for parish council since Father Michael had taken over.

"What can I do for you—that's my line," said Father Michael, placing his elbows on his knees, hands clasped in front of him. He still had the puppy dog eyes which had seduced his classmates all through high school; the church had given him the equivalent of a vasectomy but hadn't neutered him. "I'm here to make you an offer."

Roger's first thoughts were of how pudgy he had become compared to the priest. Not yet thirty, Roger was already falling victim to frozen pizza and Elis Getson's baked goods, which they sold at the PetroPump. Father Michael was still trim, his chest firm. Just a few years earlier, there seemed less difference between them. Father Michael had buried Raymond Niese—the young priest's first funeral mass. If Roger had not been so shell-shocked by the loss, he might have found the event full of errors: inappropriate readings, disjointed prayers, awkward pauses at the grave site. But Roger was numb then and, with regards to his father's death, still numb now.

Raymond Niese's health had been declining: arthritis, heart palpitations, prostate cancer, and migraines. His body was pulling apart. But it had been the untimely collapse of Lowell Glidden's old hay barn that killed Raymond, falling beams pummelling him to death. It took half a day to dig him out. Two milk cows had also been killed.

The entire immediate family showed up for the wake and funeral: younger brother Allan, older brother David, David's wife Emily, their mother, now Sarah Carruthers, and her husband Eddie. All through the proceedings, the off-Island visitors took all their cues from Roger, as if spending his youth in his father's company had better prepared him for coordinating the man's death. Roger had to pull David aside to ask for money. Allan, who had been rumoured to be living in Montreal, was too weepy to say or do much other than sneak out to drink bourbon in the backseat of Roger's car.

"What do you figure you'll do when you get the loose ends tied up?" David had asked Roger. "You should put that grubby little place on the market right away." Raymond had left the house/trailer and the property to Roger alone.

"I'm not selling."

"It's hardly a cottage property, Roger. No water views. No foundation.

It'll fall to pieces over the course of a winter or two."

"I'm staying."

David had always assumed his brother had been placed in Raymond's care to look after their not-quite-of-this-world father.

"What for? It's not like you've got anything going on. No girlfriend. A lousy job."

"I wouldn't know how to manage anywhere else."

"You're hardly managing here, I'd say. How long have you worked at that gas station? You smell like motor oil."

Raymond had never been the best Catholic. When Roger came knocking at the rectory, Father Michael had given serious thought about whether the man should be buried in the care of the church. Some parishioners had fully expected Raymond's ex-wife to take him back to Ontario where he had, presumably, been born and which would have freed Father Michael from the burden of deciding. Of course, no one could blame his family for wanting to bury him on the Island; nobody wants to transport a corpse between provinces. Raymond got his Catholic burial in St. Bernard's parish graveyard. He was harmless enough.

Through it all, Father Michael heaped graciousness and flattery on Roger, praising him for the simplest of decisions, the funeral home, the burial plot, the hymns. Even now, five years afterward, the priest's eyes were full of a generalized pity toward Roger, as if Raymond had infected his son with a painful chronic disease. Roger straightened his back. Father Michael had an offer for him. An offer for the Super Summer Follies '89.

"You don't have to...."

"Sure, the Union Road ball diamond is a good location. Being here is good for the talent. They can run home to change, that sort of thing."

"I got it all figured out."

"I'm sure you do, up to a point. But did you know that every tent in the province has already been rented that weekend?" It was true. There were six particularly grand weddings in Prince Edward Island the same weekend as Super Summer Follies '89. If it rained—and there was at least a thirty percent chance of that—the Union Road ball diamond would turn into a mudpit.

What Father Michael was proposing, then, quite generously, was moving the event to the St. Bernard's Parish Hall. It would not hold as many people as the ball field, no. But the concert could take place over a couple of days—a full-fledged festival. Now, how about that. If the weather cooperated, there could be outdoor stages in the adjoining field where the church picnic was held in August.

"It's not what Beatrice and I talked about," said Roger.

"Beatrice has been known to get ahead of herself," said Father Michael. She took her duties as lay eucharistic minister much too seriously and was said to boss around Father Euseb Arsenault on matters that were not the business of a layperson. The book club Beatrice had joined, it was said, devoted much of its discussion time to material of a religious nature, including Protestant, Muslim and Buddhist thought. Father Michael thought Beatrice should stick to advising pageant girls on which shade of lipstick was best for the bathing-suit portion of competitions.

"I don't think that's a fair thing for you to say, Father."

The conversation was tenser than Father Michael expected. He chose not to mention that Father Eloi Poirier, the parish priest in Mont-Carmel, the main church in the mostly French-speaking Evangeline Region, had attended and loved The St. Louis-St. Edward Follies '88. Father Poirier, a good decade or so older than Father Michael and the greatest challenge to Father Michael's power in the diocese, had had his parish council move ahead on a Follies-inspired church concert, slated for August 1989, called the Mont-Carmel Music Festival. The Wellington Co-op had already come on as a sponsor and a singer from Sainte-Anne de Beaupré in Quebec had agreed to make a guest appearance, so long as the cost of her return bus ticket was covered. People were talking about Father Eloi's music festival as far away as Summerside.

There was little need, really, for Father Michael to dream up his own crowd-pleaser since there was a proven commodity here in his backyard. The affiliation with St. Bernard's could help take the Super Summer Follies to the next level.

Normally, Father Michael would leave things with Roger, allowing what he said to sink in. But that evening the priest had a dinner engagement with the bishop in Charlottetown, an authoritarian originally from Halifax who thought he was running a raj that required constant tribute. Father Michael wanted to serve up the Super Summer Follies '89 during dessert.

"...And the rent for the hall—negligible. What you'll be paying won't cover the utilities. It's a gift from the church, so to speak."

"Let me think about it." The temperature of the Old Schoolhouse seemed to drop.

"Now, Roger," Father Michael's hand gently found its way to the bony peak of Roger's knee. "This isn't all about you or, I hate to say it, even, God bless her, Beatrice Perry. It's about the people of St. Louis and St. Edward, who are all of them members of St. Bernard's parish. In their hearts, at least. Let's work together to make the best decision for them."

"But it's my...," Roger stopped at this possessive pronoun that seemed to prove Father Michael's point.

"I took the liberty of talking to Ms Perry this morning," said Father Michael. "She doesn't think it's a problem."

Roger felt tears coming on. But no. He had to focus. He looked up at the bare lightbulb dangling over Father Michael's head.

"Okay," said Roger. "We'll have to survey the place, count the electric outlets, test the weight the stage can hold."

"Of course," said Father Michael. "You'll run it how you see fit. You can do your inspection or whatchamacallit this evening, if you want. The Catholic Women's League will be there, if you don't mind having ladies there, clucking and whatnot, and I'm sure you don't."

The priest straightened his back and brought his hands back to his knees. A Buddhist would have taken him for the Enlightened One, moments after a great meal.

★

The change of venue for Super Summer Follies '89 had far more repercussions than expected. And like a controversy that would shake up St. Louis-St. Edward almost twenty years later, these side effects were ignited by *The Spectator-Herald* and the paper's idiosyncratic processes.

"I shouldn't really be stepping in, no, I should not, but I wanted to extend you an uncommon courtesy," Caroline MacPhail told Roger over the hisses and rattles of his telephone party line. He was at home eating canned mushroom soup and a dinner roll.

"But I'm not advocating for abortion," Roger said. A particularly sharp click a moment earlier led Roger to believe that his declaration was heard not just by Caroline MacPhail, but perhaps by the Doucettes up Union Road or the Pendergasts down Union Road.

"I'm not keen on how the Catholics go on about it either, all the gory details, the way they delight in gawking at bloody fetuses and the whole horror show. You'd swear it was a personal affront to the supposedly Virgin Mary. But, really, Roger, what you're trying to say here doesn't make any sense."

Caroline was still buzzed from having made her 11:30am deadline. She had been working on a series of stories about how the environmental assessment panel would go about determining if a fixed link from Prince Edward Island to the mainland would bring economic and environmental catastrophe on the province. Today's story "End to the Island Way of Life?" focused on the effects on the family, without explicitly mentioning the possibility of increased prostitution, mainland booze, and illegal drugs. Quite an achievement, Caroline thought.

A year earlier, 59.46 percent of Islanders had voted in a plebiscite for a bridge or a tunnel—a zip-line would have pleased some people—across the fourteen kilometres that separated them from the rest of the Americas. The repercussions were infinite. A bridge would reduce the trip to Champlain Place mall in Moncton by at least an hour. It would also reduce the revenue of the police department of the town of Borden, whose issuance of speeding tickets would drop when Islanders no longer had to rush through the dumpy little town to make the hourly ferry departure.

Prior to the vote, Premier Joe Ghiz, a politician best known for his nonchalant usage of the word "scintilla," had implied that the threshold for pushing ahead on the fixed link was sixty percent. Caroline was still confident the province would respect the 0.54 percent worth of reluctance, no matter how badly the federal government wanted to save money on ferry subsidies. Premier Ghiz was a lawyer, who expected the Is to be dotted and the Ts to be crossed. That 0.54 percent gap would haunt him for the rest of his life, but Caroline was sure he'd honour it.

Or so she had written in an editorial fourteen months ago. She was increasingly unsure. She had been at *The Spectator-Herald* for five years and was astonished daily by Ghiz's capacity for political expediency. "Province Expects New Bridge Proposals to Pass with Flying Colours," she wrote that morning (reporters were encouraged to write their own headlines—it saved the publisher/editor, Basil Johnston, from having to read all the stories). Caroline fully expected tomorrow's story to be something like, "Environmental Assessment Process Crashes Fixed

Link on the Rocks." Fishermen were whining and complaining about the aversion of crustaceans to concrete, gravel, and the rumbling of eighteen-wheelers overhead. But fishermen were known for their complaining. That's how they filled all that spare time they had on their hands.

After filing her front-page story, it was time to clear up the other dribs and drabs of work the reporters shared amongst themselves. *The Spectator-Herald* presses shook the whole building underneath her feet as Caroline transcribed the letters page correspondence that Basil had chosen for the next day's newspaper. She was free to edit as she saw fit, as long as she didn't add back in what Basil had already censored with his big black marker.

Roger's letter was already half gone by the time it reached the plastic inbox tray on Caroline's desk.

"I am just making it completely clear that Super Summer Follies is not affiliated with West Prince Pro-Life Action Alliance," Roger told Caroline.

"But they're the main sponsor of your event."

"Technically. I've already told them they can't speak or get on stage with their T-shirts on. We can't afford to have the banners reprinted. So I have to have this letter published."

"But it makes you look like PEI's Dr. Henry Morgentaler."

"Abortion? I have nothing to say about abortion. Nothing! I'm trying to bring a little creativity to West Prince. The show should not be judged by the signage."

"That's not how people are going to read it." By "people," Caroline meant everybody in Prince County; *The Spectator-Herald* had eighty-seven percent household penetration, bested only by *Compass*, the 6pm show on CBC TV, which reached ninety-two percent of all Islanders each weekday evening, ninety-four percent Up West. The two media outlets made for an ideal Greek chorus in West Prince, and Caroline had become a pretty good judge of how things would play to "people."

"Show me where the hell it says I support abortion."

"You will not use that language with me." Caroline had left her father's evangelical church when she was a university student. When she married soon after getting her B.A., she started attending her husband's more moderate independent Christian congregation in St. Eleanors, though the devil still lurked over her shoulder.

"Roger, half your performers will cancel if this letter is published."

"They won't. They want to let their light shine. That's more important than politics."

"Uh, it's life, not politics," said Caroline. "Shouldn't you just take this up with Father Michael? You're still Catholic, aren't you?"

"Run it. I accept the consequences."

"Dear Basil cut out some of the softer parts."

Roger hung up the phone. What was left of his soup was cold. He took a swig of apple juice. The phone rang again.

"Good afternoon, Roger," said Beatrice. "How are you this fine day?" Her voice was tart.

"Uh, just finishing up lunch, Ms Perry."

"I'm so sorry to disturb you. I don't know how to put this. I heard about the letter."

"Who told you? Caroline!"

"Oh, there's a clever one!" said Beatrice. She had actually heard from Basil Johnston, who had tried to court her years ago, but there was no sense in not implicating Caroline. The reporter was, indeed, a clever one. The most likely of the four *Spectator-Herald* reporters to take a publishable photo at a beauty pageant, music competition, or cheque presentation, it wouldn't hurt to have Caroline take a greater interest in the Follies. "Oh, Roger. Don't ruin everything. Nobody'll even notice the pro-life banner."

"But...."

"You should have thought of all this before you cashed the cheque from the Knights of Columbus."

"I didn't know!"

"Roger, everybody knows the Knights is the men's auxiliary to the Pro-Life Alliance. Don't blame other people for your failure to keep up. Now get on the phone to *The Spectator-Herald* before I do."

"You've put your heart and soul into this show."

"I'm an Alliance member, Roger. I'm not very active, and I'm not completely in agreement, but it's what Catholic ladies do. Now get on the blower to Caroline and withdraw that letter."

Roger called *The Spectator-Herald*'s newsroom.

"His royal Basil heard me call you," said Caroline. "Things have changed since we last spoke."

"In the last two minutes?"

Basil had decided he would not let Caroline retract the letter on Roger's behalf. Basil was, quite truly, sympathetic to other people's second thoughts. His second thoughts meant he got very little work done in the run of a day. But Basil had selected Roger's letter for publication, and if it was to be unselected, a little begging would be required.

"Basil even typed up the letter himself, with two of his bony fingers."

"I won't. I won't. I won't call him."

"That's good, because Basil'd want to see you in person."

"Never!"

Three hours later, after much pacing around his front yard (there was little room for pacing in the house/trailer), Roger arrived in Summerside at the reception desk of *The Spectator-Herald's* editorial department.

Caroline, the only reporter to have less than a decade under her belt, sat on the far side of the room, next to the sports department. Her desk was angled in such a way that she could choose not to look toward the reception desk. This was handy when people arrived with handwritten obituaries, wedding notices, and wedding write-ups, which were as painful to transcribe as the phoned-in notices and announcements. The rule was: you take it, you type it. A reporter accepted a dense chicken scratching on foolscap and three days later she was being balled out for spelling three bridesmaids' names wrong. A six-person Bangkok sex show could unfold in reception and Caroline would not see it.

Roger rang the bell on the front counter, which delivered him straight into the hands of the publisher/editor. Basil was too busy brushing crumbs off his shirt to shake hands.

"Roger Niese? Hm!" The name came across his desk no less than once a day in some letter or news item submitted by someone from Up West. Now that the young man was here in the flesh, Basil realized there might be a broad array of issues that might be quickly sorted out. Perhaps this abortion letter episode was for the better. He ushered Roger into his tiny office.

Basil started with what he could most easily remember.

"I have here a request from you for a public service announcement." Basil pulled a form from among the thousands of stacked pieces of paper in the room. Without so much as looking, Basil could quickly pull from a pile, say, an Anne Landers column that had caused outrage months earlier. That the clipping's curled corners might bring with it a misplaced chicken bone from a lunch from two years ago was something others were not supposed to notice.

"Yes!" said Roger, suddenly overjoyed at the sight of the sheet of paper he had sent in a few weeks earlier. Receipt had not been acknowledged and Roger wondered if the "Run every day possible until July 1" plea he had written made a strong enough case against the "two free insertions only" rule. He was not sure what exactly an editor did, but this man had half-moon glasses, a banker's vest, and his own coffee-scented office; this circumstance surely meant Roger was being taken seriously.

"Do you not understand our rules about church notices needing to run in the Saturday 'Church Roundup' section?" Basil had spent the better part of a decade modifying and remodifying the form to make it excruciatingly clear.

"It's not a church event!"

"The address given...."

"I know, I know. It's a community event."

Basil Johnston wrinkled his nose.

"So it's like a student function?" said Basil, his finger sliding down the form until it hit the 'Educational Event' check box.

"No, it's for everybody. Beatrice Perry is helping me with it."

"Oh, Beatrice Perry. An elegant lady. Ah! Ah! So, more like a pageant."

"Yes," said Roger, defeated. "Like a pageant with singing and dancing and plays. And with men."

"Some people find female impersonation funny," said Basil, "but I am not some people. Kensington's just mad for it during their harvest festival. They can keep that to themselves. Now, our photo policy—"

"I know, I know. No more than fifteen people in a shot."

"And giant cheques?"

"The amount needs to be legible in the photo."

"Good, good," said Basil. "But that's not why you're in my office today, is it?"

"Yes, thank you. About the Supper Summer Follies '89 and the Pro-Life Alliance...."

"Very controversial. Very unpopular opinion. We could get a few new subscriptions out of it."

"You'll run it?"

"I'm told you don't want it to run."

Roger always felt he held the truth deep inside him. When others disagreed with him, he felt that either they weren't looking closely enough at the facts, weren't being honest with themselves, were caving into social pressure, or weren't hearing him right. He had gone over these four obstacles in his head for some time. If he could overcome them, people would understand he knew the truth. This was not so narcissistic or messianic as it sounded because Roger believed that everybody knew the truth deep inside them. But Roger was determined to dig it out.

For example, in a letter to *The Spectator-Herald* over the winter, Roger wrote a twenty-six-step plan to determine, once and for all, whether there should be a fixed link from the Island to the mainland. Arriving at the twenty-sixth step, one could not fail to see that a tunnel was the best idea, a bridge the worst, with the status quo somewhere in between. When he submitted this irrefutable document to *The Spectator-Herald,* the letter had been slashed for length. Only steps one, six, and nineteen were printed.

"On principle, I think...."

"Caroline thinks they'll run you out of West Prince, all the way back to Ottawa."

"What did Caroline say? No, I don't want to know what she said."

"She's a clever one!" said Basil. "On the front page every day. Her typo rate is astonishingly low. Sometimes she's salacious. That's why I keep such a close eye on her. Some of what she submits, you wouldn't want her parents reading it. Not her father, anyway."

"Can I see the edited letter?"

Basil turned his computer screen in Roger's direction. Roger read the letter aloud. "Speaking on behalf of The Super Summer Follies '89, I wish to clarify.... No relationship with the West Prince Pro-Life Action Alliance.... Father Michael Chaisson tricked me into signing the contract.... Fooled people into believing a fetus has more rights than a woman who has seen things in the world that only she has seen.... Detestable signage.... Pro-choice feminists should not conclude that there is a lack of sympathy for their point of view.... Nothing in the program references these fascist beliefs....' Do you think I need to say that the people in the Action Alliance are not evil?" Roger believed women should be free to make their own decisions. Not that he thought Debbie Arsenault shouldn't have had Michael's baby—something he had thought about a lot—but that she should have had more choices.

The more choices, the better.

"The letter is already 650 words. But. Do you know what? Why don't we ask one of the reporters to give it a rewrite? Caroline!"

"No, no! Don't call Caroline! I withdraw it."

It was hard to tell if Caroline's smirk was prompted by the situation she had been summoned into or if she had been listening to an amusing story before Basil called her into his office. Basil offered his star reporter his chair. She read the letter silently, moving her mouth to signal to observers that they shouldn't interrupt her.

"It's the implication of double-dealing that makes the letter so damning," she proclaimed. "The name calling—who Up West knows anything about fascism? We should take out the part about Father Michael's promise...."

"But that's the only reason I agreed to letting St. Bernard's host us!"

"It complicates things." Caroline cocked her head like a puppy in a staged photo for a fundraising calendar. "Let's call Michael right now."

Basil beamed, looking dreadfully impressed with Caroline's problem-solving ability. On the other side of the desk, Roger's increasing panic was squeezing his head like fingers on a pimple.

"Father Chaisson! Michael! Caroline MacPhail here! At the *Spectator-Herald*. Yes, yes. I know! Oh, you're so bad! Oh my! Well, I have Roger here, Roger Niese. Yes, right here."

Caroline dropped the receiver to her chest. "Father Michael says hello!" Up the phone went again before Roger could say anything.

"Yes, now I don't know if you know about this letter Roger has written."

The letter had seemed like the simplest solution. Roger could not imagine a conversation with Father Michael about his betrayal without raised voices. His plans had backfired. Humiliation was everywhere he looked. Roger felt his tear ducts dilate.

"I retract!" said Roger. "I retract! Please destroy the letter. He grabbed the original paper copy from the desk, crumpling it as he shoved it in his pocket. "Forget it! He won."

Roger dashed out of the newsroom and down the stairs to Water Street before the reporter and publisher/editor could reply. He'd find out if his retraction had been honoured by reading the paper. As he turned to go to his car, he nearly ploughed over a person coming towards the *Spectator-Herald's* entryway.

"Mercy!" Beatrice brought her beaded white purse up to her face as if to defend herself.

"Bea.... Where are you going?"

"I'm just dropping off some photos at *The Spectator-Herald.*"

"Yeah, right! Photos!"

"Tone, Roger!"

Roger turned his head away from her to hide his reddening face and eyes.

"Oh Roger, be a man. So much fury over so little!"

"I'll call you later, I will." Roger kept his back toward her, waving goodbye to her over his shoulder. Then he scurried to his car and drove as fast as he could back Up West.

Flat and straight, through ugly woods, swamps, and marginal farmland, the drive along Route 2 was mind-numbingly dull, which helped account for the region's poor tourism numbers. Roger sometimes felt trapped in Up West life, but he saw no escape. Moving into the orbit of his mother or either one of his brothers would be pure masochism. Charlottetown? He didn't know a soul there. He was stuck on the Union Road and whatever made it tick. He glared at the turnoff signs to the "Evangeline Region," where they seemed to work harmoniously to great success.

Beyond the O'Leary turnoff, the landscape grew more familiar, as he regularly had to drive as far as O'Leary to run errands. By the Alberton turnoff, Roger's mental inventory of what was where became that much stronger. He knew who had let their grass grow too long, who had visitors' cars in their driveway, whose kids were playing too close to the road. As he turned onto Union Road, Lester Shaw, who was pumping gas at the PetroPump, waved at his car. His sulk had receded enough that he was able to wave back.

The next day, Beatrice showed up on Roger's front step with a young woman in tow. Oddly, Beatrice did not introduce her immediately. The young woman shuffled nervously from foot to foot, nearly knocking over an antique milk can. Beatrice shot her a smile that seemed like a scowl.

"Good afternoon, Roger. Back in business?"

After several minutes discussing the Super Summer Follies '89 as if the letter-to-the-editor incident had never happened, Beatrice cocked her head.

"Oh, I almost forgot!"

She then introduced her companion as Marla Bowness from Kensington, whom Beatrice was mentoring for the upcoming Miss Community Gardens pageant. It was a long way for Marla to drive, but it was clear she needed some coaching. She was a broad-shouldered, easy-going gal with a mess of curly hair. Her collar and sleeves were all flipped and twisted, her posture abominable. She was a bit younger than Roger.

"I hope Beatrice is taking good care of you," said Roger.

"I'm in excellent hands," said Marla, smiling sweetly.

"Are you going to put on some tea?" Beatrice asked.

While Roger was filling the kettle, Beatrice set a pile of possible short plays for the Super Summer Follies on his kitchen table. For a while, Beatrice and Roger spoke as if they were distant colleagues who rarely met in person. The chill gradually lifted. Marla didn't say much; she was too busy grinning and laughing as if Beatrice and Roger were swapping joke after joke.

A month later, Roger found himself in a medium-distance relationship with Marla Bowness. That summer she was working at the Bank of Nova Scotia in Kensington but wanted to start her own dress shop—bridal gowns, prom outfits, pageant outfits. Representing the bank in Miss Community Gardens was just the beginning. Beatrice's support on the pageant side of things would be priceless, she told Roger. Putting one foot daintily in front of the other. Keeping your head up, your shoulders straight, your smile intact. This sort of eternal wisdom didn't change with the whims of American fashion editors.

Each of their dates was a meal in Summerside, a fifteen-minute drive for her, about an hour for him. Marla would have thought nothing of driving across the country to help out a friend, but Roger didn't want to take advantage of her kindness. He paid for all their meals.

The relationship was friendly and undefined. Roger never made a sexual move. The people around them expected it might grow into something, but neither party took any responsibility for shaping the future. Circumstances did their job for them. Roger, wrapped up in his organizing duties, cancelled dates, and asked for favours. As the Super Summer Follies '89 approached, Marla was telling her friends more about the festival than about how it was going with her alleged boyfriend.

"You're his assistant!" declared her best friend Sharon Heaney, who was to be married that summer to her high school beau.

"There's nothing wrong with being a little supportive," said Marla.

"Better than being an old maid, I suppose."

On the weekend of the Super Summer Follies '89, Marla was officially in charge of running messages to the volunteers who didn't have walkie-talkies. She was also responsible for giving half-hour curtain-call warnings to the performers, who might be on the site or who might be getting ready at home. St. Bernard's Parish Hall didn't have enough backstage area for everyone—nor was booze welcome there. Over the course of the weekend, there were thirty musical acts, four short plays, seven monologues, twelve sketches, and five speeches, none of which made any reference at all to abortion or reproduction. References to relationships of any kind rarely went further than the hilarity of courtship.

Unofficially, Marla spent most of the Super Summer Follies '89 following behind Mitchell, making sure he didn't injure himself. She did her best to be unobtrusive. There was row seating both inside the St. Bernard's Parish Hall and on its lawn, but Mitchell refused to put on his helmet. He had one seizure on Saturday, in the middle of James and John Arsenault playing a folk song they had learned in their high-school music class, and one on Sunday, in the middle of "Farmer Brown Comes A-Courtin'," which starred Alex Oulton from Alberton, who now ran a dairy bar in what had been Roger's Acadian museum. Marla caught Mitchell both times. She made a show of her surprise at the coincidence of her being so near at hand.

Mitchell would have broken his nose or cracked his skull if it wasn't for Marla. Her good work likely extended the life of her relationship with Roger beyond what was reasonable. She had heard him light up telling stories about this girl he knew in high school, Debbie Arsenault, something she had seen before in a boyfriend who had turned out to be gay. Marla couldn't compete with a one-track mind.

The Super Summer Follies '89 were an unquestionable success, both artistically and financially. Roger wouldn't take a cent of the profits; Beatrice claimed only the seventy-five dollars she billed for her "talent consultant" services.

Roger had made Father Michael promise that no money would go to the West Prince Pro-Life Action Alliance. Profits would instead go to

St. Bernard's parish and Catholic Children's Aid.

The Mont-Carmel Music Festival that summer attracted less than half the crowd; Father Eloi Poirier announced it would not be a regular event.

Super Summer Follies '89 highlights varied depending on whom you were talking to. The plays were thought to be amazingly funny. Material from the monologues and sketches was repeated in conversation for months afterward. For "Music Box Dancer," Susan Kennedy was joined on stage by Heather Shaw, a tiny waif that her father, Lester Shaw, whisked away the moment she walked off the stage. The next week, Linda Shaw took Lester to court to reduce his access to his daughter.

Kate Pineau's "Ste. Anne's Reel" closed the festival, though most attendees missed her. Patrons, many of them half-cut, were anxious to extricate their cars as quickly as possible from the mess of vehicles in the parish's two lots and on the sides of the Palmer and Thompson roads. Also, most people assumed the Buchanan Family Singers were the finale and the girl who took the stage afterward was just playing a rollicking sort of exit music.

But Roger was so blown away by Kate's medley of reels, he didn't even notice people leaving. As she came off the stage, he hugged her with adoration, not consolation.

"You're the star, honey, you're the star," he said, a grin on his face so big, Kate wondered if he was high. Though Roger didn't know it at this moment, he had found the North Star for his professional career, the factor he'd consider in all future decisions as an impresario.

"I think I might have been okay," she said. Her daughter Krystal was hanging on her hip, sucking on a Creamsicle. Her youngest one, Sherrie, was with her grandparents, who were in the fourth row, waiting for the crowds to disperse.

"No, you're going places, lady."

"Oh Roger, you're sweet," said Kate, who just wanted to go sit down somewhere. "I ain't going anywhere."

The attendees who did stay to see Kate Pineau play would make a legend out of that performance. Nobody could argue against their declaration of a genuine miracle. She was the girl wonder with the fiddle which spoke in tongues. That she was a Pineau from Skinner's Pond, someone reputed to get around with Arnold Crozier, a single mother with two kids, made it all the more impressive.

"A virtual unknown from perhaps not the best family background finished things off in grand style," wrote Caroline in *The Spectator-Herald*. Caroline hadn't seen the performance either, but based her critique on what she had heard people saying when she was filling up at Lester Shaw's PetroPump for her drive back to Summerside. "Her reels made you feel like you were living in a long-ago era and maybe that's the gift the Follies give to the Island. A flashback. The only glitch in the weekend of programming was when the washrooms backed up on Sunday, a problem quickly remedied by the hospitable parishioners." Caroline spared gentle *Spectator-Herald* readers a description of how this problem was solved.

The Super Summer Follies '89 had nothing but sun the whole weekend, for which Father Michael thanked God at mass the following weekend. They could have held the festival in the field by the Old Union Road Schoolhouse, after all.

CHAPTER 9

A PORTION OF THE CHAIN-link fence had been cut and pulled apart. Hidden behind a withered apple tree, the gap had long ago been forgotten. The kids who had made it had grown up and bought homes of their own far away from the rail corridor in this tiny village in northern New Brunswick.

Thanks to this forgotten family history, Roger Niese now stood in a stranger's snow-filled backyard on New Year's Eve without having torn any clothing. The conductor and various manic porters had ordered everyone to stay on the train for their safety and, incidentally, in case the police wanted to ask questions. Under normal circumstances, Roger would have been the first in line to offer testimony, but this time he didn't feel qualified.

Besides, he had other things on his mind. For starters, the recent realization that his mother seemed to have fallen into an interminable depression, of which her husband Eddie and Roger's two brothers would not speak. That part of his Christmas visit to Ottawa would take some time to process.

But Roger had an even more immediate concern, for which, at this hour, there was no solution, only triage. Hopefully, the yard's owner was home. There was no other way to the street than through the house. It took six bouts of knocking to get an answer. The residents ignored the first five, unable to believe someone had gained access to their backyard.

"Yeah?" said the man, his plaid shirt hanging open to reveal a body haloed with wiry grey hair.

"I'm from the train." Roger pointed theatrically at the visible cars. The light poured from the windows into the backyard. A few yards down, you could see the flash of police and ambulance lights. "Someone's dead."

"You ain't the killer, are you?" asked the man, not exactly joking. He sized up Roger: tall but nervous, the type would overthink every punch.

Roger heard variety-show patter blaring from a TV.

"No, no. We were talking on the train. The dead man, God rest his soul. I was talking to him—before I came to ask you a favour. He was a smoker. But I don't think lung cancer would make you tip over just like that, would it? Probably a heart attack. Anyway, he was a smoker. The girl next to him. McGill student. Set her hair on fire. Tipped his cigarette right into her."

"Does she need a fire extinguisher?" The man snorted a laugh at his own joke. "Is that what you're here for?"

Roger laughed nervously. There was some information he was holding back about his part in the train crisis. He had talked to the young lady in question in the bar car, as the train pulled out of Montreal. She had complained of the "old fart" seated next to her. Roger had walked her back to her seat and made conversation with the man, a recent widower from Fredericton, who had been visiting his eldest daughter in Ottawa. Roger had asked the McGill student if she wanted to change seats. It was right in front of the man—too obvious. She declined. Five minutes later, her hair was sizzling.

"No, no, no. I just want to borrow your phone. It's long distance, but I'll pay for it. No worries."

The man hadn't stepped back from the door to allow Roger room to move forward. In fact, the man squared himself in the door frame. Roger finally took a step back to demonstrate he would advance his cause only by persuasion.

"It's a dire emergency back on Prince Edward Island. Very dire. Could affect the direction of the rest of my life."

"Islander, eh? Got a daughter who went to vet school in Charlottetown. Hung out with a Jollimore girl. Know any Jollimores? They were all as happy as pigs in shit."

"Can't say I do." Roger looked at his watch. "Do you mind? This is the second time this train's been delayed. I should have been home already. We hit a snowmobiler in the woods somewhere in Quebec. He's still alive, you'll be pleased to know."

"You seem cursed!" the man said. "Well, I've lived long enough to handle someone the devil is picking on." He stepped aside.

"Not that I'm making excuses, but the snowmobiler was drunk," said Roger. "Put us back four hours."

The kitchen's most obvious purpose at this moment was a repository for Christmas gift wrap, boxes, plastic clamshell packaging, half-eaten boxes of crackers, half-eaten bags of chips, and plastic rings emptied of frozen shrimp. Through the door to the living room, Roger could see gifts fanned out under the tree in a large three-quarter circle that ate up a good chunk of the room. It made Roger think of an Up West Christmas habit, where the lady of the house would scuttle around on her knees around the tree, showing each gift to visitors, announcing who it was from, and explaining the gift's significance. When Roger stepped into the living room, a lady in a flowered dressing gown, apparently the man's wife, smiled and gave Roger a jaunty wave.

"He needs the phone, sweetie," said the man. That "sweetie" wiped away some of the fear Roger had of this suspicious man.

"Of course, of course! From the train!" the wife said as she had been expecting an outpouring of railway refugees. She found a heavy black rotary dial phone amongst a pile of knitted dish towels sitting on an electric organ.

Roger dialed the number. The phone at the West Prince Acadian Centre at the Miminegash Wharf rang and rang. Nobody answered. Left to his own devices, Roger would have let it ring forever but grew self-conscious at being watched so anxiously.

"My colleague must be running around like a chicken with her head cut off." Rather than hang up the receiver, he held it against his chest. "I really, really need to talk to her. Do you mind if I try again in a few minutes? I'm worried something's gone wrong." Roger nervously looked in the direction of the train, wondering how quickly he could get his boots back on if it started to move again.

"Tracey! Stand watch, will you? This guy's got some calling to do." Again, Roger heard sweetness in the man's bark. Roger turned around to see in the room's far corner a young woman sitting in a La-Z-Boy upholstered in almost the same brown as the carpet and the wallpaper. The chair was tipped so far back Roger had missed her at first. Over the years he had gotten better at scanning around to make sure he smiled and waved at everyone he might come across in the run of a day, but sometimes he got so lost in his head he forgot.

"I'm so sorry," said Roger. He stepped aside as Tracey slumped her way to her position in the kitchen doorway where she could watch the train without leaving the living room. Despite her baggy flannel PJs, Roger could tell she was as thick as a frayed piece of string. "I didn't introduce myself. Roger. I'm from St. Louis-St. Edward on PEI. On my way back from visiting my mother in Ottawa."

"I'm Gerry Tillard," the man of the house called out to him. "That's Rose, my wife. That one, that's Tracey."

Physically, Tracey Tillard looked to be mid-twenties. But there was something about her manner and movements that suggested that, no matter how nature worked, her body had no intention of venturing beyond its teens. Her hair was seventies-style, long and straight like a brown waterfall. Her big glasses made her face look tiny. Everything looked oversized on her.

"Maybe," said Mr. Tillard, "I'll take a walk up to the corner. See if the local Mounties have anything to say."

"I'm not a big fan of the police," said Tracey when the door had slammed behind her father. "Dad thinks they can do no wrong, but I think they're just as likely to go bad as anyone else. Maybe more so."

"Tracey!" said Mrs. Tillard.

"No, she's right, I suppose. She's entitled to her feelings," said Roger.

"Her feelings? Well, that's enough foolishness for one night. I'm going to do something useful. There's always dishes and at Christmas, it's a full-time job," said Mrs. Tillard. Tracey shifted to her left foot and tipped herself to the side to let her mother pass through the door.

"Do you mind if I...." Roger held up the receiver.

"Do what you got to do," said Tracey. "Nobody in this house will stop you from doing anything, no matter how crazy it is. They'll tsk-tsk you to death, but that's the worst of it."

"Tracey!" Mrs. Tillard growled from the kitchen.

"They let me go to L.A. to be an actress when I was eighteen. Paid for my ticket! It was a loan until I got my first part! Can you believe it!"

"They had confidence in you."

"They wouldn't know bad acting from a pack of cards."

Roger had a hard time dialing because he couldn't take his eyes off Tracey, who, for her part, was facing him rather than the train in the backyard. He got a busy signal, then a number-out-of-service message, then two minutes of ringing before a ragged-breathed Beatrice picked up.

"Good evening, West Prince Acadian Centre, Beatrice Perry speaking."

"Beatrice!"

"Roger! What's happened? Where are you?" She had been thinking the worst for most of the day.

"I can't talk long. I'm in New Brunswick. My train's been delayed. Twice delayed...."

"Two dead, apparently, Beatrice!" Tracey called out.

"Who's that?"

"A family is letting me use their phone. Beatrice, I need you to find a new DJ. Somebody left an old *Spectator-Herald* in the overhead bin on the train. I read it this afternoon. Michael DesRoches was sentenced to jail last week. Going to be in Sleepy Hollow for a while. Selling pot. To kids, I believe. Anyway, he's going to be a no-show tonight."

"What?" said Beatrice, who now regretted her habit of avoiding the court reports because they were none of her business, really. "I knew all along he was bad news. It's seven o'clock! We open the doors in two hours."

"Sorry, sorry, sorry. Mitchell will get Lester Shaw to be the DJ. He'll be available. Lost his drivers' licence a few weeks ago. Somebody will have to pick him up. He'll do it for a cut of the bar sales."

"Roger! I hardly needed to add an item to my to-do list."

"And ask Jesse Perry to lend us a few life jackets."

"Life jackets!"

"In case someone gets drunk and decides to take a walk outside," said Roger.

The building that for years had been the Shea Family Lobster Co-op was now home to the West Prince Acadian Centre. Right on the Miminegash Wharf, a fishing net's throw from the fishing boats, the building provided views of the harbour and the beach, a picturesque if smelly place for an ambitious cultural enterprise. Though it was a nice place for a meander in the summer and fall, it was less hospitable in the winter—it was a virtual block of ice this New Year's Eve. But the location came with government funding for restoring what had been a derelict building. Roger had become tremendously skilled at effectively filling out forms for government funding—just enough desperation mixed with the right amount of proof of concept. If he needed letters of support, he'd ask the cadre of entertainers he had in his overstuffed Rolodex.

Of the mishmash of wood-slat buildings along Miminegash Harbour's north side, the old Shea Co-op was the largest. Three cars could drive simultaneously when they rolled up the big garage-style doors, so long as the drivers were sober. If you parked them tight, you might fit eight vehicles inside, though Roger had forbidden this.

Roger didn't like to open the big roll-up very often. He wanted what was inside the West Prince Acadian Centre to be a surprise to visitors, like a hot and sour soup on the menu of a burger joint. The wooden shingles on one side were painted blue, the next side white, the next side red, with yellow stars scattered here and there like barnacles that couldn't be removed. The fourth side, which was only a few inches away from the next building, was left unpainted.

Inside the West Prince Acadian Centre, there was an array of Mexican-bright colours on the walls. Lobster traps and farm implements hung from the ceiling. Aside from the folding chairs that were brought out for sit-down functions, there were a dozen barrel chairs lined up against the bar, which, with all the flags and ropes and pulleys strung around it, made people feel like they were on a pirate ship.

The West Prince Acadian Centre had opened that August. The original opening date was June, as stated in the listing in the official *PEI Visitors' Guide*. But various changes Roger made had caused several postponements. There was a price to pay for the delays. Six tourists from Quebec who had attempted a visit in July wrote letters of complaint to the Island tourism marketing board about driving that far Up West only to find the destination was a mess of carpenters and electricians. For their suffering, the complainers were sent two-for-one coupons for the Anne of Green Gables house in Cavendish and a hand-written apology note from Premier Joe Ghiz.

Since August, the West Prince Acadian Centre had hosted eight weddings, five dances, three ceilidhs. There had been two clogging demonstrations and sixteen random Acadian music "happenings," most of them starring Kate Pineau.

The parking was inadequate, the building drafty, but Roger had quickly grown a reputation for pulling out all the stops when it came to decoration. You'd swear sometimes he spent more money on crêpe paper and balloons than the Centre made in rental fees and ticket sales. The whole thing was an achievement for Roger, something a lot of men would have been satisfied with; it paid his bills. But there was always something compromised about it that made him pick and pick at things until he drove the talent crazy.

"I'm also worried about the power," Roger told Beatrice over the phone. "I didn't pay the last bill or two."

"Roger!"

"I don't think they'll do it on New Year's. Mitchell should be there in a bit with a generator...."

"Is that what he's doing out there, freezing his hands off?"

"....but if you call Maritime Electric and feel them out, whether they're going to hit the switch tonight or not, we can save Mitchell from buying the gas."

"Heaven forbid we spend forty dollars to keep the lights on."

"How are ticket sales?"

"People around here don't buy in advance, Roger...."

"But how many?"

"Fifteen."

"Including....?"

"Mitchell, Kate, yourself, and myself. Arnold Crozier."

"I see."

"Noel Pineau said he might buy one, if Betty Ann hasn't made other plans."

"Awww."

"Bad news!" interjected Tracey.

"Roger," said Beatrice. "Is there somebody there with you?"

"Mister...."

Roger had wound himself up in the phone cord, weaving his way around the room. Tracey waited for him to turn around to face her before she continued. "...we don't have a discount plan or anything. You must already be looking at seven dollars or so. I'm wondering what you can afford."

"Okay," he said to Tracey, then brought the receiver back to his mouth. "I'm so, so sorry, Beatrice. I won't be there in time."

"That's the way the cookie crumbles. But any grease I get on me from steering this mess, you'll be paying out of your own pocket to clean it up."

Roger hung his head like a scolded child. He put down the phone and looked at Tracey.

"I won't lie to you and tell you I wasn't listening," she said, "but I have to say I couldn't figure out much of it except you don't have a lot of money and you know a lot of criminals."

"This is our first signature New Year's event."

"Now that sounds especially fancy. Signature event? And you're not even there. Just getting other people to do your work for you? What would Noam Chomsky think?"

"Who's that?"

"Smart guy. American. Linguist? Pretty critical of capitalists."

"What does he have to do with me?"

"So, this is a business of yours?"

"It's a community centre."

"Government funded?"

"Um, kinda. We have a board."

"But you're the boss of it, I bet."

"Why do you say that? Who's betting?"

The phone rang. Tracey took it from Roger, picked up the receiver, said "'Lo!" and then listened silently for a few minutes before she said "Bye!"

"It was Daddy. At the police station. Lord! The train's going to be here for at least another hour. Maybe longer. The roads are poor. The coroner's coming from Moncton. The one in Bathurst's drunk already. It's New Year's Eve! I'll bring you a cocktail. Something fruity?"

"Really? Maybe I should... They might make an announcement... I'd better...."

Roger had planned to track down whoever was in charge of the investigation and find out all the details. If the wait was substantial, he might be able to organize some entertainment; there had to be a fiddle somewhere on the train.

"Have a seat. I don't mind playing a 1950s housewife for a bit. It's been my New Year's dream for just ages now."

Tracey dashed to the kitchen. There was clinking, glugging, and the hissing sound of a pop bottle opening. Roger got up and walked to the chair on which his host had been enthroned and let his eyes roam over the books which had fallen off her lap, over the arm of the chair, and onto the books pyramided beside the chair. Among several word-search workbooks and perhaps a half-dozen different Farmer's Almanacs were works by Agatha Christie, Michel Foucault, Gabriel García Márquez, and Marshall McLuhan, and no fewer than four volumes whose titles contained the phrases "A History of," "Short History," and "Brief History."

"Where'd you go to university?" Roger called out to the kitchen.

"One with Dorothy Parker in the curriculum? Now that's an academic program I'd finish." Tracey laughed, returning to the living room with two glasses of fizzy reddish liquid, each garnished with a pineapple wedge and cherry. She set the drinks on the coffee table and wiggled herself back into the cocoon of her reading material. Roger took a seat on the couch where she had placed him before, but on the end closer to her, further from the television.

"Or were you asking me about the Foucault? You wonder if he's ever going to get to the point after all his qualms. Bloody qualmer. He's so busy pointing out what we can't say about madness and power and sex, I'm hard-pressed to think what we can say about them except they're all quite thrilling."

Roger blushed.

"I can't help notice that the word 'sex' jumps at you in an otherwise academic sentence. Or was it the word 'power' that aroused you? Do you study anything?"

"I, uh, tried UPEI."

"Tried. That's a nice way of putting it. I tried three times, sixteen thousand dollars of Daddy's money, which kept mom up nights. She's next door now, with my grandparents. The houses are connected through the laundry room. Just so you know I didn't kill her." Tracey took a drink but not a breath. "Maybe if I could have skipped under-grad and went straight to a Master's, it would have been different. Undergrads are insufferable."

"I wouldn't know," said Roger.

"Acadia was especially repulsive. But I didn't like Mount A either. Or UNB. I should have gone to Ontario. No, that would have been worse. You'd think their multiculturalism would liberate them, but it just sets them looking for new ways to signal privilege and status." She took an-other drink. "But what am I on about? You're in the middle of a crisis. A genuine crisis!"

"It's not a crisis."

"It's a little crisis, at least. Maybe a little worse than looking for your glasses for an hour only to discover they're on your head. Do you trust this Beatrice person?"

"I don't want to keep you from anything," said Roger. He was conscious of the snow melting off the boots he left in the porch. Was there a consensus growing among the train passengers about the cause of death? The estimated time of departure? The estimated time of arrival in 1993? Roger sometimes had difficulty distinguishing between hunger, physical discomfort, anxiety, an oncoming bowel movement, or a new idea he was compelled to tell somebody. He felt something like this now, perhaps a new idea, and wondered if, whatever it was, would require action. But still. This couch was comfy. The drink was sweet. This woman kept dishing up distractions.

"I'm not asking you to keep me. I could never be a kept woman again."

"Tracey!" Mrs. Tillard called out. She had reappeared in the kitchen. "Don't let your showing off how clever you are take you places you don't want to go."

"I mean, tonight. It's New Year's. I'm sure I'm interrupting your plans."

"You're sure? Look around this house, me in my pajamas. You tell me what plans I have. You haven't even seen this town yet, but I'm sure you can guess. You're from PEI, after all. It can't be much more stimulating."

At "PEI," Roger was reminded again of the dance in Miminegash and the to-do list he should have been plowing through. Posting the liquor permits. Putting duct tape over the gap in the garage doors where the snow drifted in. Tending to—some may call it fawning over—the entertainers. Making sure Beatrice was satisfied with everything.

"I can see you're bored out of your mind! Jesus. And I haven't even gotten started. Another drink?" Tracey grabbed Roger's half-empty glass and bounced to the kitchen. He sat discombobulated.

"I'm so sorry," he said when Tracey returned with freshened concoctions, more pink this time. "I didn't mean to be rude. I'm organizing a New Year's dance back on the Island. It has to be a success...."

"Or what? They'll hunt you down with pitchforks?"

"We have to make some money this year...."

"Oh, capitalism again! Is there no human endeavour capitalism doesn't gobble up!"

"Money's only a means to an end. It's about the success of the centre. Reviving Acadian culture, building the community...."

"Acadian culture? That's rich. The Acadians are the Jews of the Maritimes. They'll get by all right. Believe me. Survive anything. Aren't you too tall to be an Acadian? I had you pegged as a WASP. Early thirties, divorced parents, right?"

As a retort was mustering itself in Roger's throat, Mr. Tillard appeared, snow falling off his boots and onto the carpet.

"You're still here? Your train's gone."

Roger ran to the back door, swinging his coat over his back, sticking his toe in his boots, and stomping down on the heels. "Bye, thanks!" he called out. He was halfway across the backyard before he realized he wasn't going anywhere.

Returning to the back step, Roger stopped for a moment and looked in the door's window like he had when he first arrived. Mrs. Tillard was carrying sheets and blankets through the kitchen into the living room. Tracey was working fruit onto the rim of two freshly filled glasses. Mr. Tillard was talking loudly like he was angry, though he fell silent when he spotted Roger in the window.

Apologies were exchanged all around. The one thing about missing a train that was running so incredibly late is that Roger wouldn't have to wait a whole twenty-four hours to catch the next one. After it was made explicit that Roger would be driven to the train station on New Year's Day, Mr. Tillard left for the Legion and Mrs. Tillard went over to her parents' side of the house.

Back in the living room, Roger and Tracey returned to their places, this time with Roger sitting atop the pile of sheets meant for him to sleep under.

"Well, the phone's there. It'll solve all your problems, I'm sure. Just leave a quarter when you're done," said Tracey. She grabbed the first magazine her hand fell upon and held it up to her face.

Mockery or not, Roger was not going to leave an invitation to use the phone unclaimed. Over the next few hours, Roger called the Acadian Centre sixteen times. Each time, he did it with a clear purpose or purposes, based on what should be happening at that moment. He'd have the phone passed from person to person, speaking to as many as six or seven people per call. Each conversation began with a series of questions, followed by a series of instructions, a few bursts of pure information, followed by a series of encouragements, and then a request to pass the phone along. By about 11pm, Roger learned that the party was sold out.

"It sounds crowded," he told Beatrice.

"You could say that." She was jammed into a corner behind the bar to give herself some elbow room. She didn't want to get Roger too excited. The New Year's Eve dance had been his idea. He had fought everyone tooth and nail to have it and had called in favours she didn't think the fledgling enterprise should yet be calling in. "It's a lovely crowd, some unexpected attendees," she said. What she meant was: everybody in Mimincgash, St. Louis-St. Edward, and a good chunk of Tignish.

"I wish I was there!"

"I wish your hands were here! We need a dozen more pairs."

For a while, Tracey pretended to ignore the stranger who had second-ed her living room as his command centre. His self-importance con-trasted strangely with his otherwise Polly Anna demeanour.

"Now," said Tracey, without putting down the *National Geographic* she was flipping through, "that call sounded like she's been beating her children and you're about to call social services."

"She wanted to know when to take out the ice cream to soften."

"I'm starting to understand why you're single. I don't think you're gay. You're soft but you're not gay. I think it's just that you're such a woman, you don't leave much room for a wifey."

"Have you ever been in love?"

"No," laughed Tracey as if he had finally got her one back.

"I have. I am. Whether I'm married or not, that doesn't matter a whit."

"Have it your way, baby. Look, it's almost midnight. You need to lay off the phone and let them celebrate."

"I want to hear them when they toast. I was supposed...."

"I was supposed to be married now. Or employed. But here I am. You're here. Let's toast ourselves."

"I had a speech."

"I'm all ears."

Aside from the long list of thank yous to people Tracey had never heard of, Roger's speech contained long sentimental passages about how Up Westers know how to party and how Acadian culture was making a comeback and bringing everybody together, and how much Acadian talent there was Up West.

"That's what you were going to say? I'm glad I'm the only one who had to suffer through it."

"You're a little mean." Roger felt mean for saying so.

"Shh, here we go."

Roger and Tracey raised their glasses toward each other and silently mouthed "Happy New Year" as if they were separated by a window. There was a masculine "whoop" from the other side of the laundry room; Roger wondered how spry Grandpa was. A few minutes later, the phone rang. Roger answered.

"Happy New Year, Roger. We had a lovely toast. One thing, though. Kate won't play," Beatrice said.

Roger could barely hear over the background noise. He made a mental note about improving the Acadian Centre's acoustics.

"Arnold Crozier says he doesn't want her playing. I was just going to put on a record, the Rankins maybe. People just want to dance. I thought you might be disappointed, so I wanted to tell you." Beatrice rarely hesitated in making decisions without Roger's input, so it would be fair to think that she mentioned this one because she wanted Roger to intervene.

"Arnold Crozier, that piece of...."

"Language!"

Arnold Crozier, who must have been mid-fifties at this time, had become one of the biggest wheeler-dealers in West Prince, rivalling Roger's former boss and mentor, Lester Shaw. After amassing a fair chunk of capital in the bootlegging business, Arnold had gone legit, his finger in several enterprises, including a few with Lester himself. Arnold's ex-wife, Marlene, and the kids had vacated the province without court approval, freeing up his alimony money for risky investments, like gambling machines, pyramid schemes, a blueberry farm, and a high-end spa development that would never break ground.

"God bless those immigrant investors!" Arnold would say, drinking beer at the Tignish Legion. "They paid their way into the country and, from what I've heard, they're in. Good for them."

Arnold had dated Kate on the sly for a while. He was acquaintances with her father, Albin Pineau, and visited the house many times before making his move. One stormy March day, Arnold was at the Pineaus sipping on rye, no ice, no water—the only drink he accepted when he was making calls. There wasn't a single car on Route 2, and Albin was in the garage looking for a hoist Arnold wanted to borrow. Kate's girls were parked in front of a video.

"You wanna eat something some time?" he asked Kate. "
By the looks of it, you'd like that."

Nobody thought Kate would ever court again. She was a single mother, but she was certainly no schemer, looking for a man to support her. If one turned up—why not? Nobody thought twice about the age difference. Fiddling for Roger's projects wouldn't pay the bills. Sherrie and Krystal were still a handful. Their grandmother, Regina Pineau, was getting too forgetful to be a reliable babysitter.

These pragmatic concerns flew in the face of what Roger wanted for Kate. Since the first Follies, Kate had been a remarkable protégé. There was such talent. But she was a strange mixture of disciplined and scattered. She showed up to about half her rehearsals, but even after an extended AWOL, always sounded better than she did the last time.

Her daughters treated Kate more like a big sister than a mother. Such a serious girl herself—bottled up, they called her—it was hard to imagine Kate had done the deed she must have done to have kids. And did it twice. Kate was the kind of girl who hung out only with other girls, looking at the ground when boys came around. She commemorated the birthdays of all her friends with handmade cards, sat at the front of the school bus, and studied hard, though she was only ever a C student. Her brother Noel called her a stupid priss until, on the third try, she got her driver's licence and was able to drive him home from parties.

When Kate got pregnant with Sherrie, Albin and Regina Pineau didn't utter a harsh word or ask who the father was. They acted as if someone had left the baby in a basket on their doorstep—a gift from God from which no moral lesson could be drawn. When Krystal came along two years later, Albin and Regina again remained tightlipped, though Regina started going to early morning mass on weekdays.

Kate didn't graduate from high school, though everybody thought she would have, if things had worked out differently. The girls, people said, had two different fathers, both smooth-talking patrons of The Regent nightclub in Summerside. Kate had no means of contacting them if she wanted to, which she didn't.

Arnold didn't seem to mind the girls, though Kate Pineau did her best to make them scarce when he was around.

"Arnold's not bad with them," she'd tell Beatrice. "A little gruff, but life can be a little gruff sometimes, don't you think?"

"Not among civilized people," said Beatrice.

Arnold had been picking up Kate from her meetings, rehearsals, and performances at the West Prince Acadian Centre. Roger didn't think much of him. Arnold never acknowledged Roger's existence, and exhibited no interest in the arts or Acadians more broadly speaking. He was Protestant Scottish but hadn't even heard of the MacKinnon family band in Richmond. Arnold claimed, on several occasions, that he didn't even know what a ceilidh was.

"That piece of trouble? Can I call him trouble?" Roger scoffed into the telephone receiver, although, at that moment, there was no one at the other end. Beatrice was in the process of passing the West Prince Acadian Centre's phone to Kate. Roger could tell from her breathing that she had her coat on.

"Kate?" said Roger.

"Roger, happy New Year to you."

"Happy New Year already?"

"I know, I know. But Arnold wants to go."

Kate wasn't apologizing to anybody for her relationship.

"No beau should ever pull you off the stage on which you belong."

"He's not pulling me any which way. I'm tired."

Since the Super Summer Follies '89, Kate had assumed a role that was a cross between trained monkey and spoiled diva. Roger got her on stage every opportunity he could. Beatrice had nothing against Kate, graceless thing she was, but wasn't interested in making anybody a star. As a girl, Beatrice had seen the Rockettes, a group where no dancer was presented as any more or less important than any other—it was a kind of egalitarian magic. Beatrice had her favourite acts, certainly, but these prejudices were vulnerabilities, not battle cries.

Mitchell, who paid attention only to women who were notably attractive or well-dressed, neither of which applied to Kate, mostly sided with Beatrice.

There were times that Roger's plans seemed to be more about leveraging Kate's talents than, as his grant applications stated, celebrating Acadian culture. At one point, the name of the organization was set to be Evangeline Unlimited. But Léonce LeBlanc, now a cabinet minister in the provincial government, thwarted this idea. Léonce had seen Follies '89, '90, and '92 and been quite impressed. Maybe Roger was worth worrying about, after all. On behalf of the Evangeline Co-op and Community Centre, Léonce LeBlanc quietly trademarked the word

"Evangeline" for use "in relation to a geographic region inhabited by people of Acadian descent; cultural centres aimed at people of Acadian descent or trading on Acadian history; and cultural festivals put on by, catering to or featuring the traits of people of Acadian descent."

Roger's ad hoc committee finally settled on the West Prince Acadian Centre. But creating an organization from scratch, and finding and renovating a home for it, was not sufficient to fully occupy Roger's attention.

★

In 1990, Roger had attended West Prince's first Friends for the Island Way of Life meeting, held at the Old Woodstock Schoolhouse. It was attended, as far as Roger could see, by a mix of farmers, Women's Institute members, and evangelicals from the nearby Woodstock United Baptist Church. Not a fisherman to be seen. Barely any Catholics. The meetings in Queens County for the group were said to be very well attended, drawing the back-to-nature types who worked at the federal Department of Veterans Affairs and lived in the hills outside Charlottetown, a small cohort of contrarian UPEI professors, and the members of the ferry workers' union. Raymond, were he still alive, would likely have been among their number.

At these meetings, held across the province in the wake of the pleb-iscite, people were warmer to the idea of a fixed link so long as it was purely in the abstract. Hardly a meeting passed where someone didn't make a plea for a tunnel. It was the details that got picked apart—the million tiny decisions that were made, and how they were made—that chiefly bugged the anti-linkers.

For most Islanders, it was about the risk. A bridge would be the biggest change the Island had ever seen. Bigger than the arrival of the French or the British implementation of the lottery that chopped the place up into sixty-seven mostly neglected territories. Bigger than the ban on pop and beer cans. No matter what the government and its scientists said, the things you never expected could happen would most definitely happen. The silty floor of the Northumberland Strait. People driving recklessly. The length of time tourists stayed. Summer cottages from away buying shorefront land. What teens wore. How lobsters tast-ed. How late bars stayed open. The number of prostitutes. If, when, and where you could shop on Sundays. Biker gangs, drug cartels. Connect to the rest of the world and nobody could predict all the threats to the Island Way of Life.

There were two mics at the Friends for the Island Way of Life meeting at the Old Woodstock Schoolhouse. They were opened to attendees right after the surprisingly short opening remarks.

Roger, it turns out, chose the wrong mic. Moderator Leo Chappell, brother of the former MLA and a postal worker from Tyne Valley, started with the mic to his left, and at that mic was Gwendolyn Czarnecki.

People on the Island pronounced her last name CHAR-nikee and she had long ago stopped correcting them. Roger had seen her on the *Compass* evening news a few times. Which told you that she was probably smart but certainly considered herself so. Gwendolyn Czarnecki was a marine biologist who had come to Atlantic Canada from Poland to study seals in the mid-1970s. She brought with her a stockpile of batik-print dresses that would last her into the second decade of the 21st century.

Gwendolyn Czarnecki did not have a mere folder, such as the one Roger held in his hand. She had a grocery-store shopping cart piled full of documents, paper sticking out of bindings at all angles. Gwendolyn started her speech with this ominous sentence: "There is some scientific data I would like to read into the record."

The fact that no one was recording the proceedings, or even taking notes, was no deterrent. Her voice was nasal. Her sentences flowed one into another without modulation. She read the values on tables and charts. She read species lists. She read snippets of Darwin.

When she was done forty-five minutes later, she had read into the record a quantity of data that, when summed up, had only one possible outcome: apocalypse. A nasty, brutish apocalypse, where erosion shrank the Island little by little, on every coast and every waterway, leaving, by the end of it, nary a place for anyone to stand, never mind farm a potato or two.

"I would like to close with a line or two from the esteemed L.M. Montgomery." Gwendolyn Czarnecki did not have to name the work from which they were drawn. "'We ARE rich,' said Anne staunchly. 'Look at the sea, girls—all silver and shadow and visions of things not seen. We couldn't enjoy its loveliness any more if we had millions of dollars and ropes of diamonds.'"

Those who couldn't remember a word Gwendolyn Czarnecki said remembered the ebullient applause that followed her speech. She spoke what sounded like the language of experts, of politicians, of scientists, of economists. It was a foreign language not many Up West could speak. She had driven all the way from Hunter River to bring them the Anti-Fixed Link Gospel. And those present were transformed into true believers.

"I have here a document produced by a researcher from Dalhousie University," said Roger, when the applause died down. But no one could hear him over the sound of chairs moving and people chatting on their way out. He spoke for five minutes and then, skipping over dozens of pages of material he had prepared, thanked everyone for their attention. When his mic was turned off, the only person remaining was Kate, whom Roger had dragged along for company. Mitchell had wisely passed on the event because of the rowed seating.

On their way to Roger's car, the two of them saw Gwendolyn Czarnecki was still in the parking lot repacking her shopping cart into her car's trunk. It was a cream-coloured 1986 Lada, very similar to Roger's own.

"Wanna say hi to her?" asked Kate.

"No, no!"

"I just thought.... She's got some big ideas, too. And you both have funny accents."

"Science without a soul won't get you very far."

Gwendolyn Czarnecki looked over at them and nodded discreetly, as if they were all in on a conspiracy. Purely out of politeness, Roger and Kate waved back.

Two weeks later, Roger hosted his own Friends of the Island Way of Life meeting at the Old Union Road Schoolhouse. Fifteen people attended, including Gwendolyn Czarnecki. Roger had no idea how the marine biologist found out about it.

There was enough space that night to disperse the chairs randomly around the schoolhouse's main room, making it possible for Mitchell to safely attend. Roger chaired the meeting and spoke first. He highlighted the Island's natural scenery, the relaxed pace of life, and the innocence of its children, all of which would be at risk if a bridge were built.

"Nicely done!" called out Susan Kennedy.

"Good for you, Roger!" called out Noel Pineau. He had been dragged there by Betty Ann and felt if he had to sit through it, he should say something.

"I have a few things to add," said Gwendolyn Czarnecki, who was seated in the corner furthest from Roger. As part of the Mitchell-proofing, the chair she ended up sitting in was facing out the back window and she had to look back over her shoulder to talk to people in the room. Gwendolyn spoke so fast Roger struggled to interrupt her position on the effect of redistributed wave patterns on south-shore erosion.

"Ten-minute time limit," Roger said. He was facing Mitchell's left side. Mitchell was in the centre of the room, facing the washrooms. "Other questions from the floor?"

"Yay, bridge! Let's go for it!" shouted Mitchell. Everyone laughed and got up to go as if the whole meeting had been a false alarm.

Gwendolyn Czarnecki sidled up to Roger after he had ushered everyone out. "Your father used to work at the university, I heard."

"How did you know that?" Roger did not make eye contact.

"Despite everything, there were several people who appreciated what Raymond did. His interest in hybrids. It was a big move coming here with a family. I couldn't have done it."

"But you're here now."

"Where are you from?"

"Here," said Roger. "On the John Joe Road, just up Union Road."

"I see. So that's where we are with this. I see. Totally." A self-pleased smile spread across Gwendolyn Czarnecki's face. "Worried I'll remind the tribe that we're a couple of come-from-aways. That none of this is our business because we weren't born here. You've got to keep your distance."

"Oh my, what a theory," said Roger. His mild hostility was toward what he saw as her more-than-platonic interest in him, which, if left unchecked, would be completely unmanageable. He was also, if he had the wherewithal to notice it in himself, jealous of her ability to dominate conversations. She was so serious and determined it made her hard to take. His hand did not make contact with her back, though it assumed a position that would have been appropriate for shoving someone out the door.

At *The Spectator-Herald*, Caroline did not know nor care why Roger and Gwendolyn Czarnecki, who were becoming the two biggest critics of the bridge to the mainland, had become rivals. But over the next couple of years, Caroline was the rivalry's victim and beneficiary. She would have stopped taking Roger's calls. She would have. Caroline was at an age where discarding high-school friendships would demonstrate she'd grown up. She'd moved to Summerside. She'd married Robert Doucette, who remained the second-most handsome guy ever to graduate from Westisle High and now had an office job with the provincial government. They had a son, Brian. She was a mother, a career woman. She was making new friends, some of them university educated. But every few calls from Roger, there was something in what he had to say.

Roger knew *The Spectator-Herald* went to press at noon, that Caroline went to lunch at 12:15pm and that at 1:15pm she checked her voicemail and started planning what she was going to write for the next day's edition. He liked to call at 1:45pm, the time she usually realized her voicemail had nothing interesting in it.

"There's no process for setting aside sections of the provincial environmental assessments like they've done," Roger would tell her. Or: "Are they going to tender the bridge without putting a limit on the bids? Are we going to pay ten billion dollars? Or, worse, five thousand dollars?"

Sometimes the story idea would start off stupid and Caroline would stare at the newsroom clock while Roger babbled away. Then Roger would drop a little bomb—"There's a clerk in the privy council office that might be able to send you a copy of the fax that was sent from the Prime Minister's Office to the Premier's Office demanding that a bridge should be built, no matter the results of the plebiscite"—and the ace reporter would scramble to catch up with her notetaking. Other times, she'd start off scribbling things down, then realize it was all leading to a poetry night, the widow Mrs. Phillippe Chaisson reading her own franglais adaptation of Longfellow's "Evangeline."

Caroline was never shy about being blunt. "Don't get all uppity with me, mister. The last cheque presentation you hauled me up there for was $488 and you know our minimum is five hundred dollars."

"It was $502 by the time you got here. We just didn't have time to change it on the big cheque."

"If you have the preliminary toxicity reports you mentioned yesterday, you can drop them off. Or you can never call again. Oh, the premier's calling. Bye."

Because *The Spectator-Herald's* publisher/editor, Basil Johnston, knew Caroline MacPhail had a relationship of some sort with Roger Niese, Caroline worried her boss would see her as playing favourites, or even flirting with a man she didn't much like. Because Robert Doucette worked in Charlottetown, and volunteered for a lot of committees, he wasn't around a lot. Caroline just didn't need her coworkers forming opinions.

To allay Basil's suspicions, she'd often take Roger's tips, then make a few other calls, getting people to speculate, just so Roger's name wouldn't appear in her stories about, as Basil dubbed the topic, "the Island's journey to connection."

For his part, Roger wasn't playing games or trying to drive Caroline mad. She had been irritated with him for so long, he no longer noticed. It was just that he had no idea which leaked documents were important nor where they ranked in journalistic importance in relation to his endeavours. Weren't clog-dancing Gallant twins as newsworthy as a secret ferry workers union meeting?

Gwendolyn Czarnecki was waging much the same campaign in the Charlottetown *Guardian*. Though Gwendolyn got on *Compass* more than Roger, her scoops were seldom as juicy. She lacked Roger's secret weapon: Phillip Sinclair. His father's old friend had been transferred from the National Capital Commission to the federal Department of the Environment where he vetted pertinent documents to make sure biological diversity played a part in Canada's future. Mr. Sinclair, based on his visit to the Island so many years ago, sentimentalized PEI as the million-acre farm. Ottawa had forced the bridge on Premier Joe Ghiz, his thinking went, the fisheries and rustic beauty be damned. If a bridge was built, the whole place would be turned into a suburb of Toronto.

Mr. Sinclair hadn't attended Raymond's funeral but sent a card on which, out of habit, he had included his phone and fax-machine numbers. In 1990, when Roger invested a sizable chunk of his inheritance in a fax machine, the first fax he sent was to Mr. Sinclair.

"Hey, Phillip!" he scrawled on a sheet of white paper. "Are you civil servants going to pave the whole province too???????"

Roger faxed the feds, he faxed the province, he faxed *Compass*, and he faxed the radio stations. As much as Caroline tired of Roger's calls, the reason she didn't cut him off altogether was because she dreaded his faxes, all of which went to the fax machine in Basil's office.

The publisher personally delivered each fax to reporters, along with thoughts and suggestions about each one.

Between the time Islanders voted on a fixed link in 1988 and the awarding of the bridge contract in December 1992, Roger had attended 117 meetings about the bridge, almost as many meetings as he had attended about establishing the West Prince Acadian Centre in Miminegash. These were halcyon days.

When the bridge contract was finally awarded to Northumberland Link Limited, lesser souls might have given the battle up and started counting construction jobs. But for the Friends of the Island Way of Life—by this time the group consisted of Roger Niese, Gwendolyn Czarnecki, and a small cohort of seniors, lefties, and members of the Pro-Life Action Alliance—the deal merely meant another entity to target.

On the afternoon of the signing, Roger faxed the successful bidder. "Why don't you admit that your massive hunk of concrete is going to kill a province's spirit along with its livelihood? Go home! Stop being a pawn of the machine!" he wrote to Vince Amato, the president of Northumberland Link Limited. By "go home," Roger did not mean, as some people who followed his letters in *The Spectator-Herald* and *The Guardian* wondered, Italy. Roger did not make any presumptions about Amato's origins. "Home" was undefined—anywhere but here.

Roger faxed Vince Amato something along those same lines almost every day. He had stopped while he was in Ottawa for the Christmas holidays; his mother had no fax machine. Sarah Carruthers and her husband Eddie Carruthers had moved to suburban Kanata and it wasn't as if Roger could walk to a Kinko's. He scrawled his notes on sheets of paper throughout the holidays. When he finally got back to PEI, he planned to fax Vince Amato a separate letter for each day he had missed.

★

Those letters to Vince Amato were packed in his suitcase, which was, at this moment on a train heading east, a train that no longer carried the passenger named Roger. Who was still on the phone pleading with Kate. As he talked, he stared at the Christmas tree of the Tillard family. The scraggly thing had obviously been dug up out of a ditch.

"Just two songs, Kate, please! Two! Arnold wants to hear you play. I'm sure he does."

"My fingers are too cold. It's rocking here, Roger. Did Beatrice tell you? The people turned away are drinking out on the wharf, freezing their asses off."

"They need to hear a good Acadian fiddle tune, Kate, or the evening will be wasted. I'm depending on you because I know you'll come through."

"Roger! I have me coat on!"

"Two songs!" Roger felt he had some traction. He leapt up from his spot on the Tillard's couch. The house shuddered when he landed. He always forgot he was a big man. "Then maybe an encore, which I'm sure you'll get."

"Arnold's waiting already, I suppose...."

"Break a leg, Kate! Break a leg."

"I think this'll be it, Roger."

"It will blow people away."

"I'm just saying, so you know. I know you don't like surprises. But this isn't getting me anywhere. And Beatrice still treats me like shit."

"I'll fix Beatrice."

"Roger, Roger. I can't be your star anymore."

"Star? Is that how you see yourself?"

"Well, I am." Kate looked at a poster over the bar. Her name took up half of it.

"Not Island-wide. Not Canadian. We're getting there, Kate, we're getting there. Just give me some more time."

"I gotta be a mum to my kids."

"Arnold Crozier is behind this, isn't he?"

"I'll be seeing you. Bye, Roger."

The phone line went dead.

"A bad breakup?" asked Tracey Tillard, who had made herself another cocktail.

"She is a genius of the fiddle, and she must share her gift with the world."

"Hm. I never knew they had any geniuses on PEI. By the way, have you read Deepak Chopra?"

But Roger was too distracted to answer. In his mind, he was standing about four feet from where he had instructed the stage to be set up at the West Prince Acadian Centre, at the end of the bar, right on the dance floor. From this imagined spot, Roger heard the first few notes of "La Betaille"—admittedly of Cajun origin. He shuffled back to the couch, spread himself out on its length, and rested his head upon the pillows Mrs. Tillard had piled there for him. He wasn't sure what Kate's second song would be, so his mind went directly to the encore, "Ste. Anne's Reel."

The phone rang.

"Are you taking calls?" asked Tracey, all secretary-like, as she went to answer it.

"Roger!" Beatrice's voice was muffled. She was at this moment crouched down behind the bar. The song "La Marmotteuse" swam around her vowels; the clanking of bottles and ice squeezed around her consonants. Kate Pineau hadn't even started playing "Ste. Anne's Reel" as her encore yet. Yes! She was playing a full set. "Roger? Someone wants to talk to you."

"But she's playing...."

"No, Roger. It's Vince Tomato."

"Who?"

"Amaretto? Armada? The Bridge Guy," said Beatrice. There were a few thumps and then Roger heard the voice of the bridge builder on the line.

"Roger Niese?" asked a deep male voice. It could have belonged to a politician if its owner had not sought the financial security ensured by obtaining an engineering degree. "It's Vince Amato, the president and CEO of NLL. You've been writing me letters?" There was a hearty laugh encased in this declaration.

Roger had at least two hundred things to say to Vince Amato. But the question had been framed in such a way that all he could say was, "Yes."

"I had hoped to find you here, at your dance," said the man who was going to end the Island way of life. "Here in, in Mimgash. It's a lovely place! Fantastic people and hospitality, I'll tell you. I've never been at such a party. You're quite the party planner."

"Mmm," said Roger. "Go on."

"I have noticed," said Vince Amato, "that the Mimgash Wharf is not in the best shape. I think the north pier—the pier on which your establishment is situated—could benefit from some concrete reinforcements. And I am willing to do that, Roger. We will do that. I don't expect it to change your feelings about the bridge. But I want to do it anyway. What do you say to that, Roger? I don't think the feds will say no."

"What do you know," Roger asked, shouting into the receiver as if he himself had to shout above the noise of partying and fiddle music, "about the precious balance of cultures of Canada's smallest province, Mr. Amato? You have successfully bid yourself into certain defeat! I don't know how much you spent to get this far, but it will have been a waste of money. A complete waste."

"I don't expect to convince you tonight, young man. But I wanted to see where you were coming from. And I can say it's from quite the rockin' time here in Mimgash! We will talk soon."

"I would wish you luck," Roger said, "except I don't."

There was some distortion in the phone's sound and, perhaps, snippets of "Ste. Anne's Reel."

"He's a handsome gentleman!" Beatrice was back on the line. "Wife is so polite, but a little full of herself." Beatrice had comped the couple drinks and wasn't about to apologize for it.

"The devil in disguise."

"You had your chat. Happy now?"

"Happy New Year, Beatrice. This next one's going to be huge."

"It may very well be."

After goodbyes, Roger finally stepped away from the phone. Silence. Silence. Silence. Then Tracey Tillard spoke up, reminding him of her presence and his current location.

"You were a right cunt there at the end."

"I had a speech prepared. He caught me off guard."

"No doubt." Tracey came close to Roger. He stepped back against the couch. In his split-second of unsteadiness, Tracey pushed Roger onto the pile of pillows there, landing herself and her extended tongue right on top of him. Roger opened his mouth and let his body catch her weight. It was the only polite thing to do. For several minutes, Tracey wiggled on top of him like a butterfly caught in a blob of glue. Then Tracey took Roger by the hand and led him upstairs.

Roger was enough of a man to know what was happening. He thought he was open to it, like he thought he was open to new ideas. He liked to meet new performers, hear new acts. But he also knew he couldn't be all there for it and felt some anticipatory guilt. He did not want this woman to get attached and then be disappointed.

"They sure as hell won't notice." She meant her parents, but Roger, though it made no sense, took her to be talking about his friends and colleagues on PEI. His chin was wet from the inaccuracy of Tracey's slobbering. His skin was damp, like the first few seconds of working hard, before measurable sweat breaks out.

From a hallway that seemed to have dozens of doors, they entered a tiny room which contained a beige two-seater couch and a wardrobe bulging with bedding packed inside.

"You do have a temper." Tracey sprawled on the couch, her legs and arms thrown this way and that. When Roger stood there passively for too long, she grabbed him by the shirt collar and pulled him on top of her.

For a large chunk of his life, Roger's virginity was the result of his saving himself for Debbie Arsenault. At an undetermined point between high school and the present, this pledge was forgotten. But like a virus, it had, in the meantime, worked itself deep into his psyche, becoming such a part of him that it was invisible to him, like being of European descent or being male. It shaped his life in such a way that he effortlessly remained celibate. Marla Bowness had given up after nine months.

Roger did register attractive women; he had not fully lapsed into asexuality. But he found all kinds of reasons not to let lust set up camp in his heart. For example, it would be unprofessional for him to flirt with the talent. Or anybody related to the talent. The community trusted him to be impartial and merit-oriented. There was always, in every encounter, a more important consideration than flirtation or seduction.

Tracey Tillard—now this was not what he expected. She was the smell of soap and the rustling of clothes in his ear. To avoid crushing her, he had to manage his weight with his knees and hands, something fictional fornicators, free of gravity, never seemed to have to do. As he steadied himself on the arm of the sofa, her hand got closer and closer to his cock. He only realized he was hard when she squeezed it.

"This is just the way to start the new year," said Tracey.

"I still feel the old year. It's still here."

"Let's scare it the fuck away."

★

When Roger made his way back to his designated sleeping spot on the downstairs couch, he saw that Tracey had lined up pillows under the bedspread, so it looked like someone was lying there in the dim lights of the ugly Christmas tree. He felt bad, not because he had had intercourse; he supposed it was normal for a man of his age, something he could check off his list of things to do. And not because Tracey was a slut or a seducer, though she was potty mouthed through the entanglement. He felt guilty for betraying Debbie Arsenault, even though he supposed she would respect him more as a sexual adventurer than as a celibate.

Even Michael Chaisson must have had his share before he took his vows. Roger envied the priest's vow of chastity. At least Michael didn't have to think about how or when to say no or yes or, worst of all, how to get to yes. Priests said "No" once and stuck with it. The voice telling you to say no—that was a valuable commodity.

★

CHAPTER 10

FIVE RAILWAY TIES, NEW enough to still be sticky with creosote, were strewn like drinking straws in the ditch at the corner of Palmer and Thompson roads. Straddling one of the ties, Roger Niese traced a trajectory in the air to figure out which direction it might have been headed. He knew where it had come from. Originally, it had come from his dreams.

Dead yellow grass, released from its prison of sharply frozen snow and ice, crunched under his feet as Roger made his way up out of the ditch to the shoulder of the road. Tire tracks were etched in the clay there, which had the consistency, typical in April, of unworked putty. If you dragged the gunk into the house, it would look like you had walked in cow shit.

"So greedy they got nothing," laughed Mitchell Gallant. He was kicking at the concrete foundations newly laid in this messy corner of what, beyond this project, would be a field of potatoes. "Idiots and assholes!"

"They got three," said Roger. He looked northeast up Palmer Road as if the culprits might have stopped there to wait for their pursuer to catch up with them. "They can't be from around here."

"I don't know, Rog. Lester Shaw's young fella. This'd be right up his alley."

Rodney Shaw, who had been given a Camaro and a cottage lot on Mill River for his sixteenth birthday, was said to be wilder than Ricky Gallant ever was, God rest Ricky's soul.

"Mean where the crazy should be," was how Mitchell described Rodney Shaw, repeating something he had heard his brother say. Rumour had it that Lester, who had been buying up much of the farm property in the area, had promised Rodney property at the corner of

Palmer and Thompson. It'd be his inheritance, if Rodney could behave himself.

The field was right across from St. Bernard's and any kind of enterprise might suit. Hardware store, bakery, variety store—you name it. But Rodney showed no signs of holding up his side of the bargain. The staff at the Sleepy Hollow Correctional Facility knew how he liked his coffee.

Roger finally got the federal and provincial governments to cough up some funding so that he might build a permanent multi-use Acadian Cultural Centre and Fun Park, the next-level successor to the West Prince Acadian Centre at the Miminegash Wharf. Lester Shaw read the stories about the project in *The Spectator-Herald* with the intensity of a code-cracker. He knew how politicians rounded their numbers off to the nearest hundreds of thousands or, as everyone saw in the case of the Confederation Bridge, the nearest hundred million. Lester also knew, from the days of the Dairy Bar Acadian Museum, that Roger wasn't much of a haggler. The sale of the five acres at Palmer and Thompson took eight months to sort out. The work it took not to mock and patronize was a challenge for Lester. So was not smelling like rye when Beatrice participated in the negotiations. It was worth all the tongue-biting when Lester got the hefty cheque for the property.

Rodney, of course, got wind of the deal his father had cut. The neighbours heard Rodney's arrival home, apparently from Montreal, which had taught him a few new curse words to shout.

Rodney had a right to be upset, people said. He was good-looking enough—in the lean way a coyote can be a handsome animal. But his good looks also worked against him. He had made cuckolds of many buddies. Roger didn't think he'd access to the manpower needed to pull off a theft that required muscle.

What would Rodney want with railway ties? He'd never build anything on that cottage lot, which was already covered with a layer of beer bottles that, his father swore to everyone at the Bloomfield Legion who'd listen, he wouldn't be cleaning up for him.

There had to be other suspects besides Rodney. There was no shortage of other hoodlums to blame. But perhaps it was more personal? Roger still believed Father Michael regularly conspired to thwart him. Father Michael certainly never said anything against the new Acadian Cultural Centre and Fun Park. But Tracey Tillard had reported many sightings of the priest's eye rolls, suppressed tsks, and sighs.

Tracey had shown up on Roger's doorstep, a bulging hockey bag in each hand, eighteen days after he had left the Tillard family home in New Brunswick on New Year's Day, 1993. Her glasses seemed even bigger on her. Her wispy arms were pulled taut by the bags. Roger barely acknowledged the remarkableness of her arrival. She explained she had come to return the $8.41 change from the money he mailed for the phone bill. More than a year later, she had not left Prince County, not even to go to the movies in Charlottetown. Every few weeks, Mrs. Tillard sent Tracey a big envelope stuffed with her mail, mostly record- and book-club catalogues.

Early on, when the length of Tracey's visit was still being measured in days, Roger wondered if she might be suitable as a wife substitute, that is, a wife in all ways except deep in the recesses of his heart. He had not seen Debbie Arsenault for so long, Roger did not find this idea too horribly distressing. Besides, Tracey, who did not seem to take much seriously, seemed like she'd understand. Quickly it became clear that this was not the role Tracey would fill. Conjugality was never in doubt. Tracey hadn't greeted Roger with so much as a hug or a kiss, but that first night at his place on the John Joe Road, she crawled into his bed, claimed her side, and then joined Roger on his.

Her sole attempt to make herself at home was moving Roger's clutter off the dining-room chair that became her magnetic north in the little house/trailer. Her clothing remained in her hockey bags, from which she extracted items as needed. Which is not to say that Tracey didn't care about her appearance. She worked her limited wardrobe with the savvy of a Manhattan secretary.

Tracey sat patiently in the truck while Roger and Mitchell wandered along the roadside, puzzling through what would only be the first of several mysteries they were to experience that day.

"We'll call the cops, that's what we'll do," Roger said to Mitchell, though his gaze lingered on the parish house for a moment.

"They didn't get nothing."

"They got two or three. Or four. Three or four is what they got. Probably realized their truck couldn't carry more. Then there were the bricks and the windows this winter."

"Oh yeah."

"And those bags of concrete."

"Right," said Mitchell, who, embarrassingly, had been the one to drop the building supplies on the lot in plain sight of the road where they sat weeks before they disappeared. The contractor, Léonce's LeBlanc Construction Limited, had at that point suggested Roger might want to take a step back from the construction project.

"Why not spend the time doing somethin' that pleases you? The Eptek Centre in Summerside. Well, don't they have a fine sports museum. Or stick your nose into the Confederation Centre in Charlottetown, a centre of the arts, par excellence. How many times you seen *Anne*? Never hurts to see the redhead another time," Léonce told Roger at one fundraiser. "Hop in your car! Community centres all over the Island. They got a dandy one there in New London. Take a gander at that one. Nice stage. Kitchen. She'd help you figure out what to put inside this barn when she's finished. If we ever finish 'er."

Not long after Léonce became a politician, he appointed his son Réné as titular head of the construction company. But Léonce, who had noticed Lester Shaw hanging around the project like a hungry puppy, handled the contracts for the Acadian Cultural Centre and Fun Park. Léonce was the one wielding the shovel during the ground-breaking the previous summer.

The LeBlancs had pretty much built the Evangeline region. Projects under their belt included the Acadian Museum in Miscouche, the Evangeline Co-op and Community Centre in Wellington, Evangeline High School and Library in Wellington, the dinner theatre Chez Michelle in Saint Raphael (at which Léonce was a regular diner), the tourist information kiosk in Abrams-Village, which was all but big enough to hold one person at a time, and the gift shop for Petey Arsenault's "House 'O Pottery," which was tucked in the woods on the road between Mont-Carmel and Cape Egmont and would be easily missed except for the massive wooden candelabra near the road.

Roger was surprised how often Léonce, the provincial cabinet minister responsible for tourism, arts, and culture, member of several boards of directors, and president of the Egmont Bay Knights of Columbus and Summerside Rotary Club, showed up to check on the project, even in the dead of winter. Hm.

"Hang quilts in the lobby? Yah think? You know they got themselves a quilts room at the museum in Miscouche, don't you? Pretty damn nice one. Does it make sense to have two? I dunno."

"It's actually a tearoom," said Roger. "The quilts are about the ambiance, to make it feel cozy. Local ladies, not the prize winners you've got down in Miscouche."

Léonce wondered how much construction would have to go over budget to keep quilts off the walls.

Léonce had been a regular visitor when Roger was running the West Prince Acadian Centre at the Miminegash Wharf, which had been one of the county's top tourist destinations before it was closed down so its funding could be directed to the new Palmer Road project. Léonce wanted to see how the place complemented or clashed with what the Evangeline Region was offering. That place didn't fit well at all. The people of St. Louis-St. Edward were nice enough, he gave them that. But they were sewing costumes and practicing tunes with an eye to pleasing their impresarios, Roger and Beatrice, not commemorating their ancestors. This new Acadian Cultural Centre and Fun Park, though, threatened to be a more professional, more institution-like enterprise. Staff would wear uniforms and give receipts, not IOUs.

The stray railway ties weren't going to relocate themselves. Roger and Mitchell wrapped their gloves in old paint rags that Roger kept in his truck. Neither of them wanted to mess up their gloves with creosote. One by one, they carried the errant ties back to the big pile on the far side of the main building's foundation. Roger didn't have a particular plan for the ties when he bought them, but one morning woke up in a delighted panic: a playground. They'd form something like a wharf, sitting next to the old fishing boat Roger'd had hauled onto the property. The boat already smelled like piss; the LeBlanc construction workers couldn't bother making the walk to the portapotty.

"Nobody's going to let their kids touch creosote," Beatrice warned. The fishing boat, for its part, had cost more to transport than buy.

"You're better off when you stick to your original plan," Tracey told Roger when she saw him sketching the playground. "You get yourself in trouble when you let something cheap or free lure you off track."

"The play-wharf was there in my brain all along, Tracey."

"Sure it was, honey," said Tracey. "Sure. Just don't let anybody give you a hangman's noose, because I don't wanna know what your brain would do with that."

If Beatrice's job was telling Roger what people expected, Tracey's job was to instigate other kinds of doubt. She went about it with unparalleled enthusiasm. But in other ways, she was low maintenance. When she first moved in, Roger worried she'd have to be entertained or chauffeured around to meet her own needs, like, he expected, finding a job. But Tracey was not to be babysat. She was at Roger's side when she thought the circumstance would be welcoming to her. When one of Roger's meetings or rehearsals or receptions threatened to be especially boring, she volunteered to drop Roger off and then run errands. In just ninety minutes, she could squeeze in a run to Summerside for a haircut, pick up a book she had special ordered at the Coles at the County Fair Mall, and buy a box of Tim Hortons Timbits. Roger stopped calculating how much gas he was putting into his truck. It was always almost on empty.

When Tracey started to seem like a permanent fixture, people were glad of it. Roger liked girls, after all. There was someone for everyone. More forebodingly: sometimes you had to leave the Island to find your match. Although Tracey seemed a bit big-feeling, maybe she'd ground him.

"She's got a mouth on her," Mitchell told Beatrice when he realized his buddy had become paired up.

"Nothing that comes out of it is very practical," Beatrice replied. "She lives in her own fantasy world. But fortunately, it doesn't have much effect on this one."

Roger lived in his own little world, too, but he was obsessed with building his. For the Acadian Cultural Centre and Fun Park, Roger was planning a configuration of smaller buildings that would surround the main building. The place mustn't be a mere hall or a theatre. It should feel like a village of Acadian-ness. The fun park, too, would be classy and Acadian in theme.

Roger liked to make things complicated, Tracey told him, because he liked explaining things, even if he didn't understand himself what he wanted. His grant applications were as long as the funding bodies would tolerate.

That morning, Roger and Mitchell had both spotted the stray railway ties at the same time. Tracey, who had been driving them over to Beatrice's for a meeting, pulled the truck over to the shoulder; the driveway was so chopped up by trucks before it froze, it would have ruined the suspension to pull in.

Tracey had the truck's heat up high as she watched Roger and

Mitchell scout around the construction site for other signs of infiltration. What a funny duo they were! Then she got bored. She looked down at her crossword puzzle. She had CBC's Arthur Black, whom she found both hysterical and awful, turned up loud on the radio. Her senses were fully occupied.

So, when a body went thud onto the truck's windshield, right in front of her face, Tracey nearly bit her tongue off.

First, she stomped on the brake. Reflexes. The truck wasn't even running. Then Tracey fell onto the horn with both hands and kept them there until Roger clambered out of the field, up the ditch, and across the driveway.

"Hey!" yelled Roger to what might have been a wind-blown scarecrow on the engine bonnet. He looked at what he had in his hand, hoping it would be a good weapon. It was a tape measure. "Get away, get away from her!"

"You! There you are, you fucking asshole." These last two words sounded awkward and stilted passing the lips of Gwendolyn Czarnecki, who never used such language. She realigned her aggression away from the truck and toward Roger. "I can't believe you!"

Roger went about pulling the woman off the truck's engine bonnet, which was surprisingly easy; Gwendolyn's body cared little about gravity. Tracey blankly slipped the truck into neutral. The vehicle rolled back, and Roger discovered Gwendolyn was not as light as he initially thought; it was just that whatever small part of her body touching the engine bonnet had been supporting ninety percent of her weight. When the truck moved, Roger was no longer able to hold her. The marine biologist fell down on the sharp frozen grass by the road.

"Oh, my goodness!" Gwendolyn reverted to old-lady speak. She was wearing a huge black parka out of which peeked a bright primary-colour-splashed scarf. "Sweet, sweet goodness! You foolish people! You careless, careless woman!"

"You do have ex-girlfriends lurking around!" Tracey felt cocky enough to roll down the truck's window. "This one's a real live wire!"

"Ms Czarnecki!" shouted Roger, finally figuring out who it was; the swearing had thrown him. "Are you hurt?"

"Aside from my pride and my trust? I don't know. Let me evaluate."

Gwendolyn, her butt and left leg dampening with each passing moment, became very quiet and still. Roger and Tracey, out of some sort of respect, joined her in this quiet stillness. Mitchell, thinking his friends must have just been killed, based on the silence following all the yelling, walked slowly and quietly from the construction zone and up the hill toward the truck. All parties could hear the stinging April wind blowing across the fields and whistling in the big oak and pine trees in front of the church.

Gwendolyn finally spoke. "My leg. I don't think it's broken. There are some scrapes. I don't know how many. A sprained arm? Perhaps."

"Lucky to be alive, you are," replied Tracey. "But my nerves have been snapped right off."

"Oh shit," said Roger.

"Oh shit," said Mitchell, arriving on the scene.

"Could you please help me up," said Gwendolyn, "and tell your wife to shut up or I will most definitely smack her."

"His wife. That's great!" laughed Mitchell. "They're not married."

A couple of cars going past gave them cheerful two-toot honks.

"Your ex is showing signs of jealousy. Interesting. Interesting," said Tracey, getting out of the truck. She carried a two-week-old *New York Times* under her arm as if she might have to swat a delinquent puppy across the nose. "I really would have thought that she'd have moved on...." Tracey slowly started to recognize Gwendolyn Czarnecki from the TV news; this was the fellow anti-fixed linker Roger had complained about. She certainly did look scrappy.

Roger shot Tracey the harshest look he could. Most of the time he was too busy with his thoughts to mind her foolishness, but he was already overwhelmed by what was happening around him.

Tracey shrugged and fell silent for a moment. She could not hold her tongue for long. "Why were you trying to make out with the truck?" she finally asked Gwendolyn.

"I have recently obtained information that has—I don't want to say corrected, even though that may sadly be the case—my opinion of you and your real goals." Not a once-bitten-twice-shy kind of gal, Gwendolyn pulled herself up on the truck's bumper and leaned crookedly against the grill.

"What do you know about railway ties, Ms Czarnecki?" asked Roger.

"Absolutely nothing."

"Hm. Let's see. Please keep answering the question. I do want to know what brought you all the way Up West today when there's not a Friends of the Island Way of Life meeting scheduled for weeks, Ms Czarnecki."

"Dr. Czarnecki, though I do appreciate the Ms. You don't get that around here very much."

Her lips locked shut like an unshucked oyster, Tracey nodded her head in agreement with the intruder.

"I thought I had found in you a brother in the Island way of life."

"Brother!" spat out Tracey. "Oh, brother!"

"But you have taken dirty money. The dirtiest money of all. And by doing so, you have tainted all of us. What am I saying—us? There is no us anymore."

"I don't know what you're talking about."

"Just because I don't live in Prince County doesn't mean I don't read *The Spectator-Herald*."

"Today's *Spectator-Herald*? Haven't seen it yet. Susan Kennedy must be running late," said Roger. A lightbulb went on in his head, "Oh, that item! That item wasn't supposed to run. I'll surely have a word with Caroline MacPhail about that."

"A word? You can't be serious," snapped Gwendolyn.

"I'm getting cold," said Tracey. "Can you state your complaint at a less glacial pace?"

"The bridge! You accepted money from NLL! The bridge company paid for your silence."

"No, no, no. That's not how it works. Nothing changed. Nothing changes. We got a little money toward this place. Some free concrete. No strings."

"The very same concrete that's going to drive down the reproductive rates of Northumberland Strait lobsters, Roger! You never cared about the environment at all."

"If this bridge gets built, and it's starting to look like it will, then the Island's going to be under a lot of pressure to change. The only thing we can do is shore up our defences. Invest in our culture."

"You don't have any credibility left."

Roger had lived with the passive-aggression of PEI so long he didn't know how to respond to direct accusations. Usually, the things he wanted to do were things that nobody else had thought of doing; his perennial problem was explaining, not defending.

He was embarrassed about how seventy thousand dollars from Vince Amato's Northumberland Link Limited (NLL) had found its way into the

Acadian Cultural Centre and Fun Park's bank account. It made sense, in retrospect, that Dr. Czarnecki was upset about it. But Roger couldn't take the credit for getting the NLL money. Dr. Czarnecki had picked the wrong target. The chief source of his embarrassment was how little he knew about it. It wouldn't be till later that he'd hear the whole story about how the Centre's integrity fell prey to a sweet talker.

★

The thing was, when Vince Amato and his wife attended the now famous 1993 New Year's party at the West Prince Acadian Centre at Miminegash Wharf, Beatrice had given the NLL president her telephone number, offering to broker a face-to-face meeting with Roger.

Mr. Amato's first call was to invite Beatrice to lunch at the newly renovated Oulton Fox House restaurant in Alberton, which wasn't cheap—a fish and chips set you back fifteen dollars.

At that time, the dining room manager was Angela Gaudet (formerly Ellsworth). After her shoplifting teenage years and a brief stint at the Miminegash fish plant, Angela had studied hospitality at Holland College and married Kevin Gaudet, who was originally from Summerside but worked at the Alberton liquor store. At Oulton Fox House, she was always offering wine so pricey that people joked that it was the same forever-unsold bottle every time.

When Mr. Amato ordered that very bottle for his lunch with Beatrice, without even so much as looking at the price, she was genuinely impressed. The gesture relaxed her; there was no way he would dare to ask her to go dutch. He was wearing a grey suit jacket and tie with jeans.

"I get the feeling people around here look up to you," said Mr. Amato, giving Beatrice a sincere smile. He was good at smiling. "You throw a great party without breaking a sweat." He poured some wine into her glass and nodded for her to try it. Beatrice was a little nervous in case the wine was corked and she didn't catch it, but he smiled again and she knew that whether it was corked or not, he wouldn't blame her for anything.

"Oh, it's nothing," said Beatrice, turning red.

"I understand you're a real going concern around here. Music, pageants, theatrical presentations."

"I do bring my own touch to local happenings."

Beatrice ordered the salmon and steamed vegetables. Vince Amato said, "That sounds delicious," and held up two fingers. He told a little joke and managed to make even Angela smile.

After the meal, Mr. Amato's hand fell on the bill as naturally as if he had been scratching an itch on his nose or brushing hair from his eyes— and what lovely black hair he had, a full head of it, though he must have been in his late forties. Beatrice's eyes lingered on the bill, but Mr. Amato, pointedly, didn't notice where she was looking.

"Well, this was fun," he said.

"Delightful!"

Angela gave him a big grin when she returned his Visa card.

"Never saw a card like this before," she said. "It's not Canadian, no?"

Beatrice watched every little movement the NLL president made with his big hands, putting the card back in his wallet, reaching into his jacket pocket—the lining looked so expensive—and pulling out another black leather object. Then there was a pen in his hand and Beatrice was so caught up in his movements that she didn't realize he was writing a cheque until the slip of paper was in her hand.

"Get that look off your face," he said. Mr. Amato's smile was full of self-satisfaction.

"I can't...."

"You don't have to. It's not a bribe or anything. It's not to you. I'll get a tax break, I think. Support the arts, they tell me."

"I can't..."

"You have to stop saying 'I.' You are on the board of a registered charity to which I have just made a donation. Just take it to your treasurer. Oh! I think you are the treasurer!"

Beatrice looked at the cheque. It was for eight hundred dollars. Not an outrageously generous figure. She had already costed out lunch at an indulgent fifty-six dollars. She could easily put the eight hundred dollars on the account at the Tignish Co-op and Roger would never even know about it.

Over the next few months, Beatrice and Vince lunched regularly. Well, Angela Gaudet called it regularly, even though Beatrice seemed thrilled each and every time. Beatrice became more and more relaxed when the bill came, her eyes taking in the lovely floral arrangements or the imitation Tiffany lighting fixtures, rather than catching a peek at the total. Beatrice had given up trying to make sense of the amounts on the cheques Vince Amato passed her at the end of each meal. $1,563. $215. $2,349. It was like a game on the Price Is Right.

The second cheque Beatrice locked in the bottom drawer of the filing cabinet in the office at the West Prince Acadian Centre at the wharf. She didn't dare take it home and she didn't dare make it look as if it was purposely hidden, so she stuck it in a folder full of outdated permits. The third, fourth, and fifth cheque also went into the folder. When the sixth was handed over and Beatrice realized the lunches might go on indefinitely, she took a good look at the West Prince Acadian Centre's accounting system. She realized could create a new "new donations" account Roger would not notice. When other donations started coming in, Mr. Amato's would, Beatrice hoped, be less conspicuous. After all, they had a new Centre to build and fundraising to do.

To keep everything as above board as possible, Beatrice set up the account with two other co-signers from the board. Mitchell was an obvious choice; he'd make a trip to the bank for the pleasure of ogling the younger tellers. She needed another co-signer. Meanwhile, Angela had witnessed too much at the lunches. Angela thought she knew everything about everything. "Sealing the deal, are we?" she said once as she watched Beatrice put a cheque in her purse.

Angela always thought Beatrice Perry was big-feeling. "Never saw the inside of a courtroom in her life," she laughed, having a cigarette at the Bloomfield Legion. "Or a cop car neither. That would take her down a peg or two."

The only solution to the Angela problem, Beatrice decided, was to appoint her co-treasurer and co-signatory for the charitable donations bank account of the Acadian Cultural Centre of Prince Edward Island Limited.

Angela accepted her appointment without a thank you or asking why. It seemed as if she was finally being shown the respect she deserved and never got. Her daughters might like a fiddling lesson or two, if it was free.

After a year of lunches—including in Charlottetown at the plush Pat's Rose and Grey Room where Beatrice had her first niçoise salad—it seemed as if the ritual might go on forever. Mr. Amato opened doors for her, complimented her, looked into her eyes as if he wanted nothing from her. She felt like a girl being courted and given access to all the nicer things PEI could offer. There was nothing to correct about him, from his wardrobe to his posture. Mrs. Amato never naturally came up in conversation, though Beatrice always asked about her.

Then one day in February, Beatrice got an unexpected call. Mr. Amato always called himself. This time it was his assistant.

"I have the promotional cheque facsimile here, Ms Perry," said a woman who sounded much too young to work for someone as important as Vince Amato. "We need to pick a time. How's about next Thursday, 3:30pm?"

In her eventual confession to Roger, after the *Spectator-Herald* item had been published, Beatrice did not describe the rest of this conversation. She was getting older and feared that every little misunderstanding raised the Alzheimer's spectre. But after a lengthy phone conversation, it became apparent that there was an oversized cheque for seventy thousand dollars from Northumberland Link Limited to the Acadian Cultural Centre of Prince Edward Island Limited, the sum of all the smaller cheques Beatrice had been given.

Beatrice was too polite to hang up. She stayed on the line as the assistant repeated, "Thursday, 3:30pm?" Then Beatrice came up with the only solution she could think of.

"I'm just so busy these days. Actually, can I let you know?"

This assistant, droopy as she might sound, was not about to let her oversized cheque go to waste. Twice a day for the next ten days, she called "to touch base" about a time for the photos. There had to be two versions, one for *The Spectator-Herald* and one for *The Guardian*; each paper required a "different" photo, even if that meant two people swapping places or someone putting on or taking off a scarf.

As a rule, Beatrice never screened her calls; emergencies lurked everywhere. But for the next ten days, she left the house before 8:30am every morning and never returned before 11pm. When she was forced to spend time at home, she turned up the volume of whatever was on CBC radio—rubbish like *Finkleman's 45s* or blessed *Island Morning* with Wayne Collins—so she couldn't so much as hear the ringing in her ears. She assumed that NLL was such a big company that someone low on the totem pole had scheduled the cheque presentation without asking Vince Amato about it. But Beatrice, who had the number for the president and CEO's direct line, was too nervous to call. She did not receive a lunch invitation after the assistant's call.

As long as there was no one to publicly accept the oversized cheque, Beatrice thought she was safe. Then, that one day in April, the same weekend someone stole railway ties from the Centre's construction site, a short item appeared in *The Spectator-Herald*.

As a rule, cheque presentation photos appeared on the last page of the news section, just before the sports section. The item in question—and this is what had people talking about it for weeks—contained no photo. But it read just like a photo caption, and it appeared on page two.

Vince Amato, president and CEO of Northumberland Link Limited, the company that was the successful bidder to build the fixed link, now specifically a bridge, from Prince Edward Island to New Brunswick and which currently awaits the conclusion of the federal environmental review, even as it dedicates itself to going ahead full-force to prepare the ground for implementation of the bridge structure, recently made a presentation to the Acadian Cultural Centre of Prince Edward Island, located in the St. Louis-St. Edward area of Prince County.

The Acadian Cultural Centre of Prince Edward Island, governed by a board of directors and accredited with charitable status, which received grants through the federal government's Atlantic Canada Opportunities Agency (ACOA), the provincial infrastructure development program, under the authority of minister Prouse Chappell, the provincial tourism growth program, under the authority of minister Léonce LeBlanc, and several other funding agencies which have been mentioned in previous news stories has accepted this presentation. The sum represented in the presentation is $70,000.

Present during the presentation was the Honourable Léonce LeBlanc, Minister of Tourism, Arts and Culture and founding member of the Acadian Museum, Evangeline Co-op and Community Centre, and many other vital and important celebrants of the history and richness of Acadian Culture. It may be noted that his son Réné LeBlanc is president of the construction company which, having made the lowest bid, won the contract to build the new Acadian Cultural Centre and Fun Park at the corner of Palmer Road and Thompson Road. "Acadian culture is everywhere and should be celebrated, regardless of the circumstances," Minister LeBlanc said.

Vince Amato, who is originally from Hamilton, Ontario, not Italy as some rumours have suggested, has been touring the province to explain the bridge concept, which he describes as "little more than a simple, unobtrusive concrete structure, repeated until it arrives on the other side," to Islanders. The team of the Acadian Cultural Centre of Prince Edward Island, responsible for the famous Super Summer Follies and other authentic Acadian talent-based experiences, must surely be glad for the boost.

These four paragraphs contained more to decode than an issue of *Pravda* during the height of the Cold War. Indeed, the story's provenance was even more complicated. Northumberland Link Limited had called the papers repeatedly to set up tentative times for a photo opportunity.

"Is the cheque worth more than $750? Can you prove it with a bank statement?" Caroline MacPhail asked. The NLL assistant started to feel she was getting the runaround. After a couple of weeks of this, a fax arrived headlined, "NLL Gives $70,000 to Building Fund of Beloved West Prince Institution."

"Pretty big money," said Basil Johnston, waving the fax in front of Caroline's face. "Surprised they didn't stretch it out. There must be a dozen photos' worth of money here."

"Seems strange," said Caroline. Strange that Roger wasn't crowing about it and also strange that he accepted it in the first place.

"You should write something. Maybe you can get some more news out of that Vince Armani guy."

On the afternoon the news release was issued, he had called Caroline about an upcoming seniors' tea party. Before Roger could start talking, Caroline played her hand. "I'll take the picture of the cheque. But you have to guarantee that I can ask the NLL guy a question or two. Otherwise, I'll make sure Helen Bernard gets sent to take the picture. As you well know, Helen hasn't figured out how to use the flash yet. You know that seventy thousand dollars is a lot of money for a picture so bad it'll end up buried in the classified section."

"What picture?" asked Roger, who was looking at the list of names of people scheduled to perform at the seniors' tea party.

"I didn't know you were in bed with the bridge people, but whatever floats your boat." Caroline was wondering if there could be a weekend feature on this topic—"Islanders Who Changed Their Minds About the Bridge: Are They Hypocrites?"—and if she could write such a piece without having to interview Roger for it.

Caroline read the fax three times to him. When it started to sink in that somebody close to him might have been doing something Roger didn't know about, Roger instantly stepped into protective mode. Whatever was going on, there must be a good reason for it. Mitchell might have gotten confused about something somebody said. Maybe Kate had come around, wanted to make up, and was secretly fundraising for the new Centre.

"I can't confirm anything, Caroline. I'm not saying it's wrong. I'm just saying that if you were to publish something like that, you might have to publish a big correction afterward."

Basil hated corrections. Especially corrections about companies like NLL he thought should be major advertisers in *The Spectator-Herald*.

"Okay, I'll wait to confirm some things."

"Confirm? What if I were to tell you that nobody from the Acadian Cultural Centre would pose for such a photo? What if that were the case?"

"Come again?" Caroline wished she had been taping the conversation—Roger turning down a photo opportunity.

"It's not something we're interested in," said Roger, trying, for the first time in his life, to sound uninterested in being written about. He was poor at being coy. But he liked how Caroline, for the first time ever, seemed to be on her back foot. He was mildly delighted, after all these years of trying to please her. It was almost as good as the buzz he got from staging a successful event.

"All right. Just this once. Just because people need a break from you. I do, anyway. It's my decision but I'm going to agree with you this time. Because it's easier for me. Not because you tell me what should or should not go into the paper because that's unacceptable. Understand?"

"Understood."

Caroline put the fax in her slush pile. The matter might have ended there. But a few days later, Basil had fished it out of Caroline's wire basket.

"When is this event happening?"

"It's not. There's no time set up. There won't be. Roger won't have his photo taken."

As soon as she said it, Caroline realized she had broken the cardinal rule of never telling Basil Johnston anything more than he needed to know.

"Indeed," said the publisher/editor. Caroline saw, behind his smudged eyeglasses, the sparkle you might see in the eyes of someone challenged to a duel.

Caroline quietly warned most of the reporters that, whatever Basil said, the item should not run, especially not without a photo. It was embarrassingly unjournalistic. But Helen Bernard, who mostly wrote about school boards, town councils, and card parties, did not overhear Caroline's pleading to the other reporters. A story was published. That strange little story in that morning's paper.

When that edition of *The Spectator-Herald* arrived in Gwendolyn's mailbox on Saturday morning, she nearly choked on her muesli. She and Roger had never seen eye-to-eye on what was wrong with the fixed link, but she had never expected him to completely flip sides. She had not merely lost an ally, if not a friend, but she had gained a new target for scorn. She sincerely believed there was still time left to scuttle the bridge project; even after some concrete had been poured, there was still time. But Roger had jumped ship at the first sight of a big cheque. What an asshole!

Gwendolyn left three messages in Caroline's voicemail, six on Roger's. When none of these messages was quickly returned, her anger prompted her to hop in her Lada and drive west. She had to see the grand project that was worth betraying your beliefs for. She would not condone vandalism—and honestly, she wouldn't dream of touching a creosote-saturated railway tie—but it would be a lie to say it didn't pass through her head. Action was necessary whatever the cost.

Now here she was, having thrown herself at Roger's parked truck, bruised and bleeding on the side of the road. Her former ally, his strange girlfriend, and his best friend were staring at her. She had their attention. She might as well make her case.

"You need to give the money back, Roger," said Gwendolyn, rearranging her backside on the truck's engine bonnet to get more comfortable. "It's blood money."

Roger, who wasn't sure exactly where the money was or how the Centre had come by it, shrugged his shoulders. Whereas another man might have been flattered that a woman with whom he shared history had jumped in a car and driven all the way Up West to confront him. There had to be some emotional attachment there. But because Roger had none for her, he didn't take it that way. What he saw was that his project was attracting attention, both positive and negative. He'd have to redouble his efforts. He'd have to be more of a man.

"Hm," Roger said to Gwendolyn.

"I didn't think lobsters had any blood," interjected Tracey.

That's when Susan Kennedy came along in her Honda. When the magnetized *Spectator-Herald* sign was attached to the side of her car, the yellow flashing light attached to her roof, people got out of her way. Spotting Roger's truck and, nearby, Gwendolyn's car on the side of the road, Susan pulled over to see what was going on. It was hard not to notice the bashed-up Gwendolyn Czarnecki, agitated and perhaps in pain. Susan did not even know what to ask first.

"Everything's all right here?" she said, eager to be corrected.

Roger, who was still more interested in his railway-tie mystery than Gwendolyn's good repair, wasn't going to indulge Susan's curiosity. "We didn't get our paper this morning."

"No? Really? Maybe it got kicked somewhere? Here's a replacement. Free of charge, as they like to say."

"I'll take it," said Tracey. She grabbed the paper and jammed it into her *New York Times* as if she was hiding a lottery ticket from in-laws. She had read *The Spectator-Herald* before Roger got up, and, seeing there was more distressing news in it than what had set off Gwendolyn, hidden it.

"Now, did someone try to run off with your railway ties?" asked Susan, noticing the filth on Roger and Mitchell's hands, the marks in the earth. She was sufficiently intrigued by what was going on at the future home of the Acadian Culture Centre and Fun Park that she was willing to let some locals wait a few minutes longer for that day's news.

"I think that might be true," said Roger.

"Who do you think might have done it?" asked Susan, who would have loved to have Roger drop a few names that she could repeat to others she ran into on her paper route. The named parties might not be responsible, but repeating the allegation was a good way to fish for other gossip about them.

"Who do you think might have done it?" Roger tossed the question back to Susan.

"Hmmm," said Susan. "I'd ask Father Michael. I mean, he's right over there. Maybe he was looking out the window."

"I think I should," said Roger suspiciously. "I wonder what he'd have to say for himself."

"You're getting all detective-like now," said Tracey. She giggled. "This could be spectacular."

"I think," said Gwendolyn, growing bored by the parochial turn the conversation had taken, "that I do require a bandage or some such medical gauzing."

"Ew," said Mitchell, noticing the smear of blood on the truck's engine bonnet.

Susan covered the front seat in her car with a blanket and drove Gwendolyn over to the parish house. The rest of them walked over. Roger hung his head. This was all so frustrating. The NLL story in the paper, the railway ties, Gwendolyn's temper, Susan's nosiness. It felt like everything was conspiring against his success.

"I was wondering about the fuss over there," said Father Michael. The parish house must have been twenty-five degrees Celsius, and the furnace was still roaring. The priest wore a blue Nike tank top and matching running shorts. "Come in, come in, come in."

Susan entered with Gwendolyn, who she left on a chair in the living room couch before going to the kitchen to put on a kettle. Susan then rummaged through the cupboards to see if she could find sweets, which the priest was regularly given but never ate. She found a selection of not-quite-stale squares and put them on the living room coffee table. That day, nobody on the Palmer Road got their *Spectator-Herald* before 2pm.

"I'm not a believer in spiritual things, Father," said Gwendolyn. "But if you have an antibiotic cream, I'd be amenable to a dab."

"A little dab'll do yah," said Mitchell, who was standing in the porch, reluctant to take off his boots.

"I'll see what I can rummage up for you, dear," said Susan. They might start a juicy conversation more easily if she was out of sight.

"Are you okay?" Father Michael asked Gwendolyn, who he recognized from the TV news. He had no idea what was going on.

"She tripped," said Mitchell. "Over at the building site. It wasn't our fault." This wasn't exactly a lie; Mitchell hadn't been looking and was just guessing.

"Oh, I see. Poor dear," said Father Michael. He was wary of the stranger, despite her familiar face. This one might go running to that Tanya Moase, the toughest reporter on CBC's evening news program, about whatever had happened to her. He'd be made to look bad. People loved to accuse priests of things these days. "Susan will get you fixed up."

Father Michael turned to Roger. "Your project is starting to come together. There'll be lots of construction activity over there by summer. I hope it's not too noisy."

"Already a lot of activity over there," Tracey said. "Crime and drama and bloodshed—imagine when the place is finished." She was taking in the tchotchkes around the room—lacquered bowls, ornate frames around landscape photos, figurines of metal and wood—wondering if they signified queerness or merely priestliness. It had occurred to her that the tension between Roger and his old high-school rival could be sexual; it might be a fun thought exercise to assign each of the men the roles of desired and desirer.

"Where do you stand on the bridge, Padre?" asked Gwendolyn. The priest leaned primly back in his straight-back chair. The sound of Saturday morning CBC radio wafted from the kitchen. "Pro or con? Where does your Jesus stand?"

"That's a few sermons' worth of questions, Mrs., Mrs...."

"You can call me Gwendolyn," the marine biologist replied, "if you say you're against the bridge. Real advocates of democracy and Earth-friendly engagements are in short supply. Fake ones can be bought for a price. Did you know the Centre took $70,000 from NLL?"

"I did not," said the priest. "But I'm not sure it's such a bad thing, to accept a bit of money from someone who wants to help out. It's not like the money's coming from drugs or prostitution."

"But environmental destruction, that's all fine for you and your Bible?" snapped Gwendolyn.

Roger sat quietly on the sofa, his hands restrained under his weight. These weren't issues he wanted to get into right now.

"You never know who's up to what," said Mitchell.

Susan arrived with a tube of cream, some bandages, and scissors. She all but threw them at Gwendolyn and then took a seat in the middle of the couch between Roger and Tracey.

"I'm sure taking money from the bridge people is not all as clear cut as, say, abortion, is it, Father?" asked Susan.

"Sin can come from anywhere," posited Father Michael. He did not want to look like he was judging whatever Roger might have done, nor did he want to let him off the hook, if it turned out that serious corruption had occurred.

"I come from New Brunswick," said Tracey.

"I'm sure your people there miss you, dear," said Susan, tartly. "And who are your folks, Miss Carneekey? From around here?"

"Irrelevant," said Gwendolyn. "And can I tell you I'm so tired of that question?"

"Down East, I suppose, then," said Susan.

"This environmental review process is ridiculous. They've already said yes, without any baseline data, and we're expected to think the project is anything but a fait accompli." Gwendolyn's energy was coming back. "Why do they bother engaging Islanders and, dare I say, other stakeholders? It's patronizing but I suppose it's all we have. The mercy of condescension."

"You didn't, ah, hear anything out on the corner last night or early this morning," asked Roger. "Did you, Father?"

"Why," said Father Michael, "I might have heard a little rumbling."

"Did you now?"

"The ripping and tearing up and down the Palmer Road," said Father Michael. "I don't have to tell you."

"I suppose you don't," said Roger.

"Those railway ties aren't free, no, they're not," said Mitchell.

"Ah, yes," said Father Michael. "I saw some out there on the side of the road this morning. Was that what you were doing over there?"

Roger took a deep breath. His frustration with the lack of concern about the real issue—getting the Centre built—came out in a tinny burst.

"I'm trying to get this playground ready, so when the centre is done and there's a play or concert going on, kids aren't left out. If they're not interested or the like. And I think that the fishing boat—it's as much a symbol of this area as anything. I'm also thinking of some climbing gym, with rope swings and monkey bars. That means you've got exercise—healthy living. What I'd also like to see is a little snack bar. Nothing too complicated. Nothing to compete with the dairy bar in Huntley or anything like that, though maybe a bit of hard ice cream. Apples when it's apple season. Kids like apples more than potatoes, I'm thinking, unless they're fries and I'm not sure if I want a deep fryer out in the snack bar. I suppose we could make them in the Centre's kitchen and bring them out. That's another approach. Could make a bit of procession, bringing the fries out. The MacKinnons could play the bagpipe, though I suppose it would mean a lot of waiting around. Depends on how busy it is. How hungry people are. I suppose if there was a running track or sports field, they'd be tuckered out and starved. Makes you think we should have gotten another acre or two. But then security, I guess...."

"Well, then," said Father Michael.

"My," said Susan, "that all sounds family friendly, at least." She thought the West Prince Acadian Centre in Miminegash had turned into an even more lawless version of the Legion; the posters for "culture" were little more than a cover for late-night parties. Which was fine. Young people were entitled to a good time. But it wasn't a place you'd hang art or host discussions about poetry. Having the Centre closer to the church, Susan figured, would have to be an improvement.

"Any other leads for us," said Tracey, "in the case of the missing railway ties. Father?"

Father Michael bit his lower lip, which was still full and sensual, even as the man himself had dried up a bit as he had gotten older. He shook his head. Roger's paranoia about the priest, Tracey thought, wasn't so out there.

"Roger, I need to find out what happened with that money," Gwendolyn blurted out. She was starting to realize that she had been the victim of her own plummeting blood sugar levels for most of the morning. The brownies had done her more good than the bandages. "Were you lied to? Was it Vince Amato himself trying to get you off his back? This could work to our advantage."

Father Michael noticed some copies of *The Spectator-Herald* sticking out of Susan's shoulder bag. "Today's? May I? I've been waiting all morning."

"Of course, Father."

As Father Michael took the paper, Tracey had something of a spasm and knocked her tea onto the priest's bare legs.

"Yikes! Ow, ow, ow," said the priest, dashing off to find himself a tea towel. Tracey leaned forward and discreetly grabbed *The Spectator-Herald* from where it had fallen on the floor. Roger saw her do it. Was she involved with the $70,000, he wondered, and trying to hide her involvement?

"What a klutz I am! Oh, what a silly thing I am!" said Tracey.

"Do you have to pay for the papers that go missing, Mrs. Kennedy?" asked Mitchell. "Does somebody not get their *Spectator-Herald*?"

"Don't worry about that, Mitchell," Susan Kennedy said. "Everybody will get their *Spectator-Herald*. I will make sure everybody knows what's going on." To several people in the room, this sounded like a threat.

"Well," said Gwendolyn, getting up. "I want you to think of what I said, Roger. Let it sink in. You can still recant. Say you were lied to, like they're lying about the environmental destruction. Say that $700,000 was thrust upon you. You can use this to bring down NLL. I know you can." She smiled meekly at the priest, who had come back into the room after pulling on a pair of track pants so as not to distract everybody with his reddened calves.

"Oh, that story about the NLL cheque! That's what you're on about. Take the money and ask forgiveness is what I say," said Susan, looking at Father Michael. She had herself gone to confession in Tignish earlier that week and found that she had had nothing whatsoever to say to Father Euseb Arsenault.

"You will figure these things out for yourself, Roger," said Father Michael. "Oh, by the way," he added, as casually as anything. "I ran into our mutual friend."

Roger instantly knew who the priest was talking about. It was the moment for which he had been waiting for years. He realized this was the reason he still went to mass, in case she ever showed up.

"Oh, who?"

"Well, remember little Debbie Arsenault? Oh, that's awful! Listen to me! Obviously, she's not little anymore. Well, didn't I see her in the Charlottetown Mall. We had a great chat."

Roger started to choke, quickly hiding it in a cough.

"Did you now? You saw her?" Roger didn't care if he sounded fake. He had to hold himself in check. He was unsure what might fly out of the Pandora's Box in his heart. He might cheer. He might fall apart. He might leap across the room and strangle Father Michael. Any reaction was possible.

"She looked very well."

"Did she now?" asked Roger. He nodded like he was being given instructions on taking a medication to ease the pain of terminal cancer.

"She looked very well. And her daughter is up living in Montreal. Apparently, a bright young woman. We wished each other the best. It was nice to see someone from the past."

The loss of blood from Roger's extremities made his skin translucent. He could not determine his emotional state, though if anyone had dared look him directly in the eyes, they might have guessed boundless grief.

Then, there it was. Disappointment. Roger didn't want to believe it was that easy to run into Debbie Arsenault or that it was that possible to so simply sum up the story of her life in the years since she disappeared from his. He resented Father Michael for doing so. The priest's casual recapping—it must have been done with malice. Roger had imagined Debbie moving from place to place—port towns, hollowed-out American metropolises—struggling to put food on the table, relying on a series of odd jobs, lovers, and underworld types to stay afloat so far from her roots. She wasn't supposed to be shopping at the Sobeys on the way home from a PTA meeting.

"Imagine that!" said Susan. "She's still living and breathing. God does watch over some people."

"So he does, Mrs. Kennedy. So he does," said Father Michael, who looked somewhat more relaxed than he had a few moments earlier.

"This is why nothing ever changes in this province. Fate! This strange faith in fate," said Gwendolyn, stomping her feet loudly as if to make sure her boots were on tight. She was back to being feisty. "Oh, why take any action? It'll all work out!"

"You say that like it's a bad thing," scowled Susan.

"See you tonight at mass, father," said Mitchell, saluting his goodbye.

"Oh, Roger," said Gwendolyn. "Sorry about that other thing in the paper. But I guess you're used to it by now."

"Sure, sure," said Roger absentmindedly. Then he thought a bit more. "Excuse me. What?" But Gwendolyn, already out on the front step, didn't hear him.

They all left the rectory property at once, each heading back to the vehicle he or she had arrived in.

"This Debbie Arsenault?" Tracey asked Roger in the truck. "She's more than your average ex, isn't she?"

"I don't know why he'd be saying it like that."

Roger was silent for a few moments.

"You okay?" Tracey didn't know another question to ask. "I'm just hunky-dory myself."

"Dreaming up a little fundraiser for Friends of the Island Way of Life. That's what I'm doing now. I guess we have to counter this $70,000."

"Is that really what you're thinking about now?" said Tracey. She was glad Roger seemed unable to tell the difference between her concerned tone and her sarcastic one; of course, maybe her concern was always a bit sarcastic. She looked hard at her lover. In bed, Roger was a playful kitten, batting at a piece of yarn caught in a sunbeam. Primal, passionate desire always seemed beyond him. But right now. Oh, right now, Roger was tormented by thwarted desire. She could see it on his face.

"And calling the police. We'll call the police about those railway ties." Roger's distress came to rest back on a problem that could be solved with ingenuity and shoe leather.

"What are they going to do, Roger? Nothing except get up in your business. And God knows you got yourself involved in a lot of business. As they might say."

"They should be up to date on what's happening right under their noses. There should be a neighbourhood watch or something."

"Or something."

Back at the house/trailer, Roger did not call the police. He puttered for a while, then decided to take his mind off things. Tracey had gotten distracted by the TV and hadn't touched her *New York Times*. Roger picked it up. Just after the arts section, he found two copies of the latest *The Spectator-Herald*, one that Tracey had accepted from Susan, one she had taken from Father Michael.

Roger went looking for the article that had caused Gwendolyn to flip out, though Caroline had already, of course, told him the gist of it.

But the first thing that caught his eye was another item.

It was a soft-news feature filling the first column on the front page and turning to page three. "Documentary Captures Pride of Acadia" declared the headline over Caroline MacPhail's byline. The heading over the page-three photo of Léonce LeBlanc, Father Euseb Arsenault, Father Michael, and, fiddle in hand, Kate Pineau was, "Interviews Done, Doc Just Needs Editing."

Clem Cormier of North Rustico, son of Ronald and Gertrude Cormier, rounded up more than just the usual suspects in his Canada Council-funded feature-length documentary about influential Acadians of Prince Edward Island. Filmed over the last year, he has interviewed more than 100 movers and shakers from North Point to Charlottetown—and beyond. If Cormier can find funders to help him finish the film, melting down hundreds of hours of footage into a feature-length documentary, Islanders will soon see the best of what Acadian culture has to offer.

"We're also so overjoyed, really, really thrilled about this exciting project," says Father Michael Chaisson. "There's just so much talent and so many people working so hard. I drive through the Evangeline region, for meetings and so on, and I see so much activity. Here in our parish, there's women's groups and the Knights of Columbus and our own funeral co-op, which I'm especially proud of."

And then later in the piece:

Kate Pineau, a parishioner of Chaisson's St. Bernard's parish, has been performing all over the Island for the past few years, making appearances at the opening of the Confederation Centre of the Arts in Charlottetown, home of Anne of Green Gables—The Musical, and The Cavendish Boardwalk.

Tracey caught a glimpse of Roger with the paper. Oh no. Her plan had failed. But then: was she going to be able to prevent him from reviewing *The Spectator-Herald*? She couldn't look at his sad, disappointed face. She grabbed the telephone and tucked herself away in the backroom beside the deep freeze.

"Kate," she said in a cheerful whisper. "Saw your picture in the paper. Looking good."

"Thanks! Who's this?"

"Tracey. Tracey Tillard. I live with Roger?" Her voice went up at the end of "Roger" like she wasn't so sure.

"Oh," said Kate, a note of uncertainty in her voice.

"I was just wondering. Maybe you don't know. I just thought I'd ask you. Why wasn't Roger in that article?"

"Oh," said Kate. "Nobody said nothing about it to me. Roger's always into everything. I thought he was in it too."

"You thought that?"

"I don't know. I just did what that guy, the documentary guy, asked. He's just a regular guy, no big talk or anything. I did the interview 'cause he asked and I did the photo 'cause he asked nice. Are you calling to give me hell?"

Tracey thought for a few seconds. "No, it was a lovely photo. I just wanted to tell you I saw it."

"Thanks."

"Oh, Kate. Did you go to school with a Debbie Arsenault?"

"Lucy Arsenault? Ralph's?"

"No?"

"Cathy Arsenault from Bloomfield?"

"No." Tracey had browsed the PEI phone book and knew this could go on for a while.

"...Oh, her. She was before my time. More trouble than Angela Gaudet, back when Angela was an Ellsworth."

"Okay, then. Thanks for your help."

Tracey went back to the kitchen where Roger was still staring at the newspaper.

"Maybe it's not finished yet," she said cheerfully. "That documentary guy. Sounds like a total asshole, if you ask me. Never heard of him."

Roger ran some water to make a cup of instant coffee. He started prattling on with inconsequential nonsense, asking Tracey if she wanted some, muttering to the coffee bottle when it nearly fell out of his hand, shushing the spoon when he dropped it on the counter, and tsk-tsking the kettle when he splashed boiling water on himself. When Roger at long last got his coffee into a drinkable state, he spoke as much to the kitchen as to Tracey.

"I have to call the architects today. I realized we forgot something. I had so much on my mind that it slipped. We all make mistakes some-times. The thing that's needed. Well, you'll laugh at it. You'll laugh when I tell. I knew it all along, though I forgot it. Not a big one, mind you. Not going to be broadcasting any hockey games or anything. Though I suppose we could go out and shoot one."

"Roger?"

"A TV studio. Just off the great hall. Just got to partition things a little differently. I suppose we could build a little shed for the kitchen pantry if they were to tell me there was no room for it."

"A TV studio?"

"All kinds of things could come out of there. But to start, I figured a weekly show. A magazine, say. Don't you think that's a dandy idea? A magazine, except on TV."

"That is a dandy idea, Roger," Tracey said as sprightly as she dared.

The next Monday, over tea in her living room, Beatrice confessed everything to Roger. She had fallen into Vince Amato's trap. The bait— his manners, his taste, his disarming smile—had been so alluring she accepted the cheques without even thinking about them.

"I must remind you of some sort of vain old lady," Beatrice told Roger.

"Never," said Roger. "You'll always be a role model."

Roger was, in truth, glad Beatrice had corrupted the Centre a little. Since his tangle years earlier with the Pro-Life Action Alliance, about anti-abortion sponsorship of the Super Summer Follies, he had grown more ethically lackadaisical. What happened backstage needed to matter less. He was moving his vision forward to move the community forward. There were many ways to do so. As embarrassing as it had been for Beatrice, her courtship of Vince Amato had helped Roger turn a corner; there were so many cedar shingles that needed to be paid for. Anything that kept away people, or dollars, needed to be sidelined.

"We might have to hire a real accountant," said Beatrice. "Didn't Betty Ann Pineau do some courses? Tracey certainly can't add two and two. I can ask around. I don't even know how much those railway ties were worth. Do you?"

Though neither Beatrice nor Roger were financial whizzes, the two of them ended up being very savvy fundraisers. Before the Centre held its grand opening, nearly everybody who lived west of Tyne Valley had donated at least twenty bucks to the cause. Some donated much, much more.

"I can't believe someone tried to steal them." Roger furrowed his brow. He always had a hard time believing people weren't on the same page he was. He was so lucky to have Beatrice, who was capable of getting everybody on her page.

"People do mean things," Beatrice told Roger. "It's rarely malice, mostly incompetence and insensitivity." The woman, best known for her expertise in keeping up appearances, had grown more philosophical after joining a book club that, over time, drifted toward theological, moral, and ethical topics. The club was hosted by a group of ladies from Charlottetown, most of them former pageant girls, all of them younger than Beatrice. They looked up to her and declared, behind her back, that she had gotten the whole aging thing just right. Beatrice liked to make a day of it when she drove to the city for the club meetings, often dining at Pat's Rose and Grey Room, her attempt to create new memories at the restaurant, so diminishing the memories of being played by Vince Amato.

"But you're saying it is malice sometimes?"

"I'm saying most of the time, no."

"Well, how can I know?"

"You don't, Roger. You just carry on."

★

That spring, the Acadian Cultural Centre and Fun Park lost a truck load of bricks, three windows, nine more bags of concrete mix, enough wiring for two houses, eight sink traps, and a nice little wood stove meant for an outbuilding of some unspecified purpose. Roger seemed the most to blame for these thefts—either because of carelessness or the target he had painted on his head. Using his own money, he replaced the windows before the contractors noticed they were gone since the discovery would prompt them to sit in their trucks drinking coffee for a half-day until Réné or Léonce LeBlanc showed up to tell them what to do about it. Roger bought the windows from Arnold Crozier for way too much money, even though they weren't the right size. Kate tried to make Arnold return the money; he agreed to buying the windows back at five percent depreciation; they immediately went to the dump.

Roger drew a small salary as director of the Acadian Cultural Centre Foundation, which had turned a bit of a profit at its Miminegash location, without counting the government funding they got for their cultural programming. It wasn't a big salary, but Roger didn't have much of a life outside his work. On the rare occasions he found himself with free time, he'd do a shift at the PetroPump and would be as likely to spend it on something for the Centre as he would on himself.

Kate and Arnold got married in August at St. Bernard's; against Beatrice's advice, she had her bridesmaids, mostly cousins, wear off-white to match her dress. The photos of the bridesmaids and white-tuxedoed ushers in front of the white church were striking. Kate, though she swore she had given up show business, kept her maiden name.

The dinner and dance were at St. Bernard's Parish Hall. Though Roger had avoided Kate through all the wedding planning, he bought the couple a nice electric keyboard, in case Kate ever wanted to form a band.

Kate did not play the fiddle at her wedding.

The full scope of the Acadian Cultural Centre and Fun Park took shape that summer. All gables and turrets and cedar shingles, it should have been on a peninsula surrounded by water, it had so many portals looking out at the world. There were six fender-benders at Palmer and Thompson roads during construction, all caused by gawking. Money came from their events, from the feds, from the province, and from an institute in the U.S. devoted to promoting Cajun culture. The foundation was given a low-interest government-backed loan. But the construction money came, for the most part, from the community. As the buildings started to take shape, a series of fundraising drives got folks from Tignish to Bloomfield to open their wallets. There were concessions, too. Tenders were issued for bids to run the restaurant, the snack bar, the gift shop. There was a rumour for a while that Roger had turned away an offer from Burger King, but this misinformation was eventually traced back to Mitchell who, at one public meeting, had talked incessantly about how they'd be the perfect tenant.

In its ongoing coverage, *The Spectator-Herald* featured a photo of the proper windows going in, the strawberry social on the newly sodded lawn, the installation of the bricks of the stone oven, the raising of the Acadian flag, and the safety inspection of the auditorium by the Prince County fire inspector.

Helen Bernard was the reporter/photographer throughout. At the strawberry social, she filled her purse with the uncut strawberries from the prep table, sticking them in plastic baggies she had brought along for that very purpose. At the flag-raising, she lifted a two-litre container of orange juice. In her caption of the safety inspection photo, she spelled Roger Niese "Roger Needs."

After the story about Clem Cormier's Acadian documentary, Roger stopped calling and faxing Caroline directly, about the Centre or about the bridge. His relationship with her no longer felt like insider access. He had always claimed he wanted to be the man behind the scenes, the one who pushed the bushel aside so the light of others could shine. But this exclusion kindled that feeling of being an outsider, someone whose best efforts would never count. Not one to rage against the system, he pouted, at least for a while.

Caroline, who was oblivious to the meaning of Roger's silent treatment, hadn't counted on a full surrender. Still, as it became clearer and clearer the bridge would be built, Caroline didn't need Roger so much anyway. NLL and the feds were the ones who knew what was going on with the project; everything else was conjecture. Phillip Sinclair had much less inside information to leak. There were fewer and fewer anti-bridge meetings. Roger wasn't attending many of them anymore. Gwendolyn was talking more and more about piping plovers, seals, and honeybees.

"The whole NLL thing has transformed from a controversial story to a business story," Caroline told Basil.

"You think so?" Basil shot Caroline a lethal look.

"The ferry workers have given it up. The mayor of Borden's already counting the taxes from the factory outlet stores they've promised."

"You trust this Vinnie Tomato guy?"

"All he's got to do is pour some concrete into the Strait. Anybody can do that. If they've got enough concrete." Caroline shrugged. She sometimes wondered if she should have moved to Toronto, got a job at a bigger publication. But Caroline could never have managed being a small fish in a big pond; there wasn't a single household in Prince County who didn't know her name.

"You think your buddy there, Roger Niese, you think he had a point?" asked Basil. "They say his father worked for the government in Ottawa."

"Oh, Roger. He probably changed his mind because now he thinks the bridge would make it easier for Evangeline to find Gabriel."

"Say what now?" Basil never had any time for literature.

CHAPTER 11

"NOW, WHY DO YOU suppose they'd have that there?"

"Same nutjob who figured these'd be nice-looking sinks?"

"You can tell by looking they paid nothing for them. Powder blue. Psss! Sat in somebody's shed since 1973. Now, this, this would cost you to do something like this. See where that pipe's going? Then it comes back out here. Another hole in the drywall. Jesus."

"All tiled like that. Now, why would they do that?"

"Must have picked the orange tiles out of the dump. Some nutjob felt the need to use them all up, every one."

Mitchell was squatting in the farthest stall in the men's washroom of the main pavilion of the Acadian Cultural Centre and Fun Park, folded over tighter than he needed to be in order to see under the stall's door. The two men must have been from Down East—maybe brought their wives Up West from Kensington or Hunter River or even Charlottetown. They were all bent over themselves. Without touching their knees on the floor, they were examining the drainpipes for the three men's room sinks which were, admittedly, an unusual shade of blue and a little too sculptural for a public washroom. More suited to someone's grand-mother's house, sticky-toed plastic frogs or crocheted toilet-paper dolls clinging to their surfaces. As for the tiles—Mitchell had specially requested the tiles under the sink to make it easier to wipe everything down. He wasn't fussy about colour himself.

"Maybe that's how they do it in Ontari-ari-o. Lots of time on their hands."

"That's right, that's right now. The fellow who runs this place. He's a little out there, isn't he?"

"Nothing shy about him. Not when a camera's around."

"Check out the fuse box. Sweet Jesus!"

Mitchell held his breath like a spy in the thick of a mission. It was not unknown for people to mumble things under their breath about Roger Niese. Usually it was people Mitchell knew; familiarity tempered the digs and dismissals. Everyone was a character, Mitchell's late brother Ricky Gallant always said. Everybody had his own way of saying exactly the same thing as everybody else. You'd know it was all the same when you got to know the person.

Then you had these men, in their baggy, pinstriped shirtsleeves, dampness under their arms, big black belts holding up their best jeans, and this was what they had to say. Picking. Picking. You didn't see Mitchell getting all uppity about Kensington's scruffy-looking grain elevator or weedy ball field. Mitchell loved the Acadian Cultural Centre and Fun Park's bright colours, its maze of buildings with their mazes of halls and rooms. It was as nice as anything they had in Summerside or Charlottetown. The place had grown right before everybody's eyes. If you had seen it being built, driven up and down the Palmer Road during the construction and expansion, everything made perfect sense.

"You heard the first reader, did yah? Queer?" one man said.

"Oh, 'precious this' and 'precious that.' Should just leave them in Halifax. Don't need to be bringing that stuff here. The ferry kept away the fairies. As far as I'm concerned, that's the single bad thing about the bridge, God bless the goddamn thing."

"You think that last one, that Indian lady is finished?"

"Doubt it. She was reading pretty damn slow."

"D'yah think we...."

"...Can't smoke in here, no way. I can't smoke at all."

"Wife still holding that over your head?... Right, right, right."

The two men took their time washing and drying their hands before reluctantly making their way back to the performance hall. When Mitchell finished what he had to do, he considered going to Roger to tell him what the two men had said about the sink and the tiles and the poet from Halifax, who seemed like a sweet guy, and the Indigenous poet from Fredericton, who had brought muffins.

The warm mid-summer sun still lit the evening air. Although the fun park had closed for the day, you could hear the echo of the laughter of children, the splash of the waterslide, the popping of popcorn. It was a far cry from the days at the Miminegash Wharf, which, in retrospect, seemed rough around the edges.

No such rowdiness bubbled at the oversized Palmer Road complex. Father Michael had laid down the law early on. On the single occasion when there was overt parking-lot drinking, the priest called in the Mounties. They made two seventeen-year-olds sit in a jail cell in Alberton for six hours, which quieted them down immensely.

Whatever lesson Father Michael's vigilance had taught Roger, it taught the few remaining members of St. Bernard's Youth Group that Father Michael was not to be trusted. Things had been going sour for a while, as the free-form gab sessions of the early generations gave way to something more formal and scripture-based. Talk of sex and dating, which the founding members took to be group's raison d'être, was now discouraged.

"We don't want to embarrass anybody now," Father Michael would say, remembering back to the night when Paul Haché, the youngest son of anti-abortion activists Doreen and Melvin Haché, had confessed he touched Tammy Pineau, the oldest girl of Betty Ann and Noel, "down there," leading to rumours at Westisle High School that Tammy Pineau was no longer a virgin. It also led to Tammy's tearful resignation from the Youth Group.

Young people had come to understand that things were different at the Acadian Cultural Centre and Fun Park. It's not like Roger intentionally wanted local teens to use the place as a dating pool. But so long as they fiddled, danced, sang, acted, dressed up in period costumes, waited on customers, bussed tables, labelled jam jars, lashed toddlers into rides, picked up garbage, and closed out the cash, he didn't care what else their hormones were having them do. There was so much talk of hooking up and breaking up, and who liked who and who hated who and who had her period and who was a homo, St. Louis-St. Edward youth had, over the past few years, earned an Island-wide reputation for being fast and sophisticated in matters of love and lust. One day the bishop asked Father Michael Chaisson about the "Sodom next door."

The Acadian Cultural Centre and Fun Park was too busy for any substantially intimate encounters to take place "on property." Like an 18th century jailer, Mitchell monitored the comings and goings in all of the Centre's corridors, rooms, pavilions, its rides and courtyards. He kept his massive key ring with him always. When he lent a key to a pretty girl, who maybe was taking the gift shop till to the main office, he would wait ten minutes, then go retrieve it from her before she forgot to return it. Mitchell had no idea how many unwanted pregnancies he had prevented over the years.

For his own safety, Mitchell avoided the performance hall when the seating was set up; for this reason, the doors were always kept closed when he was around. His seizures had gradually grown more severe and harder to predict. He now wore his hockey helmet every waking hour. Roger did what he could, always experimenting with how chairs could be arranged or, if possible, breaking gatherings into smaller groups so there might be a mix of sitting and standing people, which seemed to take the edge off Mitchell's seizures. But the groups renting the performance hall were less interested in the alternatives to row seating. The Black Crow Poetry Festival was an especially big deal; it could get more than 100 people at a reading—its organizers were not interested in alternatives to row seating. Mitchell would have to patrol elsewhere for the week.

For the first couple of years of operation, Roger had been able to keep the Centre's offerings mostly Acadian—if you were generous with the definition of Acadian. Sometimes it was just a matter of the hosts wearing costumes (a scruffy black vest over a white dress shirt and baggy pants might do) while hosting a crokinole tournament. Or an introductory story about an especially funny mi-carême prank at the beginning of an A.A. meeting. At the very least, the surnames in the guest book matched the names in the graveyard across the road. But someone whose name nobody recognized, a Murphy from Charlottetown, had written a letter to *The Spectator-Herald*—not even the writer's own paper, *The Guardian*, but *The Spectator-Herald!*—complaining about how his tax dollars had built the place, and who were the St. Louis-St. Edward Acadians to keep their precious castle all to themselves? The board reluctantly established a formal non-discriminatory booking policy allowing for non-Acadian-themed rentals.

This week's rental, the Black Crow Poetry Festival, was sponsored by Northumberland Link Limited. Roger winced when he saw the flyer, but that was all. People did what they had to do; on this island, coincidences were the rule, not the exception. But even years later, Beatrice Perry did not like to talk about Vince Amato who had eventually moved back to Ontario and moved onto his next concrete project.

The "Island way of life" seemed to be working for the poetry festival organizers, Douglas and Cynthia Borenstein-LaPierre, a husband and wife originally from Montreal. The organizers had enough money to fly in poets from Halifax, Montreal, Toronto, and even Edmonton—a city not known for its poetic output. Yet they asked for the subsidized rental application like it was their God-given right. Beatrice wondered if the Borenstein-LaPierres had burnt bridges Down East, coming Up West as a last resort. Beatrice was sure she had never set eyes on them before. Roger made them pay twenty percent in advance to hold the dates.

At least the Black Crow Poetry Festival crowd didn't seem the kind who would steal a coffee maker. The Borenstein-LaPierres owned a recording studio somewhere in the hills of Breadalbane, releasing compact discs of Celtic and generic "Atlantic Canadian roots" music (nary a French-language title among them). They also ran a printing house. Cynthia Borenstein-LaPierre stamped over-saturated images of vines and birds onto recycled paper imported from British Columbia. The couple, well into their fifties, no longer stank of patchouli like they would have a decade or two earlier. These days, Cynthia Borenstein-LaPierre smelled like basil and Douglas LaPierre smelled like fresh tobacco. She wore a cobalt blue batik dress; he wore a Palestinian scarf under his greying beard. Roger took note of the couple giving direction to Tanya Moase, the star reporter these days on the evening news show *Compass*. He felt a burst of annoyance. *Compass* never came for his events, but Tanya Moase would drive all the way to St. Louis-St. Edward to talk to the same people she lived down the street from in Charlottetown. Go figure.

Caroline MacPhail had also shown up to cover the event for *The Spectator-Herald*, though she spent most of the time talking to old classmates she had fallen out of touch with over the years. The paper's readers weren't, she thought, much for reading descriptions of people reading things. She'd write up most of her story based on interviews, which she'd do during breaks.

A steadfast contingent of the poetry festival attendees wore lavender, silk scarves, and fake pearls, dragging their bored, sweaty husbands along to do the driving. White wine drinkers, the lot of them, which was a relief for Mitchell. It didn't stain like red or stink like spilled beer. If Mitchell had his way, the Centre would serve only white wine and Sprite. He didn't care about the men who went out to their cars for a shot during intermission, just so long as bottles didn't get broken.

When Roger's brother Allan held his infamous party—his "whatever," Tracey called it... now, that had been a sweet son of a sticky mess. People were pulling squashed maraschino cherries off the bottoms of their sneakers for weeks.

At first, Allan's unexpected appearance Up West seemed like good news. When Raymond Niese had died, people thought it was sad Roger didn't have any family left on the Island. It was a tough life. The woman he lived with wasn't the sort to bake a birthday cake. Or even the sort to pick one up at Save-Easy. If there weren't to be any youngsters in the house/trailer on the John Joe Road, maybe a lazy brother would fill the void.

Arriving with a roughed-up suitcase and an air mattress, Allan was assigned the room in the newly built second-floor extension. It was a good thing he showed up in July. The tiny space wasn't insulated; the following winter Roger chilled his beer up there. The second-floor room also lacked stairs. Entry and exit were through a trap door into the kitchen or a tiny window that didn't shut right. It made it very difficult for Allan to come home after a night of drinking, so there were many nights Allan did not return home to the John Joe Road at all.

Allan's first public outing was the St. Bernard's famous parish picnic the previous August, where he walked around with the confidence of a successful former parishioner, barely recognizable under the new pounds and wrinkles. Parishioners dutifully tried to place him until they realized the man had some connection to Roger.

"Oh, Christ, there's more than one of them," Susan Kennedy muttered under her breath.

Though he didn't let on, Allan must have been impressed with how many people his brother knew. Roger had something to say to everybody who let him say something. For a chunk of the day, until the cake auction, Roger ran a wheel game. Spins were free and won you tickets to Acadian Culture Centre events and passes to the Fun Park. Roger wore a fur trapper's hat, something, perhaps, an early Acadian might have worn, that Roger had bought off a teenage clog dancer from Rustico.

Many attendees approached Roger's booth thinking it was the chocolate wheel and so, despite spins being free of charge, were disappointed.

"You're in luck," Roger told the winners. "This gets you access to not only the noon happening any weekday, but you can use any of the amenities, except for the paddle boats, which cost three dollars unless you have a day-pass ticket. We had to charge that, elsewise people would hog the paddle boats. The Ferris wheel you can ride for a dollar-fifty for the first ride, regular price after that. You have to pay for your photo with Evangeline and Gabriel, but you can hang out with them for free, clown around with them all you like. That's free, too."

"Is it now?" said Ronald Corcoran, spotting the chocolate wheel over by the pony rides and slowly walking backward in that direction. "I have half a mind to take you up on that." The undertaker wasn't crass enough to hand out business cards but had discovered the benefit of showing his face at happy events.

Allan deferentially shook hands with everyone from twelve-year-old altar boys to ninety-two-year-old grannies to the guy giving the pony rides, who openly fretted that his probation officer might catch him out in the community. Anybody other than family would have chewed their left arm off to avoid all this. Tracey, for one, spent the day in Cavendish.

That summer, people started seeing Allan all over the place, leaving poor Roger trapped at home without his Ford pickup truck. Allan would be sitting in the PetroPump parking lot after midnight or tearing up Route 2 at five in the morning. Tracey, who was usually so extraordinary at living in her own little world, started complaining to Roger and others about Allen. Particularly about how much money Roger was giving him. Who knew where any of it went? It certainly wasn't the gas tank.

Allan started volunteering to be a bartender at Centre events and insisted on knowing how every button on the till worked, where the supplies were kept, how the alarm system was activated and deactivated—the whole kit and caboodle. Beatrice started to suspect he was less interested in serving drinks than in casing the joint. When, finally, Allan asked Roger if he could host a dance party—and subsequently sent a proper request letter to the board—Beatrice was relieved. It seemed less likely she'd arrive at the Centre one morning to find the place stripped bare.

Roger apologized for not giving Allan a weekend night; that would have felt like nepotism over profits; Roger, at this time in his life, felt little attachment to his blood kin. He tolerated Allan more for the secret talents the man might have tucked inside him than any special connection they had forged as brothers. In Roger's mind, his brother was still a toddler; the man living with him now was more like a roommate. At the same time, he couldn't say no to Allan's proposal or, as Tracey put it, "couldn't say no to any project he could micromanage."

"It's funny, someone like that Allan Niese showing up after the bridge opened," Angela Gaudet joked one day at the Tignish Co-op. She had been the sole board vote against Allan's party. "He'll be taking over the place any day."

Come-from-aways, it seemed, were driving up real estate prices, especially waterfront properties. There was a sense that PEI might be on the verge of turning into Toronto East. Charlottetown had more Tim Hortons per capita now than even Hamilton, Ontario, though the franchise hadn't dared to stick its nose west of Summerside. The bridge hadn't been open a year, and there was Allan, asking the customer service reps at the Zellers in Summerside if they could bring in some brand-name jeans he had seen in a Zellers in Ottawa.

Bridge proponents didn't think there was anything wrong with being able to buy the clothes and food you saw advertised on TV. The losing side wondered what they'd think when farmers were forced to rent their land from New Brunswick industrialists.

"I'm fine with the come-from-aways if they stay close to Charlottetown," Susan told Angela. "I can never find any parking there, anyway."

"I'll keep my distance from the capital, thank you very much," replied Angela.

As the date of Allan's Surf and Sand Night drew closer, the host became more and more mysterious. He had borrowed four hundred from the Centre for marketing—which he planned to pay back out of the five-dollar cover charge. Tracey thought that was an outrageous admission price. She complained to Beatrice and others about the whole thing.

"You know, I haven't seen a single Surf and Sand Night poster anywhere from Tyne Valley to Tignish. I've been flyering all over for the next 'Acadian Happening with Special Guest Stars—The MacKinnons from Richmond.' Believe me, I would have noticed."

Allan must have overheard Tracey during one of her rants. In very short order, magic-marker-on-lined-paper posters appeared on the bulletin boards of the O'Leary and Tignish Co-ops, as well as the Alberton Save-Easy. But the posters had the wrong date. And the decimal had disappeared from the price.

"Really?" Tracey snapped at Allan, whom she caught in the Centre's snack bar drinking an unpaid-for Coke.

"I can't think with you n-n-nagging at me," said Allan. He had less hair than his older brother. Nothing but a friar's crescent circled his skull. Though inclined to mention fashion designers by first name, his wardrobe consisted of baggy sweatshirts hanging over jeans with various zippers and leather strips stitched to them.

"I usually proofread what the Centre publishes, to prevent mistakes like these," said Tracey. She owned six dictionaries and referred to them frequently. It helped her pass the time. She had moved out of Roger's house/trailer around the time the Acadian Cultural Centre and Fun Park opened. Those who thought she'd head home to New Brunswick were surprised to see her setting up housekeeping on her own in a little farmhouse close to Miminegash. When people heard of the move, they wondered how Tracey would support herself. Then *The Spectator-Herald* reported that Tracey was the successful candidate for the position of gift shop manager at the Acadian Cultural Centre and Fun Park. This job, as far as Beatrice could tell, involved sitting behind a counter all day and looking perturbed when people interrupted Tracey with a question.

"Whatcha spend the marketing money on?"

"You're going to feel like a fool when this is the biggest money-maker this shithole has ever seen."

"If that's a bet, I am in like Flynn." Tracey spit on her right hand for a shake, but when she looked up, Allan was disappearing down the hall. He hid in the Centre's broadcast room until he was sure she had gone away.

That night at the house/trailer, Allan told his brother that Tracey was looking tired and premenstrual. Roger should give her a night off. Say, the night of the Surf and Sand Night party.

"Doesn't she have a boyfriend or something she should be doing something with?"

"Hm," said Roger, who had not visited Tracey at her new home and so hadn't noticed how many of his father's books she had taken with her when she moved out. He was sad to have lost her as a sexual companion. That part had been pleasant, a way to take his mind off work. But her comments were rarely helpful, though, thankfully, they were too absurdist to be hurtful. But his time with Tracey had, surprisingly, been lonely. If he was going to go through life never expressing his feelings, and barely ever hearing his partner's genuine feelings, then he might as well have the house to himself and a truck that had the same amount of gas in it as when he last drove it.

"We'll see. If she feels like working, I hate to leave the gift shop unattended. Your crowd—they'll buy a few of Kate Pineau's CDs, won't they?"

Kate now had six albums in all. Three had been recorded during the early years, before she split with Roger. Three had been compiled by Roger from live performances without Kate's permission, though she wasn't the type to make a fuss about such things.

"Sure, sure," said Allan. He knew, to keep on his brother's good side, that he must always say that Kate Pineau CDs would sell, that there was amazing potential in her music taking off big. Allan was, therefore, forced to endure Tracey for the duration of the first and only Surf and Sand Night.

The night came. Patrons scurried across the road from the St. Bernard's church parking lot to the Acadian Cultural Centre and Fun Park. Looking out the window of the parish house, Father Michael couldn't help noticing that one of the first arrivals was wearing an aquamarine taffeta gown and matching headpiece that was woven into the limpest blonde wig this side of Eastern Europe. Her escort wore an equally poofy concoction in a melon colour, evidently an old bridesmaid's dress.

Taking the tickets of these two beauties, Tracey noticed that neither patron had bothered to shave her legs, perhaps figuring it would be dark enough in the performance hall that it wouldn't matter. At Tracey's brightly lit shop counter, though, she recognized the twins of a pair of white pumps she had bought for herself at the County Fair Mall in Summerside. On the pair worn by this guest, the backstrap had been removed, so the wearer's heels could extend several inches beyond the shoe's length.

When the first wave of customers cleared, Tracey went to tell Beatrice of her suspicions. Beatrice was across the lobby, touching the earring of a crossdresser who hadn't bothered to stuff breasts into the top of his flappers' gown.

"Your grandmother's grandmother brought them from Ireland?" Beatrice was asking. "That's grand. Really grand!"

Tracey waited for the fawning conversation to end.

"Beatrice, there's something strange about these ladies."

"Ladies are ladies," said Beatrice. "The right clothes and the right manners—they have that. Some people could take a few lessons, couldn't they, dear?"

Beatrice had become particularly benevolent in recent months. She had met a man who had dropped by the Centre one day looking for Roger. They had had a charming lunch together, punctuated by flirty laughter and compliments.

Before Roger could make an appearance, the man decided he had to rush off. So many things to see and do while he was visiting the Island. He was from Ottawa, this Phillip Sinclair, but he and Beatrice kept in touch with letters, phone calls, and, once Beatrice got the hang of it, email. This mostly long-distance relationship—Phillip booked himself into a room at The Glenn several times since that first chance encounter—was perfect for Beatrice. It didn't take much of her time or attention but filled a gap in her life, conspiratorial intimacy, that Roger and the Centre could never address. It felt glamorous, too, having a lover who lived in another city, a lover she enjoyed being cagey about.

"Phillip is a little disappointed that Northumberland Link Limited is sponsoring our next concert series, after all you two did to stop the bridge," Beatrice told Roger one afternoon.

"Mr. Sinclair has never sent us a cheque," said Roger, failing to ask why Beatrice had been talking to his father's old friend, "so he has little say in the matter."

"Roger, don't be so harsh about Phillip," said Beatrice, again hoping that, maybe, just maybe, Roger would ask why she was not only talking to the man but defending him. She was discreet, certainly, at the request of Phillip himself, but Beatrice hated to leave questions hanging.

"True, his moral support has been impressive," said Roger, unable to pick up a clue he didn't want to find.

"Yes," said Beatrice, "his moral support."

On the night of Surf and Sand, the auditorium hall filled up, as did the parking lot, with many cars from New Brunswick and Nova Scotia. There were escorts, too, in tuxedos, military uniforms, firefighters' coats. Beatrice found the uniforms especially thrilling. Tracey, though, put a "Retour en 15 minutes" sign on her counter and went to find Roger. He had been demoted to Allan's errand boy for the night, carrying chairs, popcorn, and cases of beer. Tracey found Roger in the little office off the auditorium stage which he liked to use when he wanted to hide from people.

"Roger, what kind of party is this?"

"One we absolutely must host every month if they keep buying booze at this rate."

"Have you seen these folks?"

"Beatrice says you've been on a bit of a tear all night. Is it because Allan doesn't get your jokes or because you don't get his?"

"Allan has jokes?" snapped Tracey. "I'm fine with it myself. I love the film *Paris Is Burning*. I'm just worried about what local people will think."

"They'll think their Centre is very well supported across the Maritimes by people of various interests." This wasn't necessarily true, Roger thought to himself, but it should be.

Stomping back to her post, Tracey found a twenty-dollar bill stapled to the note, "Admission for two. Keep the change." She laughed aloud. She had a price. She bought some Glosette raisins and pocketed the rest of her tip.

There wasn't a single fight the entire Surf and Sand Night. After the guests had drunk all the beer the Centre had on hand, they cleared out the vodka and the rum. Panicking, Allan called Lester Shaw, whom he had befriended one day in a video gaming parlour in Tyne Valley. The businessman showed up at 1:10am, carrying several cases of distilled liquor in Mason jars.

"Rodney made this shit," said Lester, who had started to accept that his son was, for the most part, an outlaw. Lester was wearing a pajama top tucked into jeans, no socks with his sneakers. "Needed to get it out of the house before the cops showed up. Two birds with one stone. Three birds, maybe. Once this shit eats up everybody's insides, you might never have to host a party like this again. You don't want some pot and coke, do you? Not that it's me asking. I'd fucking deny it in court."

"I don't think so," said Roger, smiling like a eunuch who had been offered a happy ending to his massage. "How much do I owe you?"

"You'll be paying this off for years, Boy Scout, but I'll take five hundred dollars now."

By last call, there shouldn't have been a soul standing. Pineapple chunks littered the main hallway. A Coke bottle of piss, cold by morning, sat in the middle of one of the reading tables in the otherwise-undisturbed library. Out back, by the oil tank, there was a shattered plastic crown, topped with tiny lights that kept flashing till the battery died the next afternoon.

As the patrons crawled back to their cars, Roger was grabbed by a big-shouldered queen from Ellerslie, who led him in a free-form tango to an extended remix of "Don't Cry for Me Argentina." As the song faded, Roger took a step back, patted his partner on the small of the back, made a little bow with his head, and dashed off to find his brother. In the lobby, Roger was accosted again, this time by Gwendolyn Czarnecki. Dressed in a green and gold salwar kameez, her hair was cut short, and her glasses had been traded for contacts.

"Playing fast and loose with the rules again, Roger," declared the marine biologist, who had tasted more than a few drops of Rodney Shaw's moonshine. "Shouldn't there be some girls here? You don't advertise as a boys' club."

"There's girls as far as the eye can see. But I'll see what I can do for you." Roger scanned the departing guests with renewed purpose.

"Nothing!"

"Where's your car, Dr. Czarnecki?"

"Who knows? Maybe I swam."

Roger walked the staggering Gwendolyn to the gift shop and propped her up against the counter.

"You got a spare room for this one, Tracey?"

A few minutes later, the gift shop manager was dragging her ward to her car, which had several sprays of vomit on its driver's door. The sober woman arranged the drunk one rather coarsely into the passenger's seat.

Gwendolyn, who had been doing some soul searching and experimenting since she realized she had lost the bridge battle and needed something else to fill her evenings, couldn't bring herself to make a pass at Tracey that night. But the two women did end up becoming friends. Tracey sent Gwendolyn home with an obscure book on botany. The next time she was Up West, Gwendolyn brought Tracey a book on French poststructuralism.

The next day, Roger didn't quite know what Father Michael was talking about when the priest showed up in the lobby demanding a meeting. The two men sat in the Centre's main dining room, looking out over the ruddy potato field that surrounded them. Lunch patrons, mostly fishermen from Miminegash Wharf, were eating fish and chips, chips with the works, chips with lobster, and chips with cheese and gravy. The debauchery of the night before had been mopped up.

"This isn't going to happen again, is it?" asked the priest.

"I can't guarantee anything, father. Allan's always been a big kid. But maybe you'll be happy to know I'm writing a memo about things that could be improved." That morning, Roger had noticed that all his brother's stuff was gone from the house/trailer, as was his brother.

"Think of people's reactions. The children! Is that fair, Roger? We were taken by surprise this time. But next time, the parish will be prepared. You might not be happy to see this reported in *The Spectator-Herald*."

"Those bottles are already cleaned out of your parking lot. I know, Father, because Mitchell and I cleaned them up ourselves, before sunrise."

Father Michael's threatened story, whatever it might have been, did not make *The Spectator-Herald*. Caroline MacPhail did receive one anonymous phone message, from a male voice that sounded slightly familiar, complaining that deviants had taken over St. Louis-St. Edward.

A week later, Allan called Roger from the Gaspé to say he was okay. He wouldn't be coming back to PEI. Could Roger mail his share of the party proceeds to a post-office box in Quebec City?

★

Since Surf and Sand, Roger had kept much closer tabs on the events put on by others at the Centre. Roger did not want to appear judgmental, but Father Michael's words had made a small impact. It could hurt ticket sales. It could hurt government funding. Roger was thirty-eight now. He could smell forty. He and the priest had intertwined lives. They were both single men. Neither of them had a family life to retreat into. Roger had to win people over, while Michael had a guaranteed contract on the affections of the community, no matter how gruff he became. No sense upsetting people for no reason.

Roger had, he felt, kept the Black Crow Poetry Festival on a short leash. He had gone thoroughly over the festival's program. He didn't recognize the names of any of the poets—not an Acadian amongst them. How did they get such big crowds? They were getting more than two hundred people every night for poetry. Maybe there was something Roger could learn.

The Borenstein-LaPierres seemed to know a lot of the audience—or, at least, a lot of the audience knew them. They served cupcakes and grapes and unpasteurized cheese during intermissions, even though Susan Kennedy, Elis Getson, and the kitchen volunteer ladies had contributed baked goods and sandwiches, which were included in the rental price.

As far as Roger could tell, from his seat in the back row, the crowd came exclusively from east of Summerside. A good number must have been tourists, some still in their sandy shorts, still wearing damp bathing suits underneath, after a day of frolicking on one beach or another. He loved the fact that people from beyond Up West were recognizing the Centre as a place worth visiting. That was how they were going to make the money they needed to keep growing. But he cared about the opinions of those east of Tyne Valley less than he cared about the opinions of his friends and neighbours, the residents of St. Louis-St. Edward. He preferred feedback to be delivered at the Alberton Save-Easy rather than on comment cards.

For the final event on the final night, a woman who was probably in her twenties, but might have been a well-polished thirty-five-year-old, stood at the centre stage mic. Amy Ferrar, the Black Crow Poetry Festival's special guest act, was wearing what looked like black medical bandages wrapped around her body from neck to ankles. The poet/performance artist had mastered the art of making her face, framed by her asymmetrically cut black hair, as expressionless as possible. The blurring of humour and irritated aggression hid deficiencies in her art and demeanour.

In the front row sat a dozen students from UPEI, wide-eyed that someone who was frequently cited in glossy magazines was a living, breathing person in front of them. The little group had zero effect, though, on lowering the crowd's average age.

A slim volume was pried open on the varnished-maple lectern in front of the poet. As Amy Ferrar read, she kept her arms lowered in front of her, opened palms facing down. Her eyes were fixed on the book. She never looked up as she slowly and methodically droned her voice. Margaret Atwood, Amy had decided, was the standard for how Canadian poetry should be read. Each syllable was a croak daring boredom.

> *My stilettos dig into your ear*
> *Like your cock penetrated my ass*
> *Just now*
> *I walk across your back*
> *Leaving what will*
> *Be scars*
> *Blood and caviar*
> *My necklace breaks*
> *Pearls scatter on the floor*
> *Like mice*
> *Or rats*
> *White splotches on satin, polyester, acrylic*
> *I can't tell*
> *If it's your cum*
> *Or mine*

The front row burst into exuberant applause; the rest of the room offered a skeptical echo a few seconds later. Chairs shifted, legs repositioned, bags moved. There was tsking and coughing. Caroline's dramatic eye-rolling was almost audible. What chatter there might have been was all being saved for the tense drive home. Tanya Moase and her *Compass* videographer stepped out into the lobby; in this age, before cellphones turned everyone into videographers, the reporter had the exclusive power to decide that this recitation wasn't suitable for broadcast.

More quickly than anyone expected, the poetess started reading again. Perhaps it was a favour, so the images of the first poem didn't leave a lasting imprint. Amy Ferrar started quietly and then grew louder, as if she was talking to someone walking away from her.

The limo is a prison
But you are not the jailer
Don't think so highly of yourself
I don't
Not of you
Not of me
Now that we are both satisfied
Satisfied?
Who am I kidding?
Nothing can fill the void in me
Nothing
You?
Like an asshole
Things must continue to pass through you
So you can be real
So you can exist
That's enough of a struggle
Being that shit

Here she lifted her eyes to the audience and started them down, by Roger's count, for twenty seconds.

Ecstasy is a lie
People tell you
To keep you coming back
For more

"We are so thrilled!" exclaimed Douglas LaPierre, dashing up to the mic with such desperate recklessness he almost collided with the performer. The former Montrealer, festival co-founder, and senior manager at the federal Department of Veterans Affairs was known to have a goat in his backyard, if four wooded acres deep in the hills of Breadalbane could be called a backyard. It was also known that he cheated on his wife with a woman who had a pottery studio on Brackley Point Road. It was also known, at least among Centre staff, that he didn't wash his hands before he helped Susan and Elis put the cheese and grapes on the serving tables. Douglas wanted everything in his life to be no fuss, no muss. That's why he had stayed in the Maritimes—no pretensions but his own. When he and Roger were negotiating the rental deal for the festival, Douglas took note that Roger did not have a hundred percent Island accent.

"Yes, we moved here when I was a kid."

"Now, I never see you in Charlottetown. You don't shop at Percy's Organic Food Stuff down on Queen?"

"Don't make it into town much."

"It's quite the hubbub. Those CBC types shop there. You must read *The Buzz*? The entertainment paper?" Douglas had a column in *The Buzz* called "Getting to LaPoint."

"We put a few ads in. Didn't get much out of it."

"City Cinema? The Farmer's Market on University? Parsley and Thyme Bistro in St. Eleanors? That's not far from you. Sweet couple from Nepean run it. You said you were from Ottawa, right?" In a province where everybody knew pretty much everybody, the two men didn't have a single soul in common.

"We are so thrilled to have one of the brightest stars of Toronto's Queen Street scene here with us," Douglas was almost swooning at the audience. "So thrilled."

The poet nodded. Not so much to accept the praise—which was a given—but in the hopes that some gesture of acknowledgement would end Douglas's extended ecstatic state.

Amy Ferrar was not thrilled. She wondered if she could get her things, get back to Charlottetown, and hop a plane back to Toronto that night, rather than Monday morning. The sagging floorboards of her motel room—Lester's Shaw's motel near O'Leary—threatened to give out at any moment, dropping her, she imagined, into a foul-smelling swamp. At this moment, she was realizing her tactical error. She had accepted a ride Up West with Douglas because he drove a Saab. Now she realized that, as organizer, he would have to stay here, at or beyond the edge of civilization, until every last hand had been shaken. Perhaps she'd have to sit there while he stacked chairs. Like a teacher ready to take names, she scanned the audience members, hoping she could spot someone she might flirt a ride out of. The patrons, noticing this, shifted in their chairs and averted their eyes, afraid to attract her attention and, they presumed, her scorn.

"The language those people from away call poetry," one audience member whispered to her husband. The husband smiled. His suggestion for celebrating their wedding anniversary had been another go at *Anne of Green Gables—The Musical*. For years to come, he could use this evening as a weapon against ill-conceived adventures.

Amy Ferrar was expected to read two more poems after Douglas's commentary and "interaction," a feature the Black Crow Poetry Festival was known for. But so frustrated with herself for her lack of foresight, and with the audience for their pathetic beguilement, she felt she couldn't go on. She just couldn't. She made a quick decision: she'd leave the stage when her host stopped blathering. What did he know about her? That she couldn't pay her rent? That she hadn't spoken to her parents for a decade? That she had never been outside of North America or inside a limousine?

"... a global sensibility that makes Canadians stand up and take notice, that chills us to the bone as it arouses our...."

Before Amy could make her move, Roger lolled out from behind the curtains at the back of the stage. He stopped to rub his left shin, which had been dinged by a drum kit, and then, with the tentativeness of a shopper unsure if there was one checkout line or two, limped to a spot between Amy and Douglas.

Douglas, who had assumed Roger was performing the duties of a stagehand coming to adjust something, let his guard down. Before he knew it, the voice of the president and CEO of the Acadian Cultural Centre of Prince Edward Island Limited, the organization that ran the Acadian Cultural Centre and Fun Park, was coming over the sound system.

"I want to thank this young lady for her reading, which I'm sure we can all say we haven't heard anything like before," Roger declared. He had his own wireless mic that he regularly carried around in the pocket of his jeans; it was set up to override all other audio inputs. The audience rumbled an assent. "She's come a long way to PEI, and to St. Louis-St. Edward, and we're proud to have her here."

Hearing the word "PEI," the audience clapped a little louder than they had for the poet herself. Even if Amy Ferrar's work left them cold, it was important they not be considered inhospitable.

It was at this point that some audience members noticed that dangling from Roger's right hand was a reddish object the size of a makeup case. The handful of attendees who knew what it was, and what Roger intended to do with it, gulped. There wasn't enough time to flee. Roger yanked the object up to his chest, grabbing the bottom of it with his left hand.

"I know we have a lot of guests here tonight from other parts of the province. Other parts of the country! Maybe this is their first time here at the Acadian Cultural Centre and Fun Park, and they're wondering, hey, where is all this Acadian culture we've been hearing about?"

The grin on Douglas's face melted into a grimace; had this moment been mentioned on the pages of the contract he had not bothered to read?

Roger clicked something on the object and, for a second, it looked like it was going to fall apart. A polyphonous moan filled the room as Roger pushed it back together.

"You're going to hear the answer, just before we serve a few refreshments, there at the back." Roger nodded to the spot where Tracey was supposed to be standing, holding up a pitcher of lemonade and a plate of cookies. His ex-girlfriend had missed her cue; she was reading on a bench out front.

"Now, this is a Cajun accordion. Which might be called a zydeco, which is what they call Acadian music further south."

Roger had taken up the accordion a couple of years earlier. What he lacked in history with the instrument, he made up for with passion. He went right at it. If he missed a note, he'd hit it harder the next time. It wasn't that he wanted to claim more time on the stage than he already claimed. Roger was hoping that by being a musician himself, he would have a deeper connection with the musicians he worked with.

Roger also hoped he might eventually be invited to join a band, though no such invitation had yet been received.

Most folk musicians who specialized in the Acadian music of Atlantic Canada, which bore little resemblance to the raucous Southern influence of Louisiana, would not have chosen the accordion as their instrument. In the Maritimes, the fiddle was the thing, followed by the piano, which was thought to be more prim and best suited for lady musicians, like Beatrice, for example. Throw in a guitar, a pair of spoons, and perhaps an Irish bodhran drum and you had yourself a party. Roger went all the way to Montreal to purchase a proper Cajun accordion. A Gallant in Piusville owned one, but the old geyser refused to sell it.

Roger's decision to take up an instrument had coincided with Kate Pineau's retirement as his star performer. Her name hadn't been on the posters since she walked out the door at that New Year's Eve party at the old Miminegash Wharf location. Roger must have asked her a dozen times to come back.

"What you pay doesn't cover gas," Kate laughed at him once. The Crozier-Pineaus lived in a new house on Route 2 in Coleman, more than a half-hour's drive away from the Centre. Crystal and Sherrie, who had been great little babysitters when Beverly, the youngest, was a baby, were running the roads themselves. They went to Evangeline School, where they could learn in a purely French environment, something they couldn't get at Westisle. The family needed two cars, one going in one direction, the other the opposite way.

Meanwhile, Arnold Crozier had been approached by Réné LeBlanc, son of the provincial cabinet minister Léonce LeBlanc, about an idea he had for a factory outlet/flea market in Wellington. Now that the Confederation Bridge was built, the government was expecting more day-trip visitors to the Island. These busy day-trippers would want to cover as much territory as possible. It made sense, said Réné, that they'd want to buy their antiques, their homemade fudge, and their discounted designer clothing, plus listen to some local Maritime music, all in one place. With his connections, Réné was the man to build such a place and Arnold was the man to run it. Kate would be a cost-efficient way to draw crowds. If Arnold was driving there a few times a day for this errand and that, then it made sense for Kate to go with him and play fiddle for whoever was there until Arnold was ready to leave.

The Wellington factory outlet/flea market lasted only six months. Kate was embarrassed about it all. For Roger, it had been salt in the wound. Staff at the Centre learned very quickly not to mention Kate's name around him, though it was still plastered on CDs sold in the gift shop and on the old posters in the Centre's "hallway of fame."

Learning how to play the accordion provided something of a balm, especially since Tracey left him. Standing in front of the audience at the Black Crow Poetry Festival, Roger squeezed out one creaky sound after another. With one knee raised to stabilize the keyboard end of the instrument, he looked like a stork. Some people wondered if this was a magic show, and if there were invisible strings holding him upright.

"You've all heard of chords," said Roger. "Well, the squeezebox, it can't do 'em. Not one bit. It's got three notes, max, at a time, but that's enough to play some beautiful tunes."

Roger talked and doodled on the accordion. Amy Ferrar stood as still as she could. She willed a subtle frown across her face hoping that someone was sharp enough to see it and come rescue her. So far, Douglas had shown himself to be of no use. He stood shoulder to shoulder with her as if the two of them were posing for a photo.

The accordion squawking went on.

"It's hard to narrow down the diverse Acadian repertoire to just a dozen songs or so, but I think I have succeeded," said Roger. Through these words, the audience was able to discern that the first official tune had started.

"Do you think the potty-mouthed lady is coming back?" someone in the audience mumbled with a dollop of hope.

Desperate, panicking, and perhaps horny, Douglas reached out and grabbed Amy's hand. She accepted his fingers between hers without looking or, for that matter, flinching. Douglas's gaze moved from Amy to his wife, who was sitting in the front row, to Amy, to Roger, and then back to his wife again.

Cynthia Borenstein-LaPierre was seated next to the UPEI students, their faces glazed from the Timbits they had brought with them and had been choking down all evening. There was some icing sugar on her lap. Looking at what was on the stage, for everyone to see, Cynthia realized, in these final hours of the festival, that her marriage was over. She was caught in a loop of whether to stomp out now or wait for the festival to end before stomping off.

So, it was with an incredible sense of relief to pretty much everyone when Mitchell came jogging down the centre aisle. There might have been a fire in the kitchen, a baby fallen out of a window, a rabid dog on the loose—whatever might end Roger's performance would be a welcome thing.

Approaching the front of the stage, Mitchell grew pale. His eyes closed. A gurgling noise rose from his throat (though nobody could hear it above Roger's accordion). His limbs froze. He was going down. In his rush, Mitchell had tempted fate and lost.

Mitchell keeled over backward, scattering a half-dozen unoccupied chairs. His body bounced on the floor like a railway tie tossed off the back of a half-ton truck. Several audience members screamed. Several audience members who had been plotting an escape tsked-tsked their regret at not having already made a move. The more cosmopolitan attendees wondered if Mitchell's collapse was merely part of Amy Ferrar's performance—violent words and violent musical notes manifesting themselves in a final violent act.

The first person at Michell's side during his seizure was a woman who had come running in after him. Though the handful of locals in attendance would later claim to have known Debbie Arsenault the moment they laid eyes on her, the truth was that nobody knew who the hell she was.

Except Roger.

"You came!" exclaimed Roger, letting the accordion drop on the stage's hardwood floor.

The declaration might have seemed coldhearted, considering that his best friend was spasming on the floor. But Roger had lived through hundreds of Mitchell's seizures. He knew Mitchell had his best recoveries when he returned to consciousness in a room that had not changed since the seizure took him out. Once you were confident that Mitchell was not going to smash against something, it was best just to pretend the seizure wasn't happening. Mitchell had his helmet on. He had already knocked the chairs out of his way. Mitchell was as fine as could be, under the circumstances.

Roger was not surprised that Debbie Arsenault had come. He jumped off the stage and dashed toward her. In his mind, he was moving in slow motion. They collided. He felt her breasts press into him.

"Debbie!"

She was too busy staring at Mitchell like a first-time murderer fascinated by what she was capable of. There was horror in her eyes.

"What the fuck have I done?" she wailed.

"You came back!"

Tracey returned from her cigarette break and knew what to do.

"Everybody," Tracey cried out. "Stop what you're doing and go back to where you were before the seizure started. It'll help. Please help!"

The people who had most noticeably moved were Debbie and Roger. Each of them retraced their steps, she back to the lobby, he back to the stage. Roger took a position next to Amy and Douglas, who were still holding hands and hadn't moved at all since Mitchell's seizure began.

Mitchell continued his convulsions on the floor. It was hard to watch. If it continued for much longer, they'd have to call a doctor.

Finally, the seizure stopped. Mitchell got his elbow underneath himself and took in his surroundings.

"Sit down! Everybody, sit down. As you were!" said Tracey, who dashed out of sight so Mitchell wouldn't notice her arrival on the scene and get befuddled.

Everybody in the audience settled into their seats. Roger played a few notes on the accordion, though he found it difficult to repeat what he had just been playing.

Though groggy, Mitchell was on his feet in a matter of seconds, again running toward the stage to complete the mission his brain had rudely interrupted.

"Roger! Roger! Debbie Arsenault is here!"

"This seems like a good time for a break," said Douglas into his mic. Pricey as it was, hosting the event at the Stanhope Beach Resort didn't seem like such a bad deal now. His wife had disappeared, and Douglas couldn't be sure she wasn't on the way back to Breadalbane to have the locks changed on their home.

Roger hopped off the stage and ran outside. He found Debbie crying behind the oil tank around the corner from the main entrance. It was where the smokers on staff hung out and there were poorly aimed butts in the grass near the milk can they used as an ashtray. Debbie was leaning against the vinyl siding and, when she saw Roger, she let herself slide down till her bum was on the grass, knees at her chin. Her white slacks would be permanently grass-stained.

"Is that poor fucker going to be all right?"

"Who?" Roger's mind was well into the future where there lurked the question of moving out of the house/trailer and into something a woman (aside from Tracey) might find more palatable.

"That poor fucked-up man! And then you didn't... and then that woman said... and who was the woman on stage holding hands with the old guy? I came thinking one thing and then, all these other things. And you just standing there like a complete asshole."

This was not how Roger had imagined their reunion. Their inevitable, fated reunion. He had a speech prepared, or some fragmented form of one that had lingered since he was a teenager. He was tempted to just stop listening to her, to dedicate his mind to the lines he needed to speak to move things forward. But that would have been rude.

"That's Mitchell Gallant, Debbie. Ricky's little brother. Remember Ricky! Oh, those were good times, weren't they?"

"Mitchell? Retarded Mitchell?"

Back when the Acadian Cultural Centre and Fun Park was being built, the day some railway ties had been stolen, Father Michael had casually mentioned to Roger that he had seen Debbie at the Charlottetown Mall. Since then, without really thinking about it, Roger had become a regular visitor to the mall, sometimes walking from end to end, then remembering a purchase he had let himself forget, and walking all the way back again. If his life's goal was to accidentally run into someone, then, for once, his absentmindedness might be useful.

Finally, the quest that he hadn't consciously set out upon bore fruit. Earlier that summer, he spotted Debbie among the graphic T-shirts in Christopher's Beach Outfitters Outlet. He was alone. Debbie was alone, too.

Roger stood in Christopher's doorway a moment. He knew it was the only exit. He was too busy thinking about what he'd say to notice how hard his heart was pounding, the burning sensation in his cheeks. He might have a heart attack. She might be the one to save him. She might be the one to let him die.

"Debbie?" Roger asked, coasting up beside her. On the day of his death, when parts of his life flashed before his eyes, he remembered how suave he had felt at that moment. All the ridges, crevices, and bits of rust on the blade with which he cut through life were, for a moment, smooth and sharp.

"What?" she replied, sounding annoyed. She was rooting through oversized hoodies, turning neatly folded sweatshirts into a jumbled pile.

Debbie's greying hair was closely cropped. She had the skin of a heavy smoker. Her white blouse and navy-blue skirt fit her as well as they'd have fit a twenty-year-old. She might have been a secretary or a waitress in an upscale restaurant on Victoria Row. She was not a farmer's wife. That was clear. Her fingernails were painted a dazzling red. Roger stared at these nails while he coughed out a list of proper nouns that he hoped would turn her confused expression into something warm and delighted. Roger. Niese. Raymond Niese. Up West. Palmer Road. John Joe Road. Westisle.

The light went on. Debbie laughed loud and long enough to cover up the moments of awkwardness that had preceded it.

"Lord! Lord. Good Lord! Well, do you know that just the other day I was thinking of all those nights I slept in your bed! Dad was complaining about not sleeping and I thought, just imagine the places I've slept in my life, what do you know, you old scarecrow!"

"You look good!" said Roger, though he wasn't quite sure he meant it. He didn't know how she looked except it wasn't how she looked when she was nineteen. But her voice. Her voice erased the years. Not a hint of apology in it.

"So do you, so do you, so do you. Oh, Lord! You caught me at a bad time. A weird time. I mean. You know my father! The alcoholic! That old alcoholic! Never fucking changes. Pardon my language!"

"Me too, busy, busy," said Roger, absentmindedly. "One thing after another. Summer's the busiest time."

"Oh, isn't it now!"

"You really should... I am involved with something up on Palmer Road. Called the Acadian Cultural Centre and Fun Park."

"Now, I think I've heard of that! God, the Palmer Road! What a place! They'd just as soon punch you in the eye as drink your beer. That's what I tell people around here. I mean, Cornwall. I'm in Cornwall now." The Charlottetown suburb of Cornwall had a bad reputation; it was alleged that on Halloween, Cornwall's young people callously set dogs on fire and stuck fireworks up the buttholes of cats.

Debbie inhaled air through her front teeth. "Well! It was great talking! So great seeing you. My lunch hour! Oh Lord, work, work, work. We'll have to do something some time. That'd be nice, wouldn't it?"

Debbie's body, Roger realized in horror, had gotten itself to the mall side of Christopher's entrance. She threw her arm up in a broad wave. Then she was off, hunching her shoulders as she scurried past the sullen teenager at the candied popcorn kiosk.

Roger had meant to tell her he loved her, had always loved her, would always love her. But the mall seemed like the wrong place for everything. She had offered no contact information. He had not thought to ask.

He wasn't sure what went wrong.

★

It hadn't gone wrong. Debbie had come to him. She was crying. She was sobbing. This couldn't be considered a casual visit.

"Oh, God, I haven't been up this way for so long."

"I know, I know, I know."

"All the memories, flooding back. Oh, my father. Now he's been a piece of work. An asshole from day one. What did I get myself into? Fuck."

Roger crouched down and leaned into her. With her up against the oil tank, he couldn't figure out how to get his arms around her. "It's okay. It's okay."

"Do you know what Michael Chaisson told me?"

"That was so long ago, Debbie."

"It was ten minutes ago. When I was on my way here. Just before Ricky's brother spazzed out. Oh, Jesus Christ." Debbie sniffed and snorted some more. "Saw him. Oh, God. It was like a confession. He said I had to let go of my past. Oh, this place! It makes my skin crawl. Amber, you know, my daughter, came up to St. Louis-St. Edward once, when she first got her licence. Curious thing! Knew I'd be pissed off. Maybe I'm always pissed off! That's what Amber says. She drove down Union Road, across Thompson Road, up Palmer Road, out Harper Road, and back onto Route 2 without taking her foot off the gas. Didn't see a single blooming thing that caught her attention. Not a fucking thing. Good for her!"

Amber, thought Roger, was probably old enough to take care of herself. Oh right. Then there was the granddaughter, Nikki. That would be another couple of decades of care and maintenance. Debbie came off as a free spirit, even though she was subordinate to so many ties.

"Family is important," said Roger, uncertainly.

"Oh yes!" said Debbie. "I love my little Nikki. Amber, I couldn't do much with. But nothing's ever going to touch Nikki. Nothing!"

"Does Amber play any musical instruments?" asked Roger, looking for ways to bring the conversation around to their shared future together.

Debbie grew still and quiet for a second. "Now, I couldn't tell you that. What I can tell you is she loves music, though nothing I'd put on myself."

"Have you thought of, I dunno, coming back? You could maybe stay in the house/trailer again. It's bigger now. I mean, you'd have your own room." So much of Roger's life had been lived as a means of self-protection, his dreams and projects part of an unconscious strategy to avoid situations where people might refuse him permission to join in theirs. But not asking to be let in could, in some cases, mean missing out on some parts of life. This moment was an opportunity. He had never before been able to corner Debbie Arsenault for an answer to something.

Debbie looked at him blankly. She wasn't startled by what he had just said. She got the gist of it, like someone accustomed to the mispronunciations of a non-native speaker.

"Weren't those the days, us together? Oh, Roger! They're such a comfort to me."

Roger had no feelings of comfort connected to those days; they had all been prologue. This adult version of him should have said, "Let's get up and out of here right now and sort out the details on the way." But they sat in silence on the damp, ashy grass. She wasn't going to make this easy. He was losing his nerve.

"There could be more in the future."

Debbie laughed. "Like I'm any good at planning."

Roger was considered to be a persistent person. Too persistent, really. But he wanted this dream to come true effortlessly. He had no idea how to proceed.

This impasse was soon interrupted. Mitchell and Tracey came around the corner of the Centre, all limbs flailing.

"Roger, Roger! Come quick!"

Roger stood up. Debbie did too. She took a couple of steps back.

"It's urgent," said Mitchell.

The feeling of being needed made Roger's heart swell. He smiled at Debbie warmly, welcoming her to come inside with him. She took another step back. Roger smiled again at her, then, not getting a quick response, turned and trotted toward his two friends without so much as wiping the dandelion fluff and grass clippings from his black dress pants. He looked back at Debbie again and saw her walking toward the parking lot.

"See you later!" she waved jovially. "Keep 'em in line, Rog, keep 'em in line!"

"Bye," he croaked.

The Black Crow Poetry Festival had not resumed after the break. The remaining patrons were clustered by the refreshment table where Susan and Elis were nervously rearranging sandwiches so they looked more appealing. No one wanted to eat anyway. Every gaze was directed toward a group of VIPs who were, at this moment, being restrained from hurting one another. Nobody was talking; there was too much screaming.

"Hypocrite! People are dying in Africa because of you! I'd call you a dangerous old queer except that's a compliment in my circles!" spat Amy Ferrar. Caroline MacPhail held her by her hands, crossed behind her back, in the middle of the hall. Stacking chairs were scattered here and there around Amy. The reporter's tape recorder was in pieces on the floor. Caroline had a good grip on the poet but didn't use much force. Amy's thrashing and kicking seemed mostly for show. Both her stilettos had been flung from her feet.

A few feet away, Douglas LaPierre held the object of the poet's scorn up against the wall, one hand on each shoulder. Father Michael huffed and puffed, but his efforts to break loose also seemed lackadaisical. On the other side of the room, Beatrice had backed Cynthia Borenstein-LaPierre into a corner and was holding her there with little more than an impatient stare. Cynthia looked past Beatrice, shuffling her scorn back and forth between her husband and the poetess.

"Oh, shut up, Miss Ferrar! You couldn't write your way out of a paper bag," yelled Cynthia. She felt—she would say later over red wine with some ladies in her book club—quite exhilarated. Oh, to be belligerent!

When, over the next few weeks, the gossip about the incident at the Black Crow Poetry Festival began to spread, Beatrice was quick to point out that she never laid hands on that come-from-away woman. Elis Getson, the person best situated in the room to be able to confirm or debunk this claim, couldn't see her hand in front of her face once her glasses had been knocked to the floor by Amy, who accidentally struck them with her stilettoed left foot.

Regardless, it must be noted that Cynthia did not leave the corner until Beatrice let her.

"Only God decides whether you're going to hell, but I wouldn't second guess him right now," Father Michael barked at the icon of that year's Queen Street West scene. The priest was red in the face. These days he had been wearing his clerical collar more and more often. Elis thought it might be too tight. The priest's puffy lips seemed on the verge of popping.

"Fucker!" barked Amy. Hearing the profanity, the half-dozen spectators who had been rooting for her changed their allegiances.

"Tsk, tsk," said Elis, looking down at the sandwiches on the floor. Any had seconded several as weapons in her battle against the priest, who had meekly brushed some sugar cubes in her direction.

"Someone, please, help me out," said Caroline. She had the faintest of grins on her face. What she wanted to do now was snap a photo. Basil would never publish it, but the negative might come in handy someday.

Caroline had set off the incident, though not as intentionally as she would have liked.

All she had wanted to do was write a colourful story, full of anecdotes and clever observations, about the Black Crow Poetry Festival, presenting it as a pageant of writers who were nationally famous but largely unheard of on PEI because Islanders didn't take literature seriously enough. She had wanted at least two quotes to drive her thesis home. She was sure, after listening to Amy Ferrar read, that the performance artist was so full of herself she'd supply some pullquote-worthy barbs about Islanders as uncouth rednecks.

At the break, Amy had been standing by herself at one end of the refreshment table. Douglas was chatting with some of the festival's richer patrons.

"Hi there," said Caroline.

"Yes?" Amy eyed the reporter with some suspicion. This proved to be well-founded. After an initial bout of empty praise and unofficial welcome to PEI, the first thing Caroline asked Amy Ferrar was if she earned enough money doing what she did to make a living.

"Toronto's a very expensive city," Amy replied.

"But you gave up sex work, which must have been lucrative. Or did you?"

Amy Ferrar stared blankly.

"There's a lot of sexual imagery in your work."

"The world is a sexual place?"

"Nice! Nice!" said Caroline, jotting the quotation down without the question mark. "But is it necessary to rub our faces in it? Considering how awful you think the world already is?"

Amy's face was, as Caroline wrote in her *Spectator-Herald* story, "unforgiving porcelain."

"It's fucked, so why not do the fucking," said Amy. Her commitment to stoicism was often overruled by her desire to make trouble.

Father Michael had inched closer and closer to the conversation, the varnished floorboards slippery beneath his size eleven shoes. In the last few years, the priest had put on some pounds. All that working out, building a body nobody could enjoy except God, had seemed pointless as he grew older. As the shape of his body grew less defined, his rhetoric grew more persnickety. He had had a falling out with the youth group a couple of years earlier, over the literal truth of transubstantiation.

Michael had lost his mother Eileen to pancreatic cancer just two years after losing his father Archibald to prostate cancer. A golden boy without the adoring eyes of his parents is not so shiny. Booze seemed like a reasonable consolation. His evenings grew long. The popularity that priesthood confers felt more like servitude. People were so needy they didn't even realize how needy they were.

"Excuse me," Father Michael said. "When you're finished, I have a response, for the record."

Caroline nodded. Father Michael stood uncomfortably close to the interviewer and subject, coughing, sneezing, and jangling his keys.

It was pointless, Caroline had decided, to ask Amy Ferrar about the sexual content of her poetry. *The Spectator-Herald* wouldn't print anything about that anyway. But as she looked into Amy's eyes—there was something sweet there along with the steely—she wanted to ask something that would get at where the artist was in life, not just the image she projected.

"You're not married, are you?" Caroline hadn't had sex with her own husband, Robert Doucette, for close to a decade now. She marvelled at people who got divorced. The hassle of having to transport children back and forth between households.

"You're not trying to pick me up, are you?"

Caroline blushed, shook her head no. Maybe there was something sensational here. "Would you define yourself as bisexual?"

"I'll leave the definitions for uptight prudes."

"Is there any other kind?"

"Uptight bitches."

Caroline ended the interview, thanking Amy profusely. She then turned to Father Michael without even pausing her microcassette recorder.

"Yes, yes, thanks so much, Caroline, for asking about my response to this so-called poetry reading," said Father Michael, his feet close together, his hands in fists in front of his family jewels, his shoulders slightly hunched. When he saw himself in this pose on *Compass* the next day—Tanya Moase interviewed in the lobby while she was avoiding hearing Amy Ferrar's performance—he thought he looked especially humble. He saw no reason to abstain from the pose in print.

"Not only as a member of Prince Edward Island's religious community, but as someone who cares deeply about the future of our children, I can only state in the strongest terms that this kind of filth should not only be deprived of government funding but should not be granted space in institutions that claim to be family friendly. If people choose to engage in sacred acts with their legally married spouse in the privacy of their bedroom, we can look the other way. But this presentation encouraged promiscuity, dangerous sexual experimentation, and acts of depravity unsuitable even within the confines of holy matrimony. I heartily condemn this event and the Acadian Cultural Centre and Fun Park for hosting it. Real Acadians would know that the work of Amy Framer isn't art, it's smut."

"Ferrar! Excuse me! I donated half of my Canada Council grant to Save The Children...."

"....Miss Framer, I gave you the opportunity to speak. I'm sure you don't want to deny the community a response."

"Are you sure I don't?" Amy lunged forward, planting her lipsticked pucker on the priest's gawping mouth. She thrust her tongue as far into his mouth as physically possible—perhaps a little further than that. Tracey later said the kiss lasted as long as it did because Father Michael was enjoying it. Beatrice, in her recapping, argued that Father Michael had been caught off guard and needed a few seconds to muster his defences.

As if to make up for his initial hesitation, Father Michael forcefully pushed Amy away. It was Amy's turn to be unprepared. She went flying back into the open arms of Douglas LaPierre. The poet would have slid to a horizontal position on the floor if her breasts hadn't caught on her host's intertwined hands.

Douglas had spent a good chunk of the break explaining to his wife why he had taken Amy's hand on stage. Now Cynthia Borenstein-LaPierre saw where her husband's arms were, bolted at him, and landed a solid slap across his face. It felt good. She tried again and swatted Amy across the cheeks too.

Both women shrieked. Douglas raised his hands above his head to show his complete surrender. Amy ended up on the floor. That's when Beatrice aptly pinned Cynthia in a corner. The rest of that evening's featured poets, who were backstage waiting for their rides back to Charlottetown, heard all the commotion and, quite wisely, chose not to come out and investigate.

Into this temporary cease-fire came a heartbroken Roger.

The faces of Caroline and Father Michael stood out among the less familiar ones. He had known them for twice as long as he hadn't known them.

"Jesus!" Roger wanted to sound affably beleaguered. But the misery of the conversation he had just had with Debbie had already stretched his voice. "Ah, Jesus, fuck. Jesus, fuck. Is there nothing you can keep your hands off of? Nothing you don't want to ruin on me? I should be able to get ahead as well as anybody else. Shouldn't I? Get out. Both of yahs. Don't make me look a second longer or I can't say what will happen."

Roger raised his accordion to his shoulder and threw it over Caroline and Amy's heads. It bounced off the wall and into the pile of soggy sandwiches on the food table before rolling onto the floor. In her re-telling of events, Elis emphasized that the sandwiches were well past their prime; it was not so much of a waste as people said. The accordion came to a stop on Amy's ankles. "Ow!" she screamed, sounding surprisingly like a child. No matter the quality of her performance, the special guest didn't deserve to be treated like this, Beatrice thought. Islanders were known for their hospitality. Perhaps the Confederation Bridge had, as some had warned, ruined the Island way of life.

Cynthia, Father Michael, Caroline, and Beatrice shook themselves loose of one another and skulked out of the auditorium. The few remaining attendees of the Black Crow Poetry Festival reluctantly turned their attention back to the stage. Douglas had gotten himself back on it. He was speaking at an inaudible volume. No one had turned the mic back on; Douglas was fine with that. It was mostly about his decision to move to PEI and that it was still a good decision, despite everything.

Roger caught Amy on the way and started to thank her for coming.

"You're not going to play again, are you?"

"Not friggin' likely." Roger laughed.

"You don't think you can drive me back to Charlottetown then, do you?" Amy batted her eyelashes out of habit.

Roger could not say no to a VIP. He went into action. If they passed anyone worth saying something to on their way to the car, Roger didn't notice. In no time, he and the performer were heading east on Route 2. For a while, Amy was quiet. She had said things to drivers before that had gotten her left on the side of the highway. By the time they got to Coleman, though, Roger's obvious distress was too severe for her to ignore. The man was on the verge of tears.

"I guess you had that accordion—or do you call it a zydeco?—a long time? Was it your grandfather's?"

"Huh?"

"Oh. You were embarrassed for your friends?"

"Huh?"

"People didn't like your playing?"

"They liked it!"

"Are you kidding? They hated that. What they loved most about to-night was me kissing the priest."

"You don't know anything about it."

"You grew up here, I guess."

"Sort of." Not having spent the first few years of his life on PEI seemed to have cost Roger something. He was not an Islander, but, in his mind, he was not a come-from-away either. He was something different entirely, though he lacked the self-awareness and self-definition to be proud of it. "Ice cream?" The service station that had fifty-cent cones was still open.

"Nope."

"Rightie." Roger did not let his foot up on the gas passing the station. "It must be exciting, living in Toronto. Big city."

"It must be weird living here. You don't know any different, I suppose."

"Maybe I should have moved to Charlottetown. Sometimes I think that. More appreciation for the arts there," said Roger. He might have fit in more in Charlottetown, that's true. But he had, somewhere along the line, misplaced the urge to fit in. He swallowed. "You're cynical, I guess. I guess you don't believe in love?"

"Oh!" Amy was unsure how the subject had come up. She loved it when someone gave her a chance to answer that question directly. Her poetry had always been an indirect response to indirect accusations. Arts journalists were too busy showing how smart they were to ask about matters of the heart.

"I do believe in love. More than anyone I know. It's my internal compass, the only thing that matters. It's just that I'm so far away from it sometimes. All the time. I don't talk about it. It's nobody's business but mine. People mistake sentiment for love. Love is bread. Sentiment is the gunk we pour on it."

Amy took great pleasure in saying this and had a few other insights she wanted to impart on Roger, about art and identity, and colonialism. Then she saw the tears running down his face.

"I know, I know, I know," said Roger. He took her hand. She hadn't had a chance to wash it since Douglas LaPierre held it. "You're smart. About love, I guess is what I mean."

"I see. Somebody broke your heart?" Looking at Roger, Amy had a flashback to her time in high school, the guys who had wooed her, their naivety, their longing, their poor sense of who they were and what they needed. The flashback made no sense—this Acadian Centre guy must be forty. Shouldn't he be passed that now?

"I'll make it work somehow."

"You've found that about life? That it works?"

"Of course! You just have to keep your eye on the prize."

"Good to know."

Amy looked at Roger's lanky arms on the steering wheel. His face was streaked with tears. She imagined making love to him would be sweet and awkward. But he made no effort to follow her to her room at the Charlottetown Hotel. Once he had escorted Amy safely to the lobby, Roger headed straight back to his car and immediately headed back Up West, never thinking to stop at the half-dozen Charlottetown bars where you might find a forty-year-old grandmother who needed to be rescued from her abusive father.

Yet Roger had not totally given up on Debbie. He was back to where he was before this visit: waiting over trying, patience over persistence. It was the best way. It was also the easiest way. He had so many other things to take care of. People were counting on him. So many things wouldn't happen if he didn't push them forward.

CHAPTER 12

TRACEY SHAW (TILLARD) REFUSED to wear the all-black outfit Mitchell wanted her to wear, not simply because she didn't want to mess her hair. No, she was sure they'd be caught. Better sneaking tactics would not save them. What would save them was looking normal and having a good excuse.

"It's all a misunderstanding," declared Tracey in a stagey voice to no one in particular. She was wearing a denim jacket over a white collared blouse, and jeans, purposely, to prove her point, too tight for a quick getaway. "You just wouldn't believe it! Wouldn't at all. I can hardly believe it myself!"

"Shhh," said Mitchell, who wore a black balaclava on his head underneath an old helmet he had painted black. Roger warned him not to pull it down over his face unless necessary.

Roger didn't expect that they'd have to make up stories or pull masks over their faces. Plan A was so masterful that a Plan B was unnecessary. He was surprised how easily its pieces fell into place, as if they had been provided to him by an unseen force, rather than practice from a lifetime of putting unlikely plans into action. Blind to our own skills, we attribute them to God, fate, or luck.

The three of them were slogging along the creek that ran across the bottom of St. Bernard's Roman Catholic Cemetery. Raymond Niese was the only Niese buried there; Ricky Gallant was one of seventy-three Gallants; the Arsenaults came in a close second. The slope was steep, the ground sticky, like marshmallows cooked over a bonfire. It had been a cool summer and now in October, the ground was soggy. Bits of barbed wire from another century were tied around trees here and there. Each step crunched broken twigs and fallen leaves. Branches had stuck themselves into Tracey's hair. Still, the route was a well-known covert approach to St. Bernard's parish house; in a few weeks, Halloween trick or treaters would come this way, armed with toilet paper and eggs.

"Watch the branch," Roger called out.

"There are thousands of 'em," said Tracey. "Got a particular one in mind?"

Beatrice was, technically speaking, having nothing to do with this. But she was watching the parish house from across the road at the Acadian Cultural Centre and Fun Park. At 10am, she'd turn the Centre's sign from "Fermé" to "Bienvenue!" and then they'd be on their own. She had waitresses, salesgirls, and interpreters to scold, as well as a busload of Québécois tourists to shoo away from the breakables. If she glanced at something amiss, she might call Roger's cellphone to utter a few words resembling a warning, but Beatrice refused to guarantee anything.

Neither could Roger be counted upon to answer her call, no matter how dire the situation. He kept the ringer of his scratched-up cellphone on mute. He didn't like other people using up his minutes. This was a challenge. The executive director, president, and chair of the Acadian Cultural Centre and Fun Park had, over the last few years, managed to get himself on pretty much every board and committee west of Richmond. Roger had even managed to climb aboard a couple of not-for-profits in Summerside after befriending Sister Mary-Margaret Shea, the nun who ran the town's food bank. A poetess who cited Emily Dickinson and Tennyson as influences, Sister Mary-Margaret was artistically generous enough to say yes to invitations to read at variety shows as far away as Tignish. She didn't like to be in the same room as Beatrice, who, as a single woman, served no purpose other than her own, but Sister Mary-Margaret got almost flirty when Roger was in the room.

In Miscouche, Wellington, Abrams-Village, and Mont-Carmel—the heart of the Evangeline Region recognized by the provincial government and tourism promotion agency—Roger remained a non-entity. For those who chummed around with Léonce LeBlanc, or on a daily basis endured the coffee at the Wellington Co-op Complex, Roger was someone you read about in the paper. Perhaps he was a fabrication, some character invented by Caroline MacPhail for the amusement of readers of *The Spectator-Herald*. He was not part of their "scene."

This hole in Roger's web of power might be blamed on Léonce and Réné LeBlanc after LeBlanc Construction was forced to spend an extra fifty-five thousand dollars, so Réné claimed, to make up for deficiencies in the Centre's construction—crooked countertops, leaks in the various roofs. LeBlanc Construction was famous for getting out of repairing so-called deficiencies. Most of its customers, including the provincial government, were content to let this record continue unchallenged, no matter how many trips to the big box home renovation stores in Summerside were needed.

"That Roger Niese is always trying to get something for free," Réné complained to his wife. "They say he charges people extra for the nineteenth hole of the mini-golf." This was true; the nineteenth hole was an elaborate miniaturized replica of Nova Scotia's Fortress of Louisbourg and accounted for more than half of the cost of the construction of the course, as Réné very well knew. There was a seventy-five-cent premium to play it.

Even the Mont-Carmel church newsletter, usually put together with painstaking comprehensiveness by Father Eloi Poirier, did not include mention of events at the Centre. Roger's efforts to coordinate the Centre's activities with Evangeline Region activities—"dividing up the summer weekends," as they say—were rebuffed.

"I'm not saying the Accents LeBlanc hold a grudge," said Roger, using the nickname he had come up with for Léonce and Réné. "I'm just saying I keep looking in my mail for invitations and they never come."

It was fine. That summer, the Centre hosted its first-ever "Lobster at Cost" Festival the same weekend as the Evangeline Region International Acadian Conference. The lobster sold out; there was still a line-up way past the St. Bernard's Funeral Co-op when they were down to serving nothing but rolls and gravy. In the last few years, tour operators catering to European tourists had added the Centre to their itinerary. Although there were only a couple of hundred of them a season, the Europeans' on-trend accessories and strangely accented English excited the Centre staff. The Europeans didn't much care for mini-golf or paddle boats, but they loved the Ev&Gab preserves, a handcrafted line of jams, jellies, and pickles Roger had concocted to keep Tracey busy, so she'd have less time to mock the customers.

The Europeans loved the Ferris wheel and the nearly constant musical performances—advertised as "old-time music" despite the drum

machine and occasional bursts of rapping—and the video show chron-
icling the saga of Evangeline and Gabriel shot in what staff learned
to call "vérité documentary" style. The shaky camera work and poor
lighting left lots to the imagination, especially in the section where the
British soldier, played by Mitchell, taunted Evangeline. But the strobe
lights that went off in the theatre during the parade scene left viewers
pleasingly dizzy. For the filming of that parade scene, all Up West had
shown up, wearing, as instructed, the closest thing they had to period
costumes. Roger had hired a helicopter for the occasion and these aeri-
al shots comprised nine minutes and forty seconds of the fifteen-minute video.

Fall was a quieter season, though the restaurant and snack bar, and
the dance and music classes, kept the Centre in business year-round.
That Friday morning, the absence of Roger, Mitchell, and Tracey might
very well be noticed. Elis Getson spent most of the day looking for
Tracey to show her latest batch of tea-cozies slated for the gift shop.

Beatrice would never have asked for help. Yet it was her predica-
ment that prompted the plan. And Beatrice had established its ur-
gency when, just a day earlier, she casually mentioned to Roger that
Father Michael Chaisson had a Friday meeting with the bishop in
Charlottetown.

The bishop, Howard MacDonald, who was from Kinkora, had "initi-
ated a dialogue" with Island clergy about the legalization of same-sex
marriage and why, despite this thing called the law, it should mean
nothing for Roman Catholics, who should ignore it until it goes away,
which it inevitably would. Father Michael had written up a clever
speech Island priests could work into a homily, or cut and paste into
letters or emails, to send to parishioners who were asking unnecessary
questions, or if, heaven forbid, the priests received a request to perform a gay wedding. Father Michael's years of being the "cool priest" to
St. Bernard's parish teen group were far behind him.

You could argue that this was because, as a young man, Michael had
strongly influenced what was going on around him and so, like someone with a brain injury, was as an adult unable to imagine that his view
was just one among many. His youthful good looks had not only bur-
dened him with a lifetime of vanity, but they had also, in attracting him
so much fawning attention, made him impatient when attention was
diverted from him. Father Michael was set on the bishop circulating
his speech widely.

Widely, of course, wasn't what it used to be. There were hardly any troops left to rally. Father Euseb Arsenault had passed away at the tender age of ninety-two, leaving Father Michael in charge not only of St. Bernard's, but also St. Simon & St. Jude's in Tignish, and St. Anne's in Bloomfield. Father Eloi was still around, in charge of Mount-Carmel, as well as Wellington and St. Philippe/St. Jacques. But Father Eloi lived in his own folk-singing, rainbow-dappled world and never read anything Father Michael sent him. A young, dumpy upstart named Ramon Ortiz from who-knows-where had taken over Sacred Heart in Alberton and St. Bernadette's in Brockton; his parishioners complained that they couldn't understand a word he said. Father Ramon Ortiz was of little use to Michael.

Since seminary, Father Michael had expected to be bishop someday. He hadn't expected he'd be one of just a handful in the running for the position. Some people in St. Louis-St. Edward noticed the increasingly far-away look in their priest's eyes; Elis said it gave her the chills.

The meeting with Bishop Howard MacDonald meant that Father Michael would be gone for at least four hours, probably closer to eight. Father Michael liked to eat Lebanese food when he was in Charlottetown and often gave into the temptation to browse the pottery on Victoria Row. An end-of-the-season sale might lure the priest into dallying into the evening.

This all made the timing of the mission crucial.

One of the pieces of information that would be included in a manual for living in St. Louis-St. Edward, if such a manual existed, was this: It takes three days for a letter dropped in the box at Gallant and Sons store to arrive at any other Prince County destination, even though the same letter would take just two days to reach Charlottetown. This meant that someone like, say, Father Michael might come home Friday, stuffed with falafel, to find a piece of correspondence mailed from down the road on Wednesday that the sender might have, by Thursday, wanted to burn.

Beatrice's rare lapse in judgment was fueled by the sort of vanity she couldn't tolerate in others. The generous mindset with which she wrote the letter made her forget its boastful and, in some eyes, heretical core message.

She had recently and discreetly been ordained a Roman Catholic priest.

Admittedly, the ordination was performed by a small group of women, mostly from Charlottetown.

Admittedly, two of them had dabbled in Wicca back in the 1980s.

Admittedly, most of them had a fashion sense that suggested a belief that mumus and sandals were all-season attire.

But the course of study had been rigorous, the vows similar to those demanded by papal ordinances. The woman who had ordained Beatrice was one of the Butler girls from Charlottetown, the oldest of five, Patty, who had broken with the family after their father, a prominent lawyer, was convicted of sexually assaulting the youngest sister.

For her part, Beatrice had no intention of celebrating mass nor any desire to hear confession. But she liked knowing she could if she wanted to. She was accustomed to listening to other people's problems.

After several years of dating, Phillip Sinclair had dropped out of the picture. His declining health prevented him from visiting PEI anymore. Though he called Beatrice frequently, he was too gentlemanly to complain about this ache or that visit to the doctor's office. Phillip wouldn't tell Beatrice what was wrong with him. He was more interested in her priesthood.

"I always knew you had a mystic side to you, but I thought of you more as a Hindu queen than a paltry disciple of Peter," he told her one day. "You should be ruling that province by now."

"Oh, fudge. It's just a little something that might come in handy."

Beatrice wasn't even sure how public she wanted her ordination to be, which was the crux of this current dilemma. She had already told Roger, Tracey, Mitchell, and a couple of other staff members about it. Everyone was so caught up in the Centre's mechanizations—casting for the new play about the expulsion of the Acadians that Susan Kennedy had written, draining water from the ponds in the fall, sourcing a new beets supplier for the pickles—they simply congratulated her and went on with their business without thinking about the religious repercussions.

But Monsignora Patty Butler pressured Beatrice to report her new status to the local Pope-approved priest. The men should know clergy-in-waiting were available if ill-health or double-bookings prevented them from executing their duties. It was important that the church knew of the women's willingness to serve. The declining ranks of priests, for a multitude of reasons, would eventually force the church to take advantage of what was on offer, menstruation or no menstruation.

Beatrice mailed the letter at Gallant and Sons Wednesday morning. That afternoon, Tracey confirmed the date of the baptism of her two girls, Samantha and Sabrina, for whom Beatrice was to be the god-mother. Needless to say, Roger was the godfather.

Tracey had surprised everyone by marrying old Lester Shaw, who had been single since his wife Linda divorced him in the 1970s. The July-November romance began, like many hangovers, at the Irish Heritage Folk Festival in Kinkora. Roger had sent Tracey to hunt for talent, espe-cially someone who could play the mandolin. Lester, who had gone that far east on a whim, didn't play anything at all, but listened seriously to all Tracey had to say. He found her flippancy calming since he never had to take anything she said seriously.

Lester, who already had two daughters close in age to Tracey, turned out to be, after all these years, a decent husband. "He doesn't look like much and he can't string two words together worth shit, but he's a smooth operator," Tracey told Roger.

"Glad you're moving on." Their relationship had, at this point, been over for more than a decade.

"It's comforting to see you're not."

Tracey Shaw always claimed that she didn't want kids because they wouldn't take her seriously and would end up hurting themselves. But she turned out to be a decent mother to her twins. Samantha and Sabrina were surprisingly pretty little things, destined to win pro-vincial and perhaps even national pageants. Beatrice was sure of it. Samantha had a slightly bigger forehead; people thought she'd be the smart one.

Beatrice, who had become a lay eucharist minister in St. Bernard's, as well as in Tignish, took charge of planning the double baptism. She had some excellent ideas for scriptures. She would give communion at the mass. She would do the second reading. She would pick the altar boys. And, of course, the music. All with Father Michael's approval.

In the midst of all this baptism planning, Beatrice realized that her announcement letter to Father Michael, no matter how gentle and respectful, might put it all in jeopardy. It was entirely possible that Father Michael might refuse to perform the baptism or refuse her as godmother. Worse, he could de-minister her. That would have been a great embarrassment. Nobody had ever removed Beatrice Perry from a position. For her to perform the baptism herself was unthinkable. Her priesthood was too fresh to guarantee the baptism would hold.

Beatrice fretted over the problem Wednesday evening, sometimes in front of Tracey, who wasn't inclined to keep any secret when the telling might amuse her. Roger got wind of it Thursday morning. He called Beatrice to his office, now located in a cedar-shingled outbuilding. The building was roughly made of two-by-fours and the walls had no gyprock or insulation. It was one of a series of undersized replicas of buildings that might have comprised a historic Acadian village main street, if historic Acadian villages had had main streets or streets at all. On summer days, costumed characters passed by his window, on their way to churn butter in front of the General Store or bake bread in The Bakery's brick oven. Today, there was just Janet Gaudet painting the boardwalk green.

Beatrice glumly took a seat in Roger's office and confessed she had made a mistake sending the letter.

"It's the girls I'm worried about," said Beatrice. "They don't need any fuss on a day like that day. Baptism photos are more precious than confirmation photos."

"Sometimes you've got to take action to make sure nothing happens," said Roger after some thought. Though he was seldom given the opportunity, he loved playing the role of counsellor and, as Beatrice fiddled nervously with her hands, he stretched out the process as long as he could. He wanted her happy, for her sake and for the Centre's. When Beatrice was anxious, she was unkind to the talent. She'd let her tiny glasses slide down her nose, catch them with her thumb and say things like "I can pretend that didn't happen, if it would be helpful to you" or "You might want to rethink the promises you make on your promotional material."

Who knew what other repercussions there might be. The tensions between the Acadian Cultural Centre and Fun Park—that is, Roger—and St. Bernard's parish—that is, Father Michael—had not diminished. The expansion of St. Bernard's Parish Hall in 2000 had been particularly galling. The Centre had just upgraded its dining room; it would now be an upscale culinary experience presided over by Phillip Sinclair's son Greg, who had been a chef in Montreal before deciding that rural life might be the buffer his cocaine habit needed. His father had talked up PEI when Greg was growing up. Later, this mystique was fed by Phillip's low-key affair with Beatrice.

"Those Islanders are more cultured than you'd think," Phillip told his son, misremembering his first trips to the province.

Working with Beatrice at the Centre, Chef Sinclair never figured out that this lovely lady was the sole source of his optimism about the life he could build on PEI.

Chef Sinclair's peasant food was exquisite, but expensive for Up West. Travel magazines in the United States and Europe went wild, but locals couldn't get their heads around one-dollar oysters, since you could just go out and pick them out of a river yourself if you needed them so badly. St. Bernard's Parish Hall, meanwhile, launched a summer lobster supper, during which it sold lobster plates for two dollars less than the Centre's Fill You Up Longfellow Lobster Supper Extravaganza Dining Room.

With his own hands, Father Michael had planted a patch of basil out back of the Parish Hall, around where men used to piss during wedding dances when the washroom lineup was unbearably long. He called it organic. It was served on almost everything coming out of the St. Bernard's Parish Hall kitchen. People—not just Susan Kennedy, who boasted about the lovely lunches she had when on work trips to Moncton and Halifax—raved about it. Chef Sinclair, who had recklessly sourced his basil from Quebec's Eastern Townships, was left scrambling.

The Acadian Cultural Centre and Fun Park didn't have much room for more cultivation. The Ev&Gab preserves business utilized most of the Centre campus that was unoccupied by the main building, the Acadian Village, the half-dozen random pavilions, the outdoor amphitheatre, innumerable playground structures, including the Ferris wheel, and the Midas Basin Pond, with its little dock and boathouse. Tracey grew raspberries, strawberries, blueberries, cucumbers, and beets along the north end of the property. In the summer of 2004, they ended up ripping up the cucumbers to compete in the basil wars.

In another shot across the bow, Father Michael introduced a concert series that stretched the definition of "spiritual music." A medieval choral ensemble kicked off the inaugural season, but gradually the talent lineup grew to include acts the Centre had for a long time billed as exclusive. Jessica and Josh Parker. Fancy Night Out. Terry Gallant. The Cormier Sisters. Sick O' More Sycamores. Dancers Alliance International. Susan and Earl Kennedy had even been asked to perform a tango at the monthly (weekly in the summer) St. Bernard's Parish Hall variety show, on the condition they didn't cross-dress, as they had done in those early Super Summer Follies shows.

Counterprogramming was a strategy seldom used on Palmer Road. If the Centre had a comedy night, so did the St. Bernard's Parish Hall. If the Centre had a Wednesday Night Céilidh, so did St. Bernard's Parish Hall. The main exceptions were the pro-life events Roger was glad to let the church monopolize. On the other side of things, Beatrice had seen to it that the St. Louis-St. Edward, St. Lawrence, Miminegash, and Tignish pageants were hosted at the Centre. Beatrice even had her own "Pageant Central" stationery and website, which was maintained by Tracey, who had taken a computer course at Holland College.

For those Up West residents who weren't emotionally invested in the rivalry, the period of this intense competition was a true delight. There was a choice of something to do many nights of the week, especially during tourism season. There were jobs or, if you didn't want to ruin your Employment Insurance benefits, cash-only contracts. It was flattering having national performers visit. Kids who studied piano or fiddle or bagpipe or clog dancing were getting pretty good. More tourists certainly meant more money. You could see it when you drove down Union, Thompson, Deblois, and Palmer roads. More lawn decorations. Bigger cars. Bigger garages. Even an outdoor pool here and there, for those six weeks a year you could use one. If Roger had ever thought much about his legacy, rather than his next big idea, this is what would have pleased him the most.

On what had been the sole unoccupied corner of Palmer and Thompson roads, Lester Shaw had built a strip mall. The Kentucky Fried Chicken outlet that opened during the strip mall's launch put the place on the West Prince map, even though the KFC franchise, operated by Lester himself, quickly went under. It was replaced by a dollar store, also run by Lester. Tracey made sure her husband sold nothing similar to what was carried in the Centre's gift shop. Up the road from the Centre, James Arsenault and his wife Marissa Arsenault (Gallant) had opened a B&B, Gabriel's Keep, in their ramshackle old farmhouse. On Union Road, Arnold Crozier opened a pizza and burger place.

Still, you had to be careful what you said or people would think you were taking sides. Beatrice was the only person in the Centre leadership Father Michael would call, the only one who would take his calls.

That line of communication could not be jeopardized. Father Michael was known to attend Centre events and even stroll its grounds. He'd tsk tsk when he came upon the thrice daily summertime performance of the expulsion of the Acadians—there were five Acadians for every British soldier. The ratio made the Acadians seem rather feeble. There was no record of the priest paying admission. Beatrice let it go. It wasn't worth squawking about. The actors, the servers, and the retail and security staff were instructed to ignore him.

Yet here they were, courting Father Michael's wrath.

Of course, Roger was not as nimble as he used to be. During their planning, he and Mitchell spent a good hour figuring out which window of the priest's house would be the easiest to break open and climb through. They had settled on the rear porch window when Beatrice, who had been eavesdropping, wordlessly set the parish house key in front of them. Elis Getson did the cleaning at the parish house. She owed Beatrice, who had tutored her granddaughter Jordan, who was failing English at Westisle.

Tracey's involvement in the scheme stemmed from the fact that her husband and her two infants were driving her crazy at home. She had to get out, even if it meant getting arrested. The Centre's bookkeeper, Betty Ann Pineau, who excelled at not asking too many questions, agreed to babysit the twins.

The trio followed the fir windbreak that divided church property from James Arsenault's farm. His potato field was tilled to a chunky mud and would stay that way for the winter, its valuable topsoil offered up to the wind until next spring's planting. The muck forced them to stay on the graveyard side of the trees, where traffic on Palmer Road could see them. They scurried until they got to the priest's shed, shivering as they ran.

The metal flashing of the shed's trim made a cracking sound when Mitchell leaned against it. They snuck a peek around the corner. A car was coming down Palmer Road. It was likely Susan Kennedy, on the way home from delivering her *Spectator-Heralds*. Nobody was more capable of spreading word of their intended crime. Roger stood perfectly still. Tracey ducked behind some shrubbery. Mitchell toyed with the combination lock on the barn door, which opened without effort; the lock had not been pushed closed.

"Wee!" said Tracey, dashing inside like an incontinent concert goer coming upon a pristine, unoccupied portapotty.

"Whew!" said Mitchell. They had already relived several of his favourite *Mission: Impossible* scenes and they weren't even in the house yet. "Gotcha! Phase one!" He laughed to himself. Roger didn't have the heart to shush him.

The shed was tightly packed with stuff: bikes and coolers, but mostly folding chairs. Mitchell dug into his pocket and pulled out a flashlight.

"Put that out!" said Roger.

"Nobody's going to see!"

"I know. The batteries are almost dead. Save the power!"

"I wonder if he has any dirty magazines hidden in here," laughed Tracey. "I'd like a souvenir."

"Shhh," said Roger. "I think I hear a car in the driveway."

They stood as still as possible for thirty seconds. Roger watched the crack in the door for shadows. Sighing theatrically, Tracey stumbled backward.

"Gross! I sat on something sticky. My jeans!"

On its own accord, the door blew open, flooding the shed with light. Tracey was leaning back on a pile of railway ties. Despite their age, their creosote glaze was still tacky.

"Somebody's going to pay for my ruined jeans. I suppose that somebody's going to be me."

"Tracey!" said Mitchell. "Go do the lookout!"

"Hm," said Roger. "Those look familiar."

Neither Tracey nor Mitchell knew what Roger was talking about, but Roger was on to something. He scanned the rafters. Fish rods, golf clubs, skis, and buoys were lined up according to length. Dusty windows, their original plastic hanging off them in tatters. There were eight or ten snow shovels. It seemed an excessive number, considering that Sean Pineau reliably blew out the priest's driveway and the church's parking lot after every snowfall.

"If it was Susan Kennedy, she's probably gone now," said Tracey. "God bless her darling little heart."

"Maybe she left muffins on the front porch," said Mitchell. "Susan Kennedy makes good muffins."

Mitchell leaned out the door to see if Susan's car was there. It was not. Without a word of warning, he scurried up to the concrete walkway that ran from the church to the parish house. His two co-conspirators followed at a brisk pace. Tracey, self-conscious of the tackiness on her rear, tried to walk with dignity. She hoped Beatrice was watching from across the road and could see her excellent posture. Beatrice would be proud. Or jealous.

Roger was wearing his pager and Blackberry phone, one on each hip. In the front pocket of his dress shirt, he had stuffed a juice box, in case his blood sugar took a dive. Over the shirt, he wore a black hoodie with pockets containing snap-off lights for his bicycle, a notepad, a pen, and a gold-coloured coin commemorating the four hundredth anniversary of Samuel de Champlain's arrival in the Bay of Fundy. Since it was issued by the Royal Canadian Mint a couple of years earlier, he carried the coin everywhere. It reminded him that history was long and his part in it was short. Samuel de Champlain lasted to age sixty-one. But he got himself on a coin. That didn't seem like an outrageous thing to aim for.

At some point, maybe in his thirties, Roger figured that, fair or not, creators were more likely to go down in history than impresarios. If he wanted to make a mark, he'd have to be an artist. He had tried his hand at writing shows—six plays and two musicals so far—but they hadn't turned out the way he wanted. His first musical, *Walking after Midnight with Patsy Cline*, ran just six days. He had written it in just four, after seeing the Confederation Centre's production of *A Closer Walk with Patsy Cline*. It was hard to say which was a bigger factor in the show's abrupt cancellation: the lawyers' letters from the Patsy Cline estate and the Confederation Centre of the Arts or Caroline MacPhail's damning review in *The Spectator-Herald*. "Those who thought these songs could not be ruined by a sloppy structure, a sloppy sense of timing, sloppy casting, and sloppy sets will sit with their mouths gaping through the entirety of this sloppy rip-off," she wrote.

The bilingual musical production that sprang purely from Roger's imagination didn't fare much better. His *Sylvain!*, based on the life of the Island's first Acadian priest, Sylvain-Ephrem Poirier, had fourteen scenes and twenty-eight songs. The scene where the aging priest desperately and irritably goes from house to house, demanding that his fellow Acadians supply him with firewood, made audiences feel especially uncomfortable. It ran for three weeks.

Although *Sylvain!*'s title role was that of the priest, Roger had conceived the role of Father Sylvain-Ephrem's sister Nancy as a star vehicle for Kate Pineau. In the play, her "dialogue" was fiddle playing, intended to portray the feeling, if not the words spoken, of the priest's most supportive sibling. Nancy, at the end of the play, gives the priest a piece of wood, but one too damp to catch fire. In the final act, Father Sylvain-Ephrem dies shivering with the cold but knowing that he was loved by someone.

Much hinged on Kate playing Nancy Bouchard (nee Poirier). Roger had invited his old friend for a drive through the national park on PEI's north shore and Kate, to his surprise, agreed to come along. The drive was the first time they had been alone together since Kate quit the Acadian Cultural Centre that New Year's Eve fifteen years earlier. Since her resignation, Kate had refused to step foot inside any Centre building, fearing Roger would make a scene. But she dutifully dragged her girls Sherrie and Krystal, and then, later, Bethany, to their rehearsals, performances, fundraisers, committee meetings, and, when they got into their teens, gift-shop shifts.

Arnold Crozier had left her in 2002. Or rather, Kate threw Arnold out in 2002. Marrying an older man meant marrying someone who had a longer list of habits than you did. Heavy drinking was one of Arnold's. Other habits included: clipping his toenails in the living room, leaving the gas stove on, and neglecting to mention where he spent the previous night. Arnold lost a lot of money on the factory outlet/flea market in Wellington. Arnold had thought he and Réné LeBlanc were equal partners, but it turned out their relationship most closely resembled that of conman and mark. He was doing better in business by himself, doing better in life living by himself.

"All right," Kate told Roger after he offered her the Nancy role for the eighth time. "I'll do it. I need something else in my life. Why not?"

Just like *Walking after Midnight with Patsy Cline, Sylvain!* was a flop. The story was impossible to follow. To save the season, Roger dropped the plot and turned *Sylvain!* into a variety show called *Classic Acadian Spirit*. It was classic tune after classic tune for two hours, then a hard stop. The songs they couldn't fit in one night, they started with the next night, so each night felt like a new production. When it became known that, at long last, Kate was performing at the Acadian Cultural Centre and Fun Park, all of Up West came out to see it. Some came from as far as Mont-Carmel, even Summerside. Kate had been sorely missed. The show didn't close until November, an amazing extension of the shoulder season. Roger wished it had all gone as planned. *Sylvain!* was a story people should know about. But he couldn't help but be pleased to have sold out so many shows, whatever it was on stage.

★

Elis Getson's key opened the front door of the parish house. The trio hemmed and hawed in the porch for a few moments. Without a word spoken, all three of them took off their shoes, leaving them in a pile on the little rug there.

"Hallooo!" called out Tracey, just loud enough to say that she had tried. "Sorry we didn't call!"

"Shush," said Mitchell, dizzy with excitement.

There was nothing on the floor in front of the door's mail slot. On the ledge by the door, they found only flyers, some still wrapped in plastic.

The kitchen counter was covered with innumerable pasta containers and cookbooks. The letter, Roger thought, was too recent for Father Michael to have stuffed amongst the recipes and expired coupons beside the bread box.

"This ain't going to be as easy as you thought," said Tracey.

"I know. We'll have to touch things," Roger sighed.

Tracey followed Mitchell upstairs. Roger wandered nervously around the ground floor, his gaze moving to the right and left as though he were taking in a hostile landscape. He was not as focused on Beatrice's letter as he should have been. There were things on his mind, things that might have been there for such a long time they were hard to recognize for what they were: suspicions. Roger opened the pantry door and leaned inside. You could have hidden three or four bodies in the space. Like the priest's shed, it was densely packed. Among the boxes of shortbreads, he spotted two toasters, six coffee pots. He went through drawers. There were at least eighteen place settings that matched the Centre's cutlery, Ikea stuff that Roger's brother Allan had sent from Ottawa, Montreal, and Toronto over the years. Nobody else on the Island had that much Ikea cutlery.

In the closet under the main stairs, Roger found three identical sundials, a half-dozen solar-powered lights, eight planters, and two custom-made brochure racks, all a little worn. All of which he recognized. Most of which he himself had purchased.

In the linen closet at the top of the stairs, Roger found twenty-two stainless steel toilet paper holders, the kind that attach to the wall with little screws, the kind a public institution buys at its peril because they're so easy to steal. The Acadian Cultural Centre and Fun Park had lost twenty-two before switching to the commercial kind that requires a special key to remove.

The biggest find was upstairs in the priest's closet, where about a decade's worth of gift-shop items lined cheap white assemble-it-yourself shelving. Flip-flops and sunglasses and lobster keychains that Tracey had curated were gathered here like a museum collection honouring a long-dead civilization. There were piles of Centre programs still wrapped in plastic bindings that must have been pulled off tables and out of boxes before they could be flipped through. Roger's insistence to the volunteer ushers that "Every program counts!" didn't seem so miserly anymore.

"I got it!" Roger heard Tracey shout.

The room that used to be the teen lounge was now a library full of shelves and filing cabinets. There was a silver metal "Inbox" tray on one of the filing cabinets. Beatrice's letter was on the top, unopened.

"Damn, it must have come yesterday!" said Roger, joining Tracey in the little room. "They're getting better, they are."

"Cool!" said Mitchell, who stood in the doorway. "So great!" He couldn't believe how well the plan had gone. He jumped up and clapped his hands, applauding his brilliance. In his excitement, he forgot the issues he had around excitement.

Mitchell felt the brain buzz that meant a seizure was coming on. Excitement turned to panic. He dashed out into the hallway. Roger and Tracey looked at each other for a moment before following.

They found Mitchell sitting on the toilet in the upstairs bathroom. The vanity there had twin sinks and a matching set of gold-gilded wall-mounted holders for toothbrushes, rinse cups, and towels. Mitchell's head was between his knees.

"Give me a minute," said Mitchell.

Tracey sat down on the linoleum floor next to her woozy friend.

"Beatrice had better appreciate this," said Tracey.

"As for me, I certainly do!" said Mitchell.

"Alrightie," said Roger. Almost absentmindedly, he wandered back to the library and found himself rummaging through the priest's mail.

At the bottom of one pile, he found a yellowed envelope with a return address of D. Arsenault in Cornwall.

Roger often wondered if God had a plan for him. He had assumed that if God had, indeed, outlined something, it would match Roger's plans. Now he saw that God's local representative had been playing an uncredited role in Roger's fate.

Roger expected that he would want to read what was in this letter. He stuffed it into the front pocket of his jeans. While his hand was in there, he felt his cellphone vibrating and then heard the first few notes of "St. Anne's Reel." He did not have to look to see who was calling.

"Someone has forgotten something," said the voice on the other end of the phone.

"Did I....?"

"Not you! The owner. Him. You know. Him. Michael," snapped Beatrice.

Roger looked at his watch. Only sixty-four minutes had passed since they struck out on their mission. Father Michael wouldn't have crossed the county line yet. But of course, if the priest had stopped at the new Save-Easy in Elmsdale to pick up some munchies for the drive east, spotted some ice cream on sale, bought eight two-litre containers, and decided to head home to drop it off before it melted, then sixty-four minutes was exactly the right amount of time for the priest to again be back at his front door. Roger dashed down the hall, his arms flailing.

"Go, go!" he ordered Tracey and Mitchell.

"I dunno," said Mitchell, looking a little groggy. Tracey shrugged and assumed a half standing position.

Roger rushed to see if the upstairs hallway's front window would give him a view of the driveway. It did not. He dashed back to the top of the stairs and slid to a halt on the woven rug there. The rug, though, did not stop. The rug kept going, making a break downstairs toward the front door until it reached the stairs' halfway point. That's when the rug left Roger, leaving Roger to tumble to the bottom all by himself.

The Acadian Culture Centre and Fun Park president, CEO, and executive director, if he had had his wits about him, would have found himself staring at Father Michael, who arrived in the porch loaded down with ice cream and apple juice, which was also on sale. But Roger was not entirely conscious. He could say nothing that was of any use whatsoever. The priest, as he dropped his foodstuffs, was a blur. A blur that exclaimed, "Sweet Jesus! What are you doing here?"

Roger gave no reply.

Father Michael circled Roger, tapping him with his foot to get a sense that there was still life inside this limp body.

"Roger," Father Michael snapped as if he was talking to someone who was drunk or lazy or both. "Roger Niese?"

Upstairs, Mitchell and Tracey had, for a few seconds, entertained the notion that Roger had purposely caused a distraction to give them an opportunity to escape. The duo peered over the railing at the top of the stairs. They saw Roger in a heap on the floor and both scrambled down in a panic.

"What's happening?" said Father Michael. "What are...?"

"Roger should explain," said Tracey, all her rehearsals forgotten.

"I'll get water," said Mitchell.

It was too late for that.

The priest drove Roger to the Alberton hospital. The receptionist at the Alberton hospital sent them to Summerside. Tracey went along, while Mitchell stayed at the Alberton hospital to wait for someone from the Centre to come pick him up. Tracey spent the forty-five-minute drive deflecting Father Michael's questions. She used a combination of outlandishness and pathos.

"Wouldn't it have been funny if we had the whole junior hockey team in there, waiting to jump out at you, sticks at the ready?" she said. "But then, poor Roger. What happened to him wasn't very funny, was it? I wouldn't have wanted to take that fall, would you?"

Roger, simultaneously groggy and animated, yelled from the back-seat.

"Got one in every port, I suppose, from here to Souris," Roger spat. "All lined up. In storage! And why wouldn't you? Who cares what anybody else thinks? That's the way we'll move forward, into the future without tearing our hair out. That's it! But that's the way we'll blow the whole shit ball up, too. Sorry for the language, father. Oh, Richmond! The dairybar's closed! Summer's over...."

"Roger," said the priest. "You've got to settle down."

"That's what me mum used to tell us. When I was a kid, this big. Told me again before she kicked the bucket. Settle down."

Roger's disorientation granted him a certain impertinence. Life events he had avoided thinking about came to the surface. Perhaps the fall had loosened memories in his brain. He hadn't come to terms with his mother's passing six years earlier. Sarah Carruthers (Niese) had died during a prolonged dispute with her second husband. Eddie had mocked her in front of friends at a dinner party. Sarah stomped off in a huff and set up camp at a motel in Nepean, stockpiling the room with an arsenal of romance fiction which she'd read as she waited for Eddie to come apologize to her. Eddie figured his wife needed time alone with her books. Sarah was dead from a stroke for two days before the motel staff found her.

"She died alone, me mum. She was in a huff. She liked being in a huff. Suited her." Roger muttered. He was crying when they stopped for the traffic light in Miscouche. His sobbing intensified when they passed the Acadian Museum, which had a special exhibition on fiddle-making.

"Shush," said Father Michael, angrily. His house had been broken into, his ice cream was melting on his living room floor, and here he was yet again suffering through having to listen to whatever passed through Roger's brain.

"Leave him alone," said Tracey. "He's suffering."

When Sarah died, David Niese took his grief and anger out on his brothers rather than Eddie. David waited two days to tell Roger, in the meantime making all the arrangements himself. Allan had found this to be a great relief; when he arrived in Ottawa, Allan had little to do other than shake people's hands and smoke cigarettes. For Roger, David's behaviour was an insult. Roger couldn't remember a time in his life when he was a mere audience member at a public function. And at his mother's funeral. His annoyance was consuming, Roger couldn't bring himself to confront David, even about the fact Roger had been described in the *Ottawa Citizen* obituary as "unmarried, working in the arts in Nova Scotia." Roger had saved his rage for later when he got back to the John Joe Road. Before he even unpacked his suitcase, Roger wrote a critique of everything that was wrong with his mother's funeral, from the flowers to the readings to, of course, the obituary. He rewrote the critique several times, finally showing his definitive version to Beatrice.

"Hm," said Beatrice. "Here, you say they should have talked more about your father, but, as you can imagine, Roger, it would have hurt Mr. Carruthers feelings."

"It's the truth!"

"It's the truth for the dead, which is the truth that will last for eternity. But what people need is the truth of the living. It's a temporary truth. It will blow away."

"It had to be written down somewhere," Roger said. "Everything that went wrong."

By the time Beatrice arrived at Prince County Hospital in Summerside, Father Michael had continued on to Charlottetown for his much-delayed meeting with the bishop. At least it was easier to blame his tardiness on an accident than a sale on ice cream.

Roger had been given a bed in a room on the second floor of the crumbling red-brick building. His window looked out on Summerside's beloved baseball diamond; Summerside was known for baseball like St. Louis-St. Edward was now known for fiddle music. He looked sullen and swollen. Sitting in a low-slung chair of tubular metal and plastic cushions, Tracey looked more like a sister than an ex-common-law wife or a gift-shop manager.

"What's wrong with you? Couldn't you have been more careful?" snapped Beatrice.

"We panicked," said Tracey. She discreetly handed Beatrice the letter, as if the patient on the other side of the room—a Doherty from Kinkora who had gotten shards of iron in his eye while using a lathe—might notice and notify Father Michael. Beatrice accepted the envelope like someone would accept a dirty diaper. She stuffed it into the disposal bin for biohazardous waste.

"You wanted it!" said Tracey Shaw. "It just about went as planned. Almost. Maybe. Kinda."

"I'm not tsking you, dear. I'm tsking Roger being here." Both of Beatrice's hands went up to call attention to the room they were in, her tasteful black purse dangling from the gold chain around her elbow.

Prince County Hospital held Roger for two days. Beatrice and Tracey took turns visiting him, bringing Michell when they could. The doctors were not pleased with Roger's blood work, which suggested the early stages of prostate cancer, as well as high cholesterol.

"I'm not giving up my shortbread cookies. I'm not," Roger told Tracey on the drive back Up West. He was so eager to get home, he didn't even notice the Acadian Museum this time or think, as he usually did in Miscouche, of how Léonce LeBlanc hadn't let him have his little museum.

"I don't think it's just that, Roger."

"So you're a doctor now?" he snapped back, drawling. "You're all up in my face with your doctor shit?"

Tracey laughed. "Your brain must still be scrambled. You sound like you just crawled out of the mud of Miminegash."

"Good for me."

Roger demanded Tracey take him to the Centre before she took him home. Several things had gone awry during Roger's two days away. Menu items had been swapped. The loonie and toonie coin bins in the petty cash box were reversed. Roger realized he'd have to draw up a memo to bring things back to normal.

He finally allowed Tracey to drop him off at his little house/trailer, which had not been "little" for more than a decade now. Roger had parked a second trailer on the backside of the house, turned a living room window into a door, and connecting the two structures with pieces of plywood leftover from when Allan had lived upstairs and wanted a closet that never got built. The new annex had no purpose, other than to store broken or duplicate items the sprawling campus of the Acadian Cultural Centre and Fun Park did not have room for.

"Eat something before you go to bed," said Tracey on her way out.

"Sure, sure."

Roger threw himself into the reclining office chair that sat in the middle of the kitchen. Since the heating duties of his vintage white porcelain wood stove had been assumed by a modern propane heater, the wood stove was now an ersatz desk where things that needed immediate attention were piled. Roger pushed some magazines out of his way, opened the oven door, and put his feet inside. He would think the memo out in his head and write it up later.

"Point one—handling cash appropriately...."

Before he could finish this thought, Roger's brain started convulsing. Roger couldn't necessarily feel the physical upheaval in his skull. What he did feel was a tingling sensation down his left arm. His words trailed off. He realized his arm was awkwardly positioned. It must have fallen asleep. He started to shake it. He shook it and shook it and before he noticed, he was shaking his left leg as well, banging it on the inside of the oven. The chair bounced on the linoleum floor and his right leg knocked over a huge pile of papers and folders. Roger put his arms out to soften his fall to the floor, but by the time he landed, he was not conscious. A few minutes later, he was dead.

Beatrice and Mitchell discovered his body the next morning at 9:14am. Mitchell had noticed at 8:30am that Roger Niese had not arrived at the Acadian Cultural Centre and Fun Park for work.

★

CHAPTER 13

BEATRICE PERRY LEFT A finely calculated distance between herself
and Kate Pineau. So finely calculated, Kate found it galling. Beatrice sat
close enough to give herself a bird's eye view of Kate's ballpoint hov-
ering uncertainly above the foolscap Beatrice had placed on the desk.
Yet Beatrice was just far enough away to avoid the sharp elbow jab that
might get her to shut up.

"How about...."

"Leave it!" Kate rolled her shoulders. The current president and CEO
of the Acadian Cultural Centre and Fun Park was growing impatient
with her ersatz mentor.

"You could...."

"Let me figure it...."

"Joey LeBlanc...."

"...is here, I know. Case closed. If we're not ready, he can tell Jeeves to
drive him around the block."

"It's a Lincoln. Might be his, might be the province's, might be
Réné's."

"I don't care if he's on a bike."

Even at age forty-two, Kate's nose remained sharp and narrow. It
sliced through the air, allowing her to move quickly. The rest of her face
had loosened and wrinkled like the faces of her peers. The way she held
up her shoulders, her neck rising from them like a turtle's—girlhood
shyness that never went away. Today Kate wore a white blouse and dark
skirt, as if she might in the next instant be asked to play in an orchestra
or wait on tables.

"Of course, you don't," said Beatrice. "Now me, I'd be wondering if
Réné is with him. That would change things."

Indeed, Joey LeBlanc kept close to the man he'd inherit his fortune from. Joey had followed his father into politics, taking up the Evangeline-Miscouche electoral district that was, some believed, the family's birthright. Since the Acadian patriarch Léonce LeBlanc passed away (colon cancer), Réné had grown too busy serving on boards of directors and being recognized in local coffeeshops to bother with real politics. Big feeling lawyers from Charlottetown thought they owned Province House, anyway. There was more money to be made in the private sector. The construction business was booming. Réné's time as a political force had been shorter than his father's. Léonce had served more than twenty years, Réné just eight. People still thought of Réné as a young man, the brute of his rec hockey team. But there was his son Joey, already a cabinet minister, a premier-in-waiting.

The Liberals had spent four years represented by a single MLA, Tim Duggan, from Down East, while the Conservatives held the other twenty-six seats. During that time, the old guard Liberals, with nary a snow plough job to offer or a cheque to award, had mostly dispersed back to the private sector. In those lean years, nobody who knew what was good for them admitted to being a Liberal, not if they wanted summer jobs for their kids. Gradually, a crop of young politicians, most of whom had never fished or farmed or learned anything outside the walls of a university, made themselves available to the party. After one Conservative scandal too many—none that brought any money to the west of the province—these young Liberal bucks swept into power, tossing twenty-eight-year-old Joey LeBlanc, B.A. in geography from UPEI, into a cabinet position like a piece of driftwood onto a beautiful white sand beach.

Traditionally, the Department of Tourism and Culture required a minister with decent to excellent looks, a minister oblivious enough to his or her surroundings to make decontextualized long speeches before a much-anticipated show or game, a minister who could, once coached, pronounce "bodhran" and who knew it was a type of drum. For the Tourism and Culture portfolio, the brain power that was required by, say, agriculture, fisheries, or education could easily be substituted with a messier sort of charm.

Joey LeBlanc—whom all of Abrams-Village suspected of going to the mainland to get his teeth bleached—proved to be a perfect fit. His ministerial advisors, who knew they had a live one, had already mapped out thirty-four community festivals he'd be attending the coming summer, not to mention a plethora of theatre and art gallery openings.

He'd hardly have time to attend cabinet meetings. Which made life much easier for Premier Gwendolyn Czarnecki. The first come-from-away premier—who had promised to govern for just four years, until a report on the long-term effect of the Confederation Bridge—was tired of beating back wannabe successors.

"Couldn't care less who he's with or what he's wearing," sighed Kate.

"You can't expect that attitude to get you very far." Beatrice couldn't avoid the tone she used with pageant contestants; it was her main bad habit.

"Further than I want, as far I can tell."

"Don't be like that." Now there was more compassion in Beatrice's voice than she intended. Kate looked tired and out of sorts. But then, Kate always looked like that, except when she was playing fiddle.

"He's not going to melt out there in his car, is he?" asked Kate. "Didn't we say 4pm? *The Spectator-Herald* isn't even here yet. We're just going to stand there with shovels and stare over at the church until Caroline MacPhail shows up? She'd love that!"

"I suppose," said Beatrice, more worn down than convinced. She sprang up to look out the window overlooking the parking lot. "Is that the CBC pulling in?"

"Don't care."

"Oh really? Tanya Moase is out there in the *Compass* van, every hair in place. Oh, if she had tried for Miss Community Gardens! Together, we might have made it to Miss World."

It was no small feat to lure the *Compass* TV crew this far west, especially in the spring when the potholes on Route 2 were dangerous. The press release, typed up by Tracey Shaw (Tillard), had crowed about the groundbreaking for a new "multimedia room," which had seating for forty-four, a projector, a movie screen, a puppet-show stage, and a pantry-sized dressing room for the puppets that were the focus of today's announcement.

The Acadian Cultural Centre and Fun Park's new stars were a felt-headed cast of post-expulsion Acadian characters including a priest, a nun, a blacksmith, a fisherman, a fiddler, a British soldier, an especially severe-looking British absentee landlord, and a gnarled old biddy who resembled Viola Léger's La Sagouine character. (This resemblance would eventually result in a short-lived legal dispute between the Acadian Cultural Centre and Fun Park and La Paye de la Sagouine in Bouctouche, New Brunswick; La Sagouine eventually settled.) The puppets, donated by the family of Noel and Betty Ann Pineau (Getson), were believed to have been sewn by Betty Ann's spinster aunt, Stella Getson. Betty Ann discovered them after dear aunt Stella had passed. The puppets looked to have never been used, the fake fur of the collars still pleasantly strokable, the cotton on the cook's apron unstained, their felt faces crisp and unwrinkled. The puppets, eighteen in all, were part of an inheritance that also included $62,544.80 retrieved from Aunt Stella's savings account. The grilled cheese sandwiches the woman had lived on for most of her adult life were, it turned out, a choice rather than a necessity.

Left to his own devices, Noel probably would have split the puppets and the money amongst their three kids, all of whom, God bless them, had set aside moodiness, boyfriends, and discomfort around old people to join Noel and Betty Ann in their faithful visits to Aunt Stella's deathbed and then to attend the funeral. The thing was that Noel, who turned out to be cleverer than anyone in high school had suspected, had just sold the slick accounting software he had created to a San Francisco company. Price tag: $15.4 million. Noel and Betty Ann never told anybody the amount of this windfall.

"We've been lucky," was as far as Betty Ann would go. They didn't need Aunt Stella's inheritance. And the couple was so tickled by their good fortune, they had become more civic-minded. Though some would cluck that Noel was just helping out his sister in her new position, the choice of benefactor was not mere nepotism. The Acadian Cultural Centre and Fun Park had taken custody of the puppets before Roger died last year, before Kate was in charge. The cash donation was payable upon the publication of a photo of the groundbreaking of the new Stella Getson Puppetry Pavilion of the Acadian Cultural Centre and Fun Park.

Aunt Stella's puppets were well-crafted. But their artistic impressiveness was not solely responsible for the *Compass* assignment desk's decision to give up star reporter Tanya Moase for the better part of a day. Tanya didn't give a flying fuck about the puppets or the pavilion.

One of Tanya Moase's ulterior motives for making her way up to St. Louis-St. Edward was to capture on-camera Joey LeBlanc's reaction to the cover photo of the new *PEI Visitors' Guide*. The photo was of a flock of remarkably ebullient young women playing beach volleyball in bikinis which no serious female athletes would consider. The questions had to be asked: Was this quiet Island province being promoted as an alternative to debauched destinations like Cancun, Daytona, or Las Vegas and, if so, who would benefit from the deposits on all the empties these libertines would leave behind? Would the Department of Public Health receive additional funding to deal with the expected increases in syphilis, gonorrhea, and other sexually transmitted diseases? Would restrictions on abortion be loosened? Who okayed the photo? Was it true that Joey and his wife, Mary Lou Arsenault from Mont-Carmel, were having marital problems? Was it true that Réné LeBlanc never approved of Joey's marriage to Mary Lou? Maybe the last couple of questions went too far, but, well, the couple had no kids, so there wasn't any harm in trying.

The look on Joey's face when he dodged these questions would surely boost *Compass's* ratings. Yet even gotcha journalism was not enough of a reason for a CBC TV crew to venture beyond Summerside. Tanya had another reason for making the trip. It was Kate Pineau. Not that the reporter had any idea who Kate was. A lover of pop, a hater of country, Tanya hadn't even heard of Kate when she was a fiddling star. Tanya just knew that there was a person of interest here for whom she had questions. Tough questions. But fair.

Was it true that the Acadian Cultural Centre and Fun Park was operating in a leadership vacuum since Roger Niese's death six months ago? Was it true the founder's estate had thrown the Centre's operations into chaos? Was it true the board was divided? Was it true that Réné LeBlanc and the board of the Evangeline Co-op and Community Centre were going to take over the Centre? Was this move a tactical one—to prevent the local Roman Catholic parish, Saint-something, from staking its own claim?

Kate sat at her desk in the Centre, pretending not to notice the parking lot filling up with media and various officials. She had no idea that she, personally, was of interest to Tanya and the *Compass* crew. If Tanya stuck her microphone in Kate's face, Kate certainly wouldn't have any answers. What she might say wouldn't be fit for broadcast on *Compass*.

Kate had avoided the Centre for months. She figured she was entitled to a mourning period. It was not hard; she had managed to avoid the Centre all those years when she and Roger had been on the outs. The first time she visited the Centre after Roger's death, just before the Christmas holidays, she found that her supposed office was being used as a crafting room. Kate admired anyone who could turn chenille bumps and Styrofoam balls into adorable owls but frustratingly couldn't figure out where to sit. For a while, she leaned up against the laser printer until it coughed up dozens of invoices for oversized Acadian flags.

At the reading of Roger's will, Kate had only been half-listening. Emily Niese, for one, thought she even dozed off. Lawyer Wayne Fraser, who had since been elected Liberal MLA for Tyne Valley-Linkletter, and who was now Minister of Education, did his best to read the will clearly and completely. His office was in what used to be the Tyne Valley post office. The renovation looked great from the outside, but the boardroom was tiny, and Wayne had had to import condo-sized office furniture all the way from Ontario. Kate squashed beside Beatrice and Mitchell. Bridget Niese stood behind her parents, her elbows occasionally resting on their shoulders. Emily interrupted and argued with Wayne through the whole thing, rapping her knuckles on Wayne's desk when others tried to speak. Bridget, who was in law school, read from textbooks she had brought with her in plastic grocery bags. The lawyer had never got to finish a single sentence.

Allan Niese hadn't made an appearance at the reading of the will. The youngest Niese brother was in Bangkok, apartment-sitting for a friend who was, apparently, in Cambodia, doing something noble or dubious.

Roger had obviously spent considerable time on his will. The one Wayne read out was the sixteenth draft, though Roger had taken care to burn the first fifteen drafts in the firepit out behind the little house/trailer.

Firstly, Roger dictated that the board hire Kate as the new executive director and president of the Acadian Cultural Centre and Fun Park. Of course, this flew in the face of having a board at all.

That part of the will might have been easily overlooked if not for the rest, and what Wayne's effort to execute it had revealed.

The Acadian Cultural Centre and Fun Park had not been properly registered as a not-for-profit. Roger, it turns out, personally owned the land on which the Centre's campus had been built. Lester Shaw, who had sold Roger the land, knew this but hadn't bothered to tell anybody until the board, now led by Susan Kennedy, tried to prevent Kate from taking charge. Stories about the kerfuffle over who would become the leader of the Centre started showing up in *The Spectator-Herald*. Lester made a run to Summerside one afternoon, and on the way stopped by Wayne's with the real-estate paperwork from the original sale of the land.

"It would bug me if a dead man didn't get everything he wanted," Lester told Wayne, sitting on the edge of the lawyer's desk. To the extent that that was true, which it wasn't, it didn't bug Lester to the extent that he'd do anything about it. It was Lester's wife, Tracey, who had sent him, paperwork in hand, to see Wayne. Tracey was pretending to be neutral but had been the one leaking the board disputes to Caroline at *The Spectator-Herald*. "Better the devil I know," said Tracey of Kate taking charge. "The last thing I need is Joey LeBlanc plopping someone in there, forcing me to sell unicorn pillows and ceramic frogs."

Roger, it turned out, also owned fifty-one percent of Acadian Cultural Centre Incorporated, through a partnered subsidiary that sold its services back to the Centre. The sprawling children's play structure—a rubberized map of the world spread out on a hill, where the kids could hopscotch the journey of the Acadians from France to the Minas Basin to PEI to France to Louisiana and beyond—had been built with his own money; Roger had collected the receipts in an envelope labelled in messy handwriting, "What I Spent on the Kids Map." Operational grants had been placed into savings accounts. Capital funds had been spent on operating expenses. There were several personal bank accounts that held money for several spin-off foundations, the purposes of which were not clear. There was no evidence he ever drew a salary, though he must have lived on something.

Nothing in Roger's will mattered, then, because he had created a situation which would, on close examination, be considered fraud. If Roger's part-ownership of Acadian Cultural Centre Incorporated was not somehow voided, fifteen years' worth of government funding would have to be returned.

"What we're left with," said Wayne, "is all wrong." The lawyer cursed his due diligence.

"You're not saying Roger was stealing?" Kate didn't like lawyer meetings one bit.

"No," said Wayne. "Mr. Niese threw everything into the same basket. I'm sure he put less into his pocket than he paid from it."

"Are you serious?" snapped Emily Niese. She grabbed her purse from the floor and held it in her gloved hand, making as if to storm out. Her daughter and husband, both of whom were more curious than greedy, did not move to go with her. Emily fell back into her chair, defeated.

"Dead serious." Wayne had always wanted to say that to an heir. "We will need to proceed... delicately."

It made sense, then, to make Kate interim executive director and president of the Acadian Cultural Centre Incorporated until everything was sorted out. The last thing the board needed was prospective ED candidates asking questions during job interviews where they should have been answering them. Everything would have to be put on hold until Roger's personal life was extracted from his somewhat less personal life. And wasn't Kate such a sweetheart to play along?

Beatrice hadn't given her a key. Most days Mitchell let Kate in, or she'd follow one of the restaurant staff in through the service entrance.

Kate struggled to get used to the felt- and gluestick-filled office that had been designated hers. It was just off the lobby, behind reception, and she could hear everyone coming and going. The screaming kids, the busloads of tourists dragging themselves to and fro for selfies. The fluorescent lights and white walls gave her a headache. The printer wasn't comfortable to sit on for any length of time. Finally, she brought in a folding card table, onto which she moved the crafting supplies, doing her best to replicate the tableau in which she had found them. She sat at her empty desk, slouching in the roller chair. She desperately did not want to be in this office. But it was what Roger had wanted her to do. She had spent so many years refusing him. Refusing a living man at least acknowledged him. Refusing a dead man was a gesture toward his nonexistence.

Kate would not refuse a dead man. She would take on this role, whatever it was, until she received a sign to do otherwise. In his obituary and in his will, Roger had called her a "special friend." It was the least she could do to show that she was special. And not in that way.

It wasn't like Kate had anything going on in her life. She couldn't so much as pick up the fiddle. She hadn't been able to play since Roger's death. People kept their distance from her. The one thing that was good about being accused of adultery with someone who had died was that nobody was overtly hostile to her; it was assumed she must be somewhat heartbroken. But Kate was still a marked woman.

Either on a whim, to escape their mother's downheartedness, or because it was time to strike out on their own, Kate's older daughters had moved to Charlottetown in November, setting up housekeeping with friends in one of the dumpy apartments across from the University of Prince Edward Island. Kate was left alone with Bethany, her youngest, who had become an agonizingly uncommunicative teenager. The 24/7 company of her three TVs and two radios held off the loneliness most of the time. The girls spent two weeks at home for Christmas, complaining nonstop about their roommates, girls from Summerside they knew through volleyball. For Kate, those two weeks were pure heaven; even Bethany behaved with a degree of civility. Before the turkey was even eaten up, though, Sherrie and Krystal piled their presents into the trunk and drove back to Charlottetown.

One morning in mid-January, Beatrice discovered Kate sitting in the office by herself. The only light came from the chrome desk lamp. Another card table had been seconded from the card-party club's storage room, this one piled with the spring concert series flyers. Beatrice was mildly annoyed but didn't have the heart to ask Kate to put the table back.

By March, the president and CEO had grown comfortable enough at the Centre to play solitaire at her desk. By April, Kate was wondering what she should be doing, and got it into her head that the reason she wasn't doing anything at the Acadian Cultural Centre and Fun Park was primarily because Beatrice wouldn't let her.

Beatrice, whose attention to detail so complemented Roger's erratic workstyle, was at the root of many of Kate's grievances. That Perry woman wouldn't so much as pour Kate a cup of tea, Kate would complain in hours-long phone calls to Sherrie and Krystal, even when Beatrice held the kettle in one hand, a box of tea bags in the other. And Tracey, still in charge of the gift shop, spent all her days reading philosophy, updating her blog, and printing to the printer in Kate's office purely to check up on what her boss was doing.

Kate knew what Tracey was thinking: Poor Kate. Drove her husband away. Slept her way into a will. Had her dirty secret spilled to the whole province. Then her daughters ran off to Charlottetown. Except for Bethany, who still lived at home and was something of a burden. Now Kate was stuck running the place she turned her back on. Tracey, of course, didn't think exactly that. The New Brunswick come-from-away assumed there had been some misunderstanding. But it was more fun to suggest and imply otherwise, partly because it drove her husband Lester crazy.

In the days leading up to the groundbreaking that spring of the Centre's Stella Getson Puppetry Pavilion, the weather made tremendous progress. The snow retreated back into the woods. The eastern white pines which peppered the property were budding. The air, for the first time since December, had smells: thawing manure, spruce, creosote, seaweed, decomposing potatoes left in the field over the winter, diesel. Beatrice tasked Mitchell with washing all the summer staff uniforms and costumes, just to freshen them up.

Soon, the average age of a Centre employee would drop precipitously as students were assigned to theatrical roles, deep fryers, and cash registers. Soon, every room would be humming, every corridor filled with school classes, waitstaff carrying platters of food, artists wondering if they could extend their murals beyond their assigned walls. Beatrice thought it was good to get the groundbreaking of the multimedia centre/puppet theatre out of the way before it all became too much to coordinate.

"I want to know what's going on around here," Kate said to Beatrice that morning. "I'm the president, aren't I? I think there are things I can be doing around here. All kinds of things."

"Okay then, Miss President. You'd like to serenade us?"

"Get away with yah. Serious things. I can be dead serious."

"Playing music is serious business around here." Beatrice would have loved to have Kate Pineau's name back on the posters.

"President stuff. What does a president do anyway?" Kate regretted this question the moment she asked it. She guffawed so it sounded like she was joking.

"For starters, his lordship—her lordship—might decide what order people should be standing in the photos for today's groundbreaking," said Beatrice. She slid a sheet of blank foolscap between Kate's elbows, knocking askew a tidy row of hearts and clubs as she did so. Beatrice smiled to herself. It was a trick question. Nobody picked the order. Each politician would scramble to claim the spot in the middle of the photo.

Kate assessed the foolscap. "Well, thank you very much." She looked up at Beatrice, whose glasses were sitting on the very tip of her nose as if about to jump off. "Shouldn't I know who's coming?"

Beatrice sighed with such exasperation that it was impossible to believe she had never been a mother. "Oh, I'll do it."

"A list of names will do."

"Will they now?"

"I can go out and introduce myself to the mucky-mucks, if you think that's the better way to play this. I heard *Compass* is coming."

Beatrice shuddered. This was the first time in a long time the reporter Tanya Moase had been to St. Louis-St. Edward. Who knew what little thing might piss her off? For almost a year, the previous government, the Conservatives, had boycotted the reporter as a punishment for her questions about a grant to the premier's brother's blueberry farm. Yet the government's refusal to take Tanya's calls or answer her questions in the lobby of the legislature did anything to stop her from embarrassing them. She pursued the truth as a sort of revenge, breaking scandal after scandal. Poor handling of potato blight alerts. Property speculation by King County cabinet ministers. Servers left untipped at Charlottetown restaurants.

The government's silence in response to Tanya's stories spoke for itself. On the election night that swept the Liberals back into power, Tanya and her videographer had driven to the Evangeline Co-op and Community Centre to interview an already half-in-the-bag Joey LeBlanc. Joey instinctively credited her for his victory: "Fank yous, Tanya. Yous is da best. I mean it, Tanya."

"No, no, no. I'll write the names down for you," Beatrice told Kate.

"Just tell me. I can read my own writing. It's other people's I don't know about."

Beatrice sighed before listing the names of those who would be in the photos for *The Spectator-Herald* and *The Guardian*. There would be, of course, Joey LeBlanc. Then: the local MLA George Getson; Noel and Betty Ann Pineau, of course, plus maybe their kids; Egmont MP Ed Montgomery, who was never any trouble; Rodney Shaw, Lester's son, who had given up drug dealing and DJing to found the West Prince Arts Association; and Father Michael Chaisson.

"And me too, I guess," said Kate.

"*The Spectator-Herald's* maximum is eight people in a photo. Caroline is very strict."

"But you might stick my niece and nephew in?"

"Optional. I don't imagine they'll show."

"What's your title again, Beatrice?"

"Hm, I suppose nobody needs to see my mug in the paper again." Beatrice always knew exactly when to step back.

"So, anyways," said Kate. "Where are these things anyway?"

"These things?"

"The whatchacallems. The Caseys and Finnegans."

"The puppets?" said Beatrice. The wrinkling up of her nose at last pushed her glasses off their perch.

"Yeah, the puppets! I've got an idea about them."

The president and CEO of the Acadian Cultural Centre clapped her hands as if she had just come up with a unifying theory for the universe.

A few minutes later, Kate arrived in the lobby to greet her guests, carrying with her a black garbage bag full of coloured felt, faux fur, doll's hair, and googly eyes. Beatrice trailed breathlessly behind.

Kate explained her plan for the photos to the dignitaries and only once was forced to strongly insist; Ed Montgomery refused to take the absentee landlord puppet offered him. He finally accepted the milkmaid. The Pineau kids didn't show and neither did Rodney. Beatrice decided she didn't want to be in the picture, so Kate made seven.

"Shame to leave a spot unused, but I'm just not up for it today," muttered Beatrice.

Tanya and her videographer remained in their van for a remarkably long time. You could see through the windshield they were talking on their phones, not to each other. This gave Caroline and *The Guardian* reporter lots of time to take their photos of the groundbreaking. Caroline art-directed her subjects, having them pose each with a floppy Acadian puppet in one hand, shovels in the other. They stood on a small plot of dead grass near the Centre's main building. The late afternoon sun was bright, but the spring air still had a nip in it.

Once the photos were taken, the little gang of officials all stepped back to check their phones, ignoring Caroline, who had pulled out her notepad to get some quotes. It soon became clear that they were waiting for Tanya to get out of the van and then they'd move back to hunker down on their shovels for the TV camera. Each of the men had discreetly tossed his puppets out of sight.

"Is my time of no value at all?" declared Caroline to no one in particular. She waved at Tanya in her van. The TV reporter noticed her and hopped out, a grin plastered over her face.

"You all look so hilarious!" said Tanya, "But just so you know, we're not shooting this rogues gallery. Ah, no, won't be shooting the shovels, the puppets, the indents in the ground you've made there. Nope, not at all."

"Oh, for God's sake," snapped Caroline with a bit more edge than the moment called for.

"Lighten up, lady," said Tanya, bouncing up and down on the balls of her feet.

"This is like a trip to the zoo for you, but these Up West people expect me to spend half my time up here. You don't think I'd like to live in Charlottetown, talk about world politics, drink wine, and eat brunch in sidewalk cafés?"

"Sad because your boyfriend's dead?" asked Tanya.

"Excuse me?" Caroline's stance approximated that of a boxer. This was not a rumour anyone had heard before.

"One of our interns once did a content analysis of *The Spectator-Herald*. She wasn't the only one who found it hard to believe this tourist trap got so much coverage on pure journalistic merit," said the TV reporter. Tanya herself was currently having an affair with CBC TV's station manager, which made her cocky, prone to lasciviousness, and highly attuned to hypocrisy.

"Your wild guess makes you look foolish." Caroline was not having such gossip spread about her. Her marriage had been shaky for years. Her husband Robert, who worked in Charlottetown and played several sports, came home only to sleep. She felt like a single mother to their son Brian. Caroline could handle this; the demands of being a daily news reporter, evaluating the importance of other people's lives and projects, helped her avoid thinking much about her own life, about where she had ended up compared to what she had hoped to achieve. Speculation, even if it was this ridiculous, was not wanted. Caroline leaned hard into the side of *Compass's* star reporter. Tanya's response could not so easily be explained as losing her footing. The top student in her Pilates class, she rocked powerfully back at Caroline, nearly knocking Caroline into a green gabled birdhouse.

Kate, who had strong opinions on how mean women could be to other women, instinctively bolted toward the two reporters. She wanted to absorb the force of any punches thrown. But she came in hard and sent both Caroline and Tanya flying in opposite directions. Kate herself landed on the ground on her hands and knees. She stood up so quickly, you wouldn't have noticed she had fallen if it wasn't for the mud all over her. The ground was cold. Kate slapped her hands together like she was removing fish guts from them.

"Heavens!" gasped Beatrice.

"Good on yah," said Noel, who thought the role of jocular trouble-maker was better for his sister than that of a doormat. His wife Betty Ann jabbed him with her elbow.

The puppets-and-shovels image ran on the front page of *The Spectator-Herald*. The *Guardian* version, which depicted the groundbreakers standing in the reverse order, Joey LeBlanc still in the middle, ran on page seven.

Compass didn't devote a single second to the groundbreaking; Joey got away before Tanya could ask him a single question. She didn't do much better with the president and CEO of the Centre.

"You can't expect me to answer anything when I'm just getting up to speed," Kate told Tanya. Or rather, told Tanya's microphone. Not once did Kate's eyes meet Tanya's. Tanya, who liked to show a lot of cleavage, was so used to this she didn't even notice.

"Maybe you like to talk out of your ass down Charlottetown way, but I want to have everything nailed down before I open my trap. Don't you think that's true, Miss Lightweight Champ? I'm standing here wondering why the Conservatives were so shy about talking to you. Do you have any answers to that, miss?"

"Is it true the place might be sold?"

"It might get hit by lightning tomorrow. How would I know?"

"Well, you're...."

"That's right. I'm the queen bee. Put that on *Compass* for all to see. I'm the queen bee. Now the queen bee's thinking this little chat is over."

Kate walked away from a befuddled Tanya Moase. Her black skirt clung to her legs. Her blouse billowed. She walked over to the Lincoln that Joe LeBlanc had arrived in.

In the driver's seat sat Réné LeBlanc, former MLA and construction mogul, just as his own dad had been a former MLA and construction mogul, and president of the Evangeline Co-op and Community Centre. He had watched the whole event without so much as showing his face. Réné rolled down the window for Kate.

"Chilly day for something like this!" he said cheerfully.

"It is, it is. You're Joey's chauffeur now?" Joey was still nowhere to be seen.

Réné laughed. "Gotta keep myself out of trouble."

"I can't imagine you very far at all from trouble, Réné. What can I do you for?"

"We should meet soon, you and I. Imagine you're figuring out things are pretty messy. Going to be hard for you to make it through this summer season."

"Oh no," said Kate. "It's all sunshine and rainbows."

"That's not what I hear," said Réné. He smiled so solicitously, he might as well have been inviting her to dance. "But maybe you're not the person who'd know."

"Getting up to speed! Just telling the *Compass* lady there."

A priest puppet fell at Kate's feet. Beatrice had thrown it at the *Compass* reporter, who had quietly crept up behind Kate, videographer at her side.

"Can I help you?" Kate asked Tanya.

"Um, just saying bye?"

"Thanks for coming. Now good riddance," snapped Kate. "See yah, I guess, if this place ever burns down."

The *Compass* crew dismissed, Kate leaned down into the window of the Lincoln, rested her elbows on the open window, her chin in her hands. Réné laughed at her.

"Nobody's ever going to be running this place like Roger Niese ran it, are they?" Réné's laugh was beautiful. You could imagine it being distilled, bottled, and sold to Santa Claus impersonators. "That one, now, he was one of a kind."

"He was!"

"So blind to what was in his way and so he walked right over everything." Looking into Réné's laugh you could see every silvery filling in his mouth. It was like he had bitten into a tin pie plate and torn off all he could. "That Ottawa family. They're going to make trouble for you. That wife! And the niece!"

"Ah?" Kate cocked her head like she did in high school when a boy made a lecherous remark. Make him repeat it.

Joey strolled up to the car. He'd been taking a dump in the main building's washroom, which he declared to be the cleanest and best built in all Up West. He gave Kate a little salute as he took his place in the passenger's seat.

"We'll talk later, missy," said Réné, who also gave Kate a salute before he rolled up the car window and pulled out of the lot. His engine had been running the whole time. Neither man wore a seatbelt.

Kate turned around to head back inside the Centre, and there was

Father Michael a few inches away from her. Kate jumped as if someone had pinched her bottom.

"Kate," said the priest, his long black overcoat billowing in the wind. "Can we have a quick word? Maybe over a coffee or tea?"

"Ah, sure." Kate figured that she'd spent most of the day dealing with people who wanted something from her. She might as well roll with it. Father Michael suggested walking across the road to the Getson Goodies Bakery in Lester Shaw's strip mall. Kate agreed, telling herself that, under all circumstances, Father Michael would be treating her. She had no intention of paying even a cent for this pleasure.

Father Michael and Kate crossed the campus of the Centre, jumping over the mini-golf obstacles before descending and ascending the deep marshy ditch. They both squeezed through a gap in the wooden fence and crossed the road. Kate purposefully dragged her feet on the asphalt to scrape the red mud off the bottom of her shoes. She looked back to see the Ferris wheel looming over St. Bernard's.

Elis Getson's granddaughter Jordan, who put in about fifty hours a week at the bakery, distractedly served them tea and biscuits. The country charm of the fleur-de-lis wallpaper and teddy bear borders was undermined by the McDonald's hand-me-down table-chair sets. Someone, perhaps Jordan, had noticed that it didn't look right and sloppily affixed floral masking tape along the tables' edges. The duo ordered a biscuit, a chocolate glazed doughnut, and a pecan tart to share, and two teas. The teas came weak and milky.

"Had a good chat with Réné?" asked the priest. Kate noticed that Father Michael's once regal nose was red and covered with veins. They were all aging, but he was doing worse than most others.

"Chat?" Kate found it difficult to talk to a priest one-on-one without feeling as if she was in confession. "Sure, sure, we had a nice little chat, we did."

"You haven't made a move, I hope," Father Michael uttered the "you" so softly it was hard to say who it applied to. "Our offer will be coming soon."

"Offer?" As someone who had expected, at most, best wishes regarding her interim and largely ceremonial position, Kate was gradually becoming aware she had taken on more than photo-ops. The dark river of politics unsettled her; she did not want to look down into it.

"We've heard that Roger didn't leave things in the best shape, organizationally. Programming—nobody has any doubt the quality is there. And to have you back, that's a wonderful, wonderful thing."

"I'm not back on stage yet, father," laughed Kate, leaning back in her seat. "I might be spending my summer handing out putters on the mini-golf course."

"Yes, the mini-golf." Father Michael seemed lost in thought for a moment. "That could be sold off."

"The Acadian Culture Centre and Fun Park could do that," said Kate. The "could" stretched out for an extra moment or two.

"Okay, okay, you're not there yet. But I want you to know that the parish is interested. I think we could have a great partnership."

"Really, now, Father. You'd be running all three corners. You're buying Lester Shaw's strip mall next? People said Roger was trying to be king of Palmer Road, but it looks like you're about to beat him, father."

Father Michael shrugged.

"If you want to write something up, I'll take it to the board. Anything else, father?" Kate tossed the last of the biscuit to the back of her mouth. Neither of them had touched the pecan tart.

"Well," said the priest. He leaned back in his chair and stared out the window. A green Trans Am sped down the road. Each of them thought "Ricky Gallant" but said nothing about it. "I was wondering if you could help me with something."

This time it was Kate's turn to shrug.

"I think Roger might have had something of mine at the time he died."

"Anything valuable, as you see it, Father?" Kate was more intrigued now than by anything Réné had said to her.

"A letter, a private letter."

"Roger with a letter of yours? Why on earth? Now that's something I'd like to know." Kate could imagine the two men writing hostile diatribes to each other on the future of West Prince.

"It was from.... Do you know the letter I'm talking about?"

"I think so, Father." She didn't but figured that saying she did might move things along more quickly.

"You might remember Debbie Arsenault?"

"Oh, that one. She was quite a handful when I knew her."

"She and I remained friends long after she moved Down East."

"Now where was that, Father?"

"Cornwall. I.... She...."

"Helped her out, did you, Father? That's some nice of yah."

"She and her family had a rough time. Her father was...."

".... A real asshole. Errol Arsenault? You don't have to tell me. Everybody knows Errol Arsenault was a real asshole. I bet they know it on the mainland."

"Debbie always struggled. Too proud to ask for help. We kept in touch over the years. We'd visit and write. I'm wondering if one of these letters might have gone astray."

"Roger's not going to tell anybody what was in it now, is he, father?"

"I suppose not. But I would like it back."

"No money in it, Father?"

"No."

"Tell you what I'll do," Kate leaned forward. "I'll ask around for you."

Roger had spent so much time mulling the mystery of Debbie Arsenault, but Roger had never landed on this. Fortunately. Or unfortunately. Depends if it's better for a man to live in false hope or for a man to live in disappointed anger.

Debbie was not so much a refugee of Up West as she was an exile, held at a safe distance from her baby's daddy. Kate wondered when the priest had stopped having sex with Debbie. If they had stopped. Sad thing, really. Priests should be allowed to marry. Kate remembered her girlhood crush on Michael Chaisson. She felt she could lean over and kiss him now. He was hardly in a position to refuse her.

No, she'd been bad enough.

"Well, actually," Kate chuckled. "I'll go look for it myself. We don't need bullshit spreading everywhere."

Father Michael's glowing red face had attracted the attention of other café patrons. Was he hearing a confession? His hands clamped so tightly on his Styrofoam cup that people, a couple of Doucettes, a Gallant, and a Perry, cringed in anticipation he'd make irritating scratchy noises. The priest wanted to correct the many assumptions that had just come out of Kate's mouth. Then he thought better of it. He had made himself vulnerable asking a favour. If Kate found the letter, she'd read it. He could barely remember what was in it himself. A thank you? Some flattery to make the next cheque come more readily? Some threat?

"Kate, you're not without sin yourself." Michael spoke sharply.

"Look where you got yourself. Into an unholy mess you're incapable of fixing. And nobody wants you fixing it."

"I suppose they don't. But nobody wanted what Roger did, either, until he did it. And look what we got." She pointed out the window toward the four acres of fun. "I never slept with him, Father. He liked my fiddle playing. For Roger, that was enough."

"Everybody loved your playing," said Father Michael, letting the cup in his hands return to its natural shape. "You'll have to play at one of our parish dances sometime."

"Wouldn't that be nice!" Kate smiled so hard she squinted.

They walked together back to the Acadian Cultural Centre and Fun Park. Kate helped Father Michael search Roger's office and everywhere else the Centre's founder liked to stuff paper. The task took hours. For sure, the letter from Debbie was not there.

By the time they gave up, there was nobody left in the building but the Tuesday card-party gang. Kate waved at them. They could let themselves out.

★

Emily Niese was on her third pair of rubber gloves when Father Michael showed up at Roger's house/trailer. Only Mitchell had been inside since Roger's death the previous October. He had cleaned out the fridge as best he could, and had been picking up the mail.

Despite the myriad cleaning products Emily had bought in Summerside, she couldn't get the crusty smell out of the place. Some of the floors had heaved over the winter. The pipes had frozen and burst, damaging the bathroom floor.

"That's twenty-five percent off the selling price," thought Emily when she saw the mess. Two weeks was what she had to sort it out. It wasn't how she dreamed of spending her time. David couldn't get time off from work, or so he said. Bridget was articling in Toronto, probably experimenting with bisexuality. Her son Gary had a slutty new girlfriend. Who knew what crisis she'd return to?

Everything Emily feared about Roger's packrat tendencies turned out to be true. It was a daunting task to make the place presentable for sale. She had hoped the idyllic PEI location, walks on the beach, wine out of tumblers, and a Margaret Atwood novel would free her from the worries of her Vancouver life. But the nearest shoreline to the John Joe Road was swampy and infested with horseflies.

Worse still, Roger's hovel appeared to be devoid of anything of any value. Emily quickly gave up on finding a stash of bonds or jewelry or musical instruments hidden away. Even the possibly collectible magazines were water- and sun-damaged.

"We met at the funeral," the priest said, his face crosshatched by the dirty screen door. For a moment, Emily wondered if the man had followed her here from The Glenn Hotel where she was staying. Her hand gripped the door handle lock in position. Her cellphone was in the living room annex. As far as she knew, there was nobody around for miles. It didn't help his case that Father Michael was wearing a red polo shirt. Polo shirts are what men wear when pretending to be humble.

"Who were you with?"

"Jesus," laughed Father Michael. "I was the grownup one on the altar."

Emily squinted through the screen. "The priest? Really."

"Really. Didn't come armed. Well, just with the Holy Spirit."

Emily laughed despite herself. She opened the door.

"Quite a job ahead of you," said Father Michael. He left his shoes in the porch and walked sock footed through the filth. The kitchen table and stove were piled with papers, some in boxes, some in plastic bags. Cardboard maquettes of various stage productions were stacked on the floor: *Sylvain!* on top of *Walking After Midnight with Patsy Cline*, which crushed *Mummers Feast: A Halloween Extravaganza*. Objects from the old Dairy Bar Museum were piled on a blue tarp. Though Emily had no idea what they were about, there was something about them that made her treat them like archeological objects.

"It's taking forever, I have to tell you. He was a sweet soul—wouldn't hurt a fly!—but as you can see, a bit of a hermit. I can just picture him in here, hidden away, thinking all this trash would help change the world."

The word "hermit" struck Father Michael as odd, both the right way and very much the wrong way to describe Roger.

"You're a brave soul."

"I am." Emily Niese pointed to the cleaning tool closest at hand. It was a mop. She grabbed it and whisked it around like an actor auditioning for the part of a maid in summer stock theatre. "What can I do for you, Father?"

Father Michael wet his lips, still plump but somewhat lost in the redness of his face. Now Emily recognized him, the endearing crinkles around his eyes. When she later described the meeting to her husband, she told him the priest stank of manure and cat. "Or maybe I'm mixing him up with the gas station attendant."

Father Michael spent several minutes explaining that, for reasons, legitimate or not, at a time that might have been long ago or might have been more recent, it may have been possible that there were some papers belonging to the parish, or something akin to the parish, somewhere on the premises, maybe out in the open, maybe hidden somewhere or maybe somewhere else altogether. It might or might not contain the name Debbie Arsenault. Michael squirmed at how unimportant his favour sounded.

Emily put her mop down. Her pump had been primed.

"I wonder.... Could this be what you're talking about...." Emily hesitated for a moment, wondering if she might be giving up something that could be used against her in some other negotiation. Her busybody side got the best of her.

"An Arsenault was in the will, you know," she said. "I think that's her, Debbie Arsenault? Why it's my job to play delivery man, I'll never know. I've never set eyes on the creature."

"Indeed!" said Father Michael. He had heard bits and pieces about what was in the will but hadn't read it himself.

"You're here to get that! Makes sense." Emily's skepticism lifted. She felt like her selfless troubleshooter self, so loved by parent-teacher associations, figure skating clubs, and charity foundations. She took her rubber gloves off by pulling on the fingers. "Let's see! Yes, yes. I remember stuffing some things in here." She pointed Father Michael toward the bedroom, which required stepping up, ducking, stepping down, then stepping up and ducking again.

Many cardboard boxes surrounded the bed. Four were marked "Debbie." The masking tape on two of them was stringy with age. Two of them were open, and Father Michael could see books, papers, and knickknacks inside.

"You wouldn't believe the detail of Roger's bequests. He was insufferable until the very end. I'm trying to figure out the difference between the Paderno frying pan and the T-Fal. Oh, the horror if somebody got the wrong one!"

"Your patience and thoroughness won't go unnoticed, I'm sure."

"By whom?"

"People around here notice things. God, too."

"Oh, right. Sure. Lovely."

"You know what I can do," said Father Michael. "I can take these to Debbie Arsenault for you."

"You're kidding! You're sure?"

"No, no, I'd be happy to do it."

Father Michael started arranging the boxes, speedily folding in the tops of the open ones before curiosity got the best of him then and there. He had a thought.

"The document I was referring to was relatively recent. Would it be in these boxes? They look older."

"The letter? I don't know anything about a letter. If it's on the bequeath list, it's there." Emily held up a stapled pile of printouts. "He was such a drip. Listen to this. 'Debbie, the Rankin Family North Country cassette reminds me of your restless ways. I listen to "Lisa Brown," who had been running around too long, and picture you. Were you in the Gaspé the summer I graduated? At least the stars over us were the same.'"

"Huh?" said the priest. There was a hint of melancholy in his grunt. Emily wondered if the priest had spent time himself gadding about the Gaspé. "This letter I'm talking about. I doubt it's on the bequeath list."

"Have you seen this place? What you see is what you get!" Emily Niese loomed over the priest who was bent over, fussing with the boxes. Emily reached out a hand to help the priest straighten himself, as she imagined he must want to do. The priest allowed her to help him up.

"Do you have a number? I can call you if I find your whatever. I wouldn't wait by the phone, though."

"That would be verily appreciated."

Back at the rectory, Father Michael went through the boxes. There were forty-fives of The Tubes, Bonnie Tyler, Elton John, and Jim Croce. Rings and necklaces that might have come from a carnival win or a vending machine. Handmade high-school dance posters carefully folded but now too crunchy to unfold without tearing. A Budweiser mirror the size of an LP. Poems by Roger Niese and poems he must have ripped out of textbooks. There was a signed copy of the Sylvain! script, about a dozen small picture frames still packaged in plastic, and an especially ornate white and gold toilet-paper holder.

As Father Michael suspected, there was no letter from Debbie Arsenault in any of the boxes. Nothing thanking Michael for the five hundred dollars he sent for his granddaughter's birthday. No "I love you, granddaddy!" in Debbie's handwriting. After encountering Emily and her mania for cleanliness, Michael figured the letter was likely in a big black garbage bag somewhere, bound for the Dock Road dump. That was an acceptable resolution. Had Roger Niese read it or not? That man never got himself set right with the world around him, thought Father Michael. Another vexation for Roger wouldn't be worth worrying about.

★

One sunny August day several years later, Debbie Arsenault found herself on Palmer Road. First time in forever. Her friend Franny, who was visiting from Montreal, thought Charlottetown and Cavendish were too busy, too expensive, and too full of "snobs." Franny liked seals and polar bears. Franny wanted to visit the windmill test site at North Cape, which she had read about in the *PEI Visitors' Guide*. Debbie couldn't figure out how Franny got from fuzzy animals to power generation, but Debbie liked to make Franny happy. Questioning Franny's motives made Franny unhappy. Franny was a big-boned and gangly Québécois, who claimed to have been sporty in her younger days. As an older woman (Debbie had just met her a couple of years ago), Franny had turned her attention to experimenting with fashion eclecticism. Today she wore peach-coloured bib overalls and, on her head, what looked like a squashed bowler hat.

In roughly the same region, Franny had also noticed, there was something called the Acadian Cultural Centre and Fun Park. The write-up in the 2009 *PEI Visitors' Guide*—the one with the cover featuring two seniors in silhouette, walking on the beach holding hands—made the place sound more fun than a barrel of monkeys.

Debbie tensed up at the first mention of going Up West, hoping Franny would drop it, like she had dropped her first two husbands. But then, just as suddenly, Debbie's mood changed. She was down fifteen pounds and fit into her favourite jeans. That morning, she had, for a change, taken a glimpse of herself in the mirror before she left home and liked what she saw. Maybe it was just Franny's gushing enthusiasm, but maybe that was enough.

"Why not?" Debbie declared. "I never knew those Acadians had any culture at all. They never did when I lived up here."

"Oh, right, this is where you're from, I guess," said Franny.

Debbie tore through Wellington, Ellerslie, Bloomfield, and Elmsdale like the two of them were fleeing the police in her Honda Civic. She flicked her signal light more than a kilometre ahead of Profit's Corner, but when the turn came, she hadn't decided she'd take it.

The two friends had the same short haircut, same streaked hair, similar plastic-rimmed glasses. They had been giggling through the whole excursion as if the Island was their private joke. At the Richmond Dairy Bar, where they stopped to have "fries with the works," the girls at the counter took them for sisters. At Getson Goodies Bakery, Jordan Getson asked them where they were from. Debbie put her hands on the counter and leaned on them as she told Jordan the story about how, on this very spot, back in the 1980s, before Lester Shaw built the strip mall, before the corner felt like Yonge and Dundas, Ricky Gallant had lost control of his car, flipped it over into the ditch and landed it right side up in the snow, not a dent on it. The car had landed exactly where that Québécois family right there was drinking scalding tea with their dried-out doughnuts.

"That so?" said Jordan. Of the two Ricky Gallants Jordan knew, one was a seventh grader at Callaghan Intermediate and the other was at St. Edward's elementary.

"It is! And we used to toilet-paper the priest's house every Halloween. That was Father Arsenault, back when Michael Chaisson was the stud of Palmer Road. Franny, Michael's the priest now. Handsome like."

"Was he now," said Jordan. She believed all priests were homosexual. Also, she wasn't sure women as old as her mother should be talking about studs at all; Jordan had had only one serious boyfriend and didn't see what the fuss was about.

"Was he, Deb?" asked Franny. She knew little of her friend's backstory and was excited to hear more. Their friendship had blossomed just in the last five or six years. They'd met on a casino bus to Niagara Falls.

"He was, indeedy, scoodle-y-do-dee." Debbie had never strung these sounds together before, but she sold it like it was her signature phrase.

"We should go see him then! If he's got a face like that on him!"

Franny thought she saw a flash of irritation on her friend's face. Then, Debbie declared: "You know, we should!"

"His car's in the driveway," said Jordan, looking out the window across the road. She was all blonde and sweet freckle-faced, but she had a sharp wit about her. It might be a laugh, watching these two horned-up tourists show up on the priest's doorstep. She watched them try to get the cinnamon bun gunk off their fingers with lightweight paper napkins. Then they were out the door.

A few minutes later, without a drop of drink in them, Deb and Franny were standing, shoulders hunched, on the priest's front step. It was Saturday afternoon and they found Father Michael home preparing for evening mass.

"Debbie Arsenault!" said the priest with staggeringly good cheer.

"Michael," she purred, stepping forward to hug him low on his waist and mashing her face into his chest. His face was puffy. His breathing seemed weird. She wondered if he had run to get the door. "Long time, no see."

"Well, yes!" Father Michael's arms hung loosely by his side.

A pause was left for Franny to pipe up and say something to distract from the horrifying awkwardness of the greeting. Franny said nothing.

"Would you come in for a cup of tea?" Father Michael did not move out of the doorway.

"We'd need two," said Franny. "We don't share cups."

"Naw, naw, naw," said Debbie. "We're just passing through."

"Are you now?" He noticed the friend's sly grin and failed to realize it was Franny's calling card. "You're not laughing at me, I hope?"

"Not at all, Father." Franny was still smirking.

"He's the one who got me off Palmer Road, Franny," said Debbie. "I had to reform my father, raise Amber right, get a decent job. Oh, the things I had to do!"

"Amber's all right!" said Franny. "And her little Nikki. Can you believe this one here's a grandmother!"

"Debbie's done well for herself," Father Michael, somewhat more relaxed, flashed Debbie a hammy smile.

"Has she now?" Debbie said dryly.

"Has she?" laughed Franny. "Has she, Deb?"

"Oh," said the priest, flustered. "I think so!"

Debbie's heart was racing. She could not put her finger on why.

Father Michael, to her, looked like he was just playing at being a priest here in this big old house, which must have been a bitch to heat.

Perhaps, Debbie wondered, she had come here to cause a scene. Otherwise, why had she agreed to come? And what a scene it would be! The teenager knocked up by the priest. Of course, he hadn't been a priest when he fucked her. Was holiness retroactive? Wouldn't Franny be tickled to see Deb put the old lech in his place? To show him who's boss. She was always the boss. He should know that. Her father had done so much of the dirty work in managing Michael Chaisson. She forgot how much she hated Errol Arsenault in those years. Her memory, as pliable as her imagination, had turned him into her debt collector and protector.

For the first few years, the Chaissons funded her exile. Debbie followed instructions. Then the money started drying up. She hadn't yet taken the secretarial course at Holland College and wasn't sure of her next step. One Saturday, just after Roger had opened the Wharf Centre in Miminegash, she came Up West to go to a dance there. Just curious. Years and years ago. She didn't remember who that person was.

The place was packed and Roger, yelling instructions at this one and that one, was too busy to notice her. Oh, what a scene that would have been! This was before Errol died and that night he was taking care of Nikki. Errol wasn't such a bad babysitter; he'd do half-assed magic tricks and make soggy French fries.

What Debbie realized at that dance, what sent her home after she gulped her rum and Coke in about six minutes, was that she didn't know a soul. And nobody knew who she was. The few people she did recognize, she had nothing to say to them. She may have been pure Palmer Road, but she didn't belong there. She never came back because she never wanted to come back. If Michael continued to send her money every once in a while, to prevent her return, she was happy to play along.

"Stay where you are," he'd write to her. "You don't want your daughter getting into the trouble you got into." Oh, go fuck yourself, Michael, she'd think. Seeing you isn't worth the gas money. Who'd think they were so high and mighty to be banishing people? Only Michael, son of a well-off farmer who thought he was better than everyone else. Only someone who had been so good-looking he thought everything that came out of his pretty mouth was live and direct from heaven.

Franny's giggling yanked Debbie out of her memories.

"Just poking at yah, Father," said Debbie. "This one here's pulling your chain too."

Franny, noticing the storm flash in her friend's eyes, nodded with enthusiasm. "I'm Franny, by the way!"

"Well," said Debbie. "We should be on our way."

Father Michael tsked and shook his head. "I know, I know. You should come to mass if you're still around this evening."

"Mass?" said Debbie. The two women giggled again. "And then maybe some confession, eh, Father?"

"Beautiful day for a drive, at least." Father Michael frowned. His thoughts darted back inside the house. "Oh, I have some boxes for you."

Debbie stopped dead. Were they gifts for Nikki, as if Father Michael might have two clues how old his granddaughter was?

"Roger left them to you. In his will," said the priest apprehensively. "You knew he passed away?"

"I did," said Debbie. The giddiness was all gone now. She had seen the obituary in the paper. She could have made the evening visiting hours for the wake. She had the car, too. She had gotten as far as getting in the car and turning over the engine. Then she thought she should change her clothes. Then Amber called about her looking after Nikki and then there was something good on TV and then it was too late.

Debbie had read, she thought, that Roger had taken up with Kate Pineau. Was glad of it. Was glad he hadn't spent his whole life alone.

"It was a very sad time here in the parish. All of Up West, really. The Island, in fact."

"Roger," said Debbie, misting up with theatrical nostalgia. In those months after Roger died, she had not returned calls from Beatrice and the lawyer. Whatever they wanted was sure to be annoying. Debbie didn't have patience for hassle. She usually needed a laugh, which was something Beatrice Perry and a lawyer, especially, could not provide. "Oh, Roger."

Father Michael carried the boxes to the car as the women stood watching the priest struggle with the out-of-shape cardboard.

For form's sake, since they were not enemies and didn't want any-one to think they were, Father Michael and Debbie hugged goodbye. Michael hugged Franny, too.

Debbie waited until Michael was inside the house, focused on whatever priests focus on, before she pulled out of the driveway. She scooted the car around the corner to the Acadian Cultural Centre and Fun Centre parking lot and, without saying a word, backed into a spot near the entrance where she figured, with all the Centre's comings and goings, her car wouldn't be noticed. She glanced across the road at the parish house; the front door was still closed.

"Where are we?" asked Franny, as if she had just woken up. "Another blast from the past? Gotta take a piss?"

"You got your magazines?"

"I do! Man, oh man, do I love my magazines." A mess of glossies—boob jobs, cellulite, and party dresses—papered the floor mat behind the passenger seat.

"Stick your nose in them, won't yah. I gotta take care of something."

Debbie climbed into the back seat with two of the boxes and went through them thoroughly. Then she went through the two boxes in the trunk.

"Junk," she thought. Aloud, though no one was in earshot, she said, "Oh, Roger. Only you'd love all this junk." She called out to Franny, whose sandalled feet were sticking out the passenger door's window: "At least it's all clean!"

"No bugs! Yippee."

Nothing in the boxes meant anything to her. When Debbie thought of Roger, she thought of his pilled flannel bedding and his father's fried eggs. Raymond Niese made them without saying a word to you while you watched the pan. She thought of the rides to school in the old Ford pickup truck. She thought of Roger's undersized bike, which he rode up and down the John James Road, too nervous to take it out on the Union Road because she had worked him up telling him about all the drunk drivers. She thought of the quarters he gave her so she could call him if she needed him. She thought of the intense quiet of the trailer when Roger stopped chattering away, when the TV was off, when the fridge stopped running. She thought of how easy it was to be alone with him when he was painting his posters or making his lists or dreaming up his schemes.

Debbie didn't mind people so much now. Didn't need to escape them. Especially if they liked to laugh, like Franny did. Franny'd laugh at Debbie's overcooked pasta, Debbie's tantrum when the phone company called offering some new Internet package, Debbie's agitation when

Franny drove too fast. Being laughed at was just fine.

"Here," she said to Franny after almost an hour of shuffling and repacking the boxes. Carloads of visitors were coming and going from the lot. The ones leaving carried shopping bags, ice cream cones, take-out containers. The brawny father of one family walked by carrying a brand-new set of bagpipes over his back.

Navigating the lobby of the Acadian Cultural Centre and Fun Park was tricky business. The teens on break from clog-dancing classes, the swarm of slow-moving seniors from an Ajax, Ontario, bus tour.

A greeter dressed as Evangeline, Kim Ellsworth, the prettiest of the summer staff and also the one who knew how to occupy herself without constantly hounding her supervisors, saw Debbie nervously put the first box on the lobby floor. Scurrying toward Debbie like a dancer emerging from backstage in the second act, Evangeline/Kim Ellsworth offered a broad, sincere smile as she gracefully picked up the box and carried it to the administrative offices, as if she knew exactly where it was supposed to go.

Franny followed the girl with the next box. By the third and fourth, the two women knew exactly where they were going.

"I'll let Mrs. Pineau know they're here," said Evangeline/Kim Ellsworth, already halfway down the hall. Her foofy blue dress might have been suited for a gala ball except for the blue apron she wore over it.

Debbie turned to her friend. "We'd better hit the road if we're going to see those windmills before dark."

"I wouldn't mind taking a gander at the gift shop," said Franny.

"Oh, jeez, you and your shopping!"

Kate arrived in the office before they could bolt. "Ladies! What do we have here?" Out of breath, she sounded like a surgeon asking the nurses what procedure she'd be performing.

"Got something for you!" said Franny. All the driving around without knowing what was going on from moment to moment had turned Franny's brain to feathers. Her mantra, "Debbie is about adventure so let yourself go with it," was starting to seem naïve.

"I better not have to pay for this," laughed Kate. She ran her hand around her mouth to make sure there weren't remnants of the fricot she had been tasting during her visit to the Mémé's Home Cooking class. The fricot had been her excuse for checking on Susan Kennedy, who Kate believed had been manipulating Elis Getson into taking all the worst students.

"Oh, no, no," said Debbie. Her stomach, which had remained patiently clenched since their visit to the priest's house, had grown restless. Debbie worried all the lurching might knock her over. Falling onto the floor, having to be carried out on a stretcher—it might be the easiest escape. Explaining the boxes meant explaining who she was. That was the problem with missing the wake and funeral, not keeping up on the gossip. People might have built a case against you, all full of nonsense and bullshit, making it impossible to clear the air. It was best to behave as if everything was laundry fresh. "Free of charge. Gratis."

Kate, who in her matching dark blue blazer and skirt might have been the director of a funeral home, sized up Debbie Arsenault, who had not introduced herself. The woman's face and talk was from Up West, but living Down East had otherwise smudged the outlines of her origin. Kate couldn't put a finger on the family. She had been trying, these days, not to ask people who their father was. It was starting to feel intrusive.

They had been a few years apart in school. But a surname would have released a flood of information. For instance, when their fathers were in their twenties, before they had kids, Errol Arsenault had jammed with Albin Pineau at parties, Albin on fiddle, Errol on guitar. Booze, rather than talent, made their playing memorable. By the time the flames of the bonfire or fireplace were throwing more shadow than heat, you could barely make out the tune for all the misplaced notes.

Or, for instance, when they were little kids, the Pineaus and the Arsenaults often sat in the same back pew of St. Bernard's, before Debbie's mother gave up on getting her family to church and then gave up on them altogether. Kate might have remembered a pink woolen hat Debbie wore in winter, or the way, if she squirmed a lot, Debbie was able to get her mother to take her home right after communion.

Or, for instance, when driving by the Arsenault house, Kate's mother Regina never once failed to mention the time she had been collecting money for the Canadian Cancer Society, and stepped into the chaotic kitchen to find Bernice Arsenault, Errol's mother, changing Debbie's dirty diaper right there on the kitchen counter on top of a pile of potato peelings.

With some effort, Kate could have matched up this young Palmer

Road Debbie Arsenault with the mythical one Roger obsessed over, the one who was a charismatic free spirit, whose departure to parts unknown suffocated his heart. The one who danced barefoot through the woods and could have every man she ever met under her thumb, if she wasn't so unconventional. The one to whom Kate should, as instructed in the will, offer a senior position at the Acadian Cultural Centre and Fun Park. "Minister of Mischief, you can call her," Roger wrote in Appendix C of the will. Appendix C had been added when he was forty-two. "If she doesn't show up for work, she still gets her paycheque. Consider it a trust fund."

Kate wasn't going to look too hard for that Debbie Arsenault.

Luckily for Kate, neither of these Debbies—Errol Arsenault's or Roger Niese's—was present in the woman who now stood in her office. This face spoke of fad dieting, long periods of singleness and some experience with illegal drugs. She didn't look like she could handle herself in a fight—both Errol's and Roger's Debbie certainly could.

In this sense, though Kate did not know it, the woman in front of her was Michael Chaisson's Debbie.

"A donation! Of course! How lovely. Now you're....?" said Kate.

"Me? Now, I'm an old friend of Roger Niese."

"How lovely!" said Kate, falling into a shtick she had picked up from Beatrice. "So many people enjoyed his concerts over the years, I can't believe it myself. If you were to get them all together in one place, the stories you'd hear!"

"I can just imagine!"

"Was there one show you especially loved?" Kate was not merely fishing for compliments; she was working on a report on audience satisfaction.

Debbie smiled and shook her head. "Can't say, can't say. All so good!"

"We should go some time!" Franny piped up. Her excitement about seeing windmills was giving way to her wondering about whether this place served a decent hot hamburger sandwich. The Ferris wheel they had seen from the parking lot might be a fine substitute for wind turbines.

"You should!" Kate was now wondering if the two women were fishing for free tickets. If there was anything of value in these boxes, she could hardly say no.

Beatrice, by contrast, would not have hesitated to direct them to the box office to make a purchase. Unfortunately, she was a weapon that could no longer be deployed. Until her eighty-third year, Beatrice had been to a doctor only four times in her life. Then it was fourteen visits, none of which did any good except make her never want to hear the word "cancer" again. The cancer had taken her final beau, Phillip Sinclair, several years earlier.

St. Bernard's overflowed for Beatrice's funeral. It might have been better attended than Roger's. Every living Island woman who had ever been in one of her pageants attended.

In the last year of her life, Beatrice had developed an edge—testing people with veiled criticism and backhanded compliments. Kate hadn't known how to take her when Beatrice came to her office one afternoon and declared, "I'm sorry about the obituary."

"Don't be sorry!" Kate lowered her head. She waited for Beatrice to dictate how she wanted her obituary to read.

Beatrice puckered her lips in intense concentration. Her gaze lingered on the tree line of the property's edge, beyond Kate's office window.

"I'm here for you," said Kate.

"No, no," snapped Beatrice. "Not mine! Roger's! So long ago, it feels like. I know. I'm sorry. So sorry about that."

Kate did not like to think of those days after Roger's death, the stares and whispering marring her grief, prolonging it, making her second guess its nature. Had he brushed against her, taking it as sex? Had his lingering after late night rehearsals been more than pure boosterism? People gossiped that she had seized control of the Acadian Cultural Centre and Fun Park, claiming some kind of common-law wife status. At a certain point, she started to believe it a little, so that it made her feel less out of touch with popular opinion. She'd be at meetings, worried about sounding smart enough, then imagine herself as the bitter grieving lover of King Roger. She'd lean back in her chair, finally asking the sharp questions an entitled woman was meant to ask. They'd answer—the education committee, the marketing committee, the food committee—as if she had a special power to report back to the late founder.

"You know, what they were saying about you, back then."

"Water under the bridge." Kate made a dismissive motion with her left hand.

"You don't know what I'm talking about whatsoever, Kate, not one scintilla."

Beatrice finally recounted the story of how Roger's obituary came to be.

Roger had written his own obituary when he turned thirty-eight, though it went through several rounds of revisions. The original version came in at more than five thousand words, when you included quotes from various poets, including the Island's own Milton Acorn. He never showed the draft to Beatrice but told her, not at all boastfully, that after he laid it out on a piece of paper in a font size similar to *The Spectator-Herald's*, that it took up an entire newspaper page. Beatrice told him Basil Johnston would never run it.

Vowing to create something more in line with the norm, Roger took to regularly reading the obituaries in *The Spectator-Herald*. At first, he found them dryly inscrutable. After all his years on PEI, the names still meant very little to him, who was related to who, whose father was whose. Faces, he knew. And talent. But names, by themselves, left him cold. What was his favourite drink? Her favourite song? Her true love? Did he love all his nieces and nephews equally? You'd never know by reading *The Spectator-Herald* obituary.

But Roger knew that an obituary style that was so pervasive must be based on time-tested profundity; that was the magic in folklore. Reading obituary after obituary over the next few years of his life, Roger gradually found a pleasure in their rhythms and hierarchy, the puzzle-solving needed to determine one branch of Arsenaults or Gallants or Gaudets from another. He took to doing them like crossword puzzles. Beatrice noticed him with his little notepad on which he drew rudimentary family trees while he read the newspaper. Finally, Roger was getting at a core piece of Island life, she thought. But by then, it was a moot point; Roger had already imposed his meaning on the community, had made stars of lesser-known people, had sidelined more prominent families. Whether that had been the proper way to do things or not, evidence showed that it was sufficient for his purposes.

Roger took a second crack at his obituary and, feeling he had written the most quintessentially Prince Edward Island obituary ever produced, stuffed it into an unsealed envelope and gave it to Beatrice the day before his forty-second birthday.

"You're going to like this one," he said.

Beatrice tsked; an obituary was a strange thing to get all puffed up about. She impatiently filed the envelope at the back of the bottom drawer of her filing cabinet. She had no intention of looking inside.

When Beatrice received the call that Roger had passed away that morning of October 17, 2007, she walked to her office without saying a word to anyone and quietly retrieved the envelope from its hiding place. "On the unfortunate event of my death," he had scrawled on the envelope. Beatrice gasped when she saw his handwriting.

"I thought it was going to be a million words. I thought I'd have to re-write it from scratch. But it was just what the doctor ordered," Beatrice told Kate. "Almost."

There were some things Roger hadn't gotten quite right. In particular, he included mention of non-relatives, like Beatrice herself, his ex Tracey, Mitchell, and, most beguilingly, Debbie Arsenault. It couldn't have been the Debbie Arsenault Beatrice thought it was. If it was, she had to be cut out immediately.

"You were mentioned, too," said Beatrice. "Of course, you know that. So many names! I was reading it over the phone to Caroline MacPhail. I had tears in my eyes. Caroline, who was also broken up about Roger's death, was snuffling, barely able to pay attention.

"And when I saw my name there in the obituary, at the beginning of the list of 'special friends,' I couldn't read it. And couldn't say Mitchell's name aloud—he was a sobbing mess in the other room. I skipped that line and the next. And Tracey? Her name no more belonged in the death notice than Debbie Arsenault's. Roger and Tracey hadn't even married, for heaven's sake. None of that needed to be publicized. It's a public record, most of all, the write-up in the paper. Your name, Kate, was a few lines down and I was so distracted, I went back to what Roger had typed up and picked up there. I didn't leave you in on purpose. But your name, his biggest talent, made a bit of sense, I suppose. Maybe that's why I said it. Caroline typed up everything I said. She's one of the more accurate ones at *The Spectator-Herald*. But! She dropped the 's' off the 'special friends' on her own accord. It made more grammatical sense, I suppose. She never read it back to me. I should have asked her to, I suppose. Ultimately, Kate, there was no sense in having all those names in there. It would have taken up a whole column."

"It would have, I suppose," said Roger Niese's "special friend" Kate Pineau.

"I didn't know you were in the will. I had no idea! I didn't think there was a connection to be made."

"Neither did I," Kate shrugged. "Accidents happen."

"They do," said Beatrice. "I think about my mistake every day. How much it hurt you and embarrassed you. How much it hurt Arnold."

"Arnold?" said Kate skeptically.

"You were a married woman. It cast a doubt on your entire marriage. I know Arnold wasn't the best husband, but nobody wants that kind of talk. If I had accidentally left in my name instead.... But that would have been just as suspicious, I suppose. Or I could have left Tracey's or Mitchell's. Debbie Arsenault's—now that would have been a riddle! No, there was no way of doing it except take them all out. Or leave them all in, which would have been ridiculous."

"Totally ridiculous."

The next time they saw each other, Beatrice was in the palliative care unit of O'Leary hospital.

★

"Now this stuff," said Kate.

"Yes, this stuff," said Debbie.

"This stuff," laughed Franny.

"Well," said Debbie. "The priest, there, across the road...."

It had dawned on her—a way to do this. Debbie wanted to spit it out before the idea dissolved. "We were taking pictures of the church. Such a pretty church! He asked us to run this stuff over here. Donations. This is a charity place, isn't it?"

Franny looked around as if expecting to see orphans and injured soldiers.

Kate screwed her face up in a look of confusion. It was a handy way to ask for an explanation.

"Belongs to Roger Niese! My old friend! The guy that whipped all this up." Debbie waved her hands in the air. "Not sure what got into him. All this stuff! But this seems like a good place for it. You'll take care of it!"

Kate was on her knees, looking into the first box. She unfolded a poster for the "We Got the Beat" dance and, easily recognizing Roger's handiwork, Kate teared up.

"Oh, this is so sweet! Roger's things. His first, uh... efforts at being a promoter. You can't imagine...."

"I hope you can do something with it."

Kate needed to thank these ladies and get them out of her hair so she could have a good cry. "Mitchell!" she called out, hoping that one of the student workers within earshot would relay the message.

Mitchell appeared so suddenly, Franny jumped and clutched her chest. Everybody burst out laughing.

"Nice helmet, dude," said Franny.

"Thankies."

"You must let Mitchell give you a tour," said Kate.

"We'd love to look around. Don't know if we have the time to do a proper tour, like real tourists," said Debbie. "This one's always in such a rush."

"Me?" laughed Franny.

Kate asked Mitchell, whose current title was assistant operations manager, to take the ladies on a guided VIP tour of the Acadian Cultural Centre and Fun Park. Mitchell, who loved giving tours, clicked his heels together and nearly whacked Debbie with his flailing elbows.

"Get it under control, dude," said Franny. "We want to make it to the Ferris wheel in one piece."

Kate shook Debbie's hand, still having no idea who she was. Both women were relieved to have completed the transaction.

"We'll take such good care of everything you brought us."

"Know you will," said Debbie, already out in the hallway.

Mitchell led the guests through the main building to the fun park's entrance. Brian Doucette, Carolyn MacPhail's son, was working the admission kiosk and waved them through without looking at their tickets.

"VIPs, Deb! That's what we are today. Who knew our little visit to the priest would pay off!" Franny had been too shy to ask if it cost anything to see the North Cape windmills. She didn't like paying more than a buck or two for entertainment that didn't include alcohol.

"Nice day for it," said Debbie, wondering how soon they'd have to be back on the road to make it to Cornwall by suppertime.

"Food's not included. Just so you know," Mitchell told them.

They started with the paddle boats, where they mostly soaked themselves. At the mini-golf course, Mitchell invoked his line-bypass privileges. Franny, delighted by all the value, insisted they get some cotton candy, no matter the price. Lester Shaw had won the tender to run the amusement-park snacks concession—perhaps without the intervention of his wife Tracey, who was still the Centre's retail manager. One of the Perry boys had failed to show up for his shift, so Lester was spinning the candy himself. Lester loved his quirky wife, though he had to tune her out much of the time. Tracey, of all of them, had changed the least over the years.

Next, the VIPs headed to the Ferris wheel. Each car was painted in the tri-colours of the Acadian flag, a yellow star on each side, three stars along the back. It was a tight squeeze with the three of them, Franny half in Mitchell's lap.

"Mitchell, I remember your brother, Ricky. We used to get around," Debbie said as they made their first rotation. In the foreground, that summer's Gabriel—a Todd Gallant from Rustico when people on Palmer Road thought they knew for a minute until they figured out they didn't—was playing pirate to a mass of kids on the old fishing boat in the middle of the fun park. As the whole grounds came into view, they could see all the people getting in and out of swan-shaped paddle boats. Franny smelled fir and ozone and fried potatoes.

They could see St. Bernard's church across the road, looking like a flimsy cardboard box painted white with milk, black with tar. You could hardly believe it had been there for one hundred years. Going higher still, they could see over the treetops, all the way to Miminegash, the muddy red of the shallows blurring the line between the shore and the strait.

"Ah, Ricky!" said Mitchell. "My Ricky." The joy of the memory trumped even the glorious landscape stretched out before them.

"Great guy!" said Debbie.

"He was!"

"Old beau?" asked Franny. She was finding the conversation hard to follow, her brain full of the view.

"No!" snapped Debbie. "Not everybody Up West was my beau."

On the downward trip, Mitchell regained his wits. He saw a posse of young teens skulking behind the washroom pavilion. He bit his lip— he'd have to check on them when the ride was over. He didn't like to talk about his brother. The memories were lovely at first, but then the sadness came.

"How about the guy who loved you so much, back in high school!" asked Franny. "Roger?"

"Franny! I told you not to...."

"Well?"

"Hey, hey, hey, hey!" barked Mitchell. His yelling, directed at the underaged smokers, was blown away on the wind and dispersed across West Prince at a volume too low to hear. He turned back toward Debbie and said with a note of consolation: "That's okay. Roger loved a lot of people."

★

Brian Doucette had done excellent work on the display cabinets in the gallery, which staff were under no circumstances permitted to call a museum—nobody wanted another lawyer's letter from the Accents LeBlanc on behalf of the Acadian Museum in Miscouche. Brian had been the star of 4-H woodworking. Every year, he took the top prize at fairs and exhibitions across the province. His napkin holders, bookshelves, and knife racks were all Platonic ideals of their form. His secret was sanding; they said he could make a lopsided house look straight if you gave him the right grain of paper. The gallery's Plexiglas sheets would pop into their display-case bases without force. Brian's display case for an 1800s wrought-iron bedframe, taken from an Acadian farmhouse, attracted more admiration than its contents.

It took Kate some time to convince herself that a Roger Niese display was the right decision. She could hear Beatrice warning against big feelings and false idols. When you took the long view of history, you had to admit that Roger certainly wasn't Acadian.

Most of the items Kate chose to display were left over from Roger's old Dairy Bar Museum: the hand-cranked drill, the chalice, and the vintage signs. Still, Kate had Brian build one cabinet especially for Roger's personal artifacts. Most of them were paper—memos, flyers, posters, and newspaper clippings.

The cassette player Roger had used to listen to audition tapes sat in the middle of the cabinet. The sound you heard when looking at the exhibit came from a CD player hidden in a compartment Brian had built in the back.

Going through Roger's massive cassette archive, Tracey had compiled her interpretation of Roger Niese's favourite songs and copied them onto a dozen CDs. They were to play continuously whenever the gallery was open. Needless to say, Kate's performances featured prominently, despite her protests.

Mitchell was in charge of changing the CDs regularly so as not to drive the gallery's volunteer staff crazy. There was only so much "Ste. Anne's Reel" anyone could take in a day.

ACKNOWLEDGEMENTS

Thanks to the Ontario Arts Council for making this project possible.

Thanks to my most excellent editor Richard Lemm.

Thanks to the friends who suffered through an earlier version of the manuscript.

Many quotes are taken from *Evangeline* by Henry Wadsworth Longfellow, 1897.